First published 2025

First printed edition published 2025 by Drollery Ltd.

Copyright © Alice Coldbreath, 2025

ISBN: 978-1-0682366-5-5

I0636074

More books available by Alice Coldbreath:

Vawdrey Brothers Series:

Book 1: Her Baseborn Bridegroom

Book 2: His Forsaken Bride

Book 3: An Ill-Made Match

Brides of Karadok Series:

Book 1: Wed By Proxy

Book 2: The Unlovely Bride

Book 3: The Consolation Prize

Book 4: Her Bridegroom, Bought and Paid For

Book 5: An Inconvenient Vow

Book 6: The Favourite

Book 7: A Most Forgettable Girl

Victorian Prizefighter Series:

Book 1: A Bride for the Prizefighter

Book 2: A Substitute Wife for the Prizefighter

Book 3: A Contracted Spouse for the Prizefighter

Reversal of Fortune Series:

Book 1: A Foolish Flirtation

This book is dedicated to my friend Anne Flosnik,

whose narration of the audiobooks has really enriched the Karadok experience.

Thank you for your enthusiasm and encouragement which has really inspired me.

Prologue

Vawdrey Keep, The Harvest Moon

Gunnilde made her way carefully up the circular steps of the Keep, carrying her platter of herb bread, oat cakes, and mead. Her friend Eden had bidden her most particularly to take it to her husband and his friend in the solar, for them to toast the harvest.

She had taken her turn kneading the bread as one of the unmarried women in the house and eyed the plaited loaf now with satisfaction. It was well risen and had a lovely golden color. She only hoped her wish to St. Alden was granted this year. She was two and twenty now, and it was high time she took a husband.

Nearing the top of the stone steps, she heard the words drifting down toward her. They were talking, she thought, pausing to check there were no crumbs on her bodice, for she had already eaten her portion of the ceremonial bread.

"You'd better watch yourself, Bev, old man," Sir Roland remarked after clearing his throat. "My wicked faery has a bee in her bonnet about that friend of hers, and you know how determined she can be when she sets her mind to something."

Gunnilde smiled to herself, reaching the top. Sir Roland often referred to Eden as "his wicked faery." It never failed to make her smile.

"You don't need to warn me," Sir Ned Bevan replied dryly. "I've known that any time this past month. Every time I so much as catch her ladyship's eye, she sends the wretched girl to fetch me something. No offense, Roly, but your wife's about as subtle as a mace."

The smile dropped from Gunnilde's face, and she froze where she stood, one hand raised to draw back the curtain. Wretched girl?

1

Suddenly it occurred to her that they might well be talking about her. Surely not? Surely, she had never given Sir Ned cause to hold her in such contempt? Her distress was so great, she missed Sir Roland's rejoinder.

"I've nothing against the girl, don't get me wrong," Sir Ned was now assuring his friend. "Nice and all that. Bit toothy," he added critically, "and a bit on the heavy side, but amiable enough if you're none too exacting in your tastes. Hal tells me there was some suitor in the making a couple of years back."

"Yes, some neighbor of her father's," Sir Roland agreed. "Slipped his halter apparently, leaving her high and dry."

There was a meaningful pause as Gunnilde's heart thudded painfully in her chest. Hal? The mention of her brother's name confirmed the horrible truth beyond all measure of doubt. She was the object of their conversation and none other. Toothy? And even worse... A bit on the heavy side. The blood pounded in her ears.

With such casual cruelty, Sir Ned dragged her greatest insecurities into the light and dissected them. A lump formed in Gunnilde's throat to hear herself discussed with such cool disdain. For some reason, she had not thought to hear such unchivalrous speech from Sir Edward Bevan of Knollesley. It seemed she should add "naïve" to her list of many faults.

"Well, I'm in no hurry to take his place," Sir Ned replied with feeling.

"You could do worse," Sir Roland said thoughtfully. "Mistress Gunnilde always seems keen to please, I'll say that for her. And likely she's generously dowered. Old Payne's got a nice spread at Tranton Vale."

"Hal will inherit the estate," Sir Ned pointed out, "as the only son."

"She'll get her portion, I've no doubt," Sir Roland replied. "A fond father does not neglect his daughter's prospects."

"Egads! If I didn't know any better, I'd think Eden had enlisted you to her cause!" Sir Ned replied with spirit.

Roland laughed. "Hardly that. But she's a nice, goodhearted girl, when all's said and done."

Sir Ned snorted. "Oh aye, I daresay Mistress Gunnilde Payne is nice enough," he said breezily. "Nice, and eminently forgettable. I've no fancy to be clapped in wedding irons for the likes of her."

A sweep of hot color suffused Gunnilde's face. Nice, and eminently forgettable. As though anyone had asked him! As though she had ever dreamed… Except, she had dreamed, hadn't she? She had been dreaming for years of a handsome knight finally turning her way.

Foolish dreams, as it now turned out. Dreams that would never come true. Without giving herself time to pause, she seized hold of the curtain with a shaking hand and hauled it back, making both knights startle where they stood.

"Lady Eden thought you might stand in need of refreshment, good sirs," she announced loudly, stepping between them. "I trust I do not interrupt a matter of great import?"

"Oh, er, course not, Mistress Payne," Sir Ned answered with bluster. "Nothing could be further from the truth. Always a pleasure." He had the grace to turn rather red when Gunnilde turned her gaze on him.

She fixed a tight smile on her face. "I'm so glad to hear it, Sir Ned. I would hate to make myself wretchedly in the way."

Her pointed words were met with an appalled silence. Sir Ned turned even redder, a hunted look creeping into his eye. At Sir Roland she did

3

not glance. Lifting the tray, she presented them both with goblets and flagon. "Mayhap you would be good enough to pour for yourselves this eve? I fear the cork is stoppered fast, but if you cannot prize it free, let me know. Perhaps my teeth could perform the office? They are so exceptionally large after all."

Sir Ned made a strangled noise in his throat, while Sir Roland made a muffled sound, she was not sure was not a stifled guffaw. Her words seemed to have robbed Sir Ned of speech, though Sir Roland at least had the presence of mind to take the tray from her trembling hands.

"So kind of you," Gunnilde said brightly, though she did not look at her host. "But then you are always kind, are you not? I suppose it is part of your knightly calling." Her voice broke over the last few words, and she turned and fled back down the staircase, stumbling as she went.

It was the single most humiliating experience of Gunnilde's life. She could not face the others in the Great Hall, not with those words still ringing in her ears. Instead, she hurried up another set of winding steps to her own temporary bedchamber, slamming the door behind her.

This was even worse than the humiliation of Sir Arthur Conway not proposing to her at eighteen as everyone in Tranton Vale had expected. At least then people had whispered behind closed doors, and she had not heard any of the gossip with her own ears. In time the scalding embarrassment had faded, and she had dusted herself off to face folk again.

Optimistically, she had thought with such a well-connected friend as Viscountess Vawdrey, new and exciting doorways would become opened to her. Instead, it was the same old story. They simply slammed shut in her stupid, provincial face.

Here she was four years later, scorned and found wanting, yet again. She would never, ever put herself in such a humiliating position again. From now on, she would stick to the role of confidante and

4

matchmaker. It suited her far better. Flinging her pillow bearer across the room, she collapsed onto the bed and succumbed to a hearty bout of tears. When the storm was over, she rolled onto her back and stared listlessly up at the timbered beams above her.

She would face facts squarely. She, Gunnilde, was not some dainty lady to be offering her token to the premier knights of the land. Clearly marriage was a lost cause for one as stout of limb and strong of tooth as she. She needed new ambitions, she told herself with a doleful sniff. Ambitions that did not include matrimony, but what else was there?

Even as fed up as she felt currently, she knew a nunnery held no appeal for her. She sat up. Eden had promised to introduce her at court. And Gunnilde had kept putting it off. She had so much preferred visiting her friend in her home, and spending time with her baby goddaughter, Agnes.

But, after all, she had always wanted to meet the Queen. She wiped her eyes. Eden always insisted that Gunnilde would benefit from some of the many opportunities at court. She suffered a moment's misgiving. But had Eden just meant the opportunity to meet eligible suitors? No, she thought, she wronged her friend. Eden spoke of court as a place of learning and culture, a place where intellect could be broadened and like minds discovered.

Before she had married, Eden had resided chiefly at court and been a member of all kinds of societies and even a patroness of the arts. She had been one of the Queen's favorite ladies-in-waiting, no less. Gunnilde's heart quickened. Could she aspire to climb such lofty heights? She had never been much of a scholar, but Eden always maintained she had much to offer. Was she right? Could Gunnilde catch the Queen's eye, and become one of her attendants? Her pulse raced. There was only one way to find out…

Two Months Later

The Royal Court at Aphrany

"Who the hells is that girl anyway?" James Wycliffe asked his brother irritably.

"Girl?" Neville glanced around, smothering his yawn. "Which girl?"

"The one with all that tow-colored hair!"

Neville eyed him with surprise. "Not like you to notice girls," he remarked, then took a look in the direction his brother was glowering. "She seems to be some connection of the Portstanleys. I think her name is Payne," he said, the effort of remembrance causing a pucker between his brows.

"Appropriate," James remarked acidly, causing his brother to look even more intrigued.

"Why? What has she done to irk you?" Neville directed a puzzled glance her way. "Looks an inoffensive sort of girl to me."

Inoffensive? James thought with a hollow laugh. Nothing could be further from the truth! "I suspect she has some personal vendetta against me," he muttered.

"Good Lord!" Neville looked even more startled. "Why should she?" He turned about to give the girl another look. "She has the reputation for being a most sympathetic listener. I'm sure I'm thinking of the right one. Someone was speaking of her only the other day. Said Mistress Payne had been disappointed in love at a young age or some such thing and now devotes herself to helping spurned lovers."

"Disappointed in love?" James echoed incredulously. "What rot. And as for a sympathetic listener, I'd wager she is merely collecting gossip." Neville seemed amused by his cynicism. "Every time I try to pay court to Constance lately, she's there, sticking her oar in and getting in the way."

Neville gave a choked laugh. "Perhaps she's vying for your attention, brother. You know how the ladies love to sigh over the perfection of your profile."

James gave an impatient gesture. "It's not that at all! The way she looks at me... Well, let us just say it is far from admiring."

Neville guffawed. "Disapproves of you, does she? I wonder why? Your conduct has always been disappointingly staid." He dug James in the side. "Found you out in some secret dishonor, has she?"

To his annoyance, James found himself coloring hotly. "Of course not!" he snapped, but the damage was done. Neville was intrigued. He should never have brought him along to this gathering. He could never depend on his younger brother to behave himself.

"Do you think that's all her real hair?" Neville mused.

"What do you mean?"

"Well, you know ladies will sometimes employ a little artifice in these matters. With hair that color, at least half of it could be flax." He laughed at James's startled expression. "You really know so very little about women, brother."

"Whereas you know altogether too much," James retorted. "Who have you been talking to?"

"Did you not hear the Bishop of Badsbury bemoaning the fraudulent practice from his pulpit only last week? Fie, for shame! To think that I

7

would pay closer attention to his holiness than you. Truly our roles have switched of late, you ogling women and me listening to bishops."

James dismissed this with the contempt it deserved and returned to his current concern. "I think she is trying to put a spoke in the wheel," he said, dropping his voice, "regarding Constance."

For the first time, Neville looked alarmed. "No, really? Your betrothal? But why would she want to do a thing like that?"

"I don't know, but I have a…bad feeling about her."

"She is friends with Constance?"

"Lately they always seem huddled together sharing confidences."

"Surely she would have introduced her new friend to you?"

James shrugged. "I believe she did, at some point."

"You believe so?" Neville repeated disbelievingly. "Yet you never even bothered to learn the girl's name! No wonder you made a poor impression." He shook his head. "Maybe your handsome face failed to distract this one from damnable rudeness. It was bound to happen sooner or later."

"I am not rude!" James did not bother to deny he was handsome. He was not vain, but his good looks had been commented on from a young age. He only wished his compositions shared equal fame.

Neville looked thoughtful. "Unfortunately for you, Mistress Payne must be more discerning than your average courtier."

James snorted. "I don't know where you got that impression. Just look at her!"

Neville cast a critical eye over the female. "Why, what's amiss? It's true she's a little homely, but she makes the best of what the gods gave her, you have to give her that. She's well-dressed enough and that hairstyle is really most up to date."

"Well dressed?" James echoed. "Her surcoat is practically hanging off her in shreds it's so…slashed about. Why, it shows off her—" Neville caught his eye, and James hastily changed the words he had been about to use. "Her undergown," he amended swiftly, "to an almost unseemly degree."

"My, my, you really have been taking a good look, haven't you?" Neville commented with a smirk. "But as a matter of fact, open-sided surcotes are the very latest thing. They say the fashion originated in Kloberg."

"Well, then it should have stayed there. It looks positively indecent."

"Indecent?" Neville looked startled by his vehemence. "Come now, James. You must have seen some other courtiers wearing them that way."

"Where?" James scanned the room. "I see no one else parading around with their gowns falling off them."

"Not here," Neville huffed. "There is not a single person of fashion present in this dismal gathering. I've never been in a room with so many dullards all at once."

James rolled his eyes. "There are several prominent courtiers present and many learned scholars."

"Fusty old ones, you mean," Neville muttered. "From the way she dresses, it seems Mistress Payne would like to run with a less sedate pack, and who can blame her? Not I."

9

James snorted rudely. "You can determine much from a woman's hair arrangement, it seems."

"I can," Neville agreed firmly. "So did the bishop. He said it a piece of great wickedness for women to dress their hair like horned beasts."

"Horned…?" James turned to survey Miss Payne's extraordinary hair arrangement again. "It does not look precisely like horns," he said uncertainly, "but I agree it hardly appears seemly."

"Lord, you're starting to sound like a fussy old cleric yourself, brother!" Neville sighed. "Your looks are wasted on you. If I had been blessed with your height and features, I would not squander such a gift as you do."

James ignored this. His brother had always favored the company of women, while James preferred that of books and music. "What else did he say on the subject?" he asked grudgingly.

"Who?"

"The bishop."

"Oh, just a lot of prosing about forwardness and licentiousness in females. Tempting the menfolk from the path of virtue and all that."

"I daresay she does," James observed darkly. Neville's eyebrows shot up. "I've observed her about court these past few days," he admitted grudgingly. "Suffice to say, Mistress Payne does not conduct herself as a respectable maiden should."

Neville made a choking sound which turned into a cough. "How so?" he asked, looking wildly curious.

"I am not about to besmirch her name," James said coldly. "You will simply have to trust my word on this matter."

10

Neville tutted, his gaze returning to Mistress Payne with renewed interest. "Well, well. Perhaps there is more to the lady than first appears. It is true, she is a buxom lass," he pondered aloud. "Some men like that. Not you, I know," he said hastily as James opened his mouth to disparage this sentiment. "Not everyone has your refined tastes, brother.

"Some of these knights are particularly crude and barbarous, and you know how they always flood to court at this time of year, with their rough speech and boisterous spirits. I daresay Mistress Payne will garner admirers enough if she continues to flaunt her plentiful hair and…person."

James frowned. "That is hardly my concern."

"Now that I think about it, I believe her name was mentioned in connection with that Fulsham business. Did you hear about his engagement with Mistress Linfield? Entered into without the guardian's consent apparently but they got their own way in the end. The scandal's good as died down by now. I heard they're living at Linfield Hall in married bliss."

"You mean, she encouraged a clandestine betrothal?" James asked with deep foreboding.

"Aye, that's the sum of it. Apparently, she and the Linfield chit were thick as thieves at one time." When James remained disapprovingly silent, Neville leaned forward. "Some say they put the cart before the horse and old Sir Joseph had no choice but to let them wed." He slanted a knowing look at his brother. It was wasted on James, who merely shrugged his shoulders.

"I don't know what you're talking about."

Neville tsked. "That is because you do not pay enough attention to palace gossip."

11

"I do not pay any attention to it," James corrected him swiftly.

"You need not sound so pleased with yourself. Perhaps if you did, you would have a good deal more patrons beating down your doors."

James gave a fatalistic sigh, suddenly weary of the conversation. "Perhaps you are right."

"Certainly I am. If you would only concern yourself a little more with popularity and a little less with scrupulous respectability, I feel sure you would be more successful. I daresay this Mistress Payne is far merrier company than Lady Constance and her ilk. I don't know why you subject yourself to such company."

"Yes, you do," James responded shortly.

Neville's expression instantly sobered. "Well, yes, I know why," he admitted in a low voice. "All the family do, and we appreciate your sacrifice. But must it be this heiress in particular? Answer me that?"

"Most readily," James replied at once. "Constance Northcott is a serious-minded young woman of impeccable breeding and large fortune who will bring decorum and grace to the role we all expect her to play at Wycliffe Hall."

Neville looked resigned. "I suppose Mother will approve of her at least."

"Undoubtedly."

"It's just…" Neville waved a hand. "Mayhap there is another with full coffers who might actually put a smile on your face, brother. Constance does not have it in her to make you happy, I'm convinced of it."

"Happy?" James echoed blankly. "That will hardly be one of her responsibilities. I will be busy at court composing, and she will be employed with the running of Wycliffe Hall. If we could entrust that to a safe pair of hands, then I will be a good deal happier, I assure you."

Neville sighed. "I suppose that is true. Have you heard much from home lately?" he asked without enthusiasm.

"I had a letter from Mother two days ago," James said shortly. "Believe me, you do not want to know its contents."

Neville winced. "The old man's on some mad start again, I daresay," he lamented. "It beats me how he manages to find the energy, let alone the funds."

"Oh, he manages," James said bitterly. "Where there's a will, there's a way, and he can always find some fool willing to extend him a line of credit. I would not mind so much if the bills did not invariably end up in my lap."

"Perhaps we should smother him in his drunken slumbers one dark night."

James shook his head at his brother's flippancy, and Neville's gaze returned to the two whispering women. "Do you know," he decided, perking up, "I believe you're right about Mistress Payne. From the glances she's darting your way, I think she is maligning you to Constance!"

"I knew it." James whipped around to glare at the offending party. He made a muffled sound of annoyance.

"Where are you going?" Neville asked in some alarm.

"To find out what her game is," James responded grimly.

*

"You will be most upset with me, Gunnilde, and I'm sure that I cannot blame you," Constance said, her pretty face troubled. "I am quite vexed with myself for not entirely crushing his pretentions in the spring."

Gunnilde eyed her friend with surprise. Her attention had wandered, for Lady Schaeffer had walked in wearing the most magnificent headpiece. It was a kind of padded roll worn high on her head in the shape of a heart, and Gunnilde was so taken with it that she turned her head to watch Lady Schaeffer's progress about the room. How wonderful it must be to be a married lady and able to wear such ostentatious headdresses!

By the time she refocused on her friend, it was clear the conversation had taken a turn. For some reason, Constance seemed to expect her to be upset with her. "What can you mean, Constance?" she asked, careful not to betray the fact she had not been listening. "I dare assure you I could never be cross with you."

Constance bit her lip, looking pained. "I hardly know how to tell you this, for I know how sincerely you admire the gentleman in question. Indeed, when I think of how fulsomely you have spoken of him these past couple of months, and with such warmth, I hardly have the heart to tell you of it and crush your expectations."

Gunnilde wished her friend would get to the point. If there was a downside to Constance, it was that she never failed to use ten words when two would do. "To tell me of…?" she prompted.

Constance took a deep breath, taking Gunnilde's hand in her own. "It pains me to have to tell you that Sir Douglas Farleigh hath renewed his interest in me." She looked grave. "I think I told you before that he attempted to pay court to me some months ago, and I quashed his efforts. Well, it seems he is not so easily dissuaded. I heartily pity you in your disappointment, Gunnilde. I need hardly add that I—"

"My disappointment?" Gunnilde echoed. "Oh no, no! You must not let such a scruple stand in your way, if that is what you imagine."

Constance stared at her, her flow quite disrupted. Then her expression changed. "Most noble friend," she breathed. "You would put your own heartache aside in such a matter to support me?"

"Oh, of course!" Gunnilde hastened to assure her. "But as a matter of fact, I do not admire Sir Douglas. I mean, I do admire him of course, excessively, but never with myself in mind. No, I always knew his heart belonged to you entirely. It is obvious even to a bystander like myself."

"It is?" Constance sounded dazed. She sat down abruptly on the nearest seat. "Forgive me, I have been so concerned with how to break this news to you that I hardly know how to react now I find I was worried over nothing!"

"Please do not trouble yourself on my account. I assure you, my heart is quite unscathed."

Constance passed a hand over her brow. "Well, I am relieved about that in any event."

It occurred to Gunnilde that she must have been far too subtle in her methods for Constance to run away with the idea that she wanted Sir Douglas for herself! Had she been wasting her breath all this time praising him to the skies? How vexing! "Might I ask how Sir Douglas renewed his suit?" she asked, hoping to further Sir Douglas's cause.

"A poem," Constance said flatly. "Here, you may read it, if you like." She retrieved it from her drawstring bag, grimacing slightly. "It…well, it does not show great delicacy of mind, I'm afraid," she said, looking pained. "You see how he rhymes need with steed."

Gunnilde scanned the lines eagerly. "I think that is quite clever," she admitted. "And you know how much a knight loves his horse. It must

15

be a point in his favor that the whole thing rhymes." She squinted down at the much blotted and crossed-out parchment. "Sir Douglas must have spent a good deal of time and effort on this."

"Doubtless," Constance said, pursing her lips. "One might have hoped he would have written it out on fresh parchment on completing it, for presentation's sake."

"He was up all night finishing it!" Gunnilde appealed, feeling quite injured on Sir Douglas's behalf. "Indeed, he looked quite haggard this morning."

"In any case," Constance said dismissively, "it does not really bear comparison to the poem Sir James sent me." She cast an approving look in the direction of that gentleman. Gunnilde followed suit, only hers was more of a glower.

She could not deny that Sir James Wycliffe was likely the most handsome man at court with his curling auburn hair and bluey-green eyes. It was only that his particular kind of masculine beauty left Gunnilde cold.

What was the point in a man having such long dark lashes and that pouty mouth? They were quite wasted on him, and besides, she preferred a more rugged type herself, weatherbeaten and battle worn.

Also, there was a cold disdain to the man that Gunnilde quite detested. Every time she had the misfortune to meet him he looked right through her and forgot her name. He seemed arrogant, unfeeling, and downright rude. "I daresay he paid the poet a pretty penny for his offering," Gunnilde sniffed, "but it is hardly the same as writing poetry to you himself, now, is it?"

Constance looked rather annoyed at this rejoinder. "He made no secret of the fact he employed an expert," she said, pressing her lips together. "I might have counseled Sir Douglas to do the same!"

16

"Did he not have a poet dedicate a poem to you last year?" Gunnilde exclaimed. "I quite understood he had, and that it left you entirely unmoved."

Constance stirred uneasily in her seat. "He did," she conceded. "I forgot I had told you of that." Gunnilde held her tongue. In truth, it had been Douglas who had told her of it, not Constance. "The poet he used, Mr. Shadbolt, was most unsuitable, almost lewd in his tone," Constance said primly. "At least Sir James had the sense to select one with an impeccable reputation."

"Was it indecent?" Gunnilde asked with a flicker of interest.

"Practically and most unsuitable for a maiden's eyes. I burned it," Constance replied virtuously.

"Oh," Gunnilde said sadly. "Not that I wanted to read it," she added hastily as Constance rounded on her with a shocked expression. "It is only that I feel sorry for poor Sir Douglas. I doubt he realized it was improper."

"Of that I have no doubt! I expect most poetry sails over Sir Douglas's head. If you had only seen the love token he sent me last summer, the most unsuitable thing. An enameled disc depicting a knight's helm, and after I had specifically told him that I did not care for jousting. What say you to that?"

"I think it sounds rather sweet," Gunnilde admitted.

Constance opened her mouth on a retort only for it to be interrupted by Sir James's sudden arrival at her elbow. "Good morning," he said, startling them both with his appearance.

"Oh, Sir James!" Constance blurted, looking about as flustered as Gunnilde had ever seen her. Doubtless she was horrified he might have heard them discussing the subject of lewd poetry.

17

"Mistress Payne," he said, looking straight at Gunnilde and surprising her greatly.

So, he had troubled to remember her name for once, wonders would never cease! Any gratification she might have felt disappeared when she saw the accusatory glint in his eye. Perchance he had heard something of their conversation after all. "Sir James," she responded coolly, dipping into the shallowest of curtseys and refusing to be intimidated.

Constance cleared her throat. "I am so pleased to see you and your brother could make the lecture," she twittered. Really, if Constance was not careful, she would be losing her reputation for composure, for she looked quite rattled. "I was afraid you might miss it, and Master Mullins sets off on his travels on the morrow not to return until spring."

Sir James appeared to consider her words with a frown. "Why would I miss it?" he asked with what Gunnilde thought a most ungallant abruptness.

Constance blinked. "I had heard that Sir Neville was indisposed yesterday," she replied in a low, sorrowful voice. "As he so often is."

His dark brows snapped together, and he gave a short callous laugh. "Oh, you mean with one of his maladies. We are fortunate that Neville was not afflicted today." His words dripped with sarcasm, and Gunnilde could not help but marvel that Constance could prefer such a suitor to earnest Sir Douglas, who was so open and artless.

Despite his good looks, Sir James was clearly in possession of a heartless, unsympathetic nature. "You are not a fond brother, Sir James, evidently," Gunnilde remarked disapprovingly.

Constance's eyes widened, and Sir James turned his gaze upon her again. "You hold perhaps an idealized view of brothers, Mistress Payne," he said with a sneer. "Not possessing one yourself."

"Quite the contrary on both points, I assure you," Gunnilde responded at once. Sir James stared at her, as though stunned by her contradicting him. "I both possess a brother and precious few illusions about his character. It does not alter my affection for him one whit."

There was a pointed silence as they sized one another up. To Gunnilde's surprise, she noticed his focus dwell a beat too long on the bodice of her gown. She glanced down, wondering if her modifications had gone awry. She had been rather enthusiastic about taking the shears to it.

The "pinking" of one's sleeves and bodice was said to be the very latest in Lasconian fashion, and Gunnilde had been keen to get ahead of the crowd. Had the new seams burst? But no, everything looked as it should. Or at least, as Gunnilde envisaged it should after hearing of the fashion.

Constance cleared her throat. "Alas, I have no brother," she sighed, striving to fill the hostile silence. "I have often lamented the fact."

"If you had a brother, you would hardly be so impressive an heiress," Sir James replied absently, his gaze still on Gunnilde. Constance drew in a sharp breath at so tactless a remark, and Sir James tore his gaze from Gunnilde to turn to his affianced with a look of some dismay.

Belatedly, it seemed to occur to him that he had blundered. A harassed look entered his eyes, and Gunnilde strove to hide her satisfaction when instead of smoothing his betrothed's ruffled feathers, Sir James made things rather worse by withdrawing even further into his habitual aloofness.

Constance, two bright pink spots appearing on her cheeks, responded in kind, and who could blame her? The man had as good as announced his attraction to her lay solely in her fortune. He had not one chivalrous bone in his body, and finally Constance seemed to have noticed as much.

19

"Well!" Constance muttered as Sir James retreated, cold and stilted till the very last. "Perhaps you were right," she said bitterly. "Perhaps I have been misled by a handsome face. That remark…" She bit her lip angrily. "It is not one I can forgive in a hurry!"

"I know," Gunnilde murmured, lowering her eyes to hide her brimming glee. At last, Constance would give sweet Sir Douglas a chance! "Sir James is clever to be sure, but as for his polished address, I am afraid I have never seen much evidence of it. He has always seemed to me a calculating and rather cold sort of man." She paused to let this sink in. "How very different he is to a stalwart knight such as Sir Douglas, whose regard a lady might depend upon," she concluded brightly.

Constance looked much struck by her words. "Yes," she pondered slowly. "Yes, I think you may be right after all. I believe I will go back now. I have…much to consider."

Inwardly rejoicing, Gunnilde retired from the field.

2

Three Days Later

"Gunnilde, what have you done now?" Harriet Portstanley hovered in the doorway looking pale as milk and practically wringing her hands.

Gunnilde turned from the looking glass where she was trying to achieve the "ram's horn" hairstyle she had heard so much about recently. Sadly, having heard only a thirdhand account of it, her efforts were largely guesswork. She regarded Harriet blankly. "Naught that I am aware," she said, lowering her hair comb. "Why?"

"You must have! Mother is simply beside herself!"

"Well," Gunnilde ventured cautiously, "I did not attend that talk on black and yellow bile that she recommended, but she knew about that for I told her as much at supper last night."

Harriet waved this aside. "It's not that! She's used to you skipping improving lectures by now. No, it's something else this time. Something far worse!" Her voice swooped low with horror.

Gunnilde considered this as she thrust another couple of hairpins into her rolled up braids. In her experience it was better to be safe than sorry when it came to the potential of her hair experimentations to tumble down. "I really cannot think," she admitted. "Shall I come now and see what vexes her?"

"It's a little late for that!" Harriet's voice wobbled. "There's a royal attendant waiting to escort you at once to the Queen's presence chamber."

"The Queen's presence chamber," Gunnilde repeated in astonishment. She had never penetrated further than the outer rooms previously. "Really?"

"You need not look so gratified! It is hardly an honor when you are called there in disgrace!"

Gunnilde's careering spirits plummeted at once. "Disgrace?"

"Why pray do you imagine Mother is so put out?" Harriet asked, sounding exasperated. "It is one thing that you are not high-minded, Gunnilde, but it is quite another to—to court scandal and dishonor as you do!" Poor Harriet's voice cracked over the last words and she gave a suppressed sob.

Scandal and dishonor? Gunnilde regarded her with dismay. "When have I ever—?"

"You cannot possibly have forgotten that whole affair with Colette Linfield and John Fulsham," Harriet said primly, though in truth Gunnilde almost had forgotten it. It had been over a month ago after all. "You were certainly implicated in that business, and if not for Mother's good name, you would have suffered the consequences, I am sure!

"You were given the benefit of the doubt that time, but let me tell you, if it were not for Viscountess Vawdrey, Mother would have washed her hands of you after that! Just look at you!" Harriet cast a despairing look at Gunnilde's hair. "What have you been doing to yourself? Where is your caul? Hurry, you must put it on and look decent."

Gunnilde patted her rolled braids. "You do not wear hair nets over this particular hairstyle," she said with a confidence she did not entirely feel. "It is a new look called 'the ram's horn.' You are supposed to be able to make out the whorl. That is the whole point."

Harriet's mouth primmed up. "I have never heard of it."

22

"Surely you heard tell of the bishop's sermon last week, highlighting the evils of lady's hairstyles?" Gunnilde replied unthinkingly.

Harriet let out a yelp of indignation. "You are not supposed to take his excellency's admonishments as fashion advice, Gunnilde!" she said, aghast.

Gunnilde bit her tongue instead of pointing out that if she had no pretensions to high-mindedness, then assuredly Harriet had none to fashion. "It was not only the bishop!" she pointed out defensively. "The letter from the Vlandivarian ambassador referred to it also! Everyone is speaking of it."

"You're beyond hope!" Harriet said, throwing up her hands. "You will be sent packing in disgrace after this; I have no doubt. Now do hurry! You cannot keep Master Winstanley waiting any longer."

Master Winstanley? Gunnilde's eyes flew wide. Everyone knew he was the Queen's favorite attendant. Setting down her remaining hairpins, Gunnilde obediently followed Harriet out of the bedchamber to find Piers Winstanley awaiting her in the hallway, resplendent in a tunic of silver and blue.

He smiled faintly at her. "Mistress Payne?" The query in his voice caused her a pang. She knew full well who he was, but he needed confirmation of her identity. She nodded and gave a little curtsey. He bowed and then made for the door without more ado, opening it and gesturing for her to precede him.

Gunnilde did so, with one backward glance over her shoulder to find Harriet and Lady Portstanley watching them with matching expressions of foreboding. She flashed them a brave smile, and then Piers followed her through the doorway and they were headed toward the royal chambers.

All the while, Gunnilde's mind raced. She did not want to be sent back to Payne Manor. How could she return when she had achieved precisely nothing thus far in her stay at court? Not only had she failed to catch the Queen's eye in the past two months, but she had also failed to forge any real lasting friendships with her fellow courtiers.

Her stepmother would not be surprised by Gunnilde's failure but still, it would sting. The only thing she had ever done which had impressed them was befriend Viscountess Vawdrey. What remained for her at Tranton Vale? Naught but her childhood memories.

Her friends and neighbors had all married and moved away. Everyone had moved on with their lives. It was the way of things. Even Hal did not reside there anymore, for as a squire now he toured the country ten months out of the year.

Gunnilde racked her brains as to what she could possibly have done to have caused the Queen's displeasure. Queen Armenal had not spoken to her once since her presentation, and even on that occasion, she had looked bored, her dark gaze barely resting on Gunnilde before it had moved away.

In spite of herself, Gunnilde's spirits rose as the attendant led her straight through the outer reception rooms, a flick of his wrist causing the guards to open the heavily decorated doors into the more select chambers peopled by the Queen's chosen few. She tried not to stare about her like the gauche young countrywoman she was, but after all, this might be her only opportunity to see the Queen's personal quarters firsthand.

A set of double doors led into the presence chamber itself, and this room seemed very grand and formal and nothing like the intimate setting of Gunnilde's imagining. The Queen was pacing about on her dais, gesturing excitedly with her hands toward a formidable-looking attendant dressed in purple.

Gunnilde knew at once this was Mistress Bartree and that she was the Queen's current favorite despite the fact there were many far younger and prettier ladies to be found at court. Around the room clustered various small groups of Armenal's chosen lords and ladies engaged in murmured conversation.

Surely, Gunnilde thought fervently, she was not the reason the Queen was looking so agitated? Her step faltered, and she cast a quick look at Master Winstanley, but his expression remained serene even as he marched right up to the dais and presented his bow.

Gunnilde stayed two steps behind him, feeling her face turning very red as the courtiers quietened down and turned toward them, their expressions openly curious.

"Yes?" Armenal said loudly. "Who is this you have brought before me?"

Piers Winstanley straightened up. "This is Mistress Payne, Your Majesty," he answered.

"Payne?" Armenal's eyes darted questioningly to her lady-in-waiting, who coughed and stepped forward to whisper in her ear. "Ah yes!" she said and turned back to Gunnilde, raking her with a keenly assessing glance. Gunnilde straightened up. It was one thing to inwardly quake before your Queen but quite another to appear poor spirited.

"So, you are Mistress Payne," the Queen mused, her eyebrows shooting up. "I see I quite wronged the bishop. I thought he was making up things to be outraged about these days, but now I see such extraordinary hairstyles do exist."

Gunnilde felt a thrill of pride run through her, even as she heard the speculative whispers of the crowd, who seemed to be drifting closer.

"I think," the Queen began hesitantly, then gave a decided nod, "that is, I am sure I will take Mistress Payne into my private sitting room for a comfortable little talk, just the two of us."

Gunnilde was sure her eyes must have bulged out of her head at this point. She stared, and she was not the only one. Mistress Bartree directed a hostile glare her way, and the rest of the room erupted in disappointed murmurings that swelled to almost alarming proportions.

"Come!" the Queen said imperiously, stepping down off the dais. "Follow me!"

Instantly, Mistress Bartree fell in step behind her, and Gunnilde trailed helplessly in their wake. "Just the two of us" seemed to include the Queen's favorite, more's the pity. She had never felt less like indulging in a tête-à-tête. Both women seemed alarming, if anything, Mistress Bartree even more so than the Queen. Still, given her lack of choice in the matter, she would have to make the best of it.

Mayhap she could even turn it to her advantage, she thought nervously, passing through two more doorways and finding herself in a smaller chamber, decorated with gold and green wall hangings. After all, she could hardly make a worse impression than she had at her presentation when her formal curtsey had gone largely ignored.

The Queen lowered herself into a seat before the fireplace as Mistress Bartree threw logs upon the blaze. "Come and sit before me, Mistress Payne," the Queen instructed. "Make yourself comfortable by the fire." Gunnilde made haste to comply, the Queen regarding her thoughtfully all the while. "You are but lately come to court, I take it?" she said as her eyes roamed over Gunnilde's face.

Gunnilde strove to hide her wince. "No, Your Majesty. I came to court in September as a guest of the Portstanley family. I was presented to you at the feast of St. Gyles..." Her words trailed off miserably, but

26

after all, she had always known she must have made next to no impression.

"The Portstanleys," Armenal repeated with a frown. "They are a cultured family, are they not, keen on enlightened thinking?" She did not sound particularly enthusiastic about the fact. "You are much in sympathy with such subjects? The arts, the sciences," she enquired politely.

"Not really, Your Majesty," Gunnilde admitted. "But the Portstanleys are intimate acquaintances of my best friend in all the world, Lady Eden Vawdrey."

"Eden? She is the great friend of yours?" The Queen sat up in her seat. She made some gesture to her lady-in-waiting, and Mistress Bartree crossed the room to open a cupboard and extract three goblets.

"She is," Gunnilde said fervently. "I am devoted to Eden."

"And she to you?"

"I believe so, she has always been most kind and generous toward me."

"You have been to stay with her at Vawdrey Keep?"

"Several times. I am godmother to her daughter, Agnes," Gunnilde offered proudly.

The Queen nodded, as though finally accepting the veracity of her claims. "But how is it that your very good friend Eden, she did not present you to me herself?"

"She wanted to Your Majesty, but you see…"

"The child rearing," the Queen decided with a sigh.

"Er…yes. And other commitments at home. A married lady's life—"

"You need not tell me of this," Armenal assured her with a wave of the hand. "I am lamentably familiar with the subject." She looked up at Mistress Bartree's approach with a tray of drinks. "I always caution you, Magnatrude, do I not, against taking such a foolhardy step?"

"You do, Your Majesty," Mistress Bartree replied in a low, rich voice, and to her surprise, Gunnilde realized the older woman was not without attraction, though she could not imagine any man being so brave as to offer for Magnatrude Bartree. The lady-in-waiting offered the contents of her tray first to the Queen and then to Gunnilde.

"They so very rarely listen," Armenal sighed. "No matter how nicely they are set up. First Eden, then Jane… I daresay someone will try enticing Magnatrude away from me next, is that not so, Magnatrude?"

"Never, Your Majesty," Mistress Bartree said fervently, then retreated to a seat a little further away from them to pour herself a cup of mead.

"Well, well, we shall see. I have all but lost faith in the loyalty of handmaidens," she said bitterly. "Experience hath proved a cruel mistress."

Gunnilde, unsure what else to say, took a swig of mead. It was good and sweet and warmed the cold pit of her stomach. She began to feel a bit better about the situation. Surely this was an honor, to sit in the Queen's private sitting room and converse with her, practically just the two of them.

"And you?" Queen Armenal asked suddenly, almost making Gunnilde spill her drink. "What are your own marital prospects? You cannot be older than one and twenty I am sure."

Gunnilde took a deep breath. "I am fully two and twenty, Your Majesty. But the truth is, I've decided against marriage after suffering a crushing disappointment in my youth." She paused to dab her eyes with her handkerchief and allow this momentous statement to sink in. "No, I have decided that the role of sympathetic listener is mine. You will not know of this, Your Highness," she said with quiet pride, "but I am in much demand to act as chaperone here at court. Many couples have need of my offices."

"Is that so? You take the strolls down the long gallery dogging the steps of the courting couples?"

"I do."

"And sit with them on the end of the bench, keeping the watchful eye as they converse?"

"Most readily, Your Highness."

"And this does not bore you?" the Queen asked incredulously. "The role always of onlooker and friend to lovers?"

"Oh no, Your Majesty! I vastly prefer it."

Queen Armenal's eyebrows shot up. "Prefer it?"

"Yes, for that way, I will never risk jeopardizing my own feelings again."

The Queen paused thoughtfully. "I see," she said after a moment's consideration. "Tell me of this misfortune you suffered in your…youth." She and Magnatrude Bartree exchanged an amused look with one another. "For I find myself most interested."

Almost without conscious effort, Gunnilde adopted a sorrowful expression. It was a subject she was most comfortable discussing by now, for she had talked of it often and again. "The tale is not an unusual one, Your Majesty," she said modestly. "Our fathers' estates were

29

neighboring, and there was an understanding of sorts that when we came of age, we would make a match of it. Alas, his father died, and nothing came of it." She dabbed her eyes, though in truth, she had no more tears to shed over Arthur Conway.

"I see," the Queen murmured. "He made you promises and played you false, the knave."

Gunnilde's eyes widened. "Oh no!" she objected. "No, no, we were both young and the betrothal was never really spoken of all that much. It was simply something that we quietly acknowledged whenever we happened upon each other. Master Conway was always most agreeable in his manner, and I grew attached to the idea that we were destined for one another, that was all.

"Later on, his sister made an advantageous match, and it was agreed he could aim higher in his choice of bride." She shrugged. "These things happen. I was embarrassed, and it was much discussed in our home county for a twelvemonth, until such talk happily died down."

The Queen frowned. "You talk like a woman of sense regarding this," she said slowly, "which only makes me more curious." She shot a quizzical look at Gunnilde as though trying to puzzle something out.

"How so, Your Majesty?" Gunnilde set down her empty goblet. The Queen gestured at once for Magnatrude to refill it, and waited until this office was performed before she resumed her speech.

"You see, Gunnilde," she said, "it makes me believe that your forswearing of husbands was not due to this youthful setback, for you took that quite in your stride." She looked at her shrewdly. "I believe there must be something you are not telling me, is that not so? Some later event of more significance, perhaps?"

Gunnilde was still basking in the fact that the Queen had addressed her by her given name when realization of her words hit. Her breath caught

30

in her throat and her cheeks grew hot. "B-but how did Your Majesty—? No one else ever surmised as much!" she stammered.

Armenal's expression became complacent. "I am considered reasonably astute in such matters," she said with a self-satisfied smile. "You see, much like yourself, I prefer to be the observer in life, but I have a good decade more of experience to draw upon. You must not reproach yourself," she said kindly. "It was inevitable that I should find you out in your lie."

"Lie?" Gunnilde spluttered. "Nay, it was not that precisely." She squirmed awkwardly in her seat. "It was more like…" Words failed her and she fell silent.

"An omission?" the Queen suggested lightly.

"Yes," Gunnilde admitted. She could not quite meet the Queen's eyes and nibbled unhappily on her bottom lip.

"You have spoken to no one of this event? Except perhaps your very good friend Eden Vawdrey."

"Oh no! I could not possibly—that is, I did not tell even my dearest friend of it," she answered guiltily. "I did not wish to—to burden her."

"I see." The Queen sat back in her chair, steepling her hands under her chin. "But you will tell to me now this significant event, will you not?"

Gunnilde raised appealing eyes to the Queen. "Oh, please, I—"

"Do not speak of it yet," the Queen said, holding up her hand. "I will even send away my good Magnatrude as a show of good faith between us." She directed a glance at her lady-in-waiting, who rose at once from her seat and swiftly exited the room, shutting the door behind her. "You see? Now…" Armenal leaned forward in her seat, her eyes gleaming. "Tell to me, please."

31

And just like that, Gunnilde told. She was careful to switch the setting to her father's house, and to leave the knights in question faceless strangers. Wisely, she kept the substance of their conversation intact. Because of this, she knew her words bore the ring of truth, for when repeating them, her voice rasped with emotion she could not falsify.

The fire crackled and the silence stretched as the Queen sat in deep contemplation, her eyes half-closed. "Yes, now it all makes the perfect sense to me," she murmured, then gave a dreamy sigh. As though emerging from her contented ponderings, she straightened up and clicked her tongue. "You have been through much, my poor Gunnilde. These knights they can be such swine." She shuddered. "So brutish. So coarse. They outrage every common decency. Never will I understand the women who are impressed by such men."

Gunnilde's expression wavered. "Well, er, I don't know that I would say that precisely…"

"And those two knights you overheard describing you so unbecomingly that time… You are sure you could not hazard a guess as to who they were?"

"Oh no, Your Majesty!" Gunnilde hurried to reassure her. "I did not recognize their voices; I dare assure you of that!" She lowered her eyes. "You see my father hosts an annual tournament, so our home is positively swarming with knights at that time of year. It could have been any one of their number."

"Yes, that is a good deal too many to narrow down," Armenal acknowledged sadly. "'Tis a pity we will never know the churl's identity, but few maidens would have had the courage to confront them there and then. I suppose your heart failed you in the moment." Her attitude in this was one of resigned disappointment.

Inwardly, Gunnilde breathed a sigh of relief. No matter how much heartache he had caused her, she would not expose Sir Ned for his ungentle conduct, not for the wide world! She felt badly though, for deceiving the Queen, who had been so kind and sympathetic to her plight.

"You must not regret confiding in me, my good Gunnilde," the Queen said, misinterpreting her expression. "Indeed, it is a good thing, for in truth, you were in some hot water when first you came to me today."

"Hot water?" Gunnilde repeated. Oh yes. In all the excitement, Gunnilde had almost forgotten she was supposed to be in disgrace.

"Yes," the Queen agreed absently, "for you have been named as a guilty party in a serious affair here at court. There has been some pother and commotion over it this morn. Still, it is of no matter now, for I have thought of a very neat solution." She beamed at Gunnilde, who was sat frozen in her seat. "And now, if you would just open the door and call to Magnatrude, then we may see about straightening this all out."

"Yes, Your Majesty," she said obediently, rising from her seat, though she felt more bewildered than ever. Whatever could Queen Armenal mean? She crossed the room and called to Mistress Bartree, who appeared so suddenly, it was almost alarming.

"Have Sir James fetched hither immediately," the Queen instructed. "Gunnilde, you will go into my bedchamber and await my summons there. You may look over my Book of Days. It is generally much admired."

Gunnilde stood amazed, but Mistress Bartree caught her elbow and directed her along the passage to the Queen's spacious bedchamber. "So, I just...sit in here?" she asked, gazing about her at the sumptuous furnishings and decoration.

Magnatrude Bartree gestured toward a stand bearing a gorgeously illustrated book gleaming with gold leaf. "Her Majesty gave you gracious instruction how to employ yourself," she said sternly. "Do not touch anything else." She backed out of the room, her beady eyes still fixed on Gunnilde till the last.

Gunnilde watched her retreat, still open-mouthed. What in heaven's name was happening? She could not seem to grasp the situation at all. And to which Sir James was the Queen referring? There were several that Gunnilde was aware of.

There was Sir James Attley of course, the knight under whose tutelage her brother was currently learning the ways of knighthood. There was also Sir James Henderson, an old crony of her father's, though it was unlikely he had been to court in the past fifty years. There was even that disagreeable Sir James Wycliffe, she reflected, pulling a face.

Sir James Attley was perhaps the most likely, she decided desperately. Mayhap Hal had come to court at last? The letter she received from home had indicated she would likely see him soon, for the last tournament of the year had taken place at the end of October and the next was not until March.

But then, why would Gunnilde find herself in hot water over Sir James Attley's appearance? A sudden uneasiness entered her soul. Sir James was a close friend of Sir Roland Vawdrey and Sir Ned Bevan… But it couldn't be anything to do with that business, she told herself firmly. It was just on her mind from the version of events she had told the Queen. Sir James had not even been at Vawdrey Keep that time.

A small page in pale blue hose appeared in the doorway, his hair almost obscuring his eyes. "If it please you, my mistress has sent me to see if you have need of aught," he said obligingly.

"Your mistress?"

He straightened up proudly, whisking his hair out of his eyes. "Mistress Bartree."

She had her own page? Why was Gunnilde not surprised? "How kind," she said brightly. "What is your name, child?"

"'Tis Unwin, miss."

"Well, Unwin, I would be most grateful if you would come and keep me company a while." She smiled at him. "It would be a great kindness in you for I am somewhat afeared sat here all alone in a queen's bedchamber."

His thin chest puffed out and he advanced into the room. "You needn't be afeared, miss," he assured her cautiously. "You have full permission to take your ease."

"Until the Queen calls me," she agreed, lowering herself onto the window seat and patting the cushion beside her.

"That won't be for a while," Unwin said with confidence as he crossed the room to join her. "That Sir James is in with her now and he'll take a time, for he'd a face like thunder." A certain relish entered his manner at the retelling.

"Sir James?" Gunnilde seized on this eagerly. She cleared her throat. "Now which Sir James would you be referring to, I wonder? Sir James Attley?" she asked hopefully.

"Attley? Nay, that's not his name," Unwin responded, shaking his head. "Isn't he the one attends the royal tournaments?"

"Yes, that is so," Gunnilde agreed absently. "Well, if not him, then perhaps 'tis my old neighbor from home, Sir James Henderson?" she ventured, however unlikely the scenario that her father's friend should journey to court. Mayhap there was some news from home, she thought, desperately clutching at straws.

"Nay, I never heard tell of any Henderson," Unwin replied, blowing his hair out of his eyes. Really, Mistress Bartree should get the child's hair trimmed. He looked at her expectantly, as though keen to hear her next guess.

"Um, well, is not that council member with the limp called Sir James something?" Gunnilde quavered.

"That's Sir Jacob Brentford," Unwin corrected her, looking smug.

"I can't think of any more," Gunnilde lied, sending the child a sidelong look.

"Would you like a clue?" Unwin asked obligingly.

She nodded. "Yes, please."

"It's that handsome one that always looks so moody. The one what writes the music."

Gunnilde's heart sank down to her slippered feet. "Not…Sir James Wycliffe," she said hollowly.

A grin broke over Unwin's face. "The very same," he said, swinging his legs. "He don't half look mad. Do you want to know a secret?" he asked, leaning in close. Almost against her better judgment, Gunnilde nodded again. "I heard tell his betrothed up and left him for another!" Unwin confided hoarsely. "Vanished in the night."

Gunnilde gasped. "Did she really?" Constance? Constance did that? Highly proper and dignified Constance ran off into the night with Sir Douglas? She could scarcely believe it, feeling both equal parts gratified and shocked. Oh, Sir Douglas must be quite giddy with joy, she thought, flushing with pleasure. How thrilled she was for him. Never had a knight striven harder to win his maiden's favor.

36

Unwin nodded, looking pleased by her response. "Only you can't tell no one," he warned. "It's all a big secret and the families don't want it to get out. The Queen herself is handling the matter and promised to seek out the guilty parties and make sure repar—repar—" He gave up on the word. "Justice is done," he concluded.

Gunnilde heart pounded. "I see," she said faintly. Now it was all starting to make a horrible sort of sense. So that was why she was in trouble.

3

James stared at the Queen. Surely, he had misheard her.

Seemingly picking up on his disbelief, Queen Armenal sat forward in her seat. "You will take her to wife forthwith for I have decided Mistress Payne will suit you admirably." She nodded as though pleased with her pronouncement. "She will more than make up for that which you have lately lost."

"I have lately lost an heiress, Your Majesty," James pointed out. He could see at once she was not pleased with his response, but it was nothing less than the truth.

"That may be so," she agreed graciously after a small pause, "but this one has an abundance of qualities to make up for this. Money is not everything, Sir James," she said with the cool assurance of the very privileged.

The silence stretched as James reflected grimly that the Queen was fortunate enough to know nothing of family debts. "To which qualities does Her Majesty refer?" James heard himself ask calmly, though all around him his carefully laid plans were crashing to the ground in ruins. The only quality he could think of was her abundance of hair, though come to think of it, Neville had intimated that was likely supplemented.

"She will never fade into the background, that one," the Queen said simply. James agreed but he was far from convinced this was a good quality. "She will no longer allow it," she continued cryptically. When he said nothing, she looked a little disappointed, then changed the subject. "She has a father who hosts the tournaments. There must be money there," she decided airily.

Who even was her father? James was fairly sure he had never been introduced. "I know nothing of her family connections," he said stiffly.

"No more do I, but it turns out she is very closely acquainted with Viscountess Vawdrey, so that must suffice." Was she? James did not think he had seen her in such company even once.

"Besides, I have decided I will give her a wedding present," Armenal said grandly. She paused for dramatic effect. "I will make her a lady-in-waiting," she announced, looking pleased with herself. "That will give your wife consequence and influence. What more can you ask for?"

James held his tongue, despite several things springing to mind. Only once the silence grew pronounced, did he ask quietly, "Do I have any choice in the matter, Your Majesty?"

"None," the Queen replied briskly. "If you do not wish to give royal offence, which presumably you do not."

As his income relied on his position at court, James closed his eyes briefly. "No, Your Majesty," he admitted.

"You must admit there is a pleasing symmetry to your marrying Gunnilde after Sir Douglas, he ran away with the Lady Constance," the Queen mused. James seethed in silence. He supposed Sir Douglas must be one of the men he had seen Mistress Payne parading about court and whispering in corners with. "Then I can consider the matter settled?" the Queen said, breaking into his thoughts.

"Settled?" James blurted, feeling panicked. Surely to gods he was not expected to play up to and flatter this woman. To express an admiration he did not feel and actually propose to her! "What of the lady?" he asked desperately. The recent memory of Mistress Payne's hostile glances allowed him the tiniest flicker of hope. She did not care for his society any more than he for hers.

"She will be led in this matter by her queen, I am quite sure of that," Armenal uttered with such confidence that James's hopes were instantly dashed. "With your permission, I will summon her, and we will see to the matter forthwith."

Despite her talk of permission, Armenal did not even look to him for his confirmation. Instead, she turned at once to some woman in purple who had been hovering in the background. "Fetch her now, my good Magnatrude. Then run along to the royal chapel and find whoever is currently on duty there. Tell them there is a ceremony I need performing. We will be along presently to see that it is done."

James stood frozen, despite his inner turmoil. What in the hells was happening? The Queen was humming to herself, a smile playing about her lips. There was something almost monstrous about the way she was toying with his life, like some kind of spoiled child with her puppets.

He had to avert his eyes for a moment, to rein in his thoughts. Words trembled on his lips that would be unwise, disastrous even to speak. He was not in control here, and he needed to remember that lest he lose his head altogether.

At least, he thought suddenly, he would not have to actively court this one. He knew instinctively that she would not have been satisfied with the kind of dry speeches he had delivered to Constance. She would have expected effort. Effort James had neither the ability nor the inclination to expend.

His shoulders relaxed infinitesimally. There was that one small comfort. Then, too, he had been rather dreading the intimacies of marriage with Constance. Before she ran off, he had owed it to his bride to be always courteous and considerate. At least with this one, there was no need for pretense and civility. He could be wholly his own horrible self.

Gunnilde Payne would just be another member of his godsawful draining family for him to endure and nothing more. Moreover, she had brought such treatment upon herself with her shameless interference in his affairs. The thought was an oddly fortifying one. He had known all along that he would be a complete failure in the role of husband. Her appearance in the doorway startled him out of the cold comfort of his thoughts.

"Ah, Gunnilde, come in," hailed the Queen. "We find ourselves in an awkward situation this morn. Perhaps you are unaware of it, but Lady Constance hath eloped in the night with Sir Douglas Farleigh." She paused, waiting to see the effect upon Gunnilde.

It was not pronounced. She turned rather red and squared her shoulders. "I did not know," she said unconvincingly. "And indeed, I am very surprised to hear of it."

The Queen smiled a pitying smile. It was plain she did not believe a word of it either. Mistress Payne bore a faintly guilty air however much she tried to shrug it off. She spared him a fleeting glance, then refocused her attention on the Queen.

What had she done with her extraordinary hair today? he wondered. It was rolled up like those puffed sweet breads the street vendors sold. Most distracting. He wondered that she could even hear through all that hair heaped on each side of her head. Instead of wearing the large buns behind her ears like a sensible woman, hers were worn so far forward they framed her face.

Belatedly, he realized he had lost the thread of conversation, for the Queen was raising her voice to attract his attention. "I have been speaking with Sir James," she said loudly, "and we have hit upon an admirable plan to rectify things. Is that not so, Sir James?"

Though he attempted to muster up the required response, James found he could manage nothing more than a nod and a clearing of his throat at this point. For the first time a hint of trepidation entered Mistress Payne's expression, and he was strangely pleased to see it. She darted

41

an alarmed glance his way, before determinedly facing forward and concentrating solely on the Queen.

"We have decided you will be wed this afternoon in the royal chapel," Armenal concluded graciously.

This pronouncement caused Mistress Payne's eyes to widen like trenchers. "To whom?" she burst out in astonishment.

The Queen looked a little annoyed. "Why to Sir James, of course! Who else?"

Mistress Payne gasped aloud at this, her head whipping around to skewer him with a disbelieving stare. This time he could well believe the Queen's words had shocked her. He took a perverse sort of pleasure in her horrified incredulity.

"What?" she yelped. "But I—I—" Her protests seemed to stick in her throat. She swallowed, then hope appeared to flood back into her eyes. "What about my father's consent?" she asked wildly, as though a drowning woman spotting land in the distance.

The Queen made a scoffing sound. "Clearly your father does not think marriage it is the priority for you, my good Gunnilde, else he would have arranged a match for you as soon as your first, it fell through, would he not?"

James's ears pricked up. So…he was not the only one with a failed betrothal it seemed.

"You must not fret over this matter," the Queen continued sagely. "Your father, he will concede to my judgment in this matter, I am sure. Did he not send you to court to mingle with the leading lights of the land and elevate your prospects?"

Mistress Payne's expression alternated from desperate to doubtful and back again. James surmised her father did not give a rush light for such things, however she could hardly vocalize this to the Queen, so for once she behaved wisely and held her tongue.

"I am sure his forgiveness will be forthcoming when he hears of your most impressive elevation to lady-in-waiting to Karadok's Queen," Armenal said slyly.

Gunnilde's expression went from anguished to dazed disbelief in an instant. It was plain she could not quite believe her ears. "M-me?" she breathed, pointing to her bodice. "A lady-in-waiting to Your Highness?"

The Queen beamed, finally pleased with the reaction she had evoked.

"Oh, Your Majesty!" Gunnilde's voice shook with emotion. "Oh, I can scarcely believe it!" She took two impetuous steps forward before she could stop herself, and the Queen extended a beringed hand. James watched through narrowed eyes as Mistress Payne hurried to clasp it.

Slowly, one of her hair buns started to unravel. He watched, strangely fascinated as it snaked loose and then swung down, a thick pale yellow expanse of hair which extended past her waist. In her distraction she barely seemed to notice the mishap.

"Oh, Your Majesty," she repeated joyfully. "I am honored beyond belief!"

"Of course you are," Armenal said indulgently. "Now turn to Sir James and give him your formal acceptance of his suit."

All pleasure drained from her expression as she turned to look at him. "I accept," she said woodenly and gave a stiff curtsey. He bowed shallowly in return. Well, at least in this, their feelings were mutual.

They were given an hour's reprieve to ready themselves before reconvening in the Queen's private chapel. James used that time to return to his palace quarters and fetch his brother. He should have at least one family member to stand beside him on such an occasion.

Fortunately, he merely felt numb by this point, so Neville's amazement washed over him instead of infuriating him further. When his brother seemed to realize there was nothing to be done except to change into his best doublet, he fell mercifully silent, though 'twas plain he was itching with curiosity.

They made their way, side by side to the Queen's chapel, sober and resigned, their moods matching for once. At the chapel they found Lady Portstanley, who James vaguely recognized, and her plain-faced daughter, whose name he did not recall. Both looked anxious and seemed determined to avoid direct eye contact.

"Did you say the Portstanleys were her guardians?" he muttered in an aside to his brother.

Neville merely shrugged. "I know precious little of the matter," he whispered back with some asperity. "Should you not have ascertained as much before you offered for the girl?"

It was James's turn to shrug. "There was no time." His brother shot him an odd look, but James was not inclined to explain, and in any case the Queen had now arrived escorted by her favorite attendant. She made way to the front pew, all wreathed in smiles and clearly overflowing with benevolence at having got her way.

Neville's head swiveled to look at him interrogatively, but he pretended not to notice. Next the bad-tempered lady-in-waiting marched up the aisle, stony-faced and accompanied by a little page with an untidy haircut.

Last, but not least, the bride appeared, her hair once more done up in two ornate whorls. She had changed her gown, James noticed, presumably for her best, which was of a deep rose hue. The sleeves of this one were mercifully intact, and he thought for a moment she had dressed modestly for the occasion.

When he joined her at the front however, he found this gown was no less flaunting than the rest of her wardrobe for it had a series of holes about the bodice, giving flashes of a paler pink undergarment peeking through.

"Sir!" the cleric said in a voice stiff with outrage, and James made haste to face front. To his surprise, he found it was none other than the Bishop of Badsbury eyeing him balefully. He had not expected such an exalted personage to perform the ceremony, but he supposed if anyone could command his participation it would be the Queen.

"Might I ascertain if we can begin?" the right reverend asked crisply. James nodded and the bishop's disapproving gaze moved to the bride. At the sight of her hair, he recoiled slightly before a look of grim determination overtook his jowly face.

Taking a deep breath, he gave a brief, if bleak overview of marital duty, before plunging without more ado into the vows. Both repeated them dutifully and toward the conclusion James was surprised to feel a jab in his side. The small page had appeared there and was thrusting a ring into his fingers.

Lifting it, he found what looked to be a devotional ring of gold decorated with raised quatrefoils and some lettering. The need for a ring had not even occurred to him. He flushed and the boy winked at him before beating a hasty retreat. Gunnilde, seeing his hesitation, held out her left hand, fingers spread.

He jammed the ring onto her middle finger, realized his error, and had to grasp hold of her to draw it back off and try again. The contact was a shock. Her hand, which he had thought would be cold and limp, was warm and jumped in his own, as though she, too, felt the shock of their connection.

"Sorry," he heard himself mutter, then slid the ring onto her fourth finger, where it passed both knuckles with ease. Instead of releasing her, he paused, holding it in place while his eyes sought her own. Afterward, he could not explain it, even to himself. He only knew that it was vital in that moment that their eyes should meet.

Their gazes clashed and the moment passed. James released her hand, feeling oddly shaken. Cornflower blue, he thought as the bishop summed up. Dimly he remembered his father's steward teaching him something about cornflowers. Something detrimental. Oh yes, that was it. They were said to be a great nuisance in agricultural circles for they blunted scythes and reduced the corn crop. Her eyes would be cornflower blue.

4

It was dark in the Great Hall, a huge fire blazed, and the room was lit up by dozens of candles. Excitedly, Gunnilde peered around, making note of all the nobles present. There was Lord Vawdrey and his countess, and there was Lord and Lady Schaeffer, and Viscount Bardulph and his wife, Lady Jane.

Further down the table were other ladies-in-waiting who Gunnilde hoped to get to know better now that she was one of their number—the beauteous Frances Lessimore, the dashing Osanna Spencer, and even the fascinating Lady Wymarka. It occurred to Gunnilde that if she worked very hard to please the Queen, she, too, might get an epithet one day.

What could hers be? Gunnilde the daringly dressed? Her heart beat faster even at the thought of it. How many times had she watched the Queen's ladies drifting around the royal gardens and fervently wished she, too, was permitted to mingle among them? Instead, she had been forced to trail sadly in the wake of Harriet and her bookish friend Winifred Hawes until she had found some acquaintances of her own among the wider court.

The trouble with the new friends she had found was that once she had helped them untangle their love lives, they invariably went off to live a happily wedded life and she never saw them again. Colette Linfield was one such.

She had really liked Colette and believed they would be friends forever, but since she had left court, Gunnilde had not received a single letter from her. The same was true of Mary Kingston. Once she had a betrothal secured, she had flitted back to rural obscurity, for she had come to court in the first place only to make her curtsey and find a spouse.

Even when Gunnilde had managed to befriend the popular Constance Northcott, it had not helped her own position one bit, for Constance moved between groups and did not seemingly mix their members of her own accord. Besides, she had only managed to befriend Constance by pretending she, too, was interested in intellectual pursuits and that had been a big fat lie.

It had not taken long before Gunnilde had found out she was sadly unsuited for any of the meetings and societies that Eden so adored. The lectures set her yawning, the music recitals set her eyelids drooping, and as for the poetry readings! My gods, the sessions left her confused and scratching her head. What in the world were these men twittering on about?

At least she did not have to pretend to be clever anymore! Gunnilde gazed proudly down at the ruby brooch with three teardrop pearls that the Queen herself had bestowed upon her. It now graced the front of her bodice, and Gunnilde could not keep her eyes from it, even as the celebration carried on around her.

The Queen and founder of the feast sat at the head of the table, toasting them and receiving congratulations on the appointment of her new lady-in-waiting. Gunnilde and her new husband sat midtable, surrounded by well-wishers and the premier courtiers of the land.

It did not really feel like a wedding celebration, but Gunnilde did not mind that, for she did not really feel married. Back home in Tranton Vale such an occasion would have been a very different affair. It would have been a joyous and boisterous occasion with much laughter, singing and shouting.

All of her family's friends and neighbors would have been there to join the festivities. Gunnilde and her stepmother would have planned every roasted joint of meat, and any troubadour in the vicinity would have been welcome to come to Payne Manor and perform for them in her father's hall.

For a moment, the contrast made her feel almost forlorn. Then she reminded herself that the groom her father had picked out for her had gone off to marry another. And in any case, she had wanted different things.

She had wanted to be a lady-in-waiting. She had wanted a place at court, and here at court, things were done differently. She nodded. Yes, this was what she wanted, and here at court, wedding feasts were not occasions of unbridled merriment. They were instead restrained and decorous.

In any event, there was music, for there were a couple of lute players strumming a tune of sorts in the gallery. There were no rousing words to sing along, and it was not the kind of tune you could clap in time to or shout out "Hie!" at the chorus, but all the same there was entertainment of sorts.

Mentally, she composed the letter home she would write, telling them of the refinement of the occasion. She would devote a whole page describing her brooch, she decided. That ought to distract them from the lack of a bride chase or any attendant horseplay. No one had even asked for her garter.

The King appeared shortly before the first course, and even he seemed well-disposed tonight, for instead of demanding who she was, he looked over Gunnilde and said, "Ah, very good, very good." Strangely, the glance he sent toward the groom was not so benevolent.

"Not going to play us a tune, are you, Wycliffe?" he asked with foreboding. "I thought I'd send for Master Robkin this eve."

Gunnilde clapped her hands with delight before noticing the Queen's frown. Quickly, she lowered her hands.

"Like the royal jester, do you?" the King asked her, looking encouraged.

"Oh yes, sire!" Gunnilde confessed. "Though I've never had the pleasure of seeing him at such close quarters before."

"A girl after my own heart!" the King pronounced, sitting back in his seat. "Well, we cannot disappoint the bride, now, can we?" he asked, turning to his wife.

Queen Armenal sighed and tilted her head in acquiescence, and the King snapped his fingers. "Have Master Robkin brought forth!" he bellowed.

Gunnilde bit her lip and glanced at her bridegroom, who was sitting very still beside her. Had she said the wrong thing? A sudden thought occurred to her. "Did you wish to perform a piece of your music for all present?" she guessed in a low voice.

"No, I did not," he replied crisply. "I can think of nothing I would like less."

Well…that was alright, then. For a moment, she had been worried she had deprived him of some great opportunity. Gunnilde relaxed.

"I do not like jesters," he elaborated unexpectedly. "Rather like cats, they always know it and determine to single me out for their attention. I imagine as a bridegroom my lot will be even worse than usual."

He did look very tense, Gunnilde reflected. Unexpectedly, her heart went out to him. Here she was all happy and content with her new position, her beautiful new brooch, and her seat at the table among all the exalted company. And beside her sat Sir James, whose lot was now tied to her own, feeling quite the opposite.

She really knew very little about the man, other than him being a cold fish and the fact he was considered an accomplished musician. What an awkward thing it must be, to write and perform music but hate to have an audience! Maybe that was why he was always so moody. "Don't

50

worry, I'll help you," she vowed aloud and shifted a little closer to him on the bench.

He sent her a startled look. "You will?"

She nodded. It was the least she could do, especially as it was partly her fault Master Robkin had been summoned. "Why do you look so surprised? Am I not your helpmeet in life now?" This question appeared to take him back even more, and seemingly he had no answer to it, for he opened and closed his mouth without saying a word.

"Is it the riddles you do not like?" she pressed on. "Or—?"

"I do not like any of it," he said shortly. "I would much rather be left in peace."

That seemed rather a lot to hope for, considering the circumstances. Gunnilde chewed her lip. "Mayhap we will be lucky, and he will content himself amusing the King?"

He sent her a skeptical look. "You think so?"

"Not really," she admitted. "But never fear. I will support you." She reached across and patted his hand reassuringly, then turned her head excitedly as jolly piping music heralded the arrival of the jester.

The next half hour, Gunnilde spent laughing so hard at Master Robkin's antics that tears rolled down her face. She did not forget her husband's plight however, and whenever the jester's attention turned their way, she would purposely command James's attention, so he did not sit there like a startled deer in the hunter's sights.

He had been quite right, she realized. The jester's attention seemed instinctively drawn to those in the crowd that did not overly relish the entertainment he offered. She needed to do whatever she could to shield her new spouse from Master Robkin's ridicule. He had been through enough this day already.

After the first few times she cupped her fingers about his ear to whisper "Pretend I am explaining the joke to you," or clapped her fingers to his cheek to turn his face toward the goblet she was holding up to him, he seemed to accept her ministrations without resisting.

Indeed, when the jester started prancing down the hall purposely toward them, he panicked and grabbed at her sleeve, turning instinctively toward her. Immediately, Gunnilde whisked up off the bench and dropped down into his lap.

Only she could see the expression on James's terse face. "Don't be afraid," she said earnestly, placing a hand on either side of his face. "Trust me." Taking a deep breath, she squashed her face up against his, squeezing her eyes shut.

James tensed for a long instant, then she felt him relax against her, his breath warm against her lips. Had he spoken? She opened one eye and saw the jester's striped tunic of yellow and blue hovering close by. Oh no!

Flinging her arms about James's neck, she crushed herself against him, determined to block out the jester and his unwanted japes. After a moment, she felt James's hands come up to rest at her waist. Cheering and whooping rang in her ears. Someone, who sounded remarkably like King Wymer, said loudly, "Lucky beggar!" and finally, the blur of blue and yellow moved away.

Gunnilde loosened her grip. She drew her face back from his. "He's gone!" she whispered, shooting him a conspiratorial smile. James was breathing hard, the expression on his face hard to read. The poor thing clearly went in mortal dread of jesters. She wondered if his aversion extended to tumblers and jugglers as well.

Seeing he was still struggling with words, she rubbed his shoulder blades. "All is well," she reassured him, turning her face to track the jester's movements. "He's making his way back to the King and Queen," she murmured, starting to lift off his lap. "Shall I—?"

"No!" he said, yanking her back into his lap, "Stay where you are for now." At her surprised look, he reddened. "He might come back this way," he muttered, dropping his gaze.

"Oh." Gunnilde nodded. "Very well." His fingers, which had been digging into her waist, relaxed their hold a little. She cleared her throat. "I'm a little thirsty," she said. "Might I just—"

"Here," he said before she could let her arms drop, grabbing his wine goblet and lifting it to her lips.

Feeling rather self-conscious, Gunnilde accepted a gulp of wine. Again, their fellow feasters cheered.

"A loving cup!" called one.

"That means you need to drink from it now," she prompted him.

"I have been drinking from your cup all night," he pointed out, his tone rather dry, but he took a swig nonetheless.

Gunnilde felt suddenly embarrassed, though she could not have said precisely why. She let her gaze wander over James's shoulder and saw his brother watching them open-mouthed. She had never had occasion to speak to Sir Neville before but realized that presently was not the best time. Things had turned surprisingly lively in the Great Hall. Even the music seemed to have taken a jaunty turn.

Abruptly someone clapped their hands, and the noise died away. "The ladies-in-waiting will now withdraw to the bridal chamber!" the Queen announced. It occurred to Gunnilde to wonder where that might be, as before now she had shared Harriet Portstanley's bedchamber. Surely poor Harriet would not be put from her own room?

She did not have long to ponder this, as her hands were caught hold of, and she was hauled out of James's lap by a pair of giggling ladies whose names she was unsure of. Gunnilde barely managed a backward glance before she was whisked away from the hall and dragged down several corridors and up a flight of stairs toward the courtiers' rooms.

It was not to Lady Portstanley's door that she was led however, but a different one. Were these the Wycliffes' designated rooms? she wondered as she was led straight into a bedchamber hung about with gloomy tapestries and illuminated by only a small fire in the hearth and a pair of candles on the mantel.

Once inside the room, the Queen's ladies spoke only in whispers as they helped divest her of her gown. Gunnilde noticed a few of them were rather standoffish and did not participate much. Lucy Melvin was one such. Instead of helping, she strode about James's bedchamber with her arms crossed and her nose in the air.

"I feel quite sorry for Constance," she muttered. "To be so soon forgotten."

"Oh, hush, Lucy!" another cautioned her as she set the Queen's brooch down carefully on a nearby table. "Do you forget—" She broke off her words and bit her lip. Forget what? Gunnilde wondered but was distracted from this when she noticed how Estrilda Rheinholdt held up her best gown, her eyebrows exaggeratedly raised.

"Do the Portstanleys have mice in their quarters?" she asked archly.

Another poked a finger through one of the pinking holes and they both collapsed into helpless laughter.

"Ignore them," a dark-haired lady recommended as she removed the many hairpins from her head. Gunnilde thought her name was Margaret something, possibly Mistress Margaret Pryor. "Goodness, you do use a lot of pins!" A rapidly growing pile of them was stacking up on the bedside table.

"I told you it was her real hair," Osanna Spencer said with satisfaction when another lady looked disappointed as Gunnilde's long braids were unwound and hung down her sides.

Lucy Melvin sniffed. "I'll not believe it until I see the braids taken out." As plucking fingers were already seeing to this, Gunnilde held her tongue.

"You see!" Osanna said triumphantly when her hair hung loose about her like a pale gold cloak.

"It is so plentiful!" Lady Wymarka Kloch marveled drawing a comb through Gunnilde's tresses. "Tell me, what do you treat it with? Crushed chickweed? Or goat's dung?"

"Neither," Gunnilde spluttered. Goat's dung? There was more giggling.

"I tell you, it is obvious when a woman's hair is bulked out with flax," Osanna said knowledgeably. "My mother has a neighbor who does it and I can see the signs from a two furlongs away!"

Lucy opened her mouth on a retort when they heard three knocks on the outer door. "The bridegroom is here!" announced a well-rehearsed voice. Instead of being brought to the marriage bed by a group of friends and family, James had been escorted by royal attendants.

The ladies-in-waiting all gasped and rushed toward the bed, pulling the covers down. "Jump in!" they entreated her, and Gunnilde made haste to follow their advice for it was a cold day in November and her thin shift did not offer much by way of warmth. They flung the blankets up around her, tucking her in.

"The bride is ready!" Frances Lessimore sang out as they all drifted out of the room.

"It seems a shame for Sir James to be wasted on the likes of her," Gunnilde heard one of them lament in retreat. "I always thought he was destined for great things."

"Such a pity!" another agreed sadly.

That feeling from earlier returned briefly, the one that made the backs of her eyes prickle. Then the door closed behind them, and she took a deep breath.

She had got what she wanted. Nothing more, nothing less.

5

James hesitated before knocking on the door, glancing around at the small group waiting at his heels. "I do not require your escort from here, gentlemen," he said stiffly.

"We will just see you inside," someone answered. James had the impression his name was Sir Lawrence something or other. "It's customary, Sir James," he added, seeing James's scowl.

"You cannot skirt custom on such occasions," chimed in another. When James met these words with stony silence, Winstanley, the Queen's attendant, gave a small cough.

"I will need to report we saw you put to bed beside your bride, Sir James," he said quietly.

"We can just stand in the doorway," Neville suggested hastily at James's answering glower.

Feeling severely goaded, James gave his brief knock and opened the door. He hoped to gods she was not naked beneath the bedsheets. She had already given everyone enough to look at all evening with her antics. The last thing he needed right now was her to give this lot an eyeful.

Inexplicably, his heart picked up its pace as he walked into the darkened room, knowing what awaited him there. Keeping his eyes averted from the occupant of the bed, he made short work of undressing, flinging his clothes down on the floor. The sooner he was under the covers, the sooner their onlookers could disperse.

Once he was down to his braies, he turned toward the bed, lifted the covers, and slid underneath them. His bed was not overly large, and the action brought him into direct contact with a warm body.

James breathed noisily out and turned his head to find his bride watching him from a golden pillow bearer. He blinked, then realized it was not a pillow bearer at all. It was her hair. She had masses and masses of the stuff. So much for Neville's theory.

Under the covers, her fingers sought his out and gave them what she presumably believed to be a sympathetic squeeze. James did his best not to yelp, but gods did the woman think he was made of stone? Clearing his throat, he lifted his head. "You can leave us now," he pronounced loudly and heard shuffling footsteps in the doorway by way of answer.

"Good night, all," the bride called after them politely. There was a chorus of answering good nights and then the door closed fast. "Are you well?" she whispered, going up on one elbow, and peering at him through the gloom.

"Yes," he lied.

"Your bed's a bit small, isn't it?" She wriggled for a bit, presumably trying to put some distance between them. Her efforts, while he appreciated the gesture, were in vain, and merely caused her soft thigh to jostle against his own. They also did absolutely nothing to alleviate his current condition, which was shamefully aroused.

"I have always found it perfectly adequate," he answered raspily, "until now."

Gods, what was wrong with him? Gunnilde Payne was not at all the kind of woman he admired, he told himself doggedly. She was… His mind went disobligingly blank. What was she? What did he know of her after all?

58

At this precise moment he knew she was warm and soft; her voice was kind and her hair was glorious. She was also lying in his bed beside him talking to him as though he were her ally rather than her enemy. This scattered his wits and made him feel an odd sort of yearning in his chest and a desperate longing in his loins. What else was there to know?

Something niggled away on the edge of his thoughts. She had done him some wrong, he vaguely remembered, despite heroically saving him from that accursed jester all evening. Oh yes, that was it. She had cost him an heiress, he recalled suddenly, but even that did not seem so very terrible at this precise moment in time.

Constance would have been as useless as him when confronted with ribald jokes and a bladder on a stick. Fucking jesters. Of course Wymer patronized them, he would, the uncultured swine. Thinking of Wymer and his piss-poor taste in the arts helped somewhat deflate the surprising hardness of his cock. He should think on that subject some more, he decided grimly.

He dwelt moodily on how much money from the royal coffers poured into the purses of grinning maniacs like Master Bobkin. How much undeserved fame and praise was heaped on his ilk, while true artists like Master Gregory, James's mentor, starved in their garrets and went to a pauper's grave. Wymer appreciated a fart joke more than a true genius.

"Are you good sleeper or a bad one?" his wife enquired politely.

James turned his head in surprise at the interruption. "I don't know," he said awkwardly, when in fact he knew himself to be a very poor sleeper. "Why do you ask?"

"I just wanted to be prepared, if we're to be bedfellows from now on," she explained.

"Prepared," James repeated blankly. Bedfellows?

59

"I sleep sound as a bell," she assured him, and he found he believed her. "You need not worry about me waking you in the night." She smiled at him reassuringly, and James's head emptied again. "Does your brother share your rooms?" she asked chattily.

"My brother?" Who? Oh yes, Neville. "Yes."

"And likely your parents too, when they come to court."

"Yes," he admitted briefly. Thank the gods that tended to be in the summer rather than the winter months. Wycliffe Hall lay just outside the summer capital and was miles away from Aphrany. "They rarely venture to the winter capital," he managed by way of grudging explanation.

"My father has not been to court in over twenty years," she confided dreamily. "Not since he was twenty-one and made his bow to the old king."

James cleared his throat. "The Portstanleys sponsor you at court?"

"Yes," she agreed, settling herself more comfortably against the mattress and sighing. The combination did all kinds of unruly things to ungovernable parts of James's anatomy. "Though they only do it for Eden's sake really. Eden Vawdrey is my greatest friend and benefactress."

Now by some miracle he did know who that was, for Viscountess Vawdrey was a patron of the arts and moved in scholastic circles. Someone had already told him they were friends though he could not remember who. Likely Neville.

Then again, Neville also thought Gunnilde wore false hair, so his information was clearly not to be depended on. "How is it that you know Viscountess Vawdrey?" he asked, willing his turgid cock to go

60

down. Gods, when had it last given him so much trouble? He almost felt light-headed from the sensation.

"She came to Payne Manor as a bride," she explained. "Her husband, Sir Roland, was competing in my father's tournament. It is held every May, mayhap you have heard of it? It is named after the locality it lies in, Tranton Vale."

He shook his head, then realized the pillow bearer impeded him. "No," he clarified. "I do not…follow the lists," he concluded tactfully, instead of voicing his true disdain of the tourneys.

"Oh, what a pity! Well, anyway, we hosted the Vawdreys and Eden was kind enough to take an interest in me. I thought she was wonderful," she enthused. "And this past January, I became her daughter's godmother. So that goes to show, does it not?" she said with shy pride. "How highly she regards me."

"Yes," he agreed. "One would not confer such an honor lightly."

His answer seemed to please her, for she beamed at him. "I hope I never let her down," she said fervently. "Her belief in me is what gave me the courage to come to court. I owe everything to Eden."

"Oh, yes?" James watched her with reluctant fascination. How could she seem so cheerful about their predicament? He supposed she had no money worries of her own, but the truth was, she was now burdened with a husband who had plenty of them. Should he inform her as such and ruin her genial mood?

He blew out a puff of air. "We should have some discussion," he said seriously. "About…how this marriage is going to function."

"Now?" She seemed a little surprised.

"Yes now, so we are fully informed from the outset and neither one of us can accuse the other of concealment."

She rolled onto her side to face him, tucking her hands under her cheek. "Yes, perhaps that would be wise," she agreed slowly. "Very well. I will hear you out."

"There was a reason I intended to marry an heiress," he said flatly. "My family depends on me for the upkeep of our family seat. My father is not…not to be relied upon."

She was silent for a long moment before asking, "You are the heir to the estate?"

"I am."

She nodded as though this explained things perfectly. "I see. And how is it that you have you supported them thus far?"

"Through my composing," he answered. "I was fortunate enough to secure the patronage of the Bishop of Hudde three summers ago. He commissioned several pieces to be performed at the cathedral in Caer Lyoness."

She looked impressed. "Have you never composed anything for the bishop here in Aphrany?"

"For Badsbury?" He shook his head. "It's well-known he strictly favors the compositions of monks over secular musicians. Today was the first time I've ever conversed with him." If conversed was really the word, he thought, remembering how woodenly he had repeated the formal vows.

"What about here at court?" Gunnilde enquired.

"A few pieces here and there but nothing substantial. I cannot seem to…" He took a deep breath. "I am not good at the acquiring of patrons," he admitted grudgingly. "Or the keeping of them."

She frowned. "I wonder why," she pondered. "You must be talented if the Bishop of Hudde thinks so." He bristled at this assumption, but she appeared not to notice. "You are popular in select circles, and you are handsome and of good reputation." She shot an interrogative look his way. "It is not because you prefer to write religious music, is it?"

"No," he answered truthfully. "I am not especially devout."

"Hmmm. And why do you suppose it is that you cannot attract patrons? What do your family think?"

He rolled his eyes. "My mother thinks my genius is not appreciated and likely will not be until I am dead. She thinks it a thankless endeavor and that I should simply…"

"Marry an heiress," Gunnilde guessed when he fell silent. Well, her wits were not lacking at any rate. "What about your father?"

"Oh, he agrees, apart from the genius part. He does not care for my style of music."

She grew quiet at this, her expression growing somber. "There will be a dowry," she said in an embarrassed voice, "but it will not be over large and likely my father will not hand it over until we have soothed his ruffled feathers. He is like to cut up rough about our unsanctioned marriage at first."

"Well, that is understandable," he conceded. His own parents would be horrified. She nodded dolefully. Looking sorrowful did not suit Mistress Payne, he thought, shifting uncomfortably and making the mattress dip. The gods knew why but he found himself casting around for something to distract her with. "You do not ask why my brother thinks I am unsuccessful," he said.

"Yes, tell me what Neville thinks," she said, brightening. Strangely, he felt a stab of annoyance that she should speak his brother's name aloud with such familiarity. "After all," she rambled on, "he is present here at court and must have some insight to provide."

James snorted but answered all the same. "He says it is because I am not personable enough. Because I do not make myself particularly agreeable and flatter folk as I should."

To his annoyance, a look of dawning comprehension crept over her face. "Oh, I see," she breathed. "Yes, of course. That does makes sense." Another pang of irritation afflicted him but before he could say something withering, she struggled up onto her elbow again, distracting him.

The sheet slipped down, revealing rather more of her than she likely realized. The fabric of her shift was filmy, and Mistress Payne was generously proportioned. Very generously. His mouth turned dry. Gods.

"But James, don't you see?" she breathed excitedly through parted lips. He saw rather more than he had bargained for. And the sight left him stunned. Then he realized she had spoken his name, and his heartbeat migrated down south. Fuck, all his hard work dwelling on disagreeable things had come undone in an instant! "This is something I can help you with!"

"What is?" James asked in a strangled voice.

"Your popularity," she answered rapturously. "Not just with the"—she broke off, as though deciding against her original choice of words—"the intellectual faction here at court," she said carefully, "but with the wider court at large."

She looked so flushed and excited that he could hardly bear to look at her. "And how would you manage such a thing?" he asked more waspishly than he'd intended.

Her light dimmed a little. "Oh, I know I am not popular right now," she said with an awkward little laugh. "You do not hurt my feelings by pointing that out, do not worry." She gave him a quick smile and a pat of his shoulder.

Hurt her feelings? James felt dazed, though that might have been because she had touched him again.

"But you see, there is my new position to take into account," she said, eyes shining once again. "And that will make all the difference."

"It will?" he asked weakly.

"Yes," she answered blithely. "I see it all quite clearly. The way before me, I mean." She sounded so assured that James was dumbfounded. It did not even occur to him to pour cold water over her scheme. They both lay quiet for a few heartbeats.

Then she asked politely, "Were you thinking of abstaining this eve? I don't mind, honestly," she hurried to add. "It has been a long day, and I quite understand that it may take you some time to adjust your expectations."

To adjust his...? Oh, she meant the fact his intended bride had switched. Instead of telling her flat that he'd no intention of consummating such an undesirable marriage, a course of action he had determined upon hours ago, he found himself clearing his throat.

"Er, yes," he heard himself respond. "It might be best if we postpone the consummation for a while. At least..." His words trailed off as he ran out of inspiration.

"I understand perfectly," she said with the utmost affability. The bedsheets rustled.

"Where are you going?" James asked, hearing her feet hit the floorboards.

"Just to extinguish the candles, never fear."

He lifted his head to watch her cross the room and blow out the candles and had to suppress a groan for he could see everything through the thin stuff of her shift. Gunnilde Payne's backside was no less voluptuous than the front.

He heard her give a puff of breath and the light dimmed. She took three steps and blew again. He tried not to remember the feel of her breath against his face at dinner when she had, well, not exactly kissed him but as near as damn it.

Now only the light from the fire illuminated the dark room. She made her way swiftly back to bed and climbed in. "All will be well, you will see," she said, collapsing back onto the mattress beside him, setting the bed to creaking. "You may depend upon me, husband, I will not let you down."

After speaking these extraordinary words, she closed her eyes, a beatific smile curved her lips. "I am so glad we had this discussion, aren't you? I just know I will get a good night's sleep now."

A good night's sleep? James reflected. When was the last time he had enjoyed one of those? It occurred to him that a man might get a good night's sleep after rolling vigorously in the bedsheets with the likes of Mistress Payne.

Those soft, pillowy breasts would likely afford a man some comfort, and as for those sizable hips and that big round arse… Well, he thought, swallowing, she would hold her own. Or at least he hoped she would.

66

He shut his eyes tight. What the hells was he thinking? Stop it, James, he told himself. Do not think about how easy it would be to simply roll on top of this woman and…gods, lose himself in her. His chest pounded. She would not even begrudge him the pleasure. She would likely say something…encouraging.

Fuck.

Think about jesters, James, he thought desperately. Jesters and empty coffers.

6

As anticipated, Gunnilde slept excellently and woke to find herself alone in the marital bed. She sat up and gazing about promptly realized she had none of her own things to make ready for the day. The bedchamber was cold, for no fire burned in the grate, yet the idea of redonning the finery of the previous day held little appeal.

Instead, she slid off the bed and grabbed the embroidered coverlet, wrapping it about her to conceal her scanty shift. With some ingenious folding she managed to fashion a sort of robe and after casting about for something to secure it with, borrowed a decorative gold braid from one of the wall hangings, tying it about her waist.

Clothing dealt with, she made for the ewer and jug in the corner. She found the bowl empty, but the jug was half-full with lukewarm water. Sloshing this into the basin, she took a hurried wash and patted herself dry with the damp cloth she presumed her husband must have used before her.

To her surprise, James apparently did not possess a looking glass, unless he had a dedicated dressing room in the vicinity. Considering the cramped nature of courtiers' quarters, she rather doubted this. Borrowing his comb, she detangled her hair and pinned up the sides with her hairpins from the previous evening.

Her appearance dealt with, she squared her shoulders and made for the door. As soon as she lifted the latch and pushed it open, the low-voiced conversation in the adjoining room abruptly halted.

"Good morning," Gunnilde said, spotting her husband and brother-in-law sat at a table next to the window. After a moment's pause, both stood from their seats and gave their muttered greetings. She fancied James stared rather hard at her choice of clothing.

"May I join you to break my fast?" Gunnilde asked brightly when no invitation was forthcoming. James flushed and moved to pull out a chair for her next to his own, indicating she should be seated.

Finding the table bare apart from a jug of ale and a few scattered sheets of paper, she looked around in surprise. "Have you already eaten this morn?" she asked.

"Er, no," James answered distractedly, drawing the sheets of paper into a loose pile. "I don't usually, and as for Neville…" He glanced pointedly at his brother as he poured a tankard of ale for her and slid it across the table.

"If I'm hungry, I usually nip over to the Ashdowns'," Neville piped up. "They're just across the corridor and we share a servant with them." He leaned forward. "The truth is," he said confidingly, "Bennett doesn't like running up and down to the kitchen more than strictly necessary. He's a disobliging fellow at the best of times."

"I see," Gunnilde replied, accepting her ale and taking a sip. Doubtless the disagreeable servant that had to be shared was all part of their straitened circumstances. Once again, she could not help but contrast this with the fare she would have received at Payne Manor after a wedding the night before. Father kept a good table.

Still, that was the country, and she knew it was unfashionable to break your fast early here in town, so mayhap that was part of it. Only two meals were served in the Great Hall, a midday meal and evening supper. Though several of the palace kitchens were staffed during morning hours, courtiers were expected to make their own arrangements to have any food collected and brought to their quarters.

"Did the Portstanleys lay on a full table at break of day?" Neville asked curiously. He sounded a little envious.

"A full table? No," Gunnilde replied. "Merely some fresh bread and cheese, mayhap a little cured meat if we were lucky."

James stood up. "I'll go and see if I can find Bennett," he said shortly. Neville looked across at her as though expecting her to refuse this offer. When Gunnilde simply thanked her new husband, his brother seemed rather surprised.

Really, though, Gunnilde could not at all see why. For all her new brother-in-law knew, Sir James might have kept her up all night with husbandly demands. She might be in dire need of sustenance! The door closed behind him and Neville Wycliffe settled back in his seat.

"So," she began, "you are my new brother-in-law. We were introduced yesterday at the wedding."

"We were," he agreed cautiously. "Though I am flattered you remember amid all the excitement."

Ignoring his wry tone, she asked, "You are my husband's younger brother?"

"I am," he repeated. "By some three years. I am but two and twenty." So, he was the same age as her. He looked younger to Gunnilde's eye but then he did not have his brother's height, so his slim frame seemed a good deal more boyish. Her own brother, at sixteen, had a far more strapping build.

"You have been knighted?" she enquired politely, though in truth this was a given fact.

"I have." He winced. "Though it was quite the ordeal and delayed twice due to my delicate constitution. Mercifully my mentor, Sir Raymond, was an understanding sort and not terribly warlike himself."

"My brother is currently undertaking the training."

70

"He has my sympathies."

Gunnilde smiled. "Hal is a healthy, outdoor type. He loves horses and dogs and exercise, though not always the early mornings."

"Ah, he is rather like you perhaps? Someone who embraces the chances life affords."

Gunnilde's surprised eyes flew to meet his. What exactly did he mean by that? Before she could ask, the door opened again, and James was back.

"Bennett is fetching some repast," he said, sitting back down beside her. He turned to look at her and cleared his throat. "I have told him you are accustomed to eating at this hour," he said. "Let me know if it slips his mind."

Neville pulled a face. "And it will slip his mind," he warned. "Our laundry is ever a source of contention. He lights our meagre fires twice a day and that is practically all he does." Gunnilde's eyebrows rose. It all sounded most dissatisfactory, but before she could comment as much, Neville rubbed his hands together.

"Now tell me, for my friends will be positively agog to hear the news. How is it that the two of you intend to spend your first day as newlyweds? I must have some small fillip of gossip to toss their way."

James frowned. "Why, I mean to spend it as I usually do," he answered. "How else? I have a long-standing engagement on the second Wednesday of every month." He cast a look at the window and Gunnilde guessed this meeting was outside of the palace.

"Fie and tush! This is no ordinary second Wednesday of the month!" Neville objected. "Surely you do not mean to abandon my sister-in-law on her first day as a wedded wife? Such behavior would set tongues wagging, make no mistake."

71

James glanced at her uneasily. "I am sure… Gunnilde," he pronounced her name after the faintest of hesitations, "has plans of her own and is accustomed to her own routine."

"Well, not really," she replied apologetically. "For you see, today marks the start of a new era in my life." Both brothers stared at her. "I am now a lady-in-waiting," she reminded them, for 'twas plain they thought she attached too much importance to the role of wifehood.

"Ah, of course," Neville replied, recovering first. "Though I am surprised the Queen expects your attendance on her today. Not very considerate of your wedded status, is she? Still, everyone knows the Queen is no lover of the institution of marriage."

"Neville," James said heavily. "Kindly guard that wayward tongue of yours."

"Why should I?" his brother responded. "Not going to repeat any irreverent thing I say at large, are you…ah?" He paused uncertainly.

"Gunnilde," she supplied with a ready smile. "And no, of course not, Sir Neville."

"Just Neville will be fine," he responded with the hint of an answering smile.

James opened his mouth but the door swinging open prevented him from speaking his thoughts.

"Got your victuals," announced a thin, reedy voice, and a servant stepped over the threshold with a tray, which he set down with a thud. "I trust it is to your liking, sir." Bennett's tone was injured, as though he had been forced to perform some act against his will.

"I told you, it is for the lady," James responded tetchily. He turned to Gunnilde. "Will this suffice?"

She looked down at the tray which held only two plates. One was piled high with buttered bread while the other held three wedges of cheese. Most likely all the cold meats had been grabbed first thing. "Amply, thank you," she responded.

Bennett sniffed and retreated, with a reproachful look back over his shoulder. Gunnilde drew the plates toward herself. "Won't you have some?" she asked politely.

"No, it's for you," James replied shortly, but she thought Neville looked a bit disappointed.

"There is plenty for the three of us," she assured them. "Here." She removed two thirds of the bread from the first plate and plunked it on her own, then transferred one of the cheese wedges from the second plate and slid it over to Neville. "Take this. James can share my plate."

"Well, if you are certain…" Neville said, brightening. "This is a rare treat, though it's a shame it is not toasted."

Gunnilde glanced over at the fireplace. The feeble thing looked on the point of extinguishing. "We should get a toasting fork," she recommended. "Then we could toast our own." She nudged the plate closer to James, but he ignored the gesture, leaning his elbow on the table.

"Did the Queen request your attendance today?" he asked.

"Not outright," she admitted. "But I am keen to commence my duties and learn what is expected of me."

Neville laughed. "The Bartree has all the choicest tasks and will not willingly relinquish any of them to you, my girl. As for the rest of them, they sit on the fringes, waiting for the chance to shine."

Gunnilde considered this as she chewed on her mouthful. "I knew Mistress Bartree was current favorite, for 'tis common knowledge," she said once she had swallowed. "But the others must have their own opportunities to serve Her Majesty, surely?"

"Oh aye," Neville agreed airily. "They fetch and carry as they're bid, but as for opportunities…" He shook his head. "No, it's no wonder they're always eloping or falling into deep disgrace. The Queen is not overly fond of any of them and gives them scant regard."

This was disheartening to hear, and Gunnilde darted a glance at James to verify this statement. He, however, did not appear to be listening. Instead, he was absent-mindedly nibbling on a piece of cheese. There, she knew he must be hungry really!

"Having said that," Neville began thoughtfully, "it's a rare thing that she arranges matches for any of them, I can really only think of one other such."

"Who was that?" Gunnilde asked with interest.

"The Lady Jane," he replied, picking up another slice of bread. "Armenal arranged her wedding to Viscount Bardulf last year. Still, it came with a price."

"It did? What was it?" Gunnilde asked, wide-eyed.

"Well, she's not her favorite anymore. The Bartree slid right into her place. Her Majesty doesn't like her ladies to get married. Before Lady Jane, it was Lady Eden that held the position but as soon as she fell from grace by running off with—"

"Neville," James cut in, lowering his cheese, "you are perhaps unaware that…Gunnilde is great friends with Lady Eden." Again, before pronouncing her name he gave the tiniest pause, as though it did not spring readily to his lips.

74

"Oh really?" Neville seemed quite unabashed. "Oh, well, you will know all about it, then."

Ignoring this, Gunnilde leaned forward. "Does the Queen have no married ladies-in-waiting apart from Lady Bardulf and Viscountess Vawdrey?"

"Oh, she has a few," Neville admitted. "But once married, they have other priorities which keep them away. She favors the Duchess of Cadwallader, but she so rarely comes to court, and Marchioness Martindale but she lives in the north now."

Other priorities? "Lady Bardulf is much at court though," Gunnilde pointed out uneasily. "And so will I be." As soon as the words left her mouth, she felt a sudden panic. After all, James had not actually told her that he would not send her packing to Wycliffe Hall. What if that was what the two brothers had been discussing when she walked in on them that morning?

Turning to him in sudden alarm, she was relieved to see him meet her searching gaze with no trace of guilt or discomfort in his own. Gunnilde relaxed. No, she was being foolish. Had they not made a pact of sorts last night? She had promised him that she would help secure him success. He had no reason to get rid of her already. Not before she had the chance to even try.

Seemingly picking up on her disquiet, James cleared his throat. "It's not really the same in any case. For Gunnilde did not serve the Queen before her marriage." This time he managed to say her name without stumbling. Gunnilde beamed at him, and his eyes fell away. He almost seemed surprised when he caught sight of a piece of cheese in his hand.

Once the food disappeared, Neville announced his intent to meet with some friends to view some new portrait in the King's state rooms. The newly married couple were left alone together. "Does your brother have any means of earning his own income?" she asked as the door shut after him.

James snorted and shook his head. "He has a good singing voice," he said begrudgingly. "But he would not dream of lowering himself by making money from it."

"Does he intend to marry an heiress too?"

James shot a hard look at her, as though suspecting some slight before answering. "I do not know. He has many friends and acquaintances here at court, but he has yet to show any inclination for matrimony."

"He is pretty enough to catch a lady's eye," Gunnilde said thoughtfully. "Though not as good-looking as you, it's true."

He made no response to this, his gaze dwelling once again on her impromptu robe. "Is that my bed cover?" he asked abruptly.

"Yes," she admitted. "I had nothing else to wear."

His fingers tapped against the tabletop. "I won't venture out today," he announced with sudden decision.

"No?" Gunnilde lowered her cup of ale. "What will you do instead?" she asked with interest.

"What we will do, madam," he said sternly, "is set about moving you into these rooms. Then this afternoon we had better…make an appearance together. As a couple. Let everyone see we are…amicably wed."

"Oh, I see!" She nodded slowly. "Yes, that would probably be just as well. Our sudden union is bound to cause quite a stir, and we should get ahead of the gossips as soon as we can."

She fancied he winced slightly at her choice of words but aloud he voiced no objection to them. "Do you have much by way of possessions in the Portstanley quarters?" he enquired.

"Nothing that could not fit into one trunk."

He looked relieved. "We should probably enlist their services."

"The Portstanleys?"

"It would look better if they appeared to sanction the match. You were under their protection before our marriage."

"Yes, that's true, but you need not worry they will say anything indiscreet for they are quite scrupulous when it comes to their reputation. They would not dream of besmirching their family name with any implication of scandal."

"I am glad to hear it," he said, turning all proper again. Gunnilde suppressed a sigh. She had thought that no one could be stuffier than the Portstanleys but James almost managed it at times. A knock at the door interrupted these depressing thoughts. They gazed at one another in open dismay. Who could that be? "You had better go back into the bedchamber," he recommended.

"Why?" Gunnilde glanced down at her covered body. "I am quite decent."

He snorted, leaving his seat and making for the small hallway. Hearing muted voices, Gunnilde stood up, undecided whether to bolt for the bedroom or not. Suddenly she recognized Harriet's voice, and, to her great surprise, felt a rush of gladness to hear it.

"Harriet, is that you?" she called impulsively. "Come in, and welcome."

There was a moment's silence before Harriet appeared in the doorway, looking extremely uncertain of herself. "I just came to—"

"I'm so glad!" Gunnilde cried, and strange to say, she really meant it. Leaping from her seat, she hurried forward to draw her old roommate in. "Will you sit and take some ale?" She seized hold of the jug before Harriet could make a reply. Looking rather dazed, Harriet sank down upon one of the hard wooden chairs. Really, they could use some cushions. The Wycliffe quarters were somewhat lacking in comforts.

"I brought your trunk with me. Or rather, Farson did," she said, naming the Portstanleys' manservant.

"That was good of you. I did not intend to put you to the trouble of packing up my things."

"Oh, it was…no trouble," Harriet said, flushing. "Mother, well, she thought we had better do it, sooner rather than later."

"It was very kind of you," Gunnilde insisted. "I am very grateful for all you have done for me."

Harriet could not meet her eye as she accepted the cup of ale and sat perched on the edge of her seat like a little bird prepared for flight. She sat gazing around the room, though truth to tell there was precious little to look at for it was sparsely furnished. Her eye fell on Gunnilde's improvised robe.

"Is that the Wycliffe crest?" she blurted in stunned accents.

Gunnilde glanced down at the embroidered sheet. "I don't know, is it?"

"Yes, it is," her husband answered from the doorway. He and Farson were carrying her trunk through to their room.

"Oh, I did not realize." She peered at the badge picked out in golden stitches. "What is it? A goat?"

"A unicorn," James corrected her loudly as they crossed the room.

"Oh, that's nice, but I think it could do with a bigger horn," Gunnilde decided.

The Portstanleys' servant muffled an amused snort. "Farson!" Harriet reproached him faintly, blushing a delicate pink.

Oh! Belatedly, Gunnilde realized the joke. "I have no complaints on that score, I assure you," she said firmly.

"Right glad I am to hear that, milady," he responded good naturedly, and shot James a wink. "No husband would like to hear such a sentiment, the morning after the bedding."

Both James and Harriet looked like they did not know where to put themselves, but Gunnilde nodded, satisfied she had put that rumor to rest, and turning back to Harriet, she took a deep breath. "We were wondering if you and your mother would care to accompany us this afternoon," she began.

7

The Portstanleys, keen to squash any hint of scandal, graciously accepted the invitation to meet outside the Queen's rooms that afternoon. After an hour holed up in their bedchamber, Gunnilde emerged in a blue velvet gown with gold brocade sleeves, apparently ready to impress her fellow ladies-in-waiting.

Despite the mismatched sleeves, James would not have thought the dress so very jarring if it were not for the fact she had swept up a good deal of the front and pinned it with a brooch to reveal the underskirt, which was of an altogether different color, a deep pink rose.

The Queen had been right; Gunnilde, it appeared, was determined she would not fade into the background. As for her hair, it seemed he had depended rather too much on the fact that once married she would be obliged to obscure her crowning glory.

Somehow, she had skirted this convention, for though a veil was duly draped over the top of her head, she had arranged two smaller puffs of hair at her temples, which evaded the covering altogether and stood out proudly for all to see.

Employing great tact, James declined to comment on her appearance, merely offering her his arm. To his surprise, Gunnilde swept a critical look over his own ensemble. "You do not intend to change?" she asked.

"I do not." There was absolutely nothing wrong with his own restrained elegance, he thought indignantly.

"Oh." She accepted his arm without further comment, and they made their way to the appointed meeting place and greeted the Portstanleys cordially. However, soon after, they found the Queen's rooms to be practically deserted.

"But where is everyone?" Lady Portstanley asked, looking about in surprise. "Last time I was here, I was jostled from pillar to post." Her mousy daughter murmured some soothing reply and both looked toward James expectantly.

"I haven't the faintest idea," he admitted. The only court events he paid attention to were educational. "Perhaps the Queen is having one of her outdoor events?" he guessed, remembering some of her summer spectacles.

"In November?" Lady Portstanley asked incredulously.

"What was that portrait viewing Neville mentioned this morning?" Gunnilde queried. "Did he not say it was in the King's rooms? I wonder if it could be that."

James shrugged. It seemed unlikely to him. "I don't think he said whose portrait it was," he added when she seemed to expect actual words by way of response.

"Perhaps it is someone exciting!" Gunnilde said, her eyes lighting up. "Let me just ask." She flitted off and James was left with the Portstanley women.

"Someone exciting?" Lady Portstanley ruminated. "I wonder, could it be some explorer or enlightened thinker, do you suppose?"

In King Wymer's state rooms? James rather thought not. "I suppose it could be," he answered diplomatically.

He turned to the daughter politely, expecting to hear her thoughts on the matter, but she stood twisting her hands together, silent as a stock.

Mercifully at this point, Gunnilde reappeared, having apparently received her answer for her eyes were agleam. She caught hold of both his own and Harriet's sleeves, drawing them closer to her. "You will

81

never guess!" she whispered with barely concealed excitement. "A new portrait of the prince, no less! Commissioned for his thirteenth birthday. Shall we go and see it?"

James suppressed a groan. He failed entirely to see what was exciting about a portrait of a royal child, even if he was heir to the throne.

"The young prince!" Lady Portstanley uttered, sounding impressed.

"Prince Raedan," Harriet breathed.

Despite their forward thinking, both ladies seemed keen to view the portrait. Given little choice, James inclined his head to show his willingness, and they turned about and made for the King's rooms.

"I wonder if he is fair-haired like King Wymer?" Harriet said to her mother as James and Gunnilde dropped behind them.

"Sure to be, child," her mother answered confidently. "His own mother's hair was fairer even than the King's."

Harriet sigh floated back over her shoulder reaching their ears. "Poor Queen Eleanor," she said sadly.

"Do you remember the King's first wife?" Gunnilde asked James.

"Barely. I saw her once at Caer Lyoness and was all but a child at the time."

"Was she beautiful?"

"Not that I remember."

"What was she like?"

James screwed up his face with the effort of remembrance. "She was pale, tall for a woman, and had a melancholy disposition."

"And her apparel?"

"I do not recall what she was wearing."

Gunnilde sighed. "Did your brother happen meet her at the same time?" she asked hopefully.

James found himself bristling at the implication Neville might have formed a more detailed impression than himself. "Neither of us 'met' her. We were merely present in the Great Hall on some saint's day or other," he answered irritably.

"I will have to ask him," she murmured.

The King's rooms were heaving, and anyone with a claim to a title seemed to have shown up that day to gawk at Prince Raedan's portrait. Seeing the press of people, even in the outer chambers, James did not feel optimistic at how long this would take.

Turning to his wife, with vague ideas of rearranging their plans, he found her eyes bright with anticipation as she surveyed the crowds. "Everyone is here!" she said, bouncing up on her toes to view the masses.

"Look!" She gave his sleeve a sharp tug. "There is the princess, with the King! I mean"—she looked around to check no one had noticed her slip—"there is Lady de Bussell," she corrected herself. "Her husband must be here too; he would not let her travel to the winter capital without him." She turned this way and that in search of Sir Armand.

James cleared his throat. "You are acquainted with the de Bussells?" he asked.

"Oh yes! For they attended Father's tournament this year, even though it is one of the smaller and most rural events on the tourney calendar. It was most gratifying, and do you know, she sat at the long table with us as kind and gracious as any lady you ever met!

"Never made any fuss or pother unlike some I could mention, and she was nothing like what everyone used to say of her before she married. Why, they used to say all manner of things about her! And all quite false and unfounded!"

Fortunately, the buzz of conversation around them was so loud that James doubted anyone could hear Gunnilde's indignant tone. "But there! You must already know this for you will have met her when she resided at court," she concluded.

"Yes."

She waited expectantly. "And was she not beauteous?"

"Er," James considered. "She was tall and seemed unhappy," he concluded.

Gunnilde eyed him with deep dissatisfaction. "Your description for every woman seems to be that they are tall and sad," she decided.

James found he was forced to defend himself. "She wore very ugly gowns when she lived here at court. She looks quite different now. Besides, I would not describe you as tall and sad."

"No? And just how would you describe her?" drawled a nearby voice, and James turned to find Viscount Bardulf regarding him with lazy amusement. As was his custom, Bardulf was dressed so eye-catchingly that James could only blame the heavy crowd for missing his approach. This afternoon he wore a tunic of azure blue decorated ostentatiously with gold thread and a gold chain about his shoulders decorated in blue stones. Fortunately, today he was accompanied, for his wife was on his

84

arm. James found Bardulf tended to temper his barbed comments somewhat when his proper viscountess was present.

"Alisander," the lady murmured now in faint reproach. "You are intruding on a private conversation."

"Nonsense, Jane, the Wycliffes are but recently wedded and must understand they are a spectacle for the rest of us to enjoy."

James stiffened but Lady Bardulf was already turning to Gunnilde with an apologetic smile.

"How do you do, Lady Wycliffe. I hope you do not feel too conspicuous in your new status, I remember only too well how wearing such events can be in those early days of marriage."

"Oh, not at all, Lady Bardulf!" Gunnilde assured her, giving her a curtsey. "I am delighted to join the Queen's ladies and most keen to embrace the opportunities it affords me."

Bardulf's eyebrows rose, and James braced himself for the worst. "But what a commendable attitude," Bardulf said, tipping his head to one side. "You must remind me, Wycliffe, from what stock such a sensible wife sprang."

"I am the daughter of Sir Aubron Payne of Tranton Vale," Gunnilde supplied helpfully, not waiting for James's reply.

"The Paynes of Tranton Vale," the viscount echoed, tapping his chin. "Hmmm...sounds somewhat familiar."

"My father holds a tournament there, every May," Gunnilde said proudly. "You have perhaps heard of it, my lord?"

"No, but then, I am no lover of the tournaments. They are so brutal," he complained, "and lacking in finesse. My poor Jane does not enjoy the

85

rowdiness of the crowds, and as for myself I do not like the hard benches in the stands. You sit there shivering in the winter months and, er, perspiring in the summer ones."

"Oh." Gunnilde's disappointment was clear for all present to hear. "I cannot imagine why your lordship should have heard tell of Tranton Vale in that case," she admitted frankly. "For it has no other claim to fame."

"I must humbly disagree!" he answered promptly. "You underestimate yourself, my dear Lady Wycliffe. For it is your own fame that has preceded you." Viscount Bardulf's eyes met James's innocently before they returned to Gunnilde. "Does not everyone whisper of Mistress Payne's daring choices when it comes to fashion? Of her philanthropic nature when it comes to aiding the cause of hopeless lovers everywhere?"

Gunnilde's eyes widened. "They do?"

"I assure you, the corridors of Aphrany positively buzz with your name these days." James glared at him, but the viscount seemed oblivious as he gave Gunnilde his most gentle smile. "I look forward with bated breath to your next move, Mistress Payne. My apologies, Lady Wycliffe, I should say.

"I cannot wait to see how you set about ousting The Bartree from the coveted position of royal favorite." He leaned in a little closer. "Might I suggest finding her a suitor?" he said slyly. "That never fails to do the trick. But I don't need to tell you that, now, do I? You're an old hand at such ploys."

Gunnilde blinked, rather a dazed look in her eye. "Er, I do not think that I would quite put it that way…"

James straightened up. "If my wife should end up supplanting the current favorite, it will be due to her own merits alone and nothing to do with subterfuge, I assure you," he said coldly.

Viscount Bardulf's smile widened, and he turned to view James full on. "Well, well, this is quite fascinating!" he said slowly. "One day of marriage and you are become quite the defensive spouse, Wycliffe. Do you know, for the first time since I have known you, you almost interest me."

"Alisander!" His wife's voice was more insistent now. "That is quite enough."

Bardulf patted his wife's hand indulgently, then turned back to Gunnilde, sketching her a bow. "Thank you for the entertainment, my dear Lady Wycliffe. My compliments to your coiffure."

Bows were exchanged, and despite the crush, the Bardulfs seemed to find a way to trickle through the crowd toward the King's state room.

"Well," said Gunnilde uncertainly, "I am not quite certain how to take his lordship. On the surface, he appears to compliment one, but his words seem to leave an aftertaste that is not altogether pleasant." She bit her lip. "When he said that about my using ploys—"

"Do not pay him any heed," James recommended, cutting across her words. "He only meant to insult me, really, not you. He can't abide me for some reason. Never has."

"Really? I wonder why?"

James shrugged. "Who knows? But every chance he has to snub or put me down, you may be sure he takes it."

He felt her gaze on his face. "I have a theory," she said suddenly. "'Tis because he is jealous."

87

James gave a start. "What?"

"That's the only thing that makes sense. Viscount Bardulf is so elegant and beautiful himself that he cannot stand having a rival moving in the Queen's circles and stealing attention away from him. He is the ambassador from her home country, is he not? And one of her great favorites."

"Rival?" James repeated. "That is not...not how men view things."

Gunnilde snorted. "You think men cannot feel jealousy?"

"Over some things, maybe, but not over something like that!"

"But certainly, they can, over lots of things. My own father fell out with his closest friend and neighbor over a horse they both coveted. It ruined a twenty-year friendship."

James took a deep breath. "Viscount Bardulf has no cause to envy my position at court," he said forthrightly. "He outranks me in every regard!"

"It is probably your masculine beauty that irritates him so much," she said. James spluttered, unable to put together a reply to such absurdity. "Only consider," Gunnilde continued earnestly, "the viscount works so hard at cultivating his appearance. His clothes are gorgeous, his accessories exquisite. Did you see his gloves? And his jewels? He does not have a hair out of place, his nails are immaculate, and then you turn up in a pair of dark brown stockings—"

"What's wrong with my stockings?"

"And a matching tunic of no distinction—"

"There is naught amiss with this tunic!"

"Yet you fill out those stockings so well, and you have such good shoulders that your clothes somehow look quite perfect, and your hair, which you barely dragged a comb through, falls just right, and in short, your natural good looks lend your overall appearance a distinction it does not really warrant. You must own, it must be very frustrating for him."

James regarded her speechlessly. "I— He—" He gave up. "Please stop."

"You know I speak sense," she said sagely.

"I know nothing of the sort!"

Feeling a tap on his shoulder, James turned about to find the Portstanleys stood looking rather forlorn. In truth, he had forgotten all about them.

"Oh, Harriet, do come stand next to me," Gunnilde urged guiltily. "We have been neglecting you." She gave James a significant look that he could only assume meant he should pay some attention to the old lady.

James had always thought Lady Portstanley a worthy woman of education and good sense. He did not really know then why he felt strangely reluctant to turn to her now and converse with her a while. Still, he did as good manners dictated and set himself to making some conversation with her while they inched their way toward the King's state rooms.

Lady Portstanley was keen to discuss some new philosopher and James listened with half an ear as he watched Gunnilde chattering away to the daughter. Harriet Portstanley was a drab sort of girl, so it was no wonder that his eye remained firmly riveted to his wife. Of course, that didn't explain why he was craning to hear whatever nonsense she was currently spouting. That part was a complete mystery even to himself.

8

It took a least an hour of waiting and shuffling forward by tiny degrees before they reached the confines of the King's state room. Gunnilde could not say that she regretted a moment of it, for she was far too busy soaking up the atmosphere. To think of it! She, Gunnilde Payne, in the very thick of things at the palace!

She knew for a fact that it would be weeks before the wider court got their chance to see Prince Raedan's portrait but she had been permitted her viewing on the very first day it had been hung! She could barely suppress her excitement. Even Harriet's desultory conversation could not dim her enthusiasm one bit.

Every so often a courtier or two would press through the crush to appear before James and offer their congratulations on his recent marriage. Their "congratulations" were naught but a thinly veiled excuse to stare first at him, and then at Gunnilde and back again, their brows arched and their words insincere as they tried to gauge how things really stood between the unlikely couple.

Still, Gunnilde did not begrudge them their inquisitiveness. Indeed, she was keen to make their acquaintance, but the first few times she had been a little anxious that James would become all starchy and offended in the face of such obvious curiosity.

To her relief, he barely seemed to react at all, other than to perform the necessary introductions. He did this in a perfunctory manner, appearing distracted and preoccupied all the while, as though his mind was currently on other things.

It occurred to her that he could be composing something, perhaps some piece to celebrate the prince's portrait? King Wymer would surely like that. She would have to encourage James to commemorate such royal occasions in future, she thought with sudden inspiration. Good wives encouraged their husbands, so the way forward was clear to her.

On finally reaching the inner sanctum, Gunnilde found the King in residence, though to her disappointment, the Queen was sadly absent.

"Sir James Wycliffe and Lady Wycliffe," the announcer intoned. "Lady Portstanley and Lady Harriet Portstanley."

After performing their bow and curtseys, the King gestured for them to view the portrait hung on the opposite wall, and they duly drifted in that direction. Gunnilde gazed keenly up at the serious boy who stared out of the canvas, stony-faced and somewhat pinched of feature.

He was not what Gunnilde had been expecting at all. Somehow she had expected a rosy-cheeked boy, fair of hair and blue of eye, rather like she imagined King Wymer must have been at that age. Instead, the prince's hair, cut very short, was a silvery sort of shade and his eyes appeared a flinty gray.

Prince Raedan had a cold stare which she imagined must be able to freeze a tutor at thirty paces. There was also a distinct lack of childish roundness to his features. One of his very white hands rested on the nape of a large and spectacularly ugly dog.

"Well, well, what do you think? Eh? Speak up," the King entreated.

"I think it is wonderful, Your Majesty," Gunnilde responded at once. "You can sort of feel his intelligence radiating from the picture."

The King grunted. "What about you, Wycliffe?"

James took on a hunted look Gunnilde was starting to recognize. It meant he had no idea what was the right thing to say. "Is it a good likeness, Your Highness?" he asked evasively.

"A good likeness?" the King looked incensed. "You think I would hire an inferior artist, is that it? Damned impertinence!"

"Such superior brushwork, Your Majesty," Lady Portstanley gushed placatingly. "The colors are so vivid. They seem to come to life before one. As though the prince stood in this very chamber before us."

"Quite," Harriet agreed hurriedly. "Oh, quite, I wholly agree."

The King snorted. "You, Hilde," he said, gesturing to Gunnilde. "You appear to have some sense. Tell me why you think this boy of mine looks intelligent."

Gunnilde cleared her throat. "Well, sire, I think he has a look of premature matureness about him. As though he is wise before his years. A look of infancy clings to most boys of that age, yet the young prince shows no sign of such childishness."

"Mmmm," the King rumbled, apparently appeased. "He is smart, so they tell me. Uncommonly smart for his age."

"What is his dog called?" James asked.

The King squinted at him, as though suspecting some slight. "Balto," he replied shortly. "None can supplant him from Dan's affections though I have offered several hounds better-looking and better behaved than that beast. He will take none of them."

Dan? Gunnilde was surprised. He did not look like a Dan somehow. Still, his partiality for his dog sounded commendable. "Do they not say that men should emulate a dog's loyalty?" she mused aloud. "They are certainly natural companions. My own brother is most devoted to his little dog, Dustin. He found him half drowned in a village ditch and no bigger than a rat."

92

"Dustin?" the King echoed, a look of disgust on his face. "What kind of a name is that?"

"Hal says it means 'valiant fighter.'"

"Oh, does it?" The King looked somewhat mollified. "Good fighter, is he?"

"Not at all," Gunnilde admitted. "He is undersized and timid, but Hal says it does not signify for he can do the fighting for both of them."

The King blinked. "He can do the fighting for both of them?" he repeated, then gave a startled chuckle. "That's a good one. Who is this brother of yours? What's his estate?"

By the time they left the apartments, Gunnilde had told the King all about Hal, Tranton Vale, and the tournament her father hosted annually. It only occurred to her as they left that she might have talked a little too much. She fancied the group who had been waiting behind theirs eyed her somewhat resentfully as they exited.

"Who was that waiting for admission behind us?" she whispered to James as they made their way out into the next room and then into the corridor.

He shrugged, glancing behind them. "I did not notice."

"I believe they were a little tired of waiting."

"I think we all were."

Gunnilde bit her lip. "Yes, but is it possible that I monopolized the King somewhat?"

At this point the Portstanleys interrupted them to take their leave for they were going straight to a lecture on astral influences. For a moment, Gunnilde experienced a sinking fear James might suggest they joined them.

She had known deep down that the portrait viewing had not been to his taste. Still, instead of taking this opportunity to be revenged on her, he simply added his farewells and watched mother and daughter walk away discussing the program of events.

"Gunnilde," he said suddenly, "if a king bids you speak, you have precious little choice in the matter. You did naught amiss."

She caught her breath. Was that the first time he had addressed her by name? For some reason, it struck her that way. When she remained silent, he turned to look at her expectantly. "Yes, I suppose that is true enough," she agreed.

"Though you might want to bear in mind it was the role of Queen's favorite you coveted, not King's," he said, glancing away.

"Oh! I hardly think I need worry about that!" she scoffed.

He leveled a wry look her way. "I notice you did not correct him about your name, Hilde."

She gave an awkward laugh. "It hardly seemed diplomatic. Besides, it is close enough, is it not? My grandmother used to call me Nilde."

For a moment he looked as though he would argue the point, then changed his mind. "You were not lying when you said you were a fond sister, were you?" he said.

The change in subject threw her for a moment. "When did I—?" Then she remembered that day when they had nearly quarreled and Constance had taken such grave offence. "Oh! No, I—I did not lie."

94

Why was he thinking of that time? she wondered uneasily. Had they not smoothed things over between them since then? "I'm afraid I was quite rude to you that day," she blurted. "I regret it now. It was simply because I felt so very deeply on my friend's behalf. I hope you can, well, overlook it now."

Without discussing it, they seemed to be heading back toward their quarters. "You felt for…Constance you mean," he said awkwardly and flushed. Interesting that he was now pausing before speaking the name of his former affianced, she observed.

For the first time it occurred to her that perhaps his feelings had been more involved than she had comprehended. She had not realized before that half of his rudeness was down to awkwardness.

"Well, to be perfectly frank, it was Sir Douglas who stood more my friend than Constance," she admitted. "You see he asked me for my help, and if you had only seen how earnestly and sincerely—"

"Sir Douglas?" he repeated in an odd tone. "It was Sir Douglas who you considered your particular friend?"

Gunnilde took a deep breath. "Yes, you see Constance and I, well, we did not exactly have the same interests in life. I knew Sir Douglas of old, for he has attended my father's tourney for several years, first as a squire and then as a knight in his own right. It was at his request that I made the effort to befriend Constance and plead his cause with her."

Oh dear, it was all so difficult. She could not possibly confess that she found Constance's company somewhat…wearing. Especially now she suspected James might admire that lady rather more than she had first thought.

"I suppose Farleigh was one of the men you were always whispering in corners with," he asked, his words cutting across her thoughts.

95

"Yes," she agreed absently.

His head whipped about to pin her with a stare. "You could at least deny it!"

Deny it? "But why would I? I just explained…" Her words faltered. Why was he looking so out of reason cross?

"Who were the others?" he demanded.

"The others? Well…" Gunnilde considered her past matchmaking endeavors. "There was John Fulsham, of course. And before him, there was Sir Thomas Crowle and Master Becker." She tried to dredge up the names of the others, but James was looking so put out that she could hardly concentrate. And they had been getting along so nicely too!

His dark brows snapped together. "I'm afraid that my wife will not be expected to conduct herself in such a manner," he said stiffly. "It would reflect poorly on my family name."

"Oh." This was disappointing as Gunnilde had enjoyed her role as a confidante very much, but she supposed she had a new focus now. "They're not at court anymore anyway," she said philosophically. "And I doubt I will come across them again anytime soon. They all moved back to the country after their respective marriages."

"I see." He retreated into silence, though he was clearly still out of sorts.

Gunnilde sighed. It seemed she had obtained a difficult sort of husband of uneven moods. It happened, she knew. Sarah Nesdin, a friend from her youth, had married an old widower with gout, well-known for his tetchiness.

At least James was young and pretty. She supposed it was his artistic temperament that was to blame. Presumably her duty lay in trying to coax him out of his sullens.

"I was wondering earlier if you might be composing some tune," she said brightly.

He flashed an impatient look her way. "What?"

"When you fell silent after we viewed the portrait."

He blinked at her. Really, his eyes were very pretty, a sort of greenish blue, with such spiky, thick dark lashes. "No," he answered shortly.

"It doesn't happen like that, then? With inspiration taking you unawares," she persisted.

"It can, sometimes," he admitted grudgingly. "Why do you ask?"

"I was just curious."

They had reached their quarters and James opened the door. "We had better dine here tonight, just the two of us," he said, gesturing for her to enter before him.

"Why?" She had been looking forward to sitting at a more prominent table in the Great Hall.

"Because we need to talk about our plans," James said heavily.

9

James suspected Gunnilde was disappointed she would not be mingling with her fellow courtiers in the Great Hall at supper, however she accepted his pronouncement without argument.

"Will Neville come back for supper?" she asked, brushing past him as she entered their rooms.

"No," he replied. "He won't be interrupting us. He prefers the company of others and never takes his meals up here if he can help it."

"Hence the Ashdowns," Gunnilde murmured thoughtfully as she walked over to the fire and plunked herself down before it.

James sent her a quizzical look. "The Ashdowns?" he repeated.

"Your neighbors across the corridor."

"Yes, I know who they are, I was just surprised that you did."

"You share your manservant, Bennett, with them, do you not?"

"Oh yes." She had a good memory for trivialities, he would give her that.

"I'll just go and find Bennett," he said, first checking the bedrooms and finding the fires unlit. Undoubtedly, he was over with the Ashdowns again. Once he had located him, Bennett returned with the utmost reluctance and set about lighting the fires. James busied himself setting out ink and parchment on the table. He glanced at the empty wood bucket.

"We will need more firewood, Bennett."

"So soon?" Bennett stood up and examined the small pile of coins on the mantel. "That's the last of them allocated for this month," he said pointedly.

James nodded and went into the bedroom in search of his coin pouch. Gunnilde jumped out of her seat and followed close on his heels. "Wait, I have some coins I can contribute," she said, hurrying to her trunk. "It is not much but—"

"Keep it," James said, turning and chinking some coins in his hand. "I have enough here."

"It is only fair," she insisted, throwing open her chest and rummaging within it. "For I suspect you usually do without or light your fires but sparingly when you are alone."

"Keep it," he reiterated. It stood to reason that the household's costs would increase along with its members. "I think you'll find I am the one who is expected to provide for a wife."

Gunnilde straightened up and regarded him with apparent dismay. "So, I am to become one of your pensioners now too?" she said, surprising him.

He shrugged. "Did you think your father would continue to pay your expenses?" he asked. "Obviously that obligation is now mine."

She flushed, dropping her eyes. "Mayhap I will receive an allowance as one of the Queen's ladies?" she suggested hopefully.

James looked skeptical. "Doubtful. The role is one of prestige and not profit. The royals do not keep their coffers full by giving with an open hand." He walked back and gave Bennett the money and instructions about fetching their supper.

Once the servant had been dispatched, he turned and found Gunnilde stood in the doorway watching him. She had thrown a dark wool mantle over her dress and looked somber. "You are used to shouldering responsibility for your family, are you not?" she observed quietly.

"I am," he said simply. "Come and sit closer to the fire. I have put out writing instruments on this table. You need to write to your family and apprise them of our marriage."

"And will you write to yours?" she asked, coming slowly into the room.

"I will," he said shortly, and sat down at the table. It was not a task he was looking forward to.

Gunnilde advanced into the room, sitting down opposite him and setting the ink pot between them. "Do you think your news will bring them to court?" she asked a little nervously.

"Who? My parents?" She nodded and he shook his head. "They never come to the winter palace. Wycliffe Hall is just outside the summer capital, and when the King is in residence there, they are at court every day. During the winter months they stay at home."

"Oh." She dipped her quill. "My stepmother would dearly love to come to court," she volunteered though he had not asked. "There was some talk of it a couple of years ago, but it came to naught as my father dragged his heels. He is not so keen to leave Payne Manor nowadays."

"He is older than your stepmother?" James enquired without much interest.

"She is three months younger than me," Gunnilde admitted.

James looked across at her, unsure how to respond. Did she resent that and dislike her stepmother? He did not know how to approach such things. "I see," he said instead.

She sighed, propping her cheek against her hand. "I am sure I do not know how I will explain the past two days," she exclaimed. "Such tidings are sure to be shocking to those at home."

"It might be best to keep things brief and strictly factual," he suggested, for that was certainly how he intended to frame things.

Gunnilde set her down her nib and started writing in very neat, round script with lots of loops and twirls, and James set about his own missives in his usual sparse manner. For the next half hour, it was very quiet in their rooms, with nothing but the scratching of quills and the crackle of logs in the hearth.

James dashed off a terse letter to his mother, another to their steward apprising him of his marital status, and a quick apologetic note to his old tutor, Master Gregory, for missing today's musical performance at Barnabus Hall, a thing he had not done since journeying to Aphrany.

The letter was really more for Justina Gregory's benefit, for she was the one who would have dressed the old man in his hat and cloak and set him on the bench by the door ready for James to collect. Old Gregory would never have remembered what day it was, but his daughter would wonder at James's nonappearance.

James described his reason as a "matter of unavoidable business," then shot a look across at Gunnilde. Ridiculous to feel furtive. What else could he call it? "A highly personal matter" perhaps, or "a family matter"? None of them seemed to quite fit present circumstances.

He noticed with raised brows that Gunnilde had covered six sides of paper with her angelic writing and still seemed to be in full flow. So much for not knowing what to say, he thought wryly.

A knock on the door heralded Bennett's return. He was bearing an armful of logs and a disagreeable expression on his face. He stomped over to the fireplace and threw them down, then turned and left again as

101

abruptly as he'd entered. Gunnilde pursed her lips but made no comment, looking instead at his folded pages.

"Have you finished your letters?" she asked.

"Yes."

"They must have been very short. Did you really stick to plain matter of fact?"

"I did." And he had skipped some of them at that.

"And pray, how did you describe me?" she asked impulsively. Before he could answer, she picked up her own letter. "I have described you as a prominent courtier of standing and influence, who is both a man of learning and culture and heir to a considerable estate in Caer Lyoness. Sir James supplements his income with the composition of music and has lately had his pieces played at the cathedral in Caer Lyoness."

James cleared his throat and picked up the first letter he had written. "One Gunnilde Payne," he read aloud, "only daughter of Sir Aubron Payne of Payne Manor."

"That's it?" She sounded disappointed.

"What else would you have me write?"

"Well, you could have made some attempt at description," Gunnilde huffed. "Even if it was only to state I am a country girl born and bred!"

"That would give them entirely the wrong impression," he said dismissively.

"How so?"

"They might think you would be content to be sent home to live quietly at Wycliffe Hall, writing inventories of bed linens," he explained dampeningly. Mother would just love that. Someone else to lord over and have jumping to do her bidding.

"Oh, well, in that case I suppose I must be grateful to you," she said, sounding anything but.

James sat back in his seat. What accomplishments would she have him describe? Mistress Payne is an arrant flirt who enjoys catching the eye of all and sundry. She has flaunting yellow hair and a pleasing buxom appearance. He gave his head a quick shake. Probably best not to let his thoughts stray in that direction.

"I would not be content to molder in the country," she added painstakingly. "If I was, I could have stayed at home and meekly done my stepmother's bidding."

"I am well aware of that," he responded crisply.

"In any case, how do you know I am an only daughter?" she asked.

He snorted. "You would certainly have told me by now if you had a sister."

She lowered her eyes. "And would your parents like a daughter to live quietly at home with them?" she asked guiltily.

He did not answer for a moment, then said, "They have a niece of my mother's who lives with them already. She fulfils that role and helps run the household."

"Oh. You never mentioned a cousin before. What is her name?"

"Rebecca."

"Is one of your other letters for her?"

"For Rebecca?" He was startled. "Certainly not. We are not on such terms. One is for our steward, Denby, and the other is for my old music tutor, Master Gregory. He lives in town and would have expected me today. I wrote him a brief note of explanation."

"He was the person you usually see on the second Wednesday of every month?" she deduced.

"Yes, we attend a musical gathering on that day. I see a lot of him when I am in Aphrany and visit with him often. I rent an attic room in his house and keep my musical instruments there."

Her eyes widened. "Oh, I see. And will I meet this Master Gregory of yours sometime soon?"

"Why would you?"

"Because he is an important person in your life, is he not?"

He paused. "Yes, he is, but he is not someone you would be interested in knowing. He is no one of consequence here at court."

Gunnilde flushed. "You think that is solely how I judge people?" she asked, two bright pink spots on her cheeks. "Perhaps it is as well you gave no description of me in your letters. Your opinion of me is far from flattering, Sir James!"

"Whereas your description of me was all flattery," he replied. "Yet relied purely on hearsay. You have never heard any of my music and we have never conversed on subjects of literature or education."

She had the grace to look a little embarrassed by his directness. "We have not," she admitted. "I myself am not much versed in such matters."

He let his eyes travel over her with disfavor. No really, he could see no purpose in having her sleeves slashed about to high heaven like that unless it was to show off her shapely upper arms. And as for her distracting hairstyles…

"It's a good thing you're a pretty woman or you would look ridiculous in some of the fashions you affect," he said sourly before he could think better of it.

If anything, his new wife looked rather pleased by this pronouncement. "I know you mean to snub me with such a remark, but I am going to take it instead as encouragement," she said, astonishing him. "For one thing, you called me pretty, which I refuse to take as anything other than a compliment, and for another, I am quite used to ignoring men's opinions on such matters. Apart from a very select few, they have nothing useful to impart."

Well! James reeled. "What select few?" he heard himself ask. Presumably, she meant her father who would have held sway in such matters previously, when it came to her manner of dress.

She hesitated. "Viscount Bardulf, for instance, is a great arbiter of such things, and my brother, Hal, has a bold style of dressing like myself which I cannot help but approve of."

James snorted. "And just how is it that you do fill your hours here at court? I have never seen you occupied with music or embroidery or any of the usual pursuits." He already knew, of course. Gunnilde Payne had spent her time flirting with knights and gossiping with other frivolous, fashionable women. It was obvious.

"You seem to have some decided opinions in how I spend my time already," Gunnilde answered pertly.

"Well," he rallied, clearing his throat. "Let us simply say that I had guessed you were not the kind to attend improving lectures."

Surprisingly, Gunnilde took exception to this. "As a matter of fact," she responded with spirit, "I have attended several of the wretched things. The Portstanleys are distressingly fond of them. Sadly, for you, I found most of them incomprehensible."

"Which ones?" he found himself asking instead of making the obvious response. She turned an enquiring look at him. "Which lectures have you attended?" he elaborated grudgingly.

"Oh." She considered this. "Well, the last one was the one with the small bald man who gets very excited and can't pronounce his Ws. He had lots of maps and tiny instruments that he used to draw lines all over them."

"Master Edcott's theories on navigation," James realized aloud. The man's oration had been rather involved. "I daresay you could have understood him if you had paid sufficient attention." She looked surprised by this assessment, so he added caustically, "You probably spent the whole time daydreaming about new shoes."

"And why shouldn't I?" she asked shamelessly. "I am fond of new shoes." She stuck out her foot and contemplated her current choice in footwear, a flimsy-looking article with more cutouts than shoe leather. Catching sight of her crimson stockings, James felt his face flush. It was not just her upper arms that were shapely. "Don't you think they are pretty?" she asked wistfully.

Her calves? He panicked. "I wasn't looking at them," he lied. Instead of tucking herself back into her skirts like a modest woman, Gunnilde Payne nodded toward her raised foot.

"Well, take a look now," she said generously, wagging her shoe. "They are of the softest Aphranian leather, and I won't tell you how much of my allowance I spent on them."

Tearing his eyes from her immodest hosiery, James spared the shoes a disparaging glance. "They look as though they are held together by ribbon alone," he concluded dampeningly.

"The lacings are all that holds them in place," she agreed with a sigh. "If the ground is damp, my stockings get soaked through."

"And how much did they cost you?" James asked before he could stop himself.

"My stockings?" She looked startled by the question, as well she might. It was highly improper for him to have asked. Except…no, it wasn't. He was the one who would be paying for them now after all. James cleared his throat and nodded, avoiding her eyes. "Fifteen shillings," she confessed promptly.

"Fifteen?" he echoed in horror. On top of everything else Mistress Payne was a spendthrift!

"I don't usually have such expensive ones," she said quickly. "I had them for a special occasion. My court presentation," she added when he could think of no response.

To his consternation, he noticed Gunnilde was now gazing at his own legs, a vaguely disapproving look in her eyes. Before he could stop himself, James found he was looking down to check naught was amiss with his own appearance.

To his relief, he found no disorder with his breeches and below them his stockings showed no holes. "You find some fault with my attire?" he asked coldly. Instead of rushing to deny such a thing as you might expect, the outrageous woman hesitated.

"Well, not fault exactly," she hesitated. "It's just…" Catching sight of the look on his face, she changed her mind. "It's nothing."

"Pray don't hold back on my account," he said sarcastically.

"Well…perhaps you are unaware of the fact, but currently, the men's fashion is for stockings to be paneled."

"Paneled?" he repeated blankly.

"Yes, so you achieve a sort of striped effect. And that shade of brown is so very…"

"So very what?" he asked, feeling goaded.

She considered this a moment. "Conservative," she decided on. Conservative? "Lord Schaeffer wears brown stockings," she added with faint condemnation.

"Lord Schaeffer is an eminently respectable courtier of seniority in the King's council."

"Yes, exactly," Gunnilde agreed at once. "He's at least sixty-five years old."

James beheld her speechlessly. Good gods. "I am not fashionable enough for you it seems, madam," he said sarcastically. "Perhaps you would prefer it if I ran around court in lime green short hose, puffed out like a popinjay."

Gunnilde flushed indignantly. "And I am not studious enough for you, Sir James, it seems," she replied at once. "You would doubtless prefer it if I ran around court fawning over scholars and dusty old tomes about mathematics and medicine!"

A cleared throat behind them made them both jump and swing around. It was Neville, stood by the door with an odd look on his face. "Sorry to interrupt," he muttered, a smile playing about his lips.

"When did you get back?" James demanded, sitting up straight in his seat. "I did not hear you enter."

"No, you were both far too absorbed to notice me," his brother answered cheerfully. "I wondered if you were coming down to supper?"

James cleared his throat. "No, we, er, thought we'd take a quiet supper up here."

"Ah, quite," said Neville. "A cozy little supper together. Sounds just the thing."

Immediately, James knew how Neville would be describing the scene to his friends. He scowled at him. "If you think for one minute—"

"She's quite right about your stockings, you know," Neville interrupted him. "You need to go bolder. Perhaps a nice plum purple or a bright pea green."

"Get out, Neville."

Neville laughed and ducked back out of the door.

Annoying swine.

10

Gunnilde finished her braid, tied it, and flung it over her shoulder. She ventured a quick look across the room at James, who had finished his wash and was now patting himself dry. Whoever would have thought that one day, she would be in a position to see the handsome Sir James Wycliffe clad only in his braies?

It was true, he was shivering and scowling at this present moment, muttering under his breath whenever he happened to stub his toe or drop his drying cloth, but even that did not detract from the fact he was fine and tall and had the face of an angel.

True, he would likely be one of the more disagreeable angels that turned up to condemn you or point a fiery sword in your direction but still…he was impressive to look at. She wondered what he must have been like as a squire.

Try as she might, she simply could not imagine him running to do his master's bidding, obliging and eager with a dagger at his hip. No, he must have been a dissatisfactory sort of squire, she thought, rather like Ancel Somers. Hal and his friends detested Ancel.

Ancel was Sir Ned's squire and famously shirked his duties and was wildly unpopular with his fellow squires. He was afraid of horses, disliked dogs, and was always trying to skip out on his obligations. She recalled Sir Ned's exasperation and experienced a pang.

Quickly, she banished both Ancel and Sir Ned from her mind. She didn't want her thoughts to go haring off in that direction. That would never do. Instead, she turned back to contemplate James in his braies. That was a much nicer subject. The damp hair at his neck was forming into clinging curls there, for he wore it quite long. "Have you ever jousted?" she asked impulsively, propping herself up on her elbow. His shoulders were nice and broad even though he was not heavily muscled.

He cast down his drying cloth onto a nearby chair. He was tidy for a man, she thought. Hal would have thrown it down on the floor. "No, I have not."

"Oh. Never wanted to?"

"No," he repeated.

"Who was your master when you were a squire?"

He cast an impatient look her way. "Why? Do you think you might have heard of him?"

"I might, if he competed. You never know." Ignoring her, he made for the bed. "You must have completed the necessary training to be a knight," she persisted. "After all, you have been knighted."

"Of course," he answered impatiently.

"My father greatly admires knights and pageantry," she said. "As do my brother and I."

Pulling back the covers, he climbed into the bed. "There are different kinds of knights, Gunnilde. Those that like jousting, wenching, and drinking till they pass out and those that do not. You happen to have married the latter, a fault entirely of your own making, I might add."

"Wine, wench, and song, you mean. Is that not what the ballad says?"

"Ballad? Which ballad?"

"I forget which one, but I'm pretty sure it had a Fair Margaret and a Sweet William in it."

"That describes at least two thirds of the wretched things," he answered with a curl of his lip. "It's always fair someone and their lover who is neither sweet nor constant."

"You are not a lover of ballads?" She turned her head sharply to look at him. "And you a musician!" In truth, she was more shocked by that than a knight who did not like jousting.

He shrugged his shoulder. "Their stories annoy me. They are always so dissatisfactory and so seldom make any sense."

"How can you say so? Why, there are so very many of them to choose from. Sad ballads, tragic ballads, ballads where they all come to nasty endings, fantastical ballads where they get transformed into beasts—"

He turned to look at her. "That is precisely my point," he interrupted. "Scarcely anyone is ever rewarded or punished as they ought to be. Cheaters, liars, even murderers frequently get away with their sins. Others suffer and perish for no reason at all. Sometimes the characters change from lover to brother, to father or son. Everyone has the same name and the story is all jumbled up and usually there is no moral within at all. It…irritates me."

Gunnilde regarded him with interest. "What about poetry?" she asked. "Do you like that?"

"It depends," he said cautiously. "The quality of poetry you come across in the palace can differ wildly."

She sighed wistfully. "I wish I liked poetry, for it is very popular at court at present."

"You do not care for it?"

112

"No, for I find poetry dissatisfactory. If you find ballads lacking, then I feel the same about poetry."

He was silent a moment, and she thought he had dropped the subject. Then all of a sudden he asked grudgingly, "What is it you find so dissatisfactory about it exactly?"

"Well, I can never make out its meaning," she explained eagerly. "On the page, it appears to be simply describing a yew tree or a cowslip and then everyone sits around and claps and says how terribly clever it is to reveal the truth about the nature of life or the humanity of man. It is all quite unfathomable to me."

Unexpectedly, James laughed.

"It is not funny," Gunnilde grumbled. "I can never penetrate the meaning, and I had to stop attending the poetry meet for I felt sure everyone would find me out."

"I expect half the people there could not understand it," he said dismissively.

"Constance even told me once that—" She bit off her words, looking suddenly stricken. "Oh, er—"

"What?" James asked. "What did she tell you?"

"Oh, I would rather not say, if you don't mind. It is not really a fit subject for your ears," she said apologetically.

"Not a fit subject for my ears?" he repeated, looking stunned.

"Yes, for you are very…proper, are you not?" She licked her lips nervously and James's expression wavered from startled to something else, then back again. "After all, you said yourself that you do not like wine, wenches, and song."

113

"When did I—? What the hells do you mean by that?" he said. "You hardly need to shield my ears from the conversation of two gently reared young women!"

Gunnilde regarded him with dismay. Oh dear, had she insulted him? "It's just that, well, I don't want you think I'm, um, trying to blacken anyone's reputation!" she gabbled, feeling her cheeks turn hot as she grew increasingly flustered. "And you see, it was purely a misunderstanding! Poor Sir Douglas did not intend any offence by it, I am sure!"

"Sir Douglas? What the hells has he to do with this?"

Feeling quite overwhelmed by the vehemence of his reaction, and her own culpability in the affair, Gunnilde covered her face with her hands. The bed lurched and suddenly, his hands were at her wrists, dragging them from her face. He loomed above her. "Tell me, Gunnilde," he said sternly. "Now."

Gunnilde stared at him, her breath coming fast. "Oh! It was…really nothing," she panted. "Just, silly really. But you see, I never dreamed that poetry could be improper, so you see, I wanted to ask her about it, but of course, Constance had burned it, so I never got to see it after all." She could not keep the wistfulness from her voice.

"Constance burned what?" he asked tersely. Gunnilde's hands were now pinned on either side of her head against the mattress and James was half on top of her. She could scarcely think, let alone breathe!

"The lewd poem!" she blurted.

James stared down at her, but to Gunnilde's surprise, instead of holding her gaze, his eyes roamed over her face, resting more on her lips than anywhere. "What lewd poem?" he asked huskily.

"The one Sir Douglas commissioned," Gunnilde admitted. "But indeed, I never got to read it, and I doubt he even realized it was lewd. Most likely he thought it was just about an acorn or some such thing."

"Most likely," he agreed, his voice still gravelly, and Gunnilde was suddenly and unexpectedly thrown into an astonished suspicion that he was perilously close to kissing her. Wasn't he? Surely not. But then…why else would he be so close and staring at her like that?

Her chest fluttered and she parted her lips expectantly as he lowered his face to hers. He was! He was going to kiss her. Gunnilde closed her eyes and angled her face toward his.

Then…nothing. She felt him move again and realized he was in retreat. She felt a sudden wild despair that he should leave her wanting like this. She should have known. Always, she seemed always destined for disappointment when it came to men.

Then it dawned on her, he was not moving away, rather the opposite. He was shifting over her restlessly and suddenly she realized what he was trying to do. He was trying to anchor himself more firmly against her.

She opened her legs to guide him, jostling her body against his own until James slid into place, exactly where he needed to be. At once she squeezed her legs together, trapping his hips between her thighs, holding him fast and tethering him to her. He gasped, and Gunnilde's eyes flew open. They stared at one another, breathing hard.

And that was not the only hard thing. His flesh was willing, she realized with stupefied gratification. More than willing, where it pressed up against her own, all hard and swollen with need, and there was nothing remotely polite about it.

James Wycliffe was keen as mustard to join his body with hers. At least, his loins were keen, who knew what torturous thoughts were whirling

115

about that pretty head of his. Oh, gods, don't let him stop, she thought desperately as her body throbbed and fluttered in a whirl of yearning. She wanted to pull him closer and demand he gave her the attention she craved. She hardly dared meet his eyes, lest he demand she release him, and oh, she did not want to!

"James," she moaned, and a panicked look entered his eyes.

"Don't," he muttered, turning his face away. "For the gods' sake, don't make that noise. I can't stand it."

Gunnilde froze. Her expression must have shown her confused dismay for he immediately froze too, releasing her wrists and rearing back from her.

"No, I—I didn't mean it like that," he said, evidently panicking. "Don't misunderstand me. I like it. I just can't—"

"Can't what?"

He hovered over her, his face blank. "Can't let the situation get out of hand," he said frustratedly. "I have not yet even kissed you." He looked so shame-faced that Gunnilde caught her breath.

Oh. She gave a relieved smile. "Well, you can remedy that easily enough."

He cleared his throat. "Are you saying my kiss would not be unwelcome?" he asked, and Gunnilde struggled a moment with the strangest impulse to laugh. James's arousal was currently straining against her belly, and here he was worrying about the propriety of a kiss.

"Do not worry," she assured him. "You can kiss me and welcome."

He stared for a long moment and then slowly, achingly slowly, he lowered his face to hers, his lips brushing against hers, oh so softly. Their breath mingled and Gunnilde whimpered. His eyes clashed with hers as he seemed to assess if she liked it or not.

Nay, she thought faintly, seeing the storm of emotions in his eyes. She had that wrong. He was trying to tell if he liked it or not. Was she his first kiss? And why, oh why did that make her heart beat so loudly in her chest that it almost deafened her?

"James?" she whispered. He did not speak, but his eyes focused more intently on her face. To her frustration he remained where he was, poised over her, unmoving. "Kiss me again," she invited, shocking even herself.

His eyes flashed, and the next second his lips were against her own again, firmer this time and less hesitant. Gunnilde gave a murmur of approval, which made him groan. Then suddenly a heavy hammering noise started. It seemed dull and distant at first and barely registered with Gunnilde before it increased in both volume and urgency until James pulled back, a look of confusion on his face.

"Open this door!" yelled a voice which Gunnilde recognized. "Open it now, I say!" As one, both turned their heads to stare at the bedchamber door, though it was surely the outer door that was pounding. "My gods, it's Hal!" Gunnilde uttered.

"Your brother?" James said, looking as befuddled as she felt. Neither of them had moved, and he was still atop of her.

"Yes. He is expected at court for the Squires' Solstice Revels," she reflected. "He must have arrived this eve and heard our news."

James cursed, then rolled off her, dragging the top sheet from the bed and wrapping it about himself. He was taking a leaf out of her book, it seemed, and she followed suit, grabbing the second blanket this time for

117

her own. She hurried out into the sitting room and heard James drawing back the bolt and flinging the door open out in the small hallway beyond.

"Where is she?" demanded a familiar voice, and then Hal was shoving his way into the room, the light of battle in his eyes. "Gunnilde?"

"Yes, here I am, Hal," she greeted him, walking forward to kiss his cheek. Goodness, he was now grown tall as her and had filled out a good deal since she had seen him in the summer. "You have heard my news, it seems," she said, placing a reassuring hand on his arm as James appeared in the doorway behind them

"Married?" Hal said blankly. "Married?" He angled a thumb at James. "To this?"

"Yes, indeed." Gunnilde took a deep breath. "And now you must greet one another as family. Hal, this is James, my husband. James, this is Hal, my younger brother."

Hal subjected James to a hard stare. "Why does he look like that?" he asked abruptly. "I don't like it."

"Undressed?" Gunnilde asked with some asperity. "Because we were abed, why else?" A chuckle drifted over James's shoulder, and Gunnilde realized Hal was accompanied. "Cuthbert?" she called out excitedly. "Kit? Is that you?"

"Aye, it's us, Gunnilde," Cuthbert called back, his blond head appearing over James's shoulder. He gave her a grin. "How are you?"

"In need of rescue?" Kit enquired, peering over her husband's other shoulder, his dark hair falling into his eyes.

"Naturally, I brought reinforcements," her brother said impatiently. "In case I needed to carry you off, slung across my pommel."

"Slung across your—?" Gunnilde gave her head a quick shake, then looked across at James, who was still blocking the doorway. In truth, he looked a little disheveled and was likely not making the greatest impression.

As though noticing the direction of her gaze, James glanced down and adjusted his bedsheet to make sure he was adequately covered. "You had better come in," he said resignedly and stood as Hal's two best friends sauntered into the room, looking about them with interest.

"Lot of good you both are!" Hal grumbled. "Waiting to be invited! I told you we were storming the place."

Kit flopped down into a chair. "Have a heart, Payne. We've been on horseback all day long. Even invading armies get fed and watered before they lay siege. You got anything to eat, Hinchliffe?" he said looking at James. "We're half-starved."

"That's not right, it's not Hinchliffe," Cuthbert said with a frown. He crossed to the table and examined the leavings on their abandoned dinner platter. Bennett never had reappeared to clear it away. "I told you," he said, selecting a chicken leg and taking a bite. "It was white cliffs I dreamed of. That's your name, isn't it?" he said, pointing toward James with his drumstick. "Whitecliff."

"Actually—" James started to correct him, but Kit gave an indignant yell and bounced up out of his chair, flying across the room to shove Cuthbert out of the way. He hovered over the abandoned meat like a carrion crow. "Trust you to secure the meatiest bone, Ames, you greedy dog!" Kit grumbled.

Cuthbert rolled his eyes, tossed down the stripped bone, and reached for another, only to get his hand slapped away.

"You've had more than your share!" Kit snapped.

Seeing Hal remain at her side, Gunnilde deduced uneasily he must really be upset. Usually, Hal's stomach and the appeasing of it was his uppermost concern.

"It's Wycliffe actually," James said loudly, directing the words at Hal. "James Wycliffe. You, I take it, are my new brother-in-law."

"That remains to be seen," Hal replied belligerently, turning to look at his sister. "How in the hells could you end up married without Father or me there to give you away?" he burst out indignantly. "It just doesn't seem lawful to my mind."

Seeing the injury in his eyes, Gunnilde patted his arm again. "If you will just be seated, brother, and allow us to extend you our hospitality, we can soon clear up this misunderstanding." She shot a significant look at James, who sighed and walked over to check the contents of the ale jug.

It must have been empty for he promptly turned and walked out of the door with it, still barefoot and clad in only his bedsheet. Was he really going to walk across the corridor in search of Bennett, half-dressed like that? It seemed strangely out of character for this husband of hers.

She turned back to the others to find them watching her with keen interest. "Who is he anyway?" Kit asked, his mouth half full. "These rooms are smaller than my uncle's, so he's not an earl."

"No title?" Hal asked, sucking in a breath and pursing his lips. "That's bad."

"Not until his father dies. Then he will be third Baron Wycliffe."

"I saw his crest," Cuthbert volunteered, and instantly Gunnilde knew he meant in a dream.

"Could you tell it was a unicorn?" she asked. "Only I mistook it for a goat." She glanced down at her bedsheet before realizing that James wore the embroidered one this time.

"Yes, for unicorns have an affinity with virgins, do they not?" Cuthbert replied absently.

Gunnilde started but luckily Hal and Kit were used to ignoring the stranger of his utterings. Was he saying that James…?

"What the devil is all this row about?" Neville complained, trailing into the room, clutching his robe shut. "It is past midnight, and you might show me some consideration for I've the beginnings of one of my sore throats…"

"Ah, Neville, I do apologize. This is my brother, Hal Payne, and these are Cuthbert Ames and Kit Montmayne, his closest friends," Gunnilde explained. "They have just arrived at court for the Solstice celebrations. Learning of my recent marriage, they rushed at once to, well, to wish us all well," she concluded optimistically.

"Ah," Neville responded awkwardly.

"Boys," she began brightly, though in point of fact, she was not sure she should address them as such anymore. They were no longer sweet little pages running around in short hose. All three of them must be around sixteen years old and took up a good deal more room than they ever used to. Still, she had started now, so she would finish. "This is Sir Neville Wycliffe, younger brother to my husband."

All three looked Neville up and down critically. Hal folded his arms. "Sir Neville, is it?" he asked skeptically. "You look a bit young to be knighted. Why, there's nary a hair on your chin!"

"I am fully two and twenty," Neville protested.

"So, then, you've been a knight all of a twelvemonth," Cuthbert commented dampeningly.

"Who knighted you?" Hal demanded.

"Sir Raymond Buxton."

"Never heard of him," Kit said, sounding unimpressed.

"Why should you? He is a courtly man of education and refinement," Neville responded smartly. "Not some ruffian brawler like your own masters, I surmise!"

Gunnilde's face fell, for Kit's master was none other than the fearsome Garman Orde, while Cuthbert served the King's champion. It was unlikely they would allow such an insult to go unchecked.

"Hah! So, you admit your master is no swordsman?" Kit retorted, flinging a chicken bone over his shoulder. To Gunnilde's surprise, he seemed entirely unruffled by the slight to Lord Twyford's honor. As for Cuthbert, he had an arm draped over the back of the bench and appeared to be making himself entirely comfortable. "I'll warrant your Sir Desmond—"

"Raymond!" Neville snapped.

"—has never had so much as a sniff of combat," Kit continued disparagingly. "I daresay," he added darkly, "that the fellow perfumes his hair."

"And what if he does?" Neville fired back. "Perfume is in much demand here at court among the eminently civilized. We do not care to smell of the stables when we consort with our womenfolk."

Hal snorted but strange to say, the atmosphere in the room seemed to have lightened considerably with the exchange of barbs. Neville, who had been complaining of a sore throat moments ago, looked positively bright-eyed and bushy-tailed. He sat himself down, and looked toward Gunnilde expectantly. "But where is James? Surely not still abed?"

The door pushed open before she could answer and her husband reappeared, carrying two brimming jugs of ale. Neville's mouth dropped open to see his brother so peculiarly garbed, but James barely seemed to notice. "Fetch the cups off the shelf, Neville," he directed him. "Enough for everyone."

Neville jumped up and the ale was poured. Gunnilde turned back to Hal, who had fallen silent. "Now, Hal," she began again. "Firstly, you must understand my marriage was at the behest of the Queen herself!"

"Seems a damned odd thing for her to have done, if you ask me," Hal muttered, casting a darkling look in James's direction.

"Well"—Gunnilde spread her hands wide—"truth to tell, neither Sir James nor myself had a lot of say in the matter. We were married by the Bishop of Badsbury in the royal chapel and the Queen's favorite lady-in-waiting provided the ring."

She held it up for Hal to examine, but he ignored such a trifle, instead focusing on James, who was now handing around the ale. "He looks a frippery fellow, not at all what I would have chosen for you, sister," he said, shaking his head. "And what's more, I cannot believe he is what you would have chosen for yourself."

Mercifully, Bennett appeared at this point bearing a large tray of cheese and savory crackers.

Kit and Cuthbert fell on this gladly and even Neville helped himself to a cracker. Casting a sidelong look at her brother, Gunnilde could tell it cost him dearly to turn his nose up, but he stuck to his principles, the light of hostility still coldly shining in his eyes.

"Is that Dustin I spy?" Gunnilde asked, hoping to direct the conversation into happier channels. Hal glanced down at the small white fluffy head peering out of his tunic.

"Aye, course it is," Hal responded. "Who else would it be?"

Gunnilde reached out a hand to pet the little dog's head. Dustin trembled with excitement and gave his shrill little bark.

"Aye, good lad," Hal said, and narrowed his gaze at James. "You like dogs, Wycliffe?" he asked with deceptive mildness.

"I do," James responded promptly and Gunnilde breathed out for though he was unaware of it, a lot had rested on his answer. Hal could never abide anyone who did not like dogs.

Her brother relaxed infinitesimally. "Own one?"

"I do not."

This was clearly a point against him. "Why not?" Hal asked suspiciously.

When James hesitated, Gunnilde cut in. "My husband does not live an outdoor life," she explained helpfully. "He is a musician."

"Oh, yes?" Hal's reply was unenthusiastic.

"Some of his compositions have been performed at the cathedral at Caer Lyoness," Gunnilde boasted.

Hal grunted. "Well, I play the lute," he pointed out, "but that doesn't prevent me from owning a dog, now, does it?" He turned back to James. "What else do you do?"

"No, I don't think you understand, Hal," Gunnilde interrupted firmly. "James gets paid for composing music. That's how good he is. He both supports his family with his earnings and maintains their seat, Wycliffe Hall."

"To which I am heir," James added quietly.

This seemed to give Hal pause. "Is that so?" he asked with a flicker of interest. "Big place, is it?"

"It is of fair size," James admitted modestly.

Hal's gaze seemed to consider whether he was the type of man to exaggerate or downplay a fact. Finally, he gave a short nod and accepted the cup of ale James extended to him. "I suppose it could be worse," he reflected. "Though mind you, I had thought one of my friends could have done at a pinch for my sister."

"One of your friends?" Gunnilde echoed incredulously. Her gaze returned to Kit and Cuthbert, who seemed to be in competition for how many crackers they could fit into their mouths at any one time.

"Aye, for in five years or so we'll all be knights, don't forget," Hal reasoned. "And Father was plainly in no hurry to find you a husband. Stands to reason that I would step in."

"In five years' time I'll be seven and twenty!" Gunnilde protested faintly.

Hal waved this aside. "I still say one of them would have suited you. Not Kit," he admitted, shooting a glance at his friend, who was laughing uproariously at something Cuthbert had said to Neville. "He's heir to an earldom, so his uncle's sure to expect someone grand, but Ames for instance."

Hal nodded in Cuthbert's direction, and seeing his furtive manner, Gunnilde realized it could not be something he had ever openly discussed with his friend. This relieved her, she would not want Cuthbert to feel snubbed, even though she had always considered him the veriest child. "He's no prospects, it's true," Hal continued in a low voice, "but he's well connected, none could argue against that."

Gunnilde did not even try. She was terribly fond of both Kit and Cuthbert, but the idea that either of them was remotely marriageable was a ridiculous one. They might not be children anymore, but they were certainly not men!

"Or there's Hadrian Kellingford," Hal continued, warming to his theme. "Old Sir Roger's appeal to get him and his brother legitimized went through but there's still some that eye him askance. A solid marriage would help his advancement right enough."

"I see," Gunnilde said weakly, still somewhat appalled but also strangely touched that Hal should have been thinking of her.

"So sorry to have put a spoke to your wheel, Payne," James cut in at this point. His manner was dry.

Hal shrugged manfully. "I won't deny it's a blow," he said, shaking his head. "But there's precious little to be done about it now, I suppose."

"That's the spirit."

Gunnilde shot James a warning look before turning back to her brother. "Come now, Hal, it is not as bad as you suppose. James is a prominent courtier, and this is not a bad match for me, now that I, too, wish to reside chiefly at court. I am a lady-in-waiting to Her Majesty Queen Armenal, you know. Only think what everyone back in Tranton Vale would say to that!"

126

Hal looked impatient. "Who cares what they might say? It is your own feelings on the matter that concern me. Last I heard tell, your ambition was to marry a knight, have your own home and five bonny children."

Gunnilde flushed, avoiding James's eye. "Well, that was before," she said firmly. "I have not wanted such things for months now."

"And when exactly do you mean to introduce my sister to your people, sirrah?" Hal asked, turning back to James. "I take it none of them were here for the ceremony either?"

"They were not," James admitted, "apart from my brother. Wycliffe Hall lies in the south, many miles from Aphrany. I have no plans to travel there till spring." He looked at Gunnilde as though uncertain of her feelings on the matter. She smiled quickly to show she supported this plan wholeheartedly.

Hal grunted, somewhat mollified to hear he was not the only one who had missed out on the proceedings.

"Who accompanied you to court?" Gunnilde asked, hoping to coax him further away from the sore subject. "Are Eden and Roland come to Aphrany for the Solstice celebrations?" She was unable to contain her excitement at the thought of seeing her friend again. Before he could answer however, Cuthbert joined the conversation.

"No, they went back to the Keep," he explained. "Roland and Eden are hosting their whole family there, now that most of the new building has been done. All the Vawdreys are traveling to stay with them for the Solstice, aye, and the Twyfords too, for as you know Eden considers the Lady Lenora very like a sister."

"Oh, of course! I'm sure they will be very merry," Gunnilde said wistfully. "Though you and Kit will be sorry to miss out on such a celebration, I am sure."

"Not me!" Kit assured her, lowering his ale cup. "There's too many squalling infants about these days. You should see them." He shuddered. "The way they carry on, and my master is bad as the rest of them!" he said indignantly. "Carting them round on his hip and feeding them pap and talking of how clever they are! Those that talk of Sir Garman Orde's ferocity would scarce credit it to see him!"

"How wonderful," Gunnilde murmured, forgetting that she was a fine courtier now. All those babies, she thought, and Eden, Lady Vawdrey, Lady Twyford, and Lady Cadwallader all such proud and happy wives and mothers. She half wished she were there for the Solstice, though poor Eden must be positively overrun with guests. Good thing she was so capable and organized. James cleared his throat, snapping her out of her reverie.

"Besides, 'tis unlikely these young fellows will miss their rural celebrations when they are here at court for far grander ones," Neville opined. "I expect some of them might even hope to lift a cup or two at the Squires' Revels. Tell me, have any of your number a decent prospect of winning?"

"Decent prospects he says," Kit echoed mockingly, tipping his head. "I should say so! Cuthbert here can swim the length of Ditton Pool without drawing a second lungful of breath. And as for myself, I'm a pretty fair long jumper. It's these legs of mine." He stretched them out for all to admire, clad as they were in burgundy hose.

Neville immediately voiced his suspicion that Ditton Pool must be more pond than lake, likely because he could not deny the length of Kit's legs.

Hal turned back to Gunnilde. "To answer your question," he said, harking back. "I came with Sir Ned. He and Attley swapped squires after he was injured at Kellingford. Did you hear about it?"

"No!" Gunnilde replied, stunned. "You never wrote of it!" Hal was here with Sir Ned? She felt suddenly a little sick. "Whyever did they swap? Who in the world would trade you for Ancel?" she asked, thinking of Sir Ned's regular squire who was known far and wide as thoroughly useless.

"Attley broke his arm, and the bones did not knit as they should, so he's gone home to lick his wounds but thought it a shame to make me miss the Revels. Instead, he suggested Sir Ned take me to Aphrany and he could take Ancel home with him. Even Ancel could not mess up fetching and carrying for an invalid when there are plenty of other servants around to help."

"Oh, that was nicely done of him," Gunnilde acknowledged. "You should not have to suffer because of the misfortune."

"And it is not as though Ancel will be missed at the Revels by anyone," Kit said scornfully. Cuthbert pressed his lips together. "Why do you look like that, Ames?" Kit demanded. "Do not tell me you will miss the little weasel!"

"Oh, I don't know," Cuthbert said vaguely. "He's not all bad."

Gunnilde was as surprised as Kit. She had on many occasions heard all three boys lambast Ancel roundly.

"You're raving!" Kit jeered. "Ever since you saved him from drowning that time, you've been soft on the churl."

"No, no," Cuthbert said hastily. "I just meant…without him around we do not know who will come in last place in every event."

"Oh." Kit seemed to accept this readily enough. "In any case, Hal has a good chance of winning the wrestling and the staff fighting events, so it made sense to send him in his stead."

129

"Oh, I am sure," Gunnilde agreed. "In any case it was fortuitous timing for us," she said, looking across at James. "For now, we both have a brother apiece to commend our marriage, do we not?"

11

Their visitors had finally left sometime in the early hours. Neville bade them a sleepy good night, and James bolted the door and made his way through to the bedchamber, somewhat surprised to find himself still barefoot and wrapped in a bedsheet. He should have gone and dressed himself decently. Even so much as a week ago, he would have done so, punctiliously.

Still, their guests had not been conventional ones. Conventional guests would have taken immediate leave upon finding their hosts already abed. A conventional host would have gone and put his clothes on, James acknowledged. But getting dressed was the last thing he had wanted to do. He had wanted to get his bride back into bed. Those kisses…

Now, however, the moment seemed to have passed, more's the pity. She had fallen quiet and distracted during the last hour. The boisterous company had more than made up for her subdued spirits, but still James had noticed the sparkle had gone out of her eye. For some reason, she was putting a brave face on things. Why?

She was inordinately fond of her brother, he knew that much, so it could not be his appearance that had discomposed her. What was it, then? The contrast of seeing her kinfolk compared to his own, he wondered, for plainly Kit and Cuthbert were like cousins to her. To his mind, Neville had slipped back into the role of squire with an almost troubling ease. He had shown no more maturity than the other boys.

Which left only him to strike the false note. The thought disturbed him. Did she regret their kissing? Mayhap she did not want their visitors to leave her to his lecherous clutches. Walking into their bedchamber he found she had shed her blanket and was remaking the bed clad in only her shift.

He cleared his throat, and silently, she held out her hand for his bedsheet. James shrugged it off and threw it on the bed. They both made haste to straighten it out and tuck it in, then climb under the covers. Gunnilde blew out the candle and silence reigned. For some reason, instead of welcoming it, James found it intolerable.

"The fire's gone out," he heard himself remark. The room was chilly now only embers remained.

Gunnilde flung a chubby leg over his own. "Better?" she asked sympathetically.

He made a noise in his throat. "Ahem, yes," he clarified. Perhaps she was not cringing away from him after all. The thought encouraged him, and he shifted a little closer until their sides fully touched from shoulder to hip. He felt warmer already.

"Are you upset you weren't invited to the Vawdrey Solstice celebrations?" he asked as the idea occurred to him. Mayhap that was why she had grown so silent and still.

"No, of course not." She sounded surprised by the idea. "I stayed with Eden almost three months in the summer. Besides, there has been so much building work at the Keep and she will have so many family members there, my poor friend will have enough to contend with."

"I'm sure your presence would have been a help rather than a hindrance," he answered with a frown.

He felt her head rustle on the pillow as though she had turned to look at him. He wished he could see her in the darkness. "Well, I hope I am always helpful and willing. After all, that is my reputation." A note of sadness entered her voice. "A nice, good-hearted girl. Nice and…eminently forgettable." Her throat closed with emotion on the last few words, and James could scarcely make them out.

132

"Nice and what?" Surely, he had misheard her?

"That was what he said." She gave a muffled sob and rolled into his side. Was she crying? James froze. What was one supposed to do with a crying near-naked woman in your bed? After a few moments of agonized indecision, he reached across to pat her shoulder, and Gunnilde's arms came up to clutch at his sides as she took a few shuddery breaths.

"Sorry," she mumbled. "It's stupid of me."

Mercifully, her tears had put a stop to the stirrings James had experienced on feeling her leg atop of his. He was not a monster. James allowed his tentative pats to become a back rub. She had rubbed his shoulders when he was confronted with that hellish jester he remembered, and took that for his inspiration.

Very likely he should say something. He cast about fruitlessly for a moment, discarding "There, there" or "Dry your tears" as beneath him. Instead, he would go for plain statement of fact. "Eminently forgettable women do not become ladies-in-waiting to Her Majesty," he said sternly. "You do not possess even half the claims of other ladies to such an honor, yet you surpassed them all to snatch the distinction for your own."

Gunnilde gave a watery sniff and settled further into his, well, by this point, it could be called nothing short of an embrace. "Do you suppose that is why half of them do not like me?" she asked in a small voice, her breath tickling the base of his throat, distracting him from the sensation of her soft, full breasts pushing up against his chest.

"Well, it certainly is not because you are nice," he replied without thinking. She gasped, and to his horror he felt her start to tremble in his arms. "Wait, no," he began in panic, "I did not mean—"

133

"Oh, James!" she gurgled, and to his immense relief he realized she was shaking with tremulous laughter. "Thank you." She sounded so sincere he was instantly relieved. Mayhap he had not made such a mess of things after all.

To his astonishment, she wriggled up the bed, her warm body brushing against his until he felt her breath on his face. Then she bestowed a smacking kiss to his cheek, disentangled herself, and rolled onto her back with a sigh.

Gods, for a minute there, he had thought… But no, that had been a dismissive good-night kiss, not like the others which had been of a more exploratory and invigorating nature. It was just as well, James told himself firmly, despite the stab of disappointment he experienced at her retreat. He felt decidedly disordered again, and the burgeonings below were back with a vengeance. It was no surprise then, when he lay awake long after Gunnilde had fallen fast asleep, watching the gray light start to filter through the window.

He lay there puzzling over the conundrum, for he could make no sense of it. Someone had told his wife that she was "eminently forgettable," and for some reason her brother's arrival at court had sparked the memory afresh.

Could one of the lads, in the thoughtlessness of youth, have uttered such words? Kit Montmayne seemed the most tactless of the bunch but so far as James had seen he reserved his scorn mostly for his fellow squires. Oh, and for babies, he recalled belatedly.

Hal had said Gunnilde wanted babies. Five of them. Oh, and a knight of her own. The recollection disquieted him. Of course, technically, he was a knight, though he had never jousted in his life. Five children though! He had never imagined himself in such a family role. Family was a burden in his experience, not something to be pursued.

Giving his head a quick shake, he returned to the problem at hand. Just who in the hells had called Gunnilde forgettable? The nice part was more understandable. She was nice, for she had a core of kindness and decency that could not be denied. She had a generous nature even if she was flaunting, flirtatious, and frivolous. But forgettable? That she was not.

He doubted her brother would have said such a thing. If Hal Payne had found his sister forgettable, he would not have had so many thoughts about her future bridegroom. Besides, he fancied Hal was also a gregarious type, when he was not in high dudgeon. His friends treated him with camaraderie, even when he was plainly out of temper.

That left only Cuthbert Ames. James found he could not suspect him either, for the boy clearly regarded Gunnilde with an open and easy affection. Ridiculous, of course, that Hal had thought to match his sister with him, but then boys did get odd notions at times. Gunnilde had clearly found the suggestion as absurd as he, so he would not dwell on that any longer, he decided firmly, for he found it strangely annoying.

So, who had made the remark? Who had wounded Gunnilde Payne so deeply that she still cried to think of it even now? Could it have been the father who had not bothered to find her a husband? Or perhaps her stepmother was the more likely culprit. Were uncaring parents the reason she had fled to court in the first place?

Then he recalled her muffled words, That was what he said. He. So no, it could not have been her stepmother. Suddenly, he remembered that cryptic utterance the Queen had given about his wife. She will never fade into the background, that one… She will no longer allow it.

What the hells? A sudden suspicion flooded his thoughts, and he turned to look at Gunnilde's sleeping face in the gray morning light. Had she confided in the Queen? And if so, why was he so damned put out about it?

12

Gunnilde awoke betimes and lay quietly so as not to disturb James, who was still in the throes of a deep, though fitful slumber. He was an uneasy sleeper, tossing and turning and muttering unintelligible words beneath his breath. She had not known that people could glower in their sleep but somehow James managed it.

It seemed such a shame that one so handsome and talented should be so worn down with cares, she thought sadly. For doubtless it was his money worries and responsibilities that weighed on him so heavily, even in his sleep. She hoped she had not added much to his burden, though she was sure she had as a dowerless bride.

In any case, she had resolved to help him, had she not? She would make promoting his cause her number-one priority, higher even than ingratiating herself with the Queen or appeasing her fellow ladies-in-waiting. James needed her aid, and she would give it to him. It was nothing less than her duty as his wife.

He had a lovely profile, she reflected, propping herself up on her elbow and eyeing it appreciatively. She had been ungenerous before when she thought such eyelashes and kissable mouth wasted on him. Why should men not be pretty after all? It did not detract from his manliness one whit, for he was both well proportioned and strong of limb.

Could he really be a virgin, as Cuthbert had intimated? Gunnilde pressed her fingers to her lips. His kiss had certainly been tentative but then, maybe he had been unsure of its reception? Once she had made it plain that she welcomed it, he had not been so hesitant.

All those ladies who had sighed over him had not been so foolish as Gunnilde had first supposed. It was funny how some people could improve on acquaintance while others did the opposite. Thoughts of the previous evening flooded her mind. In truth, James had held his own quite creditably against Hal and his entourage.

For a minute she had feared he would turn all stuffy and formal and be unequal to the task, but no, he had taken it all in his stride. He had not even seemed bothered about being swathed in a bedsheet for their visit. Mayhap her kisses had fortified him for the ordeal, she thought, a smile crooking her lips. Her gaze returned to James's perfect profile.

It seemed a crime that such a pretty mouth should remain unkissed. No, she shook her head. She was being ridiculous. Even if James was a virgin, he would surely have snatched a few kisses over the years. He could scarcely have avoided such a thing, not with his face. Even she had been kissed, for pity's sake, despite her large teeth and hefty person.

She grimaced. What a stroke of bad luck that Sir James Attley should have broken his arm. Having two Sir Jameses at large might have caused some confusion but it would have been far preferable to having Sir Ned Bevan in close proximity.

She had hoped it would be a good few months until she was forced to see him again. Months she would have spent recovering her composure, so that when she next beheld him it would be with cool indifference. Instead, here she was a scarce two months later confronted with the horrible prospect of seeing him again.

Clearly, she was not recovered for she had blubbed like an infant the night before, wretchedly exposing herself! At least James had been her only witness, and he would hardly betray her. Indeed, he had done his best to console her, despite the fact her words had doubtless thrown him into utter confusion.

Bless the man, he was quite useless at pretty speech, in spite of his appearance! That had certainly been why he had commissioned a poet to write that poem for Constance, and very likely why he did not like ballads.

In any case, she thought, cheering up, things had changed a good deal since she had last seen Sir Ned. For one thing, she was a married woman. For another, she had two months' experience at court under her belt.

Lastly, and most importantly, she was now a lady-in-waiting to the Queen herself. She was no longer quite as forgettable as she had been. She would do her best to avoid Sir Ned, but when their paths did inevitably cross, she need not run and hide or be ashamed.

The door latch sounded, startling her, and Gunnilde shrank instinctively into James's side. He turned abruptly, slinging an arm around her and dragged her in close, resting his head upon her breasts with a gusty sigh. Oh. He would be mortified if he was to wake like this, she thought, peering over blankets.

As she had suspected, it was Bennett plunking down a pitcher of water for their morning ablutions, a sour look upon his face. She mouthed her thanks, not daring to speak the words aloud in case she woke her sleeping husband.

As it was, Bennett shutting the door smartly behind him achieved that. She felt James jolt against her before lifting his head.

"Good morning," she greeted him. He regarded her with bleary incomprehension. "I don't think you slept very well last night. Mayhap you should put your head back down for another hour," she said sympathetically.

His gaze fell to where his head had been resting, and he swallowed. "Er, no," he said, tearing his gaze away and clearing his throat. "I, er, don't think that's a good idea." He rolled away and swung his legs out to sit on the edge of the bed.

"I didn't actually mean to lie on me," Gunnilde clarified. "I was not offering myself as a pillow bearer." He made no reply, merely rubbed his eyes and yawned. "What will you do today?" she asked curiously. "Go and see your Master Gregory?"

"Yes, I had better. For this morning at least." He turned to look back over his shoulder at her. "Unless you would rather have my escort somewhere?"

"No, no," she assured him. "You should definitely go. I mean to attend the Queen in her chambers today."

"I could meet you there, this afternoon, perhaps," he offered after hesitating.

She smiled at him. "That would be most agreeable, thank you."

Gunnilde urged James to get washed and dressed first, for she knew he would be quick, and she intended to take her time over her appearance. Sure enough, he was up and ready for his day in very little time.

"I'll leave you to ready yourself," he said, hovering in the doorway a moment, and then he was gone.

Gunnilde dressed with the greatest care. First, she donned her finest shift, her scarlet stockings, and her second-best gown of bright blue silk, along with the brooch the Queen had gifted her. Next, she wrapped her widest girdle about her rib cage, so that it sat high, cinching her in at her smallest point.

The girdle did not really bear close inspection for it was not of great quality, but the enameled buckle was pretty and Gunnilde told herself that the gold-colored thread made it look far costlier than it really was.

She did not need to consider shoes, for it had to be her favorites, the highly impractical ones with the cutouts. If she knew she was not leaving court, then they would always be her slipper of choice.

Once satisfied with her dress, she turned her attention to her hair. Today, she decided that instead of braiding her hair before rolling it into buns, she would simply twist it and then twine a very thin ribbon around the length to add detail. Fortunately, she had some blue ribbon which would match her gown pretty well.

It was trickier to wrap the hair this way, for it did not feel so secure, however, she fancied this modified technique gave a clearer view of the overall "whorl" effect, and once one side was completed, she admired herself in the small looking glass she had brought with her from home.

She could really do with a larger one such as the Portstanleys had in their chambers, Gunnilde thought glumly, for she had grown accustomed to seeing her whole head and not just sections of it at a time, however she made do and completed the second "horn" a lot quicker than the first.

Lastly, she pinned her gauzy veil to the back of her head and drew on her new white tippets which she was convinced everyone would be wearing soon. They slipped up and over your sleeves and buttoned up to form a band encircling your upper arm. A fall of wide ribbon then extended down in a graceful fall of fluttering fabric from your elbows. The longer they extended, the more heavily they were frowned upon as frivolous trip hazards.

Gunnilde specified hers were to be so long that they scraped the floor. If one was going to adopt a new fashion, then she felt sure it should be followed to the furthest possible degree. There was no point in half measures when it came to this kind of thing.

Giving a pleased nod, she walked out into the sitting room and found a cup of ale but no bread awaiting her there. Swallowing her drink, she pondered the shared servant situation. Clearly Bennett was determined to be disobliging. She could only imagine that the Ashdowns paid the lion's share of his wage. At least, she certainly hoped that was the case considering the precious little he did for the Wycliffe brothers.

After draining her cup, she made her way out of the courtier's quarters and proceeded along to the Queen's chambers at a steady yet sedate pace, on the lookout for any acquaintance she might know to nod or speak to. She had just reached the long corridor when she spied Lady Winifred Hawes, Harriet's bookish friend, coming from the opposite direction.

Winifred's step faltered and she stifled a gasp. For a moment it looked as though she might turn and flee.

"Good morning, Winifred," Gunnilde greeted her, affecting not to notice her strange behavior.

"Oh, er…Gunnilde. I scarcely recognized you. You look so…different." She stole an aghast look in the direction of Gunnilde's horns.

Gunnilde doubted marriage had changed her looks so vastly. Instead, she suspected Winifred was uncertain if she was in disgrace or not and ought to be publicly acknowledged. "I am just on my way to the Queen's quarters," she said airily, "to assume my new role as lady-in-waiting to Her Majesty. Had you heard?"

Winifred's eyes widened. Clearly, she had not heard this momentous piece of news. This was not surprising considering the staid company Winifred kept. Neither she nor Harriet were ever abreast of current court happenings.

Winifred congratulated her generously and asked if she was attending some lecture that afternoon with Harriet and her mother. Gunnilde happily informed her that she was not. Winifred expressed sadness that

141

she would not see her there, and Gunnilde prepared to walk on, but Winifred's hesitant expression halted her.

"Is there something else you would ask me, Winifred?" she asked encouragingly.

"I just—pray might I ask—" She took a deep breath. "What are those white streamers hanging down from your elbows?" Winifred enquired timidly.

Gunnilde beamed at her. "They are called tippets and originated in Vlandivar," she told her, though she was not entirely sure about that part. When Viscount Bardulf had worn a pair two months ago, he had made that claim, or so Gunnilde had heard. "Are they not elegant?" She held up one arm to show their full glory.

Winifred beheld them with a silent and admiring oh.

"You should get some made up, Winifred," Gunnilde suggested kindly. "They do not have to be floor length like mine, if you are not daring enough. You could get some down to your knees. Then they need not trip you up as you go up steps."

"And—and what do they signify?" Winifred asked, looking intrigued.

"Signify? Why nothing at all! Except an interest in new manners of dress."

"I see," Winifred replied, still looking dazed. Politely, they took their leave of one another, and Gunnilde sailed on her way, amused to think that Harriet's friend might have some gossip to impart for once. Perhaps she would whisper of Gunnilde's appointment to the Queen at this afternoon's lecture? It pleased her to think it might be so.

On reaching the Queen's rooms, she walked once around the outer room, smiling and nodding to all who met her eyes, and then walked through the double doors, into the inner sanctum. She felt a thrill when the guards let her through unchallenged, and Piers Winstanley, glancing up, smiled at her. What a good-looking lad he was, she thought. It did one good to see him.

"Good morning, Lady Wycliffe," he hailed her. "The Queen will be out shortly."

She took her cue from this that she should await her appearance in this chamber. "How is Her Majesty this morn?" she enquired, halting before him.

He pulled a face. "She is perhaps a little out of temper but will be all the brighter for seeing you, my lady, if you can catch her attention. Some light conversation would doubtless distract her." He lowered his voice. "If you will pardon my saying so, The Bartree does not possess such arts to distract her when Her Majesty has need of it. I will be glad to have another around who possesses the talent."

"The art of 'light conversation' you mean?"

"I do. Ah," he said, turning, "here they are now."

The Queen walked into the room, resplendent in olive green and gold. She mounted the dais looking neither to the left nor right of her, a carefully blank expression on her face. Close on her heels followed the funereal gloom of Magnatrude Bartree.

"I see what you mean," Gunnilde murmured. The Queen, it seemed, was not in a genial mood. Over the next hour she summoned no one to her and did not descend once to mingle with her courtiers. Gunnilde drifted around hoping to catch her eye but seemingly failing.

Whenever she tried to approach the other ladies-in-waiting, they appeared to relocate like a flock of restless birds, dispersing and fluttering away from her. It was hard to believe it was not deliberate.

143

Finally, Mistress Bartree descended the dais to fetch the Queen some refreshment, and Gunnilde glanced across at the Queen to find her watching her. Armenal inclined her head, and Gunnilde sank into a curtsey.

Queen Armenal beckoned, and feeling highly gratified, Gunnilde hurried at once to hasten up the steps. "Good morning, Your Majesty," she greeted her queen, all smiles. Queen Armenal's eyes were dull. Was she ill?

"How are you, Gunnilde?" she asked with a faint smile. "Enjoying your new status as wedded wife?"

"Oh," Gunnilde considered. "Yes, I think so, Your Majesty," she said tentatively. "I think we will deal very well together eventually."

"Eventually?"

"Yes, for I have already realized how I can be of help to my husband and—"

"Wait!" The Queen held up one slender beringed hand. "First you must be seated, Gunnilde. Draw up one of those footstools and make yourself comfortable." Gunnilde dragged one of the plump cushioned low stools in front of the Queen and sat herself down. "Magnatrude will return presently with some refreshment. Now, continue."

"What was I saying?"

"How it is you can aid this new spouse of yours in his endeavors," the Queen prompted.

"Oh yes. Well, I have decided I simply need to inspire him with a love of ballads and then everything will be much easier for him. You see, at the moment he sells cathedral music to bishops, but he needs more commissions in order to make a proper living from it."

"And you think that the ballads, they will prove more popular?"

Gunnilde nodded. "Certainly, I do. Religious music is all very well but everyday folk want something more enjoyable and uplifting and not so…so—"

"High-minded?" the Queen suggested.

"Exactly, Your Majesty. I have never commissioned a piece of music personally but if I was to, then I would want it to be something that I can hum or sing at my own leisure, not something I will struggle to remember, or that will take upward of three instruments to perform."

The Queen looked thoughtful. "Have you heard any of his music performed?"

"I have not, Your Majesty, at least not to my knowledge."

"He has performed in the palace several times and I am sure I am not surprised. With his looks, I daresay there's many who would pay a pretty penny merely for his presence at their feasts. He is very handsome, is he not? Some might say the handsomest man at court." She sent a piercing look in Gunnilde's direction.

Gunnilde shook her head. "He would not like that at all, Your Majesty," she said earnestly. "He has very refined feelings and would probably feel cheapened by such an experience. Being treated like a paid performer, I mean." The Queen looked taken aback by such frankness. "You must own, Your Majesty, that being a composer sounds more respectable than being a troubadour," she continued apologetically.

"Yes," Armenal acknowledged after a small pause. "There is something in what you say. I suppose there might be some awkwardness about such an arrangement. Poor Sir James is hampered by his social standing when it comes to exploiting his talents it seems."

Her tone was rather dry, Gunnilde thought, folding her lips, determined to say no more on the subject. She certainly did not want to put the Queen out of humor with her husband. That was the opposite of her intent!

"Ah, here is Magnatrude now," the Queen said, sitting up straighter.

Gunnilde's heart sank a little as the older woman climbed the steps to the dais with a measured stately step. She carried a silver salver with little dishes of nuts, dried figs, and dates. Behind her came her little page carrying a tray with pitcher and goblets.

"Draw up another chair, Magnatrude, and be seated here with us. Gunnilde here has been telling me how she means to further her husband's cause."

Magnatrude Bartree sent Gunnilde a cold look as she set down her tray before the Queen. Unwin added his items to the small table and fetched his mistress another of the low cushioned seats.

"Thank you, Unwin, now go and take some refreshment yourself," Mistress Bartree bade her page, briefly touching the top of his head. He smiled up at her and retreated down the steps. Gunnilde watched the brief interaction with interest. So…Mistress Bartree was not all glares and hostility. Not when it suited her!

"Now, Gunnilde, repeat to me what you said about encouraging Sir James to broaden his palate when it comes to music," the Queen instructed. Gunnilde did so. "Is she not ingenious, this protégé of mine?" Armenal demanded, eyes dancing. Gunnilde was glad to see the gleam back in her dark eyes, even if the amusement was at her expense.

Magnatrude's lips twisted into some grim semblance of a smile. "It seems a somewhat convoluted plot to my mind," she said dismissively. "What Sir James surely needs is a rich patron. Any wily wife would go about securing such a thing as a matter of urgency. But perhaps Lady

Wycliffe has already realized this," she said, looking deliberately from the Queen to Gunnilde and back again.

Catching her meaning, Gunnilde gasped and felt her cheeks grow warm. "I dare assure you, Mistress Bartree, that such a thing was not my intention in the slightest!" she said hotly.

Magnatrude Bartree's back stiffened even further. "I am sure I do not know what I said to cause offence—"

"Oh, yes you do, madam!" Gunnilde interrupted her. "You plainly implied that I am set about cajoling a royal appointment out of the Queen, even at this moment! But to put things plainly, I do not think such a thing would suit him at all!"

Magnatrude Bartree's rather sallow face reddened. "I simply meant," she began carefully, "that for one situated as Sir James it would be untenable to—"

"I think I might be permitted to know my own husband rather better than you, madam!" Gunnilde cut in sharply. "Thank you kindly for your consideration!"

It occurred to Gunnilde that things had turned rather quiet elsewhere in the receiving chamber. She took a quick scan of the room and found to her dismay that everyone seemed to have drifted a good deal closer, and many appeared to be actively craning to hear their words.

"But why do you say this, Gunnilde?" the Queen asked with surprise, dragging her attention back from the crowd. "Why would an official appointment, say, as royal musician, not suit Sir James?"

Gunnilde darted a look around the dais. "Could you bid everyone to move away, Your Majesty? I do not wish to discuss such private matters with an audience."

Mistress Bartree looked shocked by such a request, but the Queen stood up at once and shooed everyone away. She sat back down. "Pour us some drinks, Magnatrude." The older woman complied at once. "Now," she said, turning to Gunnilde, "tell me, for I am all agog."

Gunnilde hesitated. "Well, firstly there is the fact James does not particularly care to perform for others. Then, secondly, I imagine that palace music would be just as select as cathedral music, perhaps more so. It would not serve to make his music hold general appeal, now, would it? Lastly…" She hesitated, then plunged on. "I had thought that perhaps the endeavor might serve to bring us closer together," she confessed.

"A man is supposed to cleave to his wife, is he not? If I can only prove my worth to James then he is sure to turn to me, is he not? You must know all about it, Your Majesty, for is that not what happened in your own case? Why, everyone knows—" She broke off awkwardly as Magnatrude Bartree let out a hiss like an enraged goose.

"No, no, she is quite right," Armenal said, holding up a hand. "You must not upbraid her, my good Magnatrude, for I dearly love to hear such unguarded speech, and such a thing is rare indeed in a palace." She sighed and settled back in her seat. "The King turned to me after I proved my worth to him in the face of overwhelming grief," she acknowledged. "I am sure it is whispered of in every corner of this castle."

"Whispers are one thing, Your Majesty," Magnatrude Bartree said angrily. "But to say it boldly to your face is another altogether!"

The Queen nodded. "Precisely. Is it any wonder then, why I am growing so fond of this young woman's society? Now, let us speak some more about how you mean to snare this husband of yours and promote his interests, for I find it all quite fascinating."

Afterward Gunnilde could not really have said what exactly she had rattled off in her eagerness to explain her line of thinking to the Queen. She knew only that she talked at great length about all manner of things, and that Queen Armenal pressed her further whenever she showed any signs of flagging.

She even ended up having to tell her of the unofficial betrothal of her youth all over again.

"And this…Master Conway," the Queen said, helping herself to a fig. "Where is he now?"

"I believe he resides with his sister and brother-in-law now. His sister Muriel is married to Sir Christopher Lelland, who is a prominent courtier."

The Queen's expression continued blank. "Is he?"

"Well, that is what they say in my home county."

Mistress Bartree cleared her throat. "I believe Sir Christopher is one of the Hamford Lellands, Your Majesty," she said, casting down her eyes.

"What is a Hamford Lelland?" the Queen asked. "It sounds like a kind of loaf cake."

Her lady-in-waiting looked pained. "His uncle played a prominent role in the battle of Adarva," she said gravely. "Being a childless man, Sir Christopher is his heir."

"Ah, I see. So, his uncle garnered glory in the late war and Wymer rewarded him with land. This Sir Christopher, is he a warlike man like his uncle?"

149

"Not at all!" Gunnilde replied. "He is a tall but stooping man and mild of speech and manner. He is several years older than Muriel. Why, his hair is already quite gray!"

The Queen nodded. "I see it all clear in my mind," she said dreamily. "And Sir Arthur, after he did not honor his late father's arrangements with your own, he married another?"

"I believe his sister had high hopes of securing him a grand heiress, but I have not heard if she actually managed to find him one yet," Gunnilde admitted.

"You should find out," the Queen said emphatically. "If her husband brings her to court, then you should hold some select gathering and invite this Muriel who thinks so highly of her brother's prospects. Then she will be forced to acknowledge you as hostess and bear witness to your triumph. I will attend as your guest of honor," she said generously.

"Your Majesty!" Gunnilde breathed. "Would you really?"

"I would. You must invite Sir Arthur also and his bride if he has one. It would be amusing to see him discomforted by your superior status. You could reserve one of the function rooms here at the palace for the purpose. This former suitor of yours, he is good-looking?" she asked.

Gunnilde considered this. "I always thought so, Your Majesty," she admitted. "His features are not distinct, but he has a pleasant smile and a neat, short beard and manners that have the distinction of a true gentleman born and bred."

Armenal looked underwhelmed by this description. "So then, he will be as nothing compared to Sir James."

"No, but few men would bear such a comparison," Gunnilde said fairly.

A bell chimed in the distance, signifying it was midday. The crowds of courtiers started moving unhurriedly in the direction of the door.

"You will not go to the Great Hall to break your fast, Gunnilde," the Queen decided. "Instead, you will accompany me back to my private rooms and join myself and Magnatrude."

Gunnilde flushed with gratification, though she dared not look toward Mistress Bartree to gauge her reaction to the invitation.

13

James returned from the Gregorys' house at midday. After finding their quarters empty and no sign of Bennett or any food about the place, he decided he would have to brave the Great Hall in search of sustenance. Yanking the door open, he found Hal Payne stood there, his hand raised as though about to knock.

"Oh, there you are, Wycliffe," he said, lowering his hand. "We thought we would come and see if you were coming down to eat." Hal was flanked again by two friends, though Kit had been replaced by a newcomer. All of them looked flushed and tousled as though they had been running exercises all morning. The new boy had grass stains up the right leg of his yellow hose.

"This is Hadrian Kellingford," Hal said, pointing his thumb toward a tanned-looking youth who was staring at James with open curiosity.

"How do you do," James said, extending his hand.

"Very well, as it happens," Hadrian asserted, shaking his hand. "You really married to Payne's sister?" he asked cheekily.

"I am." Kellingford, thought James. Was that not another of Hal's friends he had thought would do for Gunnilde? James shut the door behind him and locked it. "We'll go down together, then, shall we?"

"Where's my sister?"

"She had plans to wait on the Queen this morning."

"Oh. What about Neville?" Hal asked, looking about as though James had stashed him somewhere.

"I have not the faintest idea," James admitted. "I have been out all morning in the city."

"Maybe we'll see them down there," Hal said, looking faintly disappointed.

"Hal wants to show you off," Cuthbert said, as they started down the corridor. "He's been telling the fellows about you all morning."

James rather dreaded to think how his brother-in-law might have described him. He glanced over his shoulder and found him deep in conversation with the Kellingford lad.

"Don't worry, he never said you were handsome," Cuthbert reassured him.

They had just reached the steps and James paused. "Mayhap he did not think it worth mentioning," he replied tersely.

"Well, I know you do not," the strange boy replied, "but most people would think it worthy of note."

James frowned at him and then started down the steps. "You have been training this morning?" he asked, attempting to show polite interest.

"Yes," Cuthbert agreed but did not seem anxious to elaborate in any way. "Sir Ned was asking after Gunnilde most particularly. He was taken aback to hear she was wed."

And what is it to him? thought James irritably. "Who is Sir Ned?" he asked aloud, then felt some vague stirrings in his memory. "Was he the one who brought you all to court?"

"Yes."

"And which one of you is his squire?"

"None of us are, strictly speaking," Cuthbert replied. "Though Hal is acting the part at present. Sir Ned's real squire is Ancel Somers."

"And who is Ancel Somers?"

"Well, now, that is the question," Cuthbert muttered, and seemed to be thinking about something else entirely. Suddenly he seemed very far away, though walking at James's side.

"Was he the one who broke his neck?" James asked, harking back once more to the conversation of the night before.

"It wasn't his neck; it was his arm. And no, that was not Ancel but Sir James Attley, Hal's true mentor. He and Sir Ned swapped squires."

"Oh yes, I remember now," James recalled. But why was the boy laboring the point? He seemed to attach some strange significance to the fact.

"Sir Ned was staying with us at Vawdrey Keep in September before Gunnilde left for court," Cuthbert said in an expressionless voice.

Slow cogs turned in James's brain. "Was not Gunnilde at Vawdrey Keep last summer?" he asked aloud.

"She was there from July to September," Cuthbert confirmed, his eyes meeting James's.

So then… James halted on the bottom step. Presumably at least some of their stays would have overlapped. A sudden suspicion sprang into his mind. Was it possible that Sir Ned was the one who had insulted his wife so grievously? The effort of remembrance was a strain. James had been distracted the previous evening and following the conversation had been difficult at times with so many present.

Thinking of it now, he could not help but wonder if it was before or after the mention of Bevan's name that Gunnilde had turned quiet and pale? He strongly suspected it was the latter. Nice, and eminently forgettable. Anyone who would describe her thus must be an arrant fool. "Who is he, this Sir Ned?" he asked bluntly.

"Sir Edward Bevan of Knollesley," Cuthbert reeled off obligingly. "He is a knight who tours the tourneys and sees more success in the melees than the jousting. He is tactical and strong and one of the closest friends of my master, Roland Vawdrey." Softly he added, "He is also riding for a fall."

"So, then he is another like Hal's former master. I suppose it is a consequence of competing." James eyed Cuthbert sidelong. "Do you claim to see into the future, Ames?" he asked abruptly.

"Oh, I get the odd glimpse or two, nothing more." The lad shrugged. "They just come to me. Like dreams."

"Like seeing white cliffs in connection with Gunnilde?"

"Something like that," Cuthbert agreed, "yes."

James was silent for a long moment. Then he asked, "And just what is Sir Ned about to break in this upcoming fall of his?"

Cuthbert smiled a rather pitiless smile. "His heart," he answered in the voice of a seer, and James shivered.

They spoke no more until they reached the hall, which was busier than usual at this time of day. James found himself scanning the crowded tables for his wife without success. "She's not here," he threw over his shoulder at Hal. "Let me just go and ask where she might be." He strode up to a table where several of the Queen's ladies were sat whispering to one another.

"Good morning, ladies," he addressed them with a small bow. "I am looking for my wife, she attended the Queen's chambers this morning, but it seems she has not accompanied you to the Great Hall."

There was a chorus of Oh Sir James and Good morrows and many smiles and the like. Belatedly, James recalled Gunnilde confessing the other ladies-in-waiting did not seem to like her very much. An uncomfortable notion crossed his mind that they might have excluded her and left her behind.

He narrowed his gaze. "You would surely have seen her there." There was much rustling of skirts and whispering behind hands until James lost patience with them altogether and turned pointedly to the nearest one. "Lady Osanna, have you any idea where I might find my wife?"

Osanna Spencer straightened in her seat. "She did not accompany us to break her fast, Sir James, for she had the distinction of being singled out by Her Highness and invited to dine with her in her private chambers."

This pulled him up short. "Is that not somewhat unusual?" he asked, glancing around the table.

"'Tis highly unusual!" cut in another of the ladies, Frances Lessimore this time. "And a thing usually reserved for her most particular favorite."

"Yes, but The Bartree is there too, so she has not been deposed yet," pointed out Patience Stanhope. A few titters greeted this and a few head tosses.

"All morning, she and The Bartree have been quarrelling over the Queen's favor!" cut in Emma Thackeray excitedly. "It has been most diverting!" The others immediately shushed her and elbowed her into silence.

"Do not pay any attention to Emma," Lucy Melvin said loudly. "For she gets the silliest notions into her head!"

"No, I do not!" Emma objected. "We all agreed they were vying for Her Majesty's attention, did we not?" Another round of shushing and from Emma's winces, a good deal of ankle kicking occurred this time. Finally taking the hint, Emma lapsed into a pouting silence.

"We've found a table," said a voice at James's side. It was Hal. "Come and join us." He gave an admiring glance around the table and bestowed a flourishing bow. "Ladies," he said and seizing James by the elbow, drew him firmly away.

"They're a pretty company of women," Hal said appreciatively. "You must introduce us later, Wycliffe," he said, steering James toward a far table.

"Well, those particular ladies are not being very kind to your sister at present!" James observed dryly.

"Aren't they?" He glanced back at them over his shoulder. "Ah well, I daresay they're just jealous." He shrugged.

James dropped down onto the bench he indicated and found himself at a table full of squires, all craning to look at him. Kit Montmayne gave him a nod and pushed an empty tankard in his direction.

"Who are jealous?" Hadrian Kellingford enquired chirpily.

"The Queen's ladies are all jealous of Gunnilde," Hal replied quite unabashed, seizing hold of a pitcher of ale from a passing servant and sloshing it into the cups.

"Oh, because she landed Wycliffe, you mean?" asked another with a snub nose and freckles. James bristled to find himself discussed so

157

openly in his own presence, but they barely seemed to notice his discomfort.

"Sure to be," opined another youth loftily. "Women are rather like cats, you know. They like to show their claws. Like to sink 'em in you too. You should watch your step, Payne. Your fondness for their company will get you in trouble one of these days my lad, mark my words!"

Hal snorted. "You fear what you do not know, Cosgrave. Let me tell you, you're missing out."

"Oh gods, don't let him get started on this again!" Kit groaned. He looked across at James. "Hal is always holding forth about women. It's one of his favorite subjects."

"Is it?" James was startled. He had certainly not had time to think about women during his own time as a squire. Or since that time, if he was honest. He eyed his brother-in-law's appearance anew. Hal was a stout young fellow with a shock of tow-colored hair like his sister's only cut much shorter. He had a confident bearing, a booming voice, and an open, honest face.

Out of his friends he was probably the least prepossessing for Cuthbert and Kit were very good-looking. Then again, Cuthbert's conversation was disconcerting to say the least, and Kit scowled too much to be considered truly amiable company. Out of the three of them, was it possible that Hal was the most popular?

"Hal's got this preposterous theory," Kit said, leaning forward, "that every woman, every woman mind you, has something pretty about her. Even if it's something like her hands or her ankles or her manner of speech."

"And I fully stand by that statement," Hal said, glancing around and hailing a servant approaching with a platter of bread. "Ah, there's the fellow." He slapped him on the shoulder and complimented his skill on balancing several trays at once.

"Hal is popular with ladies and servants alike," Cuthbert commented quietly. "They all like him. Young or old. My own granny says she would swap me for him given half the chance."

Hal laughed at something the servant said, and James noticed him set down a second lot of bread likely intended for another table. There was an inelegant scramble and James was grateful there were two lots, or he would have ended up entirely breadless.

"Hal may be popular," Kit said waspishly, "but is it any wonder when he's so indiscriminate in his tastes? He'll woo anyone who gives him the time of day!" Snub Nose hooted with laughter.

"Montmayne speaks true," said Cosgrave. "Payne spent over an hour holding Hortense Latimer's hand and parading her about at Areley Kings as though she was some fine lady in need of escort," he said derisively.

"And what if I did?" asked Hal through a mouthful of bread. "She's a very nice girl. I'll wager I had a better time of it than you did, Cosgrave. You got booted from the bohort and your master gave you a thick ear for your pains, did he not?"

The other boys laughed, and Cosgrave looked sulky. "A good time?" he jeered. "Why, 'cos she sneaked you half a dozen pies after supper."

"They were excellent pies," Hal reminisced fondly. "A good mix of sweet and savory. Besides, Hortense is a good talker once she gets going. You just have to give her a chance. Told me all her hopes and fears, gave me a tour of the grounds there and said she would look out for me next year." Hal looked smug.

159

"You'd better hope she doesn't set her sights on you in earnest!" Kit warned, shaking his head. "Or you'll be for it!"

"She's betrothed now," Cuthbert announced, surprising everyone greatly.

"Is she?" demanded Snub Nose. "First I've heard of it and she's my second cousin! To whom?"

Cuthbert squinted his eyes. "Some long-standing friend of the family, I think. Name begins with a J. Jacomb?" he suggested uncertainly.

"Is it Jacobson?" Hal asked excitedly.

Cuthbert's shoulders relaxed. "Yes, that is it."

Hal whistled. "Good for her."

"Henry Jacobson?" Snub Nose looked stunned. "Fancy his offering for her! I know that's what her mother and sisters were praying for, but I thought it a vain hope, truth to tell!"

"You've been cut out, Payne!" Cosgrave guffawed. "I doubt you'll get your tour of Areley Kings next year!"

"I disagree," Hal said complacently. "For all she may be married, I'll wager she still stands my friend. We shared a perfect summer's afternoon. One does not forget such a thing and one should not."

The other boys looked flummoxed by such a sentiment. Fortunately, a second wave of servants appeared bearing large platters of sliced gammon and eggs poached in milk and topped with cheese. The boys cheered, and pulling their knives from their belts, they fell upon the platters, dragging the meat onto their plates with wild, uncouth enthusiasm.

He had almost forgotten what it was like to be a squire, James mused as he watched the food disappear with astonishing rapidity. A few tidbits made their way into Hal's tunic from which a small snout and a pair of bright, shiny eyes protruded, but the rest was consumed as by a pack of slavering wolves.

Cuthbert nudged the eggs closer to James, who made haste to help himself before the platter was seized and dragged to the opposite end of the table. "You have to be quick," Cuthbert warned. "Or you'll end up with an empty belly, else."

"So I see" was James's rejoinder.

Though his own master had been no tourney-goer, they had attended the high feasts well enough, so he knew what a scrimmage it could be. Such occasions though had been far from the norm in his own training. He fancied it must be rather different for squires who followed the tournament circuit.

"Do you enjoy being squire, Ames?" he asked Cuthbert impulsively.

Cuthbert shrugged. "I do, in the main. It has both good and bad sides, like most things in life."

A scuffle had broken out on the far side of the hall. A table overturned with a crash and a splintering of broken vessels. The boys all jumped up onto their feet, craning to see the parties involved. Hadrian leaped up onto the bench to get a bird's-eye view. "It's Peterson," he announced excitedly. "He's got Bauer in a headlock!" Hal whooped and all the boys left their empty trenchers to fly across the hall to form a large, noisy circle around the combatants.

James sighed. At least during the royal summer and autumn tournaments they had reinforcements of the royal guards to keep participants in check. These Squires' Revels seemed entirely unsupervised. If present company was a true representation, then most of them had not even been accompanied by their mentor knights into the capital.

Glancing around the hall, he could see precious few figures of authority, just a lot of bewildered and distressed courtiers. Getting to his feet with some reluctance, James started in the direction of the scuffle.

14

Gunnilde gazed around the room in bemusement. She had returned to their rooms in quiet triumph after spending her day basking in the Queen's approval, only to find all the menfolk of her family cluttering up the sitting room and covered in cuts and bruises.

"And then Wycliffe seized hold of Bauer by the scruff of his neck and dragged him off Peterson," Hal explained.

Gunnilde shot an astonished look at Neville, who was sat next to Hal and listening with an avid attention. She would never have dreamed he was so keen on fighting! At least his nice clothes weren't ripped or disordered like the others.

"Shook him like a dog with a rat," Kit interceded with satisfaction. "Then shoved him to one side and turned his attention to Bauer—"

"Who had practically jumped onto his back by this point," Cuthbert interrupted.

"Naturally, I could not let that insult to my family pass," Hal said with a modest cough. "So, I entered the fray at this point to knock some sense into Peterson."

"Unfortunately, his cousin Sorenson took exception to that," Kit put in. "So, he and his cronies all jumped on Hal—"

"So, we had to enter the fray," Cuthbert finished reasonably. "You see, it all makes perfect sense when you simply consider the facts."

Gunnilde's gaze swept over them with gathering disapproval. Hal was sporting a bloody nose, Cuthbert a fat lip, and Kit a bleeding cut upon his brow.

"I appreciate that you have only just come to court," she began with dignity, "but you boys simply cannot disport yourselves in such a vulgar fashion here at the palace! It is thoroughly disgraceful behavior!" she scolded them all roundly. "Brawling in the Great Hall itself! What will the Queen say? I am a lady-in-waiting now, and my family's conduct will be a reflection upon my own!"

"We did not start it," Hal protested.

"That is neither here nor there," Gunnilde retorted. "I for one should not be surprised if the Squires' Revels were entirely canceled thanks to such unruly conduct!"

The boys appeared immediately chastened. There was much scuffling of feet and scratching of necks. The latch sounded at that moment and James walked in, holding something to his eye. "Bennett will bring us some ale presently." His step checked on noticing Gunnilde. "Ah, there you are," he said, looking suddenly self-conscious. "I apologize I did not come and find you this afternoon." He lowered the poultice to reveal what looked suspiciously like the beginnings of a blackened eye. "But you see—"

Gunnilde let out a small scream and they all jumped.

"What happened to your eye, James?" she squawked, hurrying forward to seize hold of him. She reached up a hand to move his hair out of the way to get a better look.

"It's nothing," he grumbled.

"We just told you at great length!" Kit exclaimed. He turned to Hal. "I told you they never listen."

Gunnilde rounded on them. "Indeed, you did not," she said crossly as she shepherded James toward a chair next to the fire. "You told me that Neville—"

"Me?" Neville squawked in surprise. "What have I to do with it? I am entirely blameless in this affair, I assure you."

"Neville wasn't even there," Hal agreed.

"No, I missed it altogether," Neville confirmed. "I was taking sops with Lady Dortington and her friend Mistress Blanche Alden. Her servant serves it with spices and wine and a sort of custard made with the milk of almonds."

"Sounds good," Hal responded with interest. "What do they call it served that way?"

"Well—"

"Would you stop talking about sops?" Gunnilde begged impatiently. "No one cares about your sops, Neville! Did you or did you not shake someone like a rat and—"

"No, that wasn't Neville," Cuthbert interjected. "That was your husband."

"But you just said—" Gunnilde broke off to look from James to Neville to Hal. "Do you mean to tell me that James was the one fighting by your side in the Great Hall?" Her jaw dropped when the boys all nodded.

"I wasn't fighting," James interjected testily. "I was attempting to break up the fight! Things escalated somewhat…"

"Who struck you?" demanded Gunnilde.

"No one," James assured her. "I took an elbow to the face. It was mere accident."

"Let me see." She steered him into a chair where he sat passively as she peered anxiously around his eye.

"It looks very red and inflamed, I hope you do not get an unsightly bruise!"

"Well, I must say, you would think she would be more concerned about her own brother," Hal huffed, scratching the top of Dustin's head. "Instead, she fusses over Wycliffe like a mother hen with her beloved chick!"

"What is in that poultice?" she asked in a low murmur, for James looked embarrassed by her attention. "Does it have leek and garlic in it?"

"No, I'm glad to say, for that sounds most unpleasant. Cuthbert made it."

"Oh." Her anxiety resided at once. "Well, he will know better than I."

"'Tis of turmeric and dandelion root," Cuthbert volunteered, revealing his excellent hearing. "It should bring the bruising right out."

Gunnilde tsked. "I hardly know whether we ought even to show our faces in the Great Hall for supper tonight," she said, straightening up.

"We most certainly will be," Hal said with alacrity. "I'm half starved!"

"I scarcely got anything to eat at midday," Kit agreed. "Cosgrave is like a bottomless pit, for all he's so scrawny. Did you see how many of the eggs he got down his gullet?"

James cleared his throat. "How went it with the Queen?" he asked.

166

"Oh, excellently!" Gunnilde confided, beaming. "She showed me many signs of great favor and I was very fortunate."

James hesitated, as though he wanted to press her further but did not like to with so many onlookers present.

"We heard you were fighting yourself today, sister," Hal said knowingly.

"Aye, fighting for the Queen's attention," laughed Kit.

"Who told you that?" Gunnilde asked with surprise.

"Mistress Rheinholdt," Cuthbert said promptly. "Hal asked her to hold Dustin when he entered the fray."

"Yes, we have struck up something of a friendship," Hal said modestly.

"You and Estrilda Rheinholdt?" Gunnilde asked disbelievingly.

"Yes," agreed Kit, "for none of the others would speak with us. They were too busy acting shocked and standoffish about the overturned table and broken pots."

"Estrilda seems a good deal more sensible than the rest of them," Hal observed sagely. "Said she would like a dog of Dustin's size for her very own. Said she would keep him in her sleeve and feed him off her own plate."

Gunnilde's eyebrows shot up, but she managed to bite back the tart reply that sprang to her lips, pointing out that Mistress Estrilda had been sadly standoffish with her! "I see," she said instead.

"So, are we taking supper in the Grand Hall or do we need to badger Bennett to bring something up to our rooms?" Neville queried.

Gunnilde looked to James. "We will be taking our supper up here tonight," she said firmly and saw his shoulders visibly lower. "But do not let that intrude on your own plans if you would like a more sociable evening." In truth, the sitting room was rather small for any more than three to dine in, and it would be a squeeze around the table.

"We'll go down. Care to join us, Wycliffe?" Hal said, turning to Neville. "You could introduce us to some of your acquaintances. We don't know many court folk yet."

Neville looked rather horrified at this prospect but ended up accepting their offer, and when the three boys took their leave shortly after, he accompanied them.

"I had better run and check in on Sir Ned," they heard Hal say glumly as they trooped out the door. "He may have some tasks for me to perform before supper. You go and find Hadrian and I'll meet you outside the Great Hall."

Cuthbert paused in the doorway. "I will let your servant know you want your supper fetched up this evening," he said, looking first at Gunnilde and then at James and closed the door behind him before Gunnilde could thank him.

"How will he know where to find Bennett?" James asked with surprise.

"It's hard to explain how he knows things. His granny is a wise woman, you see." James blinked at this but otherwise made no comment. "Are you sure your eye is not paining you?" she asked, dropping down into the seat opposite him.

"My eye is fine," he said briefly. "Tell me more about how you passed your day. Were the Queen's other ladies any friendlier this afternoon?"

"Not really," Gunnilde admitted. "They whispered and stared at me a good deal, but I affected not to notice." She shrugged. "They will doubtless come around, eventually."

"Perhaps relations will improve with Mistress Rheinholdt at least, if she and Hal are to become friendly."

Gunnilde was skeptical. "I think you will find that is more likely to be the result of her surprising fondness for small dogs than any great charm on Hal's part."

"On the contrary, I have it on good authority that Hal is very successful with the ladies," James said, surprising her greatly.

"Who in the world told you that?"

"Cuthbert."

"Oh." She could not really disparage Cuthbert's assessment of such things for he so often spoke with such uncanny truth. Still, it seemed most unlikely to her. "I cannot picture it somehow." She gave a gurgle of laughter. "Likely because I still remember him sticky with figs and rolling in the dirt."

James smiled back at her faintly. "Neville is popular with old ladies," he volunteered. "They like to cosset him and feed him remedies for his various maladies."

"Hal might be surprised, then, when Neville introduces him to his closest friends, and they turn out to be grandmotherly types."

"He might well be," James agreed. "Did you know the Ashdowns are a pair of elderly sisters?"

"No, for I have not met them yet." How funny that the red swelling about his eye did not detract from his good looks one whit, she thought.

169

"I'm sorry the boys dragged you into their dispute today," she said earnestly.

"It wasn't really their dispute. And I was not dragged." He considered her for a moment, his head tipped to one side. "What are those things on your arms?" he asked.

"My tippets," she replied promptly, holding up her arms. "I saw Viscount Bardulf in a pair a couple of months ago and had my tailor re-create them from a drawing I made. His were red though and he wore them over a black tunic. They looked very dramatic." James frowned. "Do you not like them?" she asked. He made a noncommittal noise in his throat. "I was thinking I could have more made up," she said, lowering her arms again. "In an array of different colors."

"I like the white," he said, "at least, with that dress."

Gunnilde beamed. "Lady Winifred Hawes may start wearing them next. She seemed to admire them greatly this morning. Would it not be amusing if they become hugely popular with ladies down to my influence?"

He did not answer at once, and when he did it was to ask, "Who is Winifred Hawes, another lady-in-waiting?"

"Goodness no. She is one of Harriet's friends and very studious and clever. You must have seen her at some of those lectures you favor. She's always at them and concentrating ferociously."

"I must have, I suppose," he murmured. "I cannot bring her to mind just now."

"Maybe because she is not particularly prepossessing," she replied sadly.

James looked discomforted. "I did not mean that the lady was not memorable," he said awkwardly. "Only that I am not good at placing faces to names."

"Oh." For a moment he looked really concerned and Gunnilde was touched. James was really proving surprisingly considerate in not wanting to cause her offence. She sent him a smile of reassurance, so that he once again relaxed.

"The Queen is encouraging me to arrange a banquet," she told him enthusiastically. "She said we could use one of the palace chambers for it."

"To what purpose?"

"Why to show off my current elevated position, of course! I was thinking I could invite my fellow ladies-in-waiting in the hope they thaw toward me a little." She hesitated. "She's also encouraging me to invite...certain people from my past."

"What sort of people?"

"The Conways," she admitted in a rush. "Muriel Conway was my closest friend growing up in Tranton Vale. She dropped me as a friend as soon as she was married. I was unofficially betrothed to her brother in my youth, but it all came to naught. Her husband is Sir Christopher Lelland. I think her husband has an official position here at court as part of King Wymer's retinue. Do you know of him?"

James scrunched his eyes then winced, feeling the bruise. "Is he one of the Hamford Lellands?" he asked.

"So Mistress Bartree says."

"Then yes. Is he the tall one or the gruff, warlike one?"

"The tall one."

James nodded. "Tell me about the brother."

"Muriel's brother, Sir Arthur? There is not much to tell. I believe he lives with Sir Christopher and Muriel now. I have not seen him for, oh, it must be over a year."

"Did you…? Were you fond of him?" he asked carefully.

Gunnilde paused. "Yes, at one time. It was terribly exciting as a young girl to look out for him at gatherings and on feast days and think that one day…"

"He would be your husband?" James concluded.

She gave a short laugh. "Yes," she admitted. "It was pleasant to think that there was someone with whom my destiny was entwined." She looked away. "But I was being fanciful, as young girls often are."

"The reason you did not want to go down for supper this evening…" James cleared his throat. "It wasn't anything to do with wanting to avoid a certain knight, was it?"

"No!" Gunnilde gasped. "Whatever gave you that idea?" she blurted, feeling her face turn red. "Has someone said something?" But really, who could have? She stared at him in confusion. Even the Queen did not know the identity of the man who had wounded her so.

At that moment the door opened, and Bennett shuffled in carrying a tray. "Got your first course," he murmured, giving them a furtive look before setting it down and placing the dishes in the center of the table before making his escape.

"First course?" James echoed in surprise, as though he was not used to getting multiple dishes when Bennett was the source.

172

"I will just go and remove my tippets," Gunnilde said. "They are so nice and white, and I do not wish to get them splattered with sauce."

Once she had shut the door behind her, she took a few deep breaths, then unbuttoned her tippets and slid them off before returning to the sitting room. She devoutly hoped there was to be no more talk of knights. She was not even sure how they had got onto that subject. On her return, James had moved to the table and was pouring out two cups of wine.

He pulled out her chair and gestured for her to be seated. Gunnilde could not help but notice how quiet he was. She did not want him thinking she was pining for Sir Arthur or dreading meeting with Sir Ned. Instead, she determined to be her usual bright and breezy self.

"Naturally, you will need to act as host at this gathering the Queen proposed," she informed him as she dug a spoon into a dish of leeks and cabbage cooked in a thick spiced broth.

"Naturally," James repeated dryly. "Am I too expected to invite anyone and rub their noses in our recent marriage?"

"I doubt very much you have a past littered with ladies who have scorned you!" Gunnilde responded, pushing the dish toward him.

"Save Constance, you mean?"

Gunnilde lowered her spoon. Oh. "Well," she said weakly. "If Constance and Sir Douglas have returned to court by then, we can certainly invite them, if you so wish."

"What about you? Should you wish to see your protégé Sir Douglas again so soon?" he asked pointedly.

There was a strange edge to his words. Was he annoyed? Gunnilde frowned as she helped herself to a couple of pastry parcels which appeared to contain a savory mushroom filling. "I would have no objection," she assured him. "If you did not."

James breathed out through his nose. "It is not likely they should return to court so soon, in any case," he muttered dismissively. "Do you want some of this?" He pushed the final dish in her direction.

Gunnilde looked at it dubiously. "What is it?"

"It appears to be carrots, radishes, turnips and…pears, I think. Pickled in something."

Gunnilde gamely took a spoonful. "Saffron and vinegar," she announced after tasting it. "It would be better served with bread and cheese," she mused. "Do you not agree?"

James shrugged. He was not a picky eater, she had realized, though neither did he seem to overly relish his food. Half the time he barely seemed to notice what he was eating. "Tell me a dish that you love to feed upon," she requested impulsively.

He frowned, no doubt believing her to still be thinking of the banquet, though in fact that had not been foremost in her mind. "I like roasted venison," he muttered, "much like the next man."

"Oh, really?"

"Why do you sound so surprised?"

"No reason. I just thought…"

"What?"

"That some unusual, refined dish might be your favorite," she admitted.

"Sorry to disappoint you," he replied sarcastically.

"Oh, but you haven't," she said firmly. "Not in any respect."

Predictably, James turned tongue-tied at this, and they ate in silence for the next few minutes. Gunnilde found her mind wandering back over her day, namely her lack of success with the other ladies-in-waiting. If Hal could succeed where she had failed what did that say about her?

There was also her falling out with Mistress Bartree to consider. Her conduct had been most impolitic, and the older woman would likely make her regret it. She also felt a little guilty that she had been so sharp with her when Magnatrude had provided the ring she now wore on her third finger. She gazed down at the gold band sadly.

"What is it?" James asked, setting down his goblet. "Why do you look so disheartened all of a sudden?"

"I am thinking of Mistress Bartree," Gunnilde admitted. "She does not like me, and she does not mean to share the Queen with me. How am I supposed to fill my new role when she jealously guards every task from me?"

James did not answer her at first, for 'twas plain he thought her question rhetorical. When he caught sight of her expectant expression, he paused and gave the matter some thought. "Well," he said slowly, "you're young and pretty, and the latest favorite. Is it not natural she should be jealous?"

Gunnilde cast aside the "pretty" comment and focused on the matter of hand. "But she has all the experience and sophistication on her side! Why can she not see things from my viewpoint? Why must I always be the reasonable one? It is not fair. Moreover, she has a mysterious and tragic past that I cannot possibly compare with," she said with a sigh. Her own tale of Arthur Conway was nothing to it, nothing at all.

175

James looked startled. "Does she have a mysterious and tragic past?" he asked with surprise.

"Yes, she does, and everyone knows of it," Gunnilde answered with exasperation. "Why is it you never know anything of your fellow courtiers?" she puzzled aloud.

Instead of answering this, James set down his knife. "How is her past tragic?" he asked, sounding like he was not entirely sure he wanted to know.

Gunnilde brightened, ignoring his grudging tone. "Well," she said, leaning forward and lowering her voice. "The way I heard tell, her castle was burned to a blackened shell when the north fell, and she was left to molder in a virtual ruin for years until her brother sent for her. And in that time, she had transformed from a young and beauteous maiden into the cold, embittered woman we all know now."

She clasped her hands together, quite entranced with the image she had created. "Can you not picture her, James? Walking up and down the ruins, growing paler and gaunter and older, rather like a ghost herself." She shivered pleasurably. "Is that not high romance?"

James did not look convinced. "It merely sounds dismal to me. And the mystery you mentioned? Wherein does that lie?"

"Ah well," Gunnilde said, holding up a finger. "I suspect there was a romance once, buried deep beneath the pyres. Who knows, but that the embers do not still smolder. Look," she said, drawing off the gold ring from her wedding finger and passing it to him.

"I have already seen it," he said, but took it all the same.

"Look closer! There is a lover's inscription running around the band."

He turned the ring to the light and read aloud, "I cannot show the love I owe." He frowned. "Doesn't sound much like an avowal of love," he said critically before passing it back.

Gunnilde was annoyed by his dismissive words. "There could be a hundred reasons why he could not outright declare himself!" she said impatiently as she slipped it back onto her finger. "You just have to use a little imagination."

"I must be lamentably lacking in imagination"—James shrugged—"for none spring to mind."

Gunnilde gave a huff of breath. "Well, what if…I don't say this is the truth of the matter, mind you, but what if her lover was committed to another?"

James appeared to be struggling with the idea of the Queen's current favorite embroiled in an illicit love affair. He shook his head and opened his mouth. Before he could answer, Gunnilde bounced up in her seat. "I can see you are about to say something disparaging, so I beg you will not trouble to speak. And before you lecture me, I will add that I have no intention of sharing that scandalous theory with aught but you. And you do not count."

"Why do I not count?" he asked, bristling at once at the perceived slight.

"Because you are my husband," she explained. "It does not signify when I confess to a scurrilous thought if it is only to you. For you are required to conceal all my faults and flaws from others as though they are your own, is that not so?"

He looked taken aback by the sentiment. "And will you perform that same office for me?" he asked, a pucker between his brows.

177

"Of course," she responded without hesitation. "It is all part of the pact of married life." She picked up her goblet and held it aloft. After a moment's pause, James echoed the gesture, and they tapped their drinking vessels together.

"To the pact of married life," he echoed, a thoughtful expression on his face.

15

James felt annoyed with his behavior as he divested himself of his clothes before bed. He had been surly company over supper he was sure, and resentful of stupid things that were of no consequence. Gunnilde would start thinking she had married a sullen fellow with nothing to recommend him.

She had carried the brunt of the conversation as it was and given him much grace. Neville always complained he was snappish and prickly in private life, but James had not cared much what his younger brother thought. It was different with a wife though. He needed to indulge her more if she was to carry on tolerating him as a spouse. He shot a sidelong look at her as she tipped her basin of used washing water out of the window.

"The rest of the jug is yours," she said, straightening the wash and dry cloths and approaching the bed. She dropped her mantle and James hastily looked away from the view of his wife in her see-through shift as she clambered into bed. He cleared his throat but disappointingly could think of nothing to say as he crossed to the washbasin and began his ablutions.

"What would you say," Gunnilde began tentatively, "if I asked you to take me out in Aphrany one evening a week?" She was lying down now with her hands folded across her stomach.

He dropped his washcloth in the basin and had to fish it back out again. "Yes," he answered briefly. "I would say yes." It was the least he could do. He did not have to turn his head to know she would be all smiles at this. It was faintly embarrassing that so little would satisfy her.

"Wait," she said guiltily, "for I have not yet explained to what type of establishment I wish you to take me."

James shook the water from his eyes and turned to contemplate her. She had started pleating the bedsheet between her fingers. He had seen her do this before. She must do it when she was nervous, he realized. She was also refusing to meet his gaze with her own. "Just where is it you wish to go?" he asked suspiciously.

"To a tavern," she answered at once. "I wish to sample the entertainment available at the taverns of Aphrany."

He might have known it would be something outrageous. Why in the name of the gods? "You wish to take fashion inspiration from tavern wenches?" he guessed wildly.

Gunnilde gave a startled laugh. "That had not occurred to me, in truth."

"You are inordinately fond of taverns?" he guessed again, scrubbing at his neck. This would be somewhat surprising, considering her avowed wish to mingle with the highest ladies in the land.

"Not especially," she admitted, "no. It is just that I thought it might be a useful exercise."

"Useful?" he echoed, lowering the washcloth. "In what way?"

"Well, to…to experience the sort of music that Aphranians wish to listen to in their free time. The music that is popular among folk at large."

James picked up the drying cloth and ran it over his neck and shoulders. "So then, this is for my benefit?"

"Yes," she agreed eagerly, sitting up in the bed. "Do you remember my saying how I mean to aid you in furthering your career?"

James had to avert his eyes. The motion set her breasts bouncing and her shift concealed next to nothing. Their truce was giving him new…unanticipated problems. He cleared his throat. "As my helpmeet?"

"Yes, precisely." She settled back on her pillows, patting the space on the bed next to her. "Come, and tell me if you think the idea has merit."

James replaced the drying cloth and walked over to the bed. "Perhaps," he lied, lifting the blanket and sliding in beside her. If she wanted, he would trail around the taverns with her, but he expected precious little by way of inspiration. "You imagine this will instill in me a newfound love of ballads and help me appeal to the masses," he guessed.

"Yes, that is my hope," she agreed readily, turning onto her side toward him. A smile tugged at his lips at her ready honesty. He gave way to it, and she immediately looked relieved.

"Do you know, I think we are becoming quite familiar with one another and settling into married life together quite nicely," she said, astonishing him greatly.

"You think so?" he muttered. They were not yet as familiar as he would have liked, if he was being entirely truthful.

"Yes, for few husbands would have taken today's events in their stride as you have," she continued blithely. "My brother and his friends are a rare handful; I am well aware."

He frowned. Sometimes he thought Gunnilde's expectations of him were rather low. "Does not every knight who eats at your father's table have to train up their own squire as a mere matter of course?"

She snorted. "Maybe so. But as I am sure you have gathered, many of the knights of this realm have shirked their duties this season by sending their squires to Aphrany unattended. It is a most shocking thing for they must know they cannot be trusted to behave themselves."

"I expect they feel in need of respite," James said, thinking of the likes of Cosgrave and Peterson and Bauer and his bony elbow. If any of them were his squire he'd make sure to abandon them at any given opportunity.

Gunnilde reached up and touched a cool hand to his swollen eye, making him startle. "Your poor eye," she lamented.

He cleared his throat again and her hand fell away. "It's really nothing."

"Indeed, it is not! It is infamous. I am quite vexed with Hal. People will get entirely the wrong impression of you and think you are some kind of rough customer." She sounded so put out on his behalf that James felt oddly gratified.

He shook his head. "Anyone who knows me will be well aware I am no fighter."

"I will be sure to tell everyone exactly how it occurred," she assured him, "so that no foul rumors spread."

"I beg you will not!" James said in alarm. "I will sound ridiculous in such a retelling. Besides, you surely do not wish to embroil your brother in the tale, lest any repercussions should arise from the incident."

Gunnilde's face fell. "You mean you, too, think the Squires' Revels might end up being canceled?"

He shook his head. "It's unlikely, I would say. They are too newly arrived for anyone to have attached names to faces yet. If they are lucky, no one will suffer any consequences for today's encounter."

She appeared relieved, then appeared to remember something, biting her lip. "Though Hal gave his name to Mistress Rheinholdt, did he not?"

182

"Yes, but if they are friendly now, it seems unlikely she will betray him."

Gunnilde seemed skeptical. "She does not seem remotely friendly to me! Besides, one of the servers may still be able to point the ringleaders out."

"And risk offending some influential family? Unlikely. You have to put yourself in their shoes."

She looked thoughtful. "I suppose that is true. Speaking of servants, Bennett was a good deal more obliging this evening, did you not think?"

He did. Four courses of food being brought up from the kitchen was unprecedented in his experience. "Most uncharacteristically so," he agreed. "Do you suppose it was down to Cuthbert's influence?"

"Cuthbert?" She repeated, and he waited for her to suggest what Cuthbert might have said to their incalcitrant servant, but when she spoke it was about something else altogether. She leaned forward and laid a tentative hand against his bare chest. "James," she said quietly.

James struggled to draw breath. "Yes," he answered unsteadily.

"You know how we were speaking of becoming accustomed to married life?"

"Yes."

"Do you feel like practicing that other matter? As we were last night, before we were interrupted, I mean?"

James's heart leaped in his chest. "The, er, the kissing, you mean?" he said hoarsely.

"Yes. Only if you want to, of course," she said quickly. "Not if—" She started to draw her hand away, but he reached up and caught hold of it fast.

"I do," he interrupted her. "I most definitely do."

"Oh." She smiled at him again, and James had the strangest realization. She was not just pretty. She was damnably pretty. He had always known she was a tempting morsel, uncomfortably so in his opinion, with her shapely form and warm, alluring voice, but somehow, he had missed the fact that the features of her face added up to the perfect sum total.

The fact hit him now squarely in the eye. Then, too, there was all that abundant hair, and the sheer force of her personality. It seemed to radiate from her, all healthy, eager goodwill and enthusiasm. Arthur Conway must be an idiot, he realized, Douglas Farleigh too. For she had favored them, had doubtless bestowed her smiles on them, yet they had squandered them in favor of someone else. He was glad he had not acted with such stupidity.

Mind you, she had neither smiled on him nor liked him till after their marriage. Did that matter? She professed herself satisfied with him now and he needed to ensure she remained that way. There was someone else too, someone whose name hovered on the edge of his consciousness. Someone else who had taken Gunnilde's good opinion for granted. Some other fool who had let her down.

Then James's thoughts scattered to the four corners for Gunnilde was kissing him and he could not hold a coherent thought in his head. Not when Gunnilde's soft lips were against his own, and her even softer body was pressing into his. His hand, almost without volition, flew to her waist, clasping and fondling her like the veriest lecher. She was so soft and pliable there. He wanted to touch her all over. He groaned and Gunnilde drew back.

184

"Is something wrong, James?" she asked in concern. "Shall we stop?"

Wrong? "No," he answered quickly. "It is just…" What could he say? "I am not much accustomed to kisses."

She blinked at him. "You have not…before?" He shook his head. "Not ever?" she marveled. "But how can that be? When you are so…" She made a vague gesture in front of his face.

James flushed. "I…was always very busy with my lessons," he said lamely. Gods, he sounded pathetic!

"No one ever caught your eye?" she wondered aloud. "Not even at a summer fair or in the square on market day?"

"Is that when you've been kissed?" he guessed shrewdly. Gunnilde started guiltily and he knew he had hit the mark. "I've never been to a fair or market day," he admitted when she did not speak. "Wycliffe Hall is rather an austere place, I suppose. We were not raised to mingle with our tenants or nearby villagers."

"What about feast day celebrations?" Gunnilde reasoned. "You must have mixed with friends and neighbors at those times."

He shook his head again. "My mother saw those as an opportunity for public prayer and private reflection. As time to catch up on one's studies."

Gunnilde's expression wavered, and her eyes filled with compassion. "Why James, you poor thing! No wonder you have not… I mean, to be raised so…so joylessly."

He should be bristling with affront at being so pitied, he realized. From anyone else, it would be intolerable, but for some reason he was not offended, far from it. Was he enjoying her solicitous concern? Inwardly, he was reeling even as he accepted her tender care.

185

She rubbed a palm comfortingly up and down his arm. "It does not matter," she declared. "We can do those things now, together. There must be a very fine market in Aphrany, I think, and next summer in Caer Lyoness there are sure to be fairs aplenty. There is absolutely nothing wrong with being chaste. I think it makes a nice change for a man to be."

"Chaste?" He was startled by the term.

"Well…" She hesitated. "The word seems an appropriate one, does it not?"

"I suppose," he agreed, still feeling rather discomposed. He coughed. "Tell me about your summer fair."

"The summer fair at Tranton Vale?" she asked, propping herself up on her elbow. Her weight distributed in a way that made his body perk up with interest. It was not just her hair that was abundant. He needed to put a little distance between them if he was not to embarrass himself.

"Well, it is a vastly noisy and busy affair," Gunnilde reminisced, happily unaware of his inner turmoil. "They come from far and wide, the entertainers and the troubadours and folk to sell their wares."

"And who kissed you there?" he asked, cutting to the heart of the matter.

She looked faintly embarrassed. "His name was Ted, and he came to the fair with his cousin to make merry."

"And how old were you?"

"Sixteen. His cousin approached my friend Muriel, and Ted and I fell in step behind them. We started talking as young people do, about our likes and dislikes. I don't remember much about him except he was very fond of mulled cider and had an amiable manner."

186

"Then what happened?"

"We talked some more and ate hot pies. He bought me a ribbon from a peddler and I…"

"Repaid him with a kiss?" he suggested. She laughed and nodded. "What happened to the ribbon?"

"I wore it till it fell apart."

"Hmmmm." He was not sure how he felt about that. "What about market day?"

"It was much the same, only this time I was eighteen. We had traveled to Greater Derring in a large party to attend the May Day market. I was invited to dance around the May pole with the other maidens."

"Your friend Muriel was with you?"

"Yes, and a few others besides. We all danced and afterward we tarried awhile in the town square."

James looked at her face, imagining her four years younger and dressed in white. "What was your swain's name this time?" he asked, careful to keep his expression impassive.

"Dickon," she replied promptly. "He was there with his uncle to buy a horse. I think my friend Rachel was his first choice in truth, but she picked another, so he made do with me."

"Dickon sounds like an idiot," he said dismissively.

"Yes," she agreed. "He was a good kisser though." Her eyes dropped to dwell on James's lips a moment.

"Was he?" Why did his voice sound like that? He cleared his throat. "What about his kiss was good?"

"Well, he did not seem in any great hurry about it. It was as though he had all the time in the world."

So...she liked being kissed slowly, James thought. That was worth knowing. "And what about the feast day?"

"The what?" She looked flustered.

"The kiss you had at a feast day."

"Oh, that." Gunnilde's eyes averted, and she turned rather pink. "That was, well, a bit different." Curiously, after being so open about the first two kisses she seemed reluctant to discuss the third.

"It was someone you knew?" he guessed and heard her faint gasp.

"How did you—?"

"Who was it?" he demanded, propping himself up on his elbow so their noses practically touched. "Conway?"

Gunnilde sighed. "Yes," she admitted reluctantly. "You're far too good at guessing games."

"When and how was it?"

"James..."

"Tell me," he insisted. "If I had any experience to speak of, I would share it with you."

188

This caught her attention, and her lips formed a silent oh. She took a deep breath. "Very well. I was nineteen and it was somehow…both better and worse."

"Better in what way?" he asked immediately.

"Well, I suppose because I had always been invested in my future husband, as I thought of him then. I believed him to be a significant person in my life. After all, the other two I had no expectation of ever seeing again."

That made sense, he supposed, though of course, he had been her future husband all along, not Conway. "Then…how was it worse?"

"Well, you see, quite honestly…"

"He was not as adept as Dickon?" James guessed.

"No, he was not. He sort of kept his mouth open a lot. Also, he had eaten fish at the feast," she confessed in a rush, "and his moustache was droopy and sort of got in the way."

James felt an unexpected pang of sympathy for Arthur Conway. "I see." He fell silent and could feel Gunnilde's slightly anxious gaze upon him. He lay back down, staring up at the ceiling. "Is there anyone else I should know about?" he asked at last.

"Anyone else?" She shook her head. "The only other person I have kissed is you."

Now it was his turn to be evasive. He did not want to ask the obvious question. Imagine being told he was a poor kisser. Still, it seemed unfair that he should take all and give nothing in this exchange. She had been so open and frank with him, and he had not been entirely truthful.

It seemed the least he could do was share his own background, however pitiful. "I did not entirely tell the truth when I said I had no experience at all," he admitted slowly. "You see, when I was fifteen something happened which—" He halted, unsure how to continue.

"Yes? Something happened?" Gunnilde shuffled closer to gaze down at his face. She looked concerned.

James huffed out a breath of air. Best to get it over with at once. "My father took me to a brothel in Caer Lyoness. He thought it was high time I learned about women and how to deal with them. He was drunk, of course." He gave her a level look. "He's often drunk," he added. Gunnilde looked so stricken and mortified on his behalf that he could hardly meet her gaze.

"He was very disappointed when it did not have the desired effect on me. In fact, it had the opposite. I was disgusted. The nudity, the lewdness of it all… I wanted nothing to do with any of it."

Gunnilde made a noise in her throat. "It must have been very shocking to you," she said carefully. "After living so sheltered a life with little to no society. To then, suddenly find yourself in such a place and surrounded by…all manner of things. Your father must be the veriest fool of a man!"

James gave a short laugh. "Well, you will find no argument from me there. When I refused to…to partake…to take my pick of the bunch, he made me wait downstairs for him for over an hour. The women were merciless in their teasing of me. They kept touching my face, telling me how beauteous I was and how I shouldn't be shy. I hated it. Their overpowering perfume, their breath on my face, the way they talked, the mocking way they laughed. Even worse, I hated the men that came through the doors. Men like my father. I never went anywhere with him again."

190

"I'm not surprised." Her expression was grave. "Did you never tell anyone, your mother for instance?"

He shook his head. "I told no one until now. My parents are rarely in accord. It would just have been another cause for strife between them."

"They have found little happiness in their marriage?"

"They have found none that I am aware of. My mother is an exacting woman with high standards and only my father's social position ever made him acceptable to her. He is a spendthrift and a drunkard and has accrued many debts over the years. That is why the estate alone does not generate enough income to sustain itself."

Gunnilde leaned across and placed a careful kiss upon his brow. "Thank you for trusting me with your story, James," she said sincerely. "I want you to know I mean to be very patient and considerate with you."

He blinked at her. That had not been his intention; however, he could see the mood had shifted. As usual, he had made things awkward. "It was not my intention to—"

"No, I know, but even so." She hovered for a moment, looking uncertain of her next move. Then she gave a small nod, and shuffled up the bed, breaking their eye contact. She grabbed her pillow and plumped it down above his own. Once she had it arranged to her satisfaction, she reached for him, wordlessly urging him closer and gently angling his head until it lay against her breast.

"Let us just lie like this awhile," she said. "Unless you find it uncomfortable."

James considered this. "It is not uncomfortable," he said, though his face felt hot, and he was not sure where precisely to put his arms.

"Good."

After a moment, he simply passed an arm about her and turned into her, fully relaxing into her cushiony warmth. He felt strangely light and unburdened and…yes, relieved. She knew everything, all about his debts, his dissolute father, and why her husband was so woefully inexperienced when it came to the wooing of women, and still she lay here by his side, her arms around him, comforting him.

He had told her of his most shameful memory, a thing he had never thought to tell another living soul. He could not quite believe he done such a thing. And yet, instead of feeling embarrassed or regretful, he felt…strangely elated.

What was it she had said before? Something about a husband and wife being duty bound to accept the other's flaws and shortcomings as their own and keep them concealed safely away from the world. Such a concept had never occurred to him before. His own parents had certainly not subscribed to such an ideology.

He closed his eyes. The notion appealed to him; how could it fail to, when he was such a flawed individual himself? Certainly, its application so far had been incredibly freeing. Not only had Gunnilde accepted his story quietly and without interruption, but she had also, at its conclusion, expressed herself firmly on his side. She had not apparently found his own part in proceedings laughable or inept. Instead of finding his disgust unfathomable, as his father had, she seemed instead to think it inevitable with the upbringing he had received.

James felt himself drifting off into dreamless sleep as her fingers touched his head, carefully sifting through his hair, her fingertips gently grazing his scalp. At this precise moment in time, it was hard to believe Gunnilde had any faults for him to hide. So, how in the world was he supposed to uphold his side of the bargain?

192

16

Gunnilde awoke early and lay abed awhile in James's sleepy embrace. He had scarcely moved a muscle all night, most unusual for him, and had remained wrapped around her until the early hours. Turning her head to look at him, she felt an almost overwhelming wave of tenderness engulf her.

James was a sensitive soul, and his father sounded an absolute brute. How dared he treat his son so? Gunnilde's chest burned with indignation at the thought of it. His mother did not sound much better either, keeping her son cooped up in the schoolroom and barely affording him any opportunities to meet anyone. No wonder he seemed such a cold fish on first knowing him. He had no notion how to make himself agreeable to others!

Lightly, she touched his hair; like everything else about the man, it was beautiful, such a rich auburn shade. He was ridiculously good-looking, but that fact no longer exasperated her. Not now she knew him better. Gunnilde had always suspected that beautiful people had things much easier than everybody else, but she was beginning to revise that opinion since getting to know James.

Nothing really seemed easy for him. From what she could make out, her husband had very few friends among his fellow courtiers. They all spoke highly of him, but they appeared more like acquaintances than anything intimate. In his private hours it seemed James did not mix with them at all.

Outside of the palace, he had his Master Gregory, of course, but he was a former teacher of James's so she was not sure that really counted. It was not as though they had met spontaneously and become lifelong friends, was it? And she knew now for a fact that he had no former loves, save for Constance, of course.

Her conscience prickled slightly to think of Constance but then, Constance could not have truly loved him back, or she would not have run away with Sir Douglas, now, would she? She, Gunnilde, would take far better care of James than Constance would have, in any case.

Constance was too reserved and proper for James, Gunnilde decided. They would never have stopped being polite and reserved with one another. They would have been one of those couples who never undressed in front of each other after thirty years of marriage.

Catching sight of the reddened, mottled skin around his eye, Gunnilde went up on her elbow and peered down at it in concern. It was definitely forming into a bruise, she thought crossly. Oh bother Hal! Why on earth had they seen fit to embroil her poor husband in their scrapes? It was too bad of them to ruin the perfection of his features like that!

James stirred at that moment, loosening his grip of her, and Gunnilde managed to extricate herself, and was half out of the bed when she heard the tap on the door. Realizing it was Bennett with the washing water, she dove back under the blanket again and huddled there until the manservant backed out of the door, his eyes still carefully averted.

"Where are you going?" James mumbled grumpily, rolling onto his back. He rubbed his eyes, then hissed, finding one swollen and bruised.

"Just to wash," she told him over her shoulder as she hurried across the floorboards in her bare feet. "What are your plans today?" she asked, splashing water into the basin. "Are you going into Aphrany?"

"I don't know," he said, then sat up to hunch over his knees. "What about you?"

"Oh, the usual," she said airily, wringing out a washcloth.

"Which is?"

194

"Attending the Queen. Trying to ingratiate myself with her ladies." She rubbed the damp cloth over her face and neck. James's frown deepened. It must pain his eye, she thought with a pang. She wished he would smile more.

"What if…" he began.

Gunnilde's shift slid down one shoulder, baring her one shoulder down to her elbow. "Whoops," she said, making a grab for it. The tie strings must have worked loose during the night. She glanced back over her shoulder and found James watching her. "Sorry," she blurted.

"You don't need to apologize on my account. If I didn't like the spectacle, I would not be looking."

It seemed such an unexpected thing for him to say that she stared at him. "You like the spectacle?" she repeated.

"Of course I do. It must be obvious to you by now, Gunnilde." He glanced away, faint color tinting his cheekbones. "It's not an easy thing for a man to hide. His body makes it rather obvious." He pulled a face.

Oh. He meant the fact she had felt the impression of his stiff manhood pressed against her the past few nights. "Well, yes," she agreed. "But that was the feel of my body in the dark, not the look of me. That is an altogether different thing."

His eyebrows rose. "Both are…pleasing to me," he said, reddening further.

"Really?" Gunnilde could not contain her gratification on hearing this. This was even better than his saying so matter-of-factly that she was pretty the previous night. She had not allowed herself to dwell on that particular compliment for she had not been sure he meant much by it. This time, she allowed the words to sink in and gave him a shy smile.

James cleared his throat. "What if I…accompanied you today, to the Queen's presence chamber?" he suggested.

Had that been what he was going to say before? Her shift slipping down her shoulder had driven his thoughts from his mind. "I would love that!" she said at once. "Then I need not trail about all forlorn until the Queen deigns to notice me."

"Is that what happened yesterday?" He frowned.

"Yes, for all the other ladies are determined to shun me as an upstart," Gunnilde said cheerfully, turning back to her ablutions.

"I shall certainly accompany you today, then," he resolved.

By the time they showed up in the Queen's receiving chambers, however, Gunnilde found her second day was a different experience altogether to the first. For one thing, she was immediately accosted by a splinter party of four ladies, headed by a bustling Estrilda Rheinholdt.

"Ah, Gunnilde, well met!" she hailed her in the friendliest of terms. "I have been looking out for you for an age and quite feared you were not gracing us with your presence this morn."

"Estrilda," Gunnilde greeted her in return. "Good morn. I have brought my husband along with me today." She gestured toward James, wondering if he was the reason for the effusive welcome. But apparently not, for Estrilda gave James the most cursory of greetings before turning determinedly back to Gunnilde.

"I had the great pleasure of meeting your brother, Master Payne, yesterday," she said airily. "A delightful young man and quite mature for his years, I thought."

196

Good grief, Gunnilde thought, seeing the pink enter Estrilda's cheeks. Was she blushing? Over Hal? "Oh…yes. He did mention your meeting and that you were kind enough to show an interest in Dustin."

"Dustin?" Estrilda looked blank.

"His little dog."

"Oh! Oh yes, of course! Dustin," she said hastily. "Such a sweet little doggy."

So…Gunnilde had been wrong. It had not been Dustin who had caught Estrilda's fancy, but Hal himself. She slanted a disbelieving look at James, but he merely smirked back at her. "I told you," he mouthed. Told her what? Oh yes, she remembered belatedly. He had claimed Hal was something of a lady's favorite. How bizarre! She could scarcely credit it.

"I do hope he will remain at court for the Solstice celebrations," Estrilda continued coyly.

"He will certainly be here until the Squires' Revels which I believe are held on the twelfth of the month."

Estrilda nodded. "How very interesting," she said. "I have always wondered what they entailed precisely, for I have never had the opportunity to attend one." She looked expectantly at her, and Gunnilde realized that Estrilda had not the first notion what the Squires' Revels even were. She took pity on her.

"As you will no doubt have gathered, they are an opportunity for the squires to prove their worth by competing in various events to show their proficiency."

The ladies stood beside Estrilda all perked up. "Pray, what sort of events, Lady Wycliffe?" enquired one. Gunnilde thought her name was Mistress Stanhope.

"Do not be so odiously forward, Patience!" Estrilda snapped at her. "I was just about to ask my friend the self-same thing!" She turned back expectantly to Gunnilde. Patience Stanhope took a step back, looking suitably chastened.

"Um, events such as wrestling and long jump," Gunnilde replied. What else had the boys mentioned? She threw a look of appeal at James.

"Archery, swimming," he listed in a bored voice. "The usual feats a squire must demonstrate before he is made a knight."

"It all sounds quite exciting," another lady twittered before Estrilda's fierce glower subdued her.

"Yes, I am looking forward to seeing my brother compete," Gunnilde agreed. "Perhaps we could watch the Revels together?" she suggested tentatively.

Estrilda was immediately wreathed in smiles. "That would be most agreeable, my dear Gunnilde," she enthused. "I would be delighted! Quite delighted! I thank you for the invitation." They curtseyed to one another and Estrilda moved on, followed by her little clique. She looked quite triumphant and threw a contemptuous gaze toward the larger group of ladies-in-waiting who were watching their interaction with aloof disapproval.

"What in heavens is happening?" Gunnilde asked James in a hushed voice.

"It appears that your brother has charmed Mistress Rheinholdt into befriending you," he answered. "But the majority of the Queen's ladies are still biding their time."

"Oh, let them," Gunnilde responded. "I have you to keep me company today in any case." She squeezed his arm, and though James looked a little self-conscious, he did not pull away.

"The Queen arrives," he said, clearing his throat, and turning her head, Gunnilde saw Her Majesty emerging from her private rooms, accompanied by two ladies this morning. One predictably was Magnatrude Bartree but the other was Countess Vawdrey, wife to the King's chief adviser.

"'Tis Eden's sister-in-law, Fenella!" Gunnilde hissed excitedly.

"Yes," James agreed.

"She only seems to attend the formal functions by and large. I do not think I have seen her attending the Queen before."

James frowned. "Was she not at the feast that followed our wedding?"

"I believe she was, but I did not get the chance to speak with her," Gunnilde said wistfully. "She and Lord Vawdrey were sat with the King."

The Queen and Magnatrude Bartree had mounted the dais by this point, but to Gunnilde's surprise, Countess Vawdrey appeared to be making her way in their direction. Gunnilde glanced about to see if there was anyone else in the vicinity she might know. Turning back, she found herself the recipient of a very warm smile.

"Good morning to you both, Sir James and Lady Wycliffe," Fenella Vawdrey hailed them, and bows and curtseys were exchanged all round. "I am so sorry not to have sought you out before. I have been most remiss in my attentions, I do hope you can forgive me." She looked so sweetly earnest that Gunnilde practically fell over herself to assure her that she had not been neglectful in any way.

"Oh, but I have indeed," she responded at once. "Eden wrote to me most particularly asking that I take an interest in you at court, Gunnilde, but you see, I was quite ill in September. Oh, nothing serious, I assure you, but such an unpleasant cough and I was not fit to be seen. And then of course, Nathan came down with it and then Stephen, my twin boys you know," she explained, looking from Gunnilde to James and then back again. "I could not bear to leave them when they are still so little."

"Oh, I quite understand!" Gunnilde hurried to assure her. "Your mothering instinct does you credit, I am sure."

"Well, my husband maintains I am the best wife and mother in all of Karadok," she replied with a laugh. "But in truth the boys are not so very young now, 'tis only that I hate to leave them for too long, despite their excellent nurse. They both have a full head of teeth and black Vawdrey hair," she said proudly. "And both are walking on two feet and even running if given the opportunity."

"Already?" Gunnilde was all admiration. "Eden has told me what fine boys they are."

"You must come and meet them," Fenella insisted. "Indeed, you must come and dine with us one evening soon."

"We would love to," Gunnilde assured her at once.

Fenella's face clouded over. "The only trouble of it is, fitting everything in. I am sure you have heard that we are all traveling to Vawdrey Keep for the Solstice and won't be in town after the eleventh."

"You must have a hundred and one things to organize before you travel to Sitchmarsh," Gunnilde sympathized. "Instead, why do I not invite you and Lord Vawdrey to attend a banquet I am holding in two weeks' time? It is to be held here in the palace on the night of the tenth."

Fenella brightened. "That is so kind of you, Gunnilde," she enthused. "And when we return from Sitchmarsh, I will make sure to invite you to our townhouse for supper." She beamed. "And you will allow me to make it up to you that I was not here to ease your passage into court life, won't you, Gunnilde?" She looked faintly anxious as she said this. "Indeed, you clearly did not need my help, for only look at you!"

Her eyes traveled over Gunnilde's ensemble with admiration. "You are quite the fine court lady. I vow I have never been half so fashionable." She eyed Gunnilde's slit sleeves and hair arrangement with interest. "I had heard, of course, of the horned hairstyles but truth to tell I could not even picture them in my mind's eye. I am very happy to finally know what all the fuss is about! Really, it looks most becoming. It is no wonder the Queen enjoys your company. She told me how you caught her eye from the outset."

This was not really true, but Gunnilde was far too taken with this flattering revision of her court debut to deny it. "The Queen is too kind," she murmured modestly, casting down her eyes.

"Yes, when the mood takes her," Fenella agreed, glancing back at the dais. "Speaking of which, I had better return to her side before I give Mistress Bartree the chance to oust me from her affections altogether." She pulled a droll face, then took her leave of them.

"Is she not lovely?" Gunnilde sighed, watching the countess cross the room.

"She seems a very pleasant woman."

She frowned at this tepid response. "You surely would not describe her as 'tall and sad.'"

"No," James agreed. Gunnilde looked at him expectantly. "She is short and plump and merry," he elaborated after a moment's contemplation.

201

"And vastly elegant and distinguished," she prompted.

"She seems quite refreshingly down to earth to me."

"I meant her manner of dress."

"Well…" His gaze returned to Fenella Vawdrey. "She is certainly wearing a lot of velvet and jewels, if that is what you mean." Gunnilde sighed. "What I meant was," he said, clearly trying to redeem himself, "she is not trying to start any new fashions. I have seen that style of dress anytime these past two years."

"Yes, but when you have the best of everything you do not need to worry about standing out from the crowd," she replied absently, her gaze sweeping the room to see if anyone was impressed by her tête-à-tête with Countess Vawdrey.

When she looked back at James, he was frowning. "I mean to buy you a new ring, Gunnilde," he said surprisingly. "You can give that other back to Mistress Bartree."

"Really? I suppose I ought," she said, lifting her hand and twisting the gold band to look at the letters inscribed around it.

"Should you like an inscription of your own?" he asked abruptly.

"Do you know, I believe I would," she answered, pleased by the thought.

"What should it be?"

"The most flowery and complimentary thing you can think of," she answered at once.

"How about 'To Gunnilde, who is neither tall nor sad'?" he suggested.

"It falls somewhat short of the mark," she laughed. "Perhaps I should be content with our initials."

"No." He frowned. "I will ponder the matter. I am sure something suitable will occur to me."

She smiled at him. "I look forward to it."

At this point, Sir Edmund Pomfritt and Lord Symmington presented their bows. Sir Edmund subjected her hair arrangement to a good many hard stares, while Lord Symmington gave her the merest of dismissive glances before asking James if he intended to attend the poetry reading that afternoon in the small chamber. James glanced at her and opened his mouth when Gunnilde interjected quickly, "Yes, of course we will be there. I am so fond of poetry, as my husband knows."

Both gentlemen looked surprised but claimed they would look for them there before moving away.

"Why did you say that?" James asked, stepping in close. He kept his voice low. "When you told me you did not care for it at all!"

"Well, if you are to be open to revising your opinion of ballads, then so must I be, to poetry."

His eyebrows shot up. "I see. Well, do not blame me if you find it dull fare."

"I will not find it dull if you explain it to me. Only you must try and do it subtly, so that others present do not know that I am a fraud."

His mouth twitched. "A fraudulent poetry lover?" A reluctant smile curved his lips.

"Precisely."

"Well, then you must do the same for me, when we are in the tavern, and they are roaring ballads to the ceiling over my unhappy head."

She laughed. "They will never find out from me," she promised.

"It can be part of our pact," he suggested.

"Our pact?"

"Our marriage pact. I will support you in this, and you me, with that."

"Always," she agreed gravely, "that and jesters."

He could not hold back his own laugh at that. "Perhaps I should have that inscribed on your ring."

Gunnilde had been about to reply when a cleared throat interrupted them. James took a guilty step back. It was Lord and Lady Gilchrist, who turned out to be a cousin of James's. They seemed nice enough, though both were clearly agog to see him with his new wife at close quarters. His swollen eye also seemed to give them pause though they were far too tactful to mention it.

"We were so sorry to miss the wedding celebrations," Lady Gilchrist said with gentle reproach. "But perhaps it was a last-minute affair, and you could not extend invitations to all the family."

"Alas, the Queen took over the arrangements," Gunnilde interrupted, saving James from any awkwardness. "She swept all before her and neither James nor myself had much by way of family representation present."

"Ah," Lord Gilchrist commented. "It was like that, was it? You cannot take offense now, Catherine. Not when they had so little say in the matter."

"There was never any question of taking offence, Godfrey," his wife assured him, a faint edge to her voice. "I was merely surprised that, well, we have perhaps said enough on that matter, and can lay it to rest," she said graciously. "Have you had news from my aunt of late, James?"

James's expression sobered. "My mother wrote to me about two weeks ago," he said grimly.

"And there is no improvement in that quarter?" she asked and tutted sympathetically. "She has a lot to contend with, indeed."

"Well, well," Lord Gilchrist said. "We must not bring down James's spirits like this! You've dashed the laughter from his lips! He has a wife now to lift him up and support him, is that not so? This is a cause for celebration, not to cast him down in a ditch!" Gunnilde beamed on him. Lord Gilchrist, she decided, was rather nice.

His wife tutted. "Weddings are usually a cause for celebration it is true, but such tidings will doubtless cause much consternation at Wycliffe Hall. Why," she said, turning back to James, "when last your mother wrote to me, she mentioned quite a different prospective bride!"

To Gunnilde's surprise, James passed an arm about her waist. "Perhaps she did," he responded coolly. "But for my part I must profess myself well pleased with the one I've got."

Lady Gilchrist looked as astonished as Gunnilde felt. Glancing up at James, she found him regarding his cousin with a challenging air.

"Oh, so it's like that, is it?" Lord Gilchrist said, rocking back on his heels. "Well, good for you, Wycliffe. Sometimes it's good to let a young person have his head in such matters. Everything can't be about duty, I've said so many a time, is that not so, Catherine? It isn't good to have the weight of responsibility always bearing down upon you. There's got to be a little room for pleasure, now and again."

"Godfrey!" his wife uttered faintly.

Lord Gilchrist puffed out his cheeks. "There now, I've said my piece," he said, "and surrender the floor." He winked at Gunnilde and led his aghast wife away.

"Your cousin looks fit to collapse," she commented.

"My mother's family are all like that," he replied dryly. "Easily shocked."

Gunnilde bit back the words that trembled on her lips. She had once thought James the same. Perhaps she had misjudged him. His hand still rested at her waist. It made her feel slightly breathless.

"I hope she does not write to your mother claiming you threw Constance over on the merest whim," she whispered. "I think Lord Gilchrist believes you cast duty to the winds in marrying me."

"There are doubtless rumors circulating," James replied, sounding unconcerned. "It is unlikely many of them will be relayed to our faces."

"You know what we ought to have done, James!" she said with sudden inspiration. "We should have invited them to our banquet!" She whipped around, dislodging James's hand, but the Gilchrists were already too far away to hurry after. Gunnilde tutted. "It did not occur to me at the time but doubtless that would smooth Lady Gilchrist's ruffled feathers."

James shrugged. He did not look particularly taken with the idea. "If you have not already sent out your invites, then you can simply add them to your list."

"No, of course I have not sent them out, for I wanted to consult with you first. You will surely have some friends and acquaintances you wish to invite along," she said encouragingly. "Tell me, what do you think to

206

taking the Squires' Revels for our theme? The Revels are held on the twelfth and our party is the tenth, so we will practically be celebrating on the eve."

James shrugged. "I thought your aim in throwing the party was to lord your new status over your former friends," he said dryly.

Gunnilde flushed. "'Tis not just for that purpose!" she stressed. "I also want to formally introduce my brother and his friends to court and… Well, it will be the first event we host together as a married couple, will it not? You must certainly invite Master Gregory and his family, and anyone else you see fit."

"Very well," James answered. "I will consider the matter."

Gunnilde looked relieved. "I should not wish to bear sole responsibility for the occasion being a success," she admitted frankly. "The likelihood of the Conways or anyone else turning up on such short notice is extremely slim. At least now we have Earl and Countess Vawdrey as well as the Queen. That means we have prestigious guests enough in attendance."

She glanced across at James, but he was frowning again. He did not seem keen to play the host, and she supposed she could not blame him. "I suppose we ought to be making our way to the poetry reading," she prompted him.

17

"Are you sure about this?" James asked Gunnilde as they filed arm in arm into the small chamber for the afternoon's poetry reading. "Last chance to flee."

She nodded, looking resolute. "I am quite determined," she said bravely. James knew she had been disappointed to have had only a couple of minutes conversation with the Queen that morning. Queen Armenal had been far too occupied catching up with Countess Vawdrey to give his wife much attention.

His wife. The phrase echoed in his mind. It was surprising how easy it was to think of her now in such terms. She was wearing one of her dresses with the slits all over the bodices again, showing the substance of her undergown. He supposed he must be getting used to her strange clothing choices by now for it barely gave him pause.

They found a bench toward the back of the room and settled there side by side, ensuring there was space enough between them and the next cluster of courtiers. He found he did not mind at all when Gunnilde shuffled up the bench to sit as close to him as possible.

"Your friends are here," Gunnilde murmured, nodding discreetly in the direction of the other side of the room. "Lord Sniffington and Sir Puffed Up with His Own Consequence."

He smirked. "They are not my friends," he answered, lowering his head and matching her low tone. "No more than Harriet Portstanley is yours."

She tipped her head to one side. "It turns out I am fonder of Harriet than I first realized," she confessed in a whisper. "And of Winifred Hawes. I should have listened to Eden and given them a fair chance. I mean to make it up to them, now I am in the position to."

"Oh? Does that mean you are inviting them to our banquet?" She nodded. "Well, I am not fond of Sniffington and Puffed Up," he whispered back. "I do not care for their society, and I shall extend them no invite." She laughed, and James noticed several heads turning their way.

He decided to ignore them. Let them stare, if they had nothing better to do. The first poet stood up and made his way to the middle of the room. Unfurling his scroll, he launched into his verse which told of a pair of seabirds, who hovered over calm oceans some days and choppy, turbulent waters another.

Verse after verse labored the metaphor as the pair of birds withstood the elements, always keeping the other in their sights and building their nest high up on the cliffs away from harm. James cast several glances at Gunnilde as the verses went on, for she wore a ferocious frown of concentration upon her face.

Finally, the poet concluded, "Oh, that we in our endeavors had the resilience of these poor creatures, buffeted as we are by life's storms, then lulled with its blue skies." A smattering of polite applause greeted his closing line, and James found Gunnilde regarding him expectantly. "Well?" she hissed, jabbing him in the ribs. "What does he mean by all that?"

James was slightly taken aback. She had not been exaggerating; Gunnilde, it seemed, struggled with even the simplest of poetry. "The last line gave away the poet's true intent," he replied quietly. "He compares the struggle of man with the habits of seabirds."

She nodded. "And what is the significance of them being a pair? He said they built a nest. Is he speaking, then, of married life?"

"Quite possibly."

"So then, what does he recommend we do? Live next to the sea? Remain ever vigilant of the daily movements of our spouse?"

James considered this. "I do not know that he purports to have any answers. He merely reflects that in some respect, dumb creatures have better instincts than we."

Gunnilde looked dissatisfied. "If he does not have any wisdom to impart, then what pray was the point of his poem?"

"Maybe he just likes seabirds."

Gunnilde beheld him suspiciously. "Are you laughing at me?"

The next speaker was introduced as a Mr. Shadbolt, and Gunnilde gave a gasp, catching hold of James's sleeve and shaking it. "I've heard of him!" she said excitedly. "Do you remember my saying about him? I am sure this must be the poet that poor Sir Douglas hired by mistake?"

"Sir Douglas?" James repeated, an unpleasant sensation in the pit of his stomach.

"You know, the—" She broke off and gazed around furtively. "The lewd one!" she whispered. "I am sure I am not mistaken! Constance said his work was most improper!"

James turned back to face front and turned a disapproving eye on a large-looking man with a suspiciously purple nose and untidy whiskers shuffling to the center of the room.

"Oh, faithless rose!" he rumbled richly. Despite his disreputable appearance, he had an impressive deeply timbred voice. "Thy dewy petals should conceal naught, but purest beauty! Instead, thou hast

210

allowed a lusty worm to burrow into the very heart of you and corrupt your tender bud with his insatiable appetite!"

James's eyebrows shot up as the poem continued, a ranting diatribe against the perfidy of roses who do not maintain their bloom, despite their caretakers toiling and tending so tirelessly to their upkeep. By the end of it, the poet was practically shaking with emotion, flecks of spit around the corners of his lips, and fist upraised as he released one final stanza condemning the duplicity of roses.

At the close, the room sat in an uncomfortable, shocked silence. Mr. Shadbolt looked around, gave a satisfied nod at their reaction, and then shuffled back to his seat. A smattering of delayed applause followed him, and Gunnilde turned to James helplessly.

"Am I to take it that Mr. Shadbolt really does not enjoy the cultivating of roses?" she ventured. When James sat silent, she continued plaintively. "In any case, it makes no sense for I am fairly certain flowers are not worm food."

"He was not really speaking of roses," James admitted.

"Oh? What pray was he speaking of?"

"I'll explain it to you later."

Gunnilde's eyes widened. "Was it rude?" she breathed. James's hesitation seemed to be answer enough, for she drew in an excited breath. "Did everyone else understand it?" she asked, scanning the room.

James shrugged. "Some certainly," he answered, seeing a mixture of embarrassed, mystified, and shocked expressions in the room.

"Shall I look disapproving too, to seem as though I understood it?"

James hesitated. He was not really fulfilling the role he had sworn to play. "Shadbolt was railing against infidelity in wives," he admitted in a murmur. "Of ladies not remaining chaste."

"How do you know he was speaking exclusively of ladies?" she whispered back.

"Women are typically likened to flowers in poetry."

"Oh. I see." She nodded.

"Then, too, there was the metaphor of the 'insatiable worm,'" he explained woodenly.

"Yes, the worm he found in the rose's bud," Gunnilde remembered, and James flushed. She paused. "Why do you look like that?"

"The worm is…representing the masculine," he explained reluctantly. "And the rose, the feminine." His throat closed over the words, and he coughed.

Gunnilde's frown intensified. "Yes, the rose is the lady and the worm the man," she reasoned aloud. "So, then the rose is at fault because—?" She cast a look of appeal his way.

"Because she allowed the worm to penetrate her petals and corrupt her," James explained in a strangled voice.

Gunnilde sat up a little straighter in her seat. "Oh!" She sat perfectly still for a moment, then shook her head. "No, you must have that wrong, James. Mr. Shadbolt could not possibly have stood up before polite company and started speaking of men's…worms!"

He regarded her solemnly. "Yet he did, I assure you."

"It would be most unseemly," she argued. "Over there is the Dowager Duchess of Rand. She would not sit there calmly while a man spoke of such indecent things! No, you must have misunderstood it." She cast an uneasy look about the room. "There are several respectable ladies here still looking quite serene."

"Mayhap they did not understand it," James conceded. "But you have to admit there are others who look quite flustered."

"Maybe they have dirty minds like yourself," Gunnilde said so earnestly that James was quite taken aback.

"I do not have a dirty mind!"

"Well…" She bit her lip. "It must be a little or you would not have leaped to such an interpretation."

She looked so apologetic that James had the strangest impulse to laugh. "Did not someone else tell you that Mr. Shadbolt's poetry was lewd?" he enquired reasonably. "Do they also have a dirty mind?"

"Who, Constance?" Doubt had clearly crept into her mind at so unlikely a possibility. "I hardly think so. Unless…" She looked down and started absently pleating her skirts.

"Unless what?" he asked, nudging her foot with his.

"Well, unless highly respectable people have secretly unwholesome minds," she said primly, rendering James quite speechless.

18

It was crowded in the Great Hall. The high table was not occupied, so it looked as though there was to be no royal presence this evening. Gunnilde felt a stab of disappointment, but this was quickly dispelled when she noticed how much busier and noisier it was than usual. It seemed that a good few more tables had been inserted into the throng.

"All the tournament rabble are turning up," Neville said cheerfully. "Now tourney season is done for the winter."

Tournament rabble? Gunnilde was surprised by this remark, for were not knights lauded wherever they went? Certainly, they were welcomed with open arms at Tranton Vale, where her father considered it an honor to host them. Something whizzed past her ear and hit an unfortunate lad to her right smack in the face. Luckily it was only a bread roll.

A roar of laughter went up from a nearby table, and James towed her in the opposite direction. "We'll sit here, I think," he said, glancing about with a hunted expression. "I can find no quieter spot."

Gunnilde, Kit, Cuthbert, and Neville sat themselves down. She wondered if Hal would turn up anytime soon. He had returned to his quarters to see if his mentor had any tasks for him to perform before supper. Maybe Sir Ned had him polishing boots or running errands down at the stables.

"It is certainly very crowded tonight," she said, noticing a bunch of ladies-in-waiting at the next table who were tutting and primming their mouths to see such antics.

"Disgraceful!" Millicent Everidge pronounced loudly to her neighbor Lucy Melvin, but for all that, Gunnilde thought her eyes were trained avidly on the newcomers, and there was a good deal of whispering going on. None of their number thought to look across at Gunnilde, she noticed, or to send a nod or a wave of acknowledgment her way.

She could not see Estrilda nor Mistress Bartree and supposed they must be dining with family or other friends tonight. Presumably the Queen was dining privately with the King. A servant halted beside her, setting goblets and wine down on their table for them.

Gunnilde had scarcely thanked him when she heard her name shouted. It was Hal, making his way toward them, waving and looking animated. Though he had spotted them, he still appeared to be looking for someone else in the hall.

"What are you waiting for?" Kit quipped as Hal halted beside their table. "A written invitation?"

"I am just looking out for Sir Ned," Hal said, swiveling round. "He said he would join us anon." Gunnilde almost choked on her wine. James produced a handkerchief, and she dabbed it to her lips.

"Keep it," he muttered when she tried to return it.

"Sir Ned won't join us tonight," Cuthbert said with quiet confidence as he poured out three more cups of wine. He looked straight at Gunnilde. "You need have no fear of that, my lady."

Gunnilde felt herself flush. Why did Cuthbert have to be so damned perceptive? A horrible suspicion crossed her mind that Cuthbert might know something of the embarrassing occurrence at Vawdrey Keep. He was Roland Vawdrey's squire after all. Could Sir Roland have repeated something of the event that occurred in September? Surely not.

She did not think for one minute that Eden's husband would have pieced together what happened, with her running off to court afterward. To Sir Roland they would have been two separate events entirely. Half

215

the time she was sure he would forget her name if not for Eden briskly reminding him of it.

No, he would have forgotten all about his friend's insensitive remarks that day, she reassured herself. He certainly would never dream of repeating them in front of his squire. Would he have repeated them in front of his wife though? She considered this a moment. This was a good deal more likely, for husband and wife were very close. Somehow though, Gunnilde could not quite believe it in this instance.

Knowing Eden's directness, she had to believe her friend would have addressed it with her frankly and at once. She would certainly have demanded that Sir Ned apologize, and as no apology had been forthcoming while she remained under their roof, she could not believe that Eden had ever been apprised of the matter. Reassured, she relaxed once more. No, Cuthbert must be acting on uncanny instinct alone.

"Why do you say that Sir Ned will not come?" Hal grumbled. "I tell you, I heard him say so with my own ears."

"He is not coming," Cuthbert repeated sagely.

Hal huffed and rolled his eyes. "Kindly drop the prophesying for one night," he begged but he sat down all the same, as though he took it for fact. "Come, Dustin, sit on my lap," he coaxed his little dog. "I can't eat soup with you teetering on my forearm."

"Is it soup?" Gunnilde asked, for now the specter of Sir Ned was dispelled, she found she was hungry.

"Aye, root vegetable and salted bacon, if I'm not mistaken," Hal replied, for he had a keen nose to match his appetite. Moments later, a large tureen of soup was placed down upon their table, and the servant started ladling it out and passing it around.

216

"Do you take your dog everywhere with you, Payne?" Neville asked critically as Hal dropped a piece of bacon into Dustin's tiny waiting jaws.

"I do," Hal responded promptly. "What else is a dog's purpose, if not companionship?"

"Even the garderobe?" Neville asked snidely and gave a guffaw.

James leaned forward. "Need I remind you your sister-in-law is present," he chided his brother. Neville looked immediately contrite and apologized though Gunnilde had not taken the slightest offense.

"I like your hair, Gunnilde. Do they wear it that way at court now?" Cuthbert asked.

"I do," she responded airily. "Apparently they wear it this way in Kloberg presently." Or was it Vlandivar? She had forgotten.

Cuthbert nodded. "I have heard they are leaders of fashion there," he responded.

"Better at dressing than fighting," Hal agreed. "Is that not so?"

Neville agreed, pointing out the ambassador from Kloberg, who was sat nearby in a soft wide-brimmed hat. Gunnilde eyed his headwear with interest and then turned to James, trying to imagine him in such a hat.

"I think it looks very distinguished," she murmured. James glanced from her face to the hat and back again without comment.

"It would look well in a better color," Hal conceded, screwing up his eyes. "Mayhap a scarlet or a royal blue."

"I believe it is called a chaperon," Neville put in, keen to show his knowledge. "But only coxcombs such as Lord Bardulf wear them at present."

"That just means everyone else will be wearing them in three months' time," Cuthbert said. "Is that not so, Gunnilde?"

"Why do you ask Gunnilde?" Kit asked, setting down his goblet.

"Clearly, my Lady Wycliffe is a leader of fashion herself, not a follower," Cuthbert answered, and Gunnilde felt a glow of pride.

"Eh? Why do you say that? Oh, you mean those puffs of hair at her brow." Hal's puzzled expression cleared. "I did wonder about those myself." He looked toward Gunnilde quizzically.

Gunnilde found herself in no hurry to explain she had created her hairstyle from the merest hearsay. Instead, she addressed Cuthbert's comment. "Lord Bardulf is such a leader of fashion that by the time everyone has caught him up in some garment, he has wearied of it already and discarded it." Neville laughed at her words while the others listened with interest.

"I am sure he would be flattered to hear you say so, my lady," Cuthbert remarked.

Gunnilde wondered, remembering Lord Bardulf's barbed words from the other day. She still felt a little hurt by the exchange though James had told her not to take it personally. Feeling her husband's eyes upon her face, Gunnilde turned to look at him, and this time he did not look away.

"You do not like the soup?" he asked.

Gunnilde glanced down. "No, I do," she assured him, dipping her spoon back into the bowl. "I was just distracted by the talk of fashion."

"You do not wear your sleeve streamers today," he commented, keeping his voice low. Despite this, Gunnilde noticed everyone at the table was following their conversation avidly.

"Sleeve streamers? Oh, you mean my tippets."

"Yes."

"I intend to wear them on the morrow."

He nodded. "Good."

Good? Gunnilde lowered her spoon. "You—you like them?" she asked, her heart giving the strangest little skip.

"Yes."

Yes? She hid her answering smile in her soup spoon. James was not looking at her now but concentrating on his food. Was he blushing? No one was talking now, and the only sound at the table was the steady slurping of soup.

Gunnilde cleared her throat. There must be some polite conversation to instill manners in the boys. "Does it seem a very long time ago that you were a squire?" she asked her husband.

"Yes, thank the gods," he replied.

"It cannot be so long ago as all that," Hal said critically. "How old are you?"

"Five and twenty."

"Well, there you have it!"

"Ever competed in a tourney?" Kit demanded.

"I have not."

Hal and Kit promptly lost interest and commenced scraping their soup bowls. He was one of those noncombatant knights, their silence seemed to say, the dull dog. Gunnilde felt the need to defend him, but while she cast about for something to say, Cuthbert spoke.

"For all that, I'll wager you serve your forty days' service a year, Sir James," he said. "As is the duty of a knight to his sovereign."

"I'll take you up on that wager," Kit said. "I'll bet he doesn't. I'll bet he pays to skip them. My own father did that for ten years," he added scornfully. "I still say it's 'cos he got too fat to sit on a horse."

"Well? Which is it?" Hal demanded when James did not speak.

Gunnilde cleared her throat. "I don't think—"

"He does serve them as a matter of fact," Neville cut in indignantly. "Tell them, James. He rides around muddy fields in the winter and dusty ones in the summer, practicing sieges and battle strategy and the gods only know what, like a good knight of the realm and true."

James frowned. "I do, but only because I cannot afford the alternative, which is to pay the penalty."

Hal relaxed, as though his own honor had been on the line. He fixed a stern eye on Kit. "And the next time you intimate a member of my own family is too fat to serve their King, I'll dunk your head in the water trough, you just see if I don't!"

"I never said he was too fat!" Kit objected. "I've eyes in my head, haven't I? I said my own father was. He had to have a special chair made last spring after he got stuck in his old one."

220

"Well, I'll thank you not to imply things," Hal retorted, somewhat mollified.

James looked up from his empty soup bowl. "And now your health has taken an upturn, Neville, you've some days to make up in your own service," he pointed out. "I can't afford to pay for you to skip yours either."

Neville groaned. "I'm only about ten days behind. I can make them up in the spring."

"And you so newly knighted," Hal said with disapproval. "You do not even carry a dagger at your hip! Why, you ought to be out there—"

"Righting wrongs and practicing at the pell?" Neville said mockingly. "We'll see if you're still so eager in four years' time, my lad! For my part, I'll wager none of you will be!"

It was not to be expected that such an inflammatory statement would be allowed to pass. All three squires immediately gave rebuttal as they helped themselves liberally to more soup.

Gunnilde leveled an apologetic look at James. "I fear you are not used to such a lively table." She remembered how dull and ponderous it was sat at table with the Portstanleys. Likely that was more the pace and tone they should be cultivating.

Ignoring this, he looked at her empty bowl. "If you want a second helping, I will need to wrestle it from them. Let me know now before they drain it dry."

Gunnilde gave a startled laugh. "I have had ample and would rather fill my stomach with roast meat. I am impressed you would perform such a feat on my behalf though. Growing boys can be feral when it comes to food."

"Like a pack of wild dogs," he agreed after the tiniest of pauses.

"Your brother seems to fit right in with them," she observed, pleasantly surprised about the fact.

"It seems Hal is right," he said dryly. "Neville's days of squire hood are not so very far behind him."

A rousing cheer went up, interrupting them, and Gunnilde looked around to see the cause. It seemed to be the appearance of servers carrying in platters of roasted meats.

"It is very jolly tonight, is it not?" Gunnilde commented, picking up her goblet and taking a sip. "I have never known it so lively."

"Jolly is one word for it, certainly."

Again, she found her heart going out to this husband of hers. She guessed he would not have had such easy camaraderie with his fellow squires back in his own day. He was too stiff and standoffish for that.

"Will there be no music tonight?" Kit demanded, glancing up at the empty gallery.

"Aye, I would have thought there would be music at the palace at every meal," Hal agreed, looking across at James as if he should know. "Music aids with the digestion, does it not? Wycliffe is a musician," he reminded his friends.

"Why don't you play us a tune now, Wycliffe?" Kit suggested.

Gunnilde leaned hastily forward. "He is eating and besides, you forget that James is primarily a composer." The three boys looked back at her as though the distinction made little difference in their book. "In any case, the King and Queen do not dine with us tonight, do not forget. If they were here with us, I am sure there would be music."

"You only play for kings and queens, Sir James, is that it?" Cuthbert asked with a challenging lift to his eyebrows. Why was he needling James like that? Gunnilde frowned at him.

"I seldom perform these days," James replied briefly.

Neville coughed. "I doubt music would be heard above the clamor in any case."

Hal frowned. "Surely, that depends on the kind," he argued. "If it were the type with a tabor where everyone claps or stamps then it would be sure to be heard."

"When people are eating, their hands tend to be too occupied to clap in time to music," James said at the same time as his brother chimed in, "That's not at all the type of music James writes, you barbarian!"

It was a rambunctious meal, and over the next few courses, the boys would frequently draw Gunnilde's attention to some knight or other they espied across the hall and regale her with accounts of their performances at recent tournaments.

"Did you hear tell of Sir Renlow at Beres Caple?" Kit wanted to know. "Gutsiest thing I ever saw in my life. His hand clearly broken; he just had Pargeter lash the lance to his arm. Went on to beat my master with the flushest hit you ever saw. Took him clean off his saddle. Twyford could not even begrudge him the win, and you know what a surly bas—what he's like," he corrected himself with a quick glance at Gunnilde.

"He is a very able competitor," Gunnilde agreed absently.

"Who?" asked Kit, looking up. "Twyford or Renlow?"

"Well, both," she admitted, "though it always takes me a moment to realize who you mean when you say Lord Twyford. I still think of him as Sir Garman Orde." She cast a sidelong look at James. Was he bored

223

by all this tourney talk? On impulse, she reached over and covered his hand with hers.

He turned his head to look at her, but when he spoke, it was to the table at large. "I know Sir Renlow d'Avenant," he volunteered surprisingly. "We were squires together."

"You know Renlow?" they clamored eagerly.

"What was he like back then?" Hal demanded.

James frowned. "No one would have expected him to excel in a tournament setting. He was…quiet," he admitted. "Modest. Kindly to animals." He seemed to struggle for more descriptors.

"A little odd?" Cuthbert suggested slyly, though strange to say it did not sound like an insult when he said it.

James nodded. "He struggled with many aspects of the training but he never gave up."

The boys all brightened. "Sounds like Renlow," Kit commented.

"If I breathe, then I strive," Cuthbert quoted.

"Is that Renlow's family motto?" Hal asked with interest.

Cuthbert nodded. "Or at least it will be. One day."

19

The boys did not accompany them on leaving the Great Hall. Instead, they bade them a swift good night with a promise of seeing them on the morrow once their training was done.

"Do you suppose they are up to something?" Gunnilde wondered suspiciously as they made their way back. "Only that farewell was rather hurried, and Hal's manner a little too offhand for my liking."

"Who knows," James replied. When she did not look satisfied with this reply, he added, "They are likely up to some mischief but there is precious little we can do to contain them."

Gunnilde sighed. "You are in the right of it, I know, but as an older sister I cannot help but be apprehensive."

"Instead of worrying about their mischief making, why do we not set about our own?" he suggested, making her catch her breath.

"Mischief making?" She echoed, her eyes widening with delight. "Pray, what did you have in mind, husband?"

"I thought we could visit our first tavern," he said, wondering if his own attempt at a casual manner struck her as false as her brother's. He did not feel remotely casual. He wanted very much to take Gunnilde out into the town, just the two of them.

"Oh yes!" she cried, catching hold of his sleeve. "I would like it above all things! Shall we set out now?"

"We need to return first to our rooms and change into our plainest garb. We do not want to encourage thieves by looking too affluent."

Gunnilde nodded. "Will we need to take someone discreet with us?" she asked, lowering her voice.

"Not tonight. I thought we would stick to the King's Row," he said, naming one of the bigger and better populated streets which was not so far from the palace. "When we venture further afield, we may have to."

Gunnilde redressed hurriedly in a bright red dress with little adornment save for some gold-colored braid at the cuffs and hem. James changed his dark tunic for an older one of similar design. Perhaps his wife had a point about his dress being unadventurous. He would have to let her have her say when next he summoned a tailor.

"You are wearing sensible footwear, aren't you?" he asked with misgiving as they donned their cloaks.

"Yes," she agreed with a gurgle of laughter. She stuck out her foot to show a red leather ankle boot. "I would not attempt to wear my others anywhere but court."

"Have you gloves?" he asked. "It is cold out."

Gunnilde nodded and held up a pair of embroidered mittens. She started pulling them on. "Are we ready?" She was all excitement, eyes aglow.

"Ready," James agreed, proffering his arm.

"Oh, wait!" she said, whipping a glove back off. "What about Mistress Bartree's ring? Should I leave that here?"

"No, you had better wear that at all times," James replied without thinking. He would not want anyone laboring under a misapprehension. "At least until I have bought you a replacement for it."

They exited the palace by way of the East Gate, which had a huge circular tower and studded gate. James exchanged a few words with the guards there, who, hearing their plans, warned him to steer clear of a certain part of town, and they passed out into the cobbled streets without more ado.

"Which tavern are we frequenting tonight?" Gunnilde asked, squeezing his arm.

"It is one of the largest in Aphrany, the King's Arms."

"And have you been there before?"

"Not for a long time," James admitted. "It must be three or four years." He cast her a quick look. "I was never much of a tavern-goer, in truth."

"I hope Hal and the others are not let loose on the city at night." Gunnilde shivered. "The guards would surely challenge them, would they not? If they attempted to escape the palace so late of an evening."

James cast a swift look at her. It rather depended on the gate and how well manned it was. Also, how susceptible the guards might be to a bit of bribery, in his private opinion. "They would certainly be questioned if they attempted to breach one of the four main gates," he answered evasively.

"Did you know they have been placed in castle barracks for the duration of their stay this time? They are not anywhere near the courtiers' rooms."

James nodded. "I heard. I suppose the guest quarters must be oversubscribed with so many traveling in for the Winter Solstice festivities."

Gunnilde gave a murmur of agreement. "Hal was quite indignant at having to share a room with so many other boys."

"I take it he is not sharing with his particular friends."

"Not initially, but there has been some swapping around from what I can make out. They all sound a law unto themselves."

"I am sure."

"They were impressed that you were acquainted with Sir Renlow. He is a great tournament favorite these days. Do you see much of him nowadays?"

James shook his head. "He is not much at court. The last time I saw him he told me he was lately married."

"And when was that?"

"It must have been the summer before last."

"I had heard he married a rich merchant's daughter," Gunnilde observed, "but he did not bring her to Tranton Vale this year. We were all quite disappointed. I wonder what she is like."

"She seemed a modest, quiet sort of woman to me," James replied, hoping this description was sufficient. "Not remotely tall or sad," he added, making her smile.

"They sound well matched, then," she said, her tone strangely wistful. What did she mean by that? Before he could ask— "She must have made quite an impression on you," she marveled. "For you to have remembered her. Why, you scarcely remember anyone!"

James cleared his throat. "She and her sister stayed at Wycliffe Hall for a month or so before either one of their marriages," he admitted reluctantly. "Her father paid my mother a handsome sum to introduce them about the county."

Gunnilde's eyes widened. "So then, you know her sister too? The sister who married Lord Kentigern and is a very famous beauty."

"I would not say I know them, either one," James answered with a shrug. "I am slightly acquainted with both ladies only."

"And was not Lady Kentigern very lovely?"

"I do not remember."

"Really?" Gunnilde sounded incredulous. "She has raven locks and the most radiant complexion you ever beheld. A lovely singing voice too. I have been fortunate enough to meet her above twice now, for you know her husband brought her to my father's house in much style and ceremony last May."

"And what does that entail exactly?" James asked.

"Well, she wore her husband's colors most boldly and unfurled his banner in the stands to sit beneath on all three days. Instead of staying under my father's roof, Lord Kentigern brought his own pavilion to stay on the grounds. It was all emblazoned with his crest and very flaunting. Everyone was most surprised for before times, he had slunk into Payne Manor as surly as a bear with a sore head, and would glare at anyone who looked too long in his direction. Why, you were lucky to get three words out of him altogether!"

They had reached the end of the street now and turned left. "Yet this time, he was different," James guessed.

"Yes!" Gunnilde agreed. "Quite, quite different! We all agreed he had never been so agreeable. He made sure to have some conversation with his hosts, and then you know, he introduced Lady Kentigern to all and sundry and made a great show of it. She told me I could call her Aimee," Gunnilde added with shy pride. "I had hoped I would see her here at court, but apparently they never come to Aphrany, for they live chiefly in Caer Lyoness for all he is a northerner." She turned her head to look at James.

"Were you not in Caer Lyoness for the summer tournament last year? There was a very famous incident where Lord Kentigern gave the tournament crown to another. Did you never hear tell of it? Oh, my heart broke for the lovely Aimee when I heard of it!"

James shook his head. "I do not frequent the tournaments," he reminded her.

"Oh, sorry, I quite forgot that fact."

He waved this aside. "What happened?" he prompted.

"When?"

"When Lord Kentigern awarded the tournament crown to another?"

"Well, they do say it quite enraged Sir Jeffree de Crecy, and everyone was expecting a huge scene to come of it, but my father says it was all just nonsense, for when they next met it was much the same as usual."

"But why should it enrage de Crecy that Kentigern snubbed his own wife? Was he a former suitor of hers?"

"No, not at all! Sorry," Gunnilde exclaimed, "I quite forgot to say, that Kentigern bestowed the crown upon de Crecy's wife, who everyone said at the time he was holding in utter contempt for being some mousy obscure country woman, and not very beauteous at all. They say she trapped him into marriage, and he was sulking about it. Then Lord Kentigern raised Lady de Crecy higher than any lady present, shaming Sir Jeffree for hiding her away."

"Well, I know that is not true," James said, glad to have some knowledge of such affairs. "For this time last year, I saw Sir Jeffree kneel in supplication to his wife and beg her to return his love in full view of the court. He certainly was not holding her in contempt at that

230

point and she did not look remotely mouselike." Indeed, she had seemed quite a forceful personality in James's opinion.

Gunnilde came to a standstill in the middle of the road, whipping around to face him. "You were not present for that?" she gasped, mouth falling open.

"I was." And very bemused, too, by the strange turn of events.

"How could you not tell me? You must give me a firsthand account at once!" She was practically starry-eyed at the prospect. "Oh, how I envy you!" his wife breathed, clapping her gloved hands together.

James caught hold of one fast in his hand and tugged her along. "Keep moving," he recommended. "The night air is brisk, and you will get cold."

"I had heard of it, of course!" she continued happily, her words coming out in white puffs of air. "How Sir Jeffree gave public penance to his wife and begged for her forgiveness for the early days of their marriage. They do say he is most abjectly devoted to her now," she said wistfully. "Would you say that is so? I have not had the opportunity to observe them together at close quarters," she said with a hint of envy.

"That was certainly the impression I gained. He made a complete exhibition out of himself just to please her and did not seem to care at all."

They had reached the main entrance to the King's Arms by this point, and James towed Gunnilde in through the entrance.

20

Gunnilde sat in the corner James had ensconced her in and gazed about her with interest. The tavern was indeed large, and the central chamber was a cavernous one of good size and proportion. The dark wood interior made it seem cozier, strewn about as it was with rough-hewn tables and chairs.

It was not well lit, though the side wall was illuminated by a huge roaring fireplace, against which three brightly dressed, though somewhat raggedy minstrels strummed their instruments and plied their trade.

The current tune was a rollicking one, the song telling of three travelers with vastly differing philosophies in life, banded together on some journey or other. They were a spoiled lordling, a crabby old scholar, and a humble miller's son.

By the time James returned with a flagon of ale and two tankards, the travelers had reached a riverbank and were being quizzed by a hermit to ascertain their purity of heart. James plunked himself down opposite Gunnilde.

She leaned forward to accept her brimming cup with thanks. "Come and sit over here beside me," she urged, patting the chair next to her own. "You will have no view of the performers from that vantage point."

James frowned but rose to his feet and rounded the small table to sit down next to her. Feeling his eyes on her, she turned her head and gave him a quick, enthusiastic overview of the story. "You will like this one," she said excitedly. "For there is not a fair heroine nor a faithless lover in sight."

He leaned in. "Are you warm enough?" he asked, possibly noting that she had not yet removed her gloves or cloak. "Should we move closer to the fire?"

"Oh no, this will do me very well," she assured him, stripping off her mittens and catching hold of his free hand. She lifted it over her head so that his arm was about her. "See? Perfectly warm now," she said, shuffling her chair closer to his and resting her hand on his knee.

She did not look at his face, for she knew it always took James a moment to adjust to anything new. She heard him clear his throat and then felt him relax at her side. A burst of laughter rang out, and Gunnilde dragged her attention back to the ballad.

The miller's son had said something foolish again, but she had no doubt that he would end up the victor of the tale, for she knew the convention well. As such, Gunnilde settled in to enjoy the saga to the utmost.

The refrain was a rousing one, and by the close of the ballad, a good deal of the patrons were singing along. "Oh, we'll travel o'er hill and dale, and will not pause to rest, no! We will not pause to rest!"

Gunnilde was merrily humming along with the rest when the minstrels came to the close of their song and the pipe player snatched off his long-tailed cap to whip around the crowd in a quest for donations. James tipped the musician, who bowed and hurried away to rattle his hat at the far side of the room.

"What did you think?" Gunnilde asked, turning to James.

"Very entertaining," he said promptly. "Though I felt the scholar's fate was rather cruel."

"True," Gunnilde agreed. "But mayhap after he tumbled down that ditch and broke his pate, he reflected on how he could be a little kinder to hapless beggars who beseech him for a crust of bread."

He gave a grudging smile. "Maybe."

"You feel no sympathy for the lord's son?" she asked. "Who wound up penniless, bare-arsed, and covered in mud?"

"He deserved it and should not have bandied with that weaver's wife."

"True," Gunnilde reflected. "Though I fear she gulled him and was in on the scheme to rob him."

"I'm sure his rich father came to his rescue eventually," James said, shifting his hand over her back. For a moment she thought he was going to remove it, but instead he just seemed to be giving her lower back a quick rub.

"In any event, you must own there was a rough sort of justice meted out to all the characters. Was not that one of your complaints about ballads?"

"It was," he agreed, then appeared to consider. "Yes, you are right. The miller's son was the least offending of the three, I suppose, though he, too, was something of a knave when it suited him."

Gunnilde nodded and took a swig of ale. "Could you play all of their instruments?" she asked, glancing over at the musicians.

James nodded. "Once I had accustomed myself to them."

"I'm not musical at all." Gunnilde grimaced. "I cannot even hold a tune." He did not seem particularly bothered by this confession. "I'm a very creditable dancer though."

"Are your feet cold?" he asked in an abrupt change of subject.

"Just my toes," she admitted for she could not really feel them anymore.

"What color stockings are you wearing?"

"Um. Bright blue," she answered after a moment's contemplation. Why did he ask?

He stood up and returned to his original chair opposite her own. "Slip your foot out of your boot," he said, "and slide it under the table. I'll warm it up for you."

"What?" Gunnilde was taken aback. "Take my foot out? In company?" She glanced about them nervously.

"It is not polite company," he pointed out. "Besides, no one would blink an eye, even if you were to put your foot in my lap in full view. We will not be so indiscreet as that," he assured her. Put her foot in his lap? Gunnilde was faintly scandalized. He patted his thigh. "Set your foot right here."

Gunnilde glanced at James's ale cup. Maybe it was stronger than his usual fare, but in truth he had scarcely touched it. Feeling the tips of her ears turn hot, Gunnilde scooted her chair closer to the table and then slipped her foot out of one red leather boot and extended her leg under the surface of the table.

She exclaimed seconds later when James's warm hand closed about her toes, guiding her heel to rest against his leg. He smiled at her and Gunnilde had no notion why she felt so suddenly breathless. He cupped his hands carefully about her toes, until they grew warmer by gradual degrees. Not as warm as her cheeks though, which she thought must now be poppy red.

In the flickering firelight he looked different somehow. Maybe it was the fault of the purple bruised eye which gave him a disreputable edge, but for whatever reason, Gunnilde could not stop gazing at him. She felt as though her eyes were inexorably drawn to him, despite their surroundings.

He was wildly handsome, of course, but he had always been annoyingly handsome, so it was not that. Whatever it was, it made her feel like she could scarcely focus on anything or anyone else present.

The musicians soon appeared again, having downed some refreshment and counted their pennies. They reintroduced themselves for any newcomers and asked if there were any particular requests for them.

A few well-known songs were shouted out by the crowd, and Gunnilde shot an anxious look at James. However, instead of looking irritable or even resigned, he seemed wholly absorbed in stroking her toes as the minstrels started piping out a well-known tune called "Fair Janet to the Bothy Came."

"At least it's a Janet," she said loudly, so he would hear her above the din. "Not a Margaret."

"There are hundreds of Janets," he replied dryly. "Probably more than there are Margarets." He stroked his thumbs firmly over the arch of her foot and cradled her heel. It was a good thing she was not ticklish. Still, she felt unaccustomedly skittish, almost nervous around him all of a sudden. How absurd!

"Why are they always so fair, that's what has always bothered me. Why do none of them have crooked teeth or an overlarge nose?" Gunnilde coughed to cover her quavery voice. It was only James. Why did her voice sound so strained? "Or do you suppose that is mere convention," she forced herself to continue. At least her voice sounded steadier. "Like all queens are described as fair and all kings good?"

"Very likely," James agreed. "Are you ready to swap feet?" Gunnilde reclaimed her foot and slipped it back into her boot, wriggling her toes. They did feel a lot less like chips of ice.

"Give me the other," he prompted. Briefly, she contemplated telling him he should not act in such a fashion in a public inn. It was highly improper. The crazy idea crossed her mind that he might be toying with her. She caught her breath. The idea was, well, she did not know what it was precisely.

But no, he would not. This was James after all. Awkward, somewhat endearing James. She was being silly, she told herself, and stuck out her foot. He caught a firm hold of it in his grasp, almost making her whimper. Pull yourself together, Gunnilde!

"You have nice ankles," he said astonishingly. Then he muttered something she did not quite catch. It sounded rather like "Shapely, like the rest of you," but she knew that could not be right.

She cleared her throat. "You are supposed to be warming my toes, not fondling my ankles," she informed him with dignity.

"I can do both."

Gunnilde shot a suspicious look at him. It occurred to her that it might be his fault she was reacting so oddly. Was he teasing her? Maybe that was why she was feeling so suddenly shy around him. Maybe she should tell him sternly to stop trifling with her.

However, James did not look remotely playful or flirtatious. He looked entirely matter-of-fact. "I like these stockings too," he continued thoughtfully, "though not as much as your crimson ones."

"My presentation stockings?" Gunnilde asked, forcing herself to speak sensibly. "The ones that cost my father fifteen shillings and scandalized you so much?" He nodded. "We could get you a pair?" she suggested, testing him.

"I'd rather get you some more." Well, thought Gunnilde. There went her notion that he was going to prove a frugal husband. "Should I send for a tailor to attend us at the palace?" he suggested, making her heart leap. "After all, we will likely need something new for your banquet."

Forcing down her instinctive excitement, she said, "Our banquet, and don't you mean a hosier?"

"That, too, but you wanted more tippets, do not forget."

"Perhaps we ought to wait until my father sends my dowry," Gunnilde replied sensibly, biting her lip.

He shrugged. "I will take it out of Neville's allowance," he answered, straight-faced, but she was pretty sure he was joking.

She leaned forward, hesitating. "James, do people sometimes find it hard to tell if you are teasing?" she asked. He looked blank, as though no one had ever commented on such a thing before. "Not me," she clarified quickly, "I can tell. I was just wondering about…others."

"I don't think I tease anyone else," he answered simply, then dropped his gaze back down to her foot.

Gunnilde opened her mouth to argue this could not possibly be true, when she found she believed him. She tipped her head to one side and settled back in her seat to watch him. The famous James Wycliffe was sat in a common inn, rubbing his wife's stockinged feet. Anyone who did not know him would doubtless think it a loving gesture that spoke of great familiarity.

What did she think of it? She was not so sure, but she certainly could not imagine him performing the office for anyone else. Did that signify anything? "Have you ever—?" She broke off.

"What did you say?" he asked, looking across at her. A rowdy discussion behind them had spilled over into heated words. He glanced in that direction before releasing her foot and rounding the table to sit back down beside her.

"Sometimes fights break out which you won't see in a private parlor," he said apologetically as she replaced her boot. "If you start to feel uncomfortable let me know and we can move on from here. There are three more taverns on this street."

"I feel entirely safe with you," Gunnilde replied truthfully. "But if you have had your fill of these minstrels then mayhap we should move on to the next establishment."

James nodded, getting to his feet and reaching down for her. He pulled her cloak tight about her and lifted her hood, fastening it under her chin. "Put on your mittens."

"Anything else?" Gunnilde asked. He was definitely acting differently tonight. She just could not quite put her finger on how.

"Yes. Stay close to me."

21

Gunnilde woke the next morning with a somewhat foggy head and only fuzzy recollections of tumbling into bed the night before. She had drunk too much mead at that last tavern, partly because the ale there was bitter, and partly to cover her nervousness.

Recalling her strange skittishness with James the night before, she almost groaned aloud. She hoped to goodness he had not noticed! James had barely wet his lips all night, she remembered, and suspected it was because he was the one responsible for their safety.

He had been surprisingly protective. Mayhap that was what had thrown her so much. It was at this point that she realized she had one leg draped over James's and an arm slung proprietorially about his waist. Oh gods!

Glancing up, she found his eyes closed and breathed out a sigh of relief. James was flat on his back and clearly fast asleep. When she tried to withdraw her arm, however, his lips moved in a muttered protest.

"What did you say?" she whispered.

"I said, don't move. I am comfortable as we are," he murmured huskily.

"Oh." Gunnilde squinted at the window, wondering about the time. "It must soon be time for Bennett to appear," she observed. That foolishly quavery quality was back to her voice again. She sounded like such a goose!

"He has already been." His eyes remained determinedly closed. "Go back to sleep. Your head must be sore."

"It isn't sore," Gunnilde said, cautiously raising it from the pillow bearer. "It merely feels a little heavy. I think that mead was rather strong in the King's Head."

"Yes," he agreed. "I think it was."

"Did you, er, enjoy yourself last night?" Gunnilde asked with some trepidation. She wished this husband of hers was not so hard to read. Had he found her trying company? Would he admit to such a thing, even if he had?

"Yes."

"Thank you for taking care of me last night," she said in a small voice. "I hope it was not too onerous a task."

His eyes sprang open. "Of course it was not." His voice was a little rougher in the morning. A little deeper. "It is my right. My responsibility, I mean." His eyelids drifted back down.

"But it meant you could not simply enjoy yourself as I did," she pointed out.

He turned his head, though his eyes remained closed. "What gave you the impression I did not enjoy myself?" he asked, frowning.

She hesitated. "You did not tap your foot or sing along."

"No," he agreed. "Yet I enjoyed myself all the same."

"Because of the entertainment?" Mayhap he had preferred the musicians they had seen later in the evening, she pondered, though he had not seemed particularly taken with any of them at the time.

"Because of"—his eyes opened a crack—"the company."

"Oh." Gunnilde's heart beat a little faster. "I think you just liked playing with my feet," she joked.

"I did like that," he admitted without a trace of shame. "I like…touching you."

Gunnilde drew back a little. "Well! You certainly speak much more frankly when your eyes are closed," she observed with an awkward laugh.

"Do I?" A smile crooked his lips. "Maybe I should do it more often."

It must be the aftereffects of the mead that made her feel so fluttery, she told herself firmly. That was all it was. The dry mouth and racing pulse must also be down to that same thing. "I wonder why you are so sleepy this morn?" she said in an unnaturally high voice. Ugh.

"Mayhap because I did not get much sleep."

"Why not?" He did not answer. "Because of me?" she guessed with dismay. She sat up as a horrible thought occurred. Oh gods, she had not been clinging to him in the night, had she? Stroking his chest and pawing him. Her face flamed. "I hope I was not too restless," she said weakly.

"You did nothing," he reassured her with a yawn. "Merely rolled over and fell into a deep slumber."

Gunnilde breathed out. Well, that was a relief. For one horrible moment she had feared she might have horribly embarrassed them both by telling him how much she liked him.

Oh. So that was it. That was why she had been behaving so foolishly. She liked him. She really liked him. She…

"You are not going to lie back down, are you?" he grumbled, struggling into a seated position beside her. He hugged his knees and turned his face to look at her, his auburn locks falling forward over his brow. "Gunnilde?"

Oh dear, thought Gunnilde, her head spinning. This was not right. This could never be right. She was not supposed to fall in love with James Wycliffe. He was not even the type of man she admired! They were to have a sensible court marriage. How in the world could this have happened?

She was still reeling from the realization an hour and a half later as she stood in the Queen's presence chamber. She had received small, fleeting smiles from Penelope Culmington and Emma Thackeray but without Estrilda present they did not quite have the nerve to separate from the herd of attendants and approach her.

Gunnilde scarcely noticed, though she vaguely wondered where Estrilda might be this morn. She was too busy dwelling on this new unexpected problem, her falling in love with her own husband. How could she have been so stupidly provincial? Court marriages did not operate along those lines. Court marriages—

Someone halted in front of her. Someone dressed magnificently in a scarlet tunic with very wide sleeves, decorated with gold medallions. Gunnilde blinked for 'twas none other than Viscount Bardulf.

"Jane tells me I must apologize to you, for my unforgiveable rudeness," he announced without ceremony.

Gunnilde straightened up. "You were rude," she agreed, flushing slightly. He did not argue, merely inclined his head and listened with apparent interest. Thus encouraged, Gunnilde gave vent to her feelings. "That implication you made about my character was most impolite and quite unfounded, I must tell you!"

243

He nodded. "Yes, I know," he agreed with a sigh. "Truthfully, I am a little disappointed you are not the scheming minx I initially took you for, but I am prepared to forgive you for that. Magnanimous of me, I'm sure you'll agree."

"Disappointed? That I am not a scheming minx?" Gunnilde repeated, feeling perplexed.

He nodded. "I rather liked the idea of the worthy Wycliffe trapped by the machinations of a cunning woman."

"Why is it you dislike him so much?" she asked forthrightly. "I will own I have my own suspicions, but I would like to hear you account for it."

He regarded her through half-closed lids. "I'll wager your suspicions are neither inaccurate nor flattering to my character."

Emboldened, she stuck out her chin. "You admit then that it is merely a matter of personal prejudice?"

"Oh, quite freely," he replied at once. "His handsomeness offends me when he puts in so very little effort." Gunnilde breathed out in astonishment that he could be so frank about his pettiness and so unashamed. "His worthiness is also tiresome," he added as an afterthought. "Though I could likely forgive him that if he had a scattering of undesirable traits. If he was stupid for instance, or clumsy, but on top of everything he must be wretchedly talented and clever."

"Oh, but he does—!" Gunnilde started to argue before she caught herself.

"Really?" His eyes gleamed. "The paragon has faults? Other than being a consummate dullard, of course."

"He is not a dullard," Gunnilde contradicted him stoutly, "and of course he has faults, though I would never betray them as a fond spouse."

"Are you one?" he asked in apparent surprise. "A fond spouse, I mean."

"Of course I am!" Gunnilde felt herself color hotly and decided to cover her embarrassment with a show of indignation. "You think because you do not like him that he is incapable of winning anyone's affection? You think very highly of your own opinion, do you not, Lord Bardulf?"

"I do," he agreed affably. "I believe everyone should have a high opinion of themselves. It is the only way to live."

"Even stupid or clumsy people?" she asked pointedly.

"But certainly, for assuredly no one else ever will."

Gunnilde pressed her lips together, feeling unaccountably disillusioned. "Well," she said flatly. "I suppose nothing remains but to thank you for your apology."

He frowned. "Is it possible you think I consider you stupid or clumsy? For I assure you I do not." She gave a faint gasp at this, turning to look at him. He smiled at her, and she turned back to face the dais where the Queen sat with his wife, the Lady Bardulf, while Magnatrude Bartree hovered behind them. "It is the only explanation for your being so offended," he added.

"What about people with overlarge teeth or imperfect figures, do you imagine them contemptible also?" she persisted, a nasty suspicion in her head.

"Certainly not. Why should I?" She shook her head, unwilling to elaborate on the subject. "I know a good many people with unfortunate looks and I do not hold that against them. After all, no one can help a regrettable physiognomy."

"You lay so much emphasis on beauty that I do not know whether to believe you."

"In my own appearance, you mean? While it is true, I hold myself to the highest standards, I do not expect others to achieve my own dizzy heights. It would be unrealistic."

"James reaches them though, does he not?" A look of annoyance flashed over his face, and Gunnilde felt embarrassingly pleased with herself. "Without even trying," she added calmly.

"Now that, Lady Wycliffe, was just plain cruel."

"Yes," she admitted. "You were annoying me."

A smile lit up his face. "Come, let us be friends," he said suddenly, taking her quite by surprise.

"Friends?" she repeated in startled accents.

"Yes, for I have decided I like you, and really I think it would be mutually beneficial."

"How so?" Any budding pleasure she had felt disappeared as a sudden suspicion crossed her mind. "Oh, you just mean because it would irritate James."

"That is not what I meant, though I admit that would not undesirable. Would he really be so irritated by our budding friendship?"

She considered this. "I'm not sure but probably not. In truth, he does not really understand why you dislike him so much. When he does think of it, he is mostly just bewildered by it."

"Of course he is," he sighed.

246

"When I told him my suspicions, he dismissed them out of hand, saying men do not think like that."

Bardulf laughed. "Such a pretty innocent," he said, shaking his head. "I do think it is a good thing he has a clever wife, for his sake."

Gunnilde felt a rush of pleasure that he should think her clever. "If we were to be friends, what would such a friendship entail?" she asked cautiously.

"Seeking one another out in a crowded room," he answered at once. "Talking of our wider acquaintance in a wholly abandoned manner and in the perfect understanding that we may lower our guards around each other without repercussion. Making it known far and wide that we hold one another in the highest esteem."

Gunnilde's eyes widened. "Really?" Try as she might, she could see no downside to such an arrangement; indeed, it would likely serve her extremely well if she could count on Viscount Bardulf's friendship, for he was both popular and influential. She glanced about the room and found almost every single lady-in-waiting had their eyes trained upon them. They either looked envious or wildly curious. "In that case, my lord, I accept."

"Good," he said simply. "And now, quickly, for I need to be somewhere else, tell me as a friend. Is Wycliffe really so negligent of his appearance as I suspect or is he simply a shockingly bad dresser?"

"He spends no time on it. He does not even possess a looking glass," she confided.

He looked appalled. "But this is even worse than I suspected," he said hoarsely. "How does he arrange his hair?"

"At most, he drags a comb through it," she answered.

He closed his eyes as though pained. "I suspected as much but still it rankles." Gunnilde eyed him sympathetically. "I once tried to start a rumor that he had scrawny calves," he admitted, "but even Jane would not support me in it."

Gunnilde clicked her tongue. James's calves, much like the rest of him, were perfect. "It is too bad," she said in a conciliatory tone, "but we must simply accept that some people are…"

"Beyond all hope?"

"Naturally flawless in their beauty," she corrected him firmly.

"Mmmm. I will have to console myself with his character defects, I suppose. You can't confide in me some undesirable habits that none know of?" he asked hopefully. "Such as the biting of his toenails or the picking of his ears. I promise I will not divulge them to anyone. It will be for my own personal satisfaction only."

"No," Gunnilde responded firmly. "He is not disgusting in any way."

"Next you will be telling me he gives alms freely and is a friend to injured animals."

"Well—" Gunnilde started but Viscount Bardulf held up one elegant hand.

"Please, no more. I cannot bear it. And now I must hasten away and tell Jane of our budding friendship, so that she will forgive and reward me accordingly. Really, she has been holding me at arm's length these past few days and it has been very hard to bear."

"Because you had offended me?" Gunnilde was startled.

"Yes, quite frankly. There is something very terrible about incurring my sweet dove's disappointment." He winced. "Somehow, you know, it is far, far worse than her wrath."

These words dismissed any fears she might have had that Lady Jane might be displeased before they had even formed. It also answered her unspoken question of how their friendship would be mutually beneficial in any way, for Gunnilde knew her own social consequence to be far below that of Viscount Bardulf. He had befriended her purely to appease his wife. She found she could live with that.

22

James lowered the sheaf of papers he had been holding. "You and Viscount Bardulf have decided to be friends?" he repeated, frowning. "Why?"

"He said it would be mutually beneficial," Gunnilde explained. "He said we could gossip with one another with perfect impunity and count on each other for high praise before others."

While James pondered this, she added, "After he spoke to me, Osanna Spencer and Patience Stanhope both condescended to head my way and make polite conversation for a while. They were really very nice and complimented me on my tippets."

"How nice of them," James said sarcastically. He was not sure how he felt about Viscount Bardulf consorting with his wife. Bardulf liked clothes and shoes and making an exhibition of himself. What if Gunnilde found she liked the flamboyant viscount better than she did her own husband? The thought was a disquieting one.

Gunnilde drew her toe across the floorboard. She was wearing her flimsy court shoes and through the cutouts he could see her stockings today were of brightest yellow. "Do you have any objection to my being friends with Lord Bardulf?" she asked. "If you do not want me to, then I will, of course, decline the offer."

James huffed out a breath. "There is no need," he said shortly. "I have not the smallest objection, why should I?" His query came out more belligerently than he had intended, but Gunnilde did not seem to notice, for she relaxed and sent him a grateful smile. Perhaps it was not an outright lie. He did want to please her after all.

It should not be so difficult to earn a wife's approbation, James reflected. Though, perhaps others found such things easier than he seemed to. "I suppose you can now invite him and Lady Bardulf to your banquet," he ventured.

Gunnilde gasped, looking up with shining eyes. "Of course! What a good idea!" She beamed at him. "Oh, well done, James!" Stupid to bask in such praise, but he could not seem to help himself. "Wait, I must start a list," she said, reaching for ink and quill.

"Perhaps not right now," he reasoned. "We said we would meet your brother and his friends in the Great Hall for supper."

"Oh, is it time to go down already?" They both walked toward the door and awkwardly halted before it. James made a grab for the latch and held it open for her. "Thank you," she quavered. Outside in the corridor, she looked rather flustered taking his arm. Why was she so on edge? Usually, she was the one who made these small gestures easy while he was the one who hesitated and turned awkward.

"Did you spend much time with Her Majesty today?" he enquired, as they started walking.

"Oh, er, yes. She was very kind and apologized for overlooking me for the past couple of days. She has not been feeling quite herself, she said, and that she has been prioritizing the company of her married ladies of late. So, it was through no fault of my own that I have been excluded."

"You are also a married lady," he pointed out, unable to stop himself.

"Oh yes, but so newly that she perhaps does not think that I count."

He frowned. "I wonder that Mistress Bartree has not also been left out in the cold, in that case."

251

"Well, I would not be surprised if she has been," Gunnilde replied. "She has been attached to the Queen's side at all times, but I fancy she has been rather ignored. She has looked bleaker than ever these past few days."

"Hmmm."

"What?" Gunnilde asked, looking up at him with flattering attention. "What are you thinking of, James?"

"It's just…did not Neville say the Queen was well-known to favor her unwed ladies? I wonder what has changed of late that she is now seeking out the married ones among their number?"

She nodded slowly. "To be sure, it is something of a puzzle," she agreed. "In any case, she said things will be back to normal soon and that I could come and help her dress on the morrow, which is a high privilege indeed."

Something about her manner seemed a little off, James thought. Surely, she should be aglow with excitement at this new development? Yet her smile looked forced and her manner strangely offhand in the retelling.

She must merely be pretending to be unaffected, he decided. Her jitteriness this eve was probably a betrayal of her true feelings. Deep down, she was nervous about further advancement and assuming new duties to the Queen. It was the only explanation that made sense. How to give her husbandly comfort, that was the question.

Clearing his throat, he reached across to pat the hand resting on his arm. Gunnilde's gaze flew to meet his own. "Do not worry," he said, hoping he sounded like he knew what he was talking about. "Her Majesty is sure to be pleased with your attentions," he said, wishing he sounded smoother in his assurances.

"Oh…Her Majesty," she said in a lackluster manner, as though she was not thinking of her at all. Who else's good graces would she be wanting to get into? James wondered uneasily.

They were approaching the Great Hall now, and James was surreptitiously observing her from the corner of his eye when someone crossed the corridor to stand directly in front of them. Someone large and bulky. They came up short, and James eyed the newcomer with disfavor. "Sir—" he started when Gunnilde gave a ragged gasp.

The tall, broad newcomer bowed, his expression very grave. "Lady Gunnilde," he addressed her, quite improperly, his voice deep and his eyes riveted to her face. Gunnilde's fingers on James's arm instantly transformed into claws as she dug them into his sleeve.

"Your name, sir?" James demanded when neither spoke, though he had already formed a suspicion as to the newcomer's identity.

"James," Gunnilde said in a strained voice. "This is Sir Ned—I mean, Sir Edward Bevan of Knollesley." She gave a feeble smile. "He is currently acting as Hal's mentor in his training. Sir Edward," she said, swallowing, "allow me to present my husband, Sir James Wycliffe."

James surveyed the knight coldly. Not that he would notice, for he gave James only the shallowest of bows. James topped this by bobbing his head in scant acknowledgment, likely the rudest greeting he had ever bestowed on anyone in his life.

"My lady," Sir Ned said raspily, two slashes of high color along his cheekbones. He raked a hand through his hair. "I wanted—that is, I hoped to have a word with you. Hal invited me to join you for supper but—"

"You must certainly join us, Sir Edward," she assured him, in a high, artificial voice. "I assure you, we will be most offended if you do not. Is that not so, James?" she asked a trifle desperately as she turned toward him in appeal.

"Of course," he answered, and Gunnilde smiled at him tremulously. Instead of releasing her grip of his arm, she now held on to it fast with both hands. Strangely, the clinging gesture soothed him somewhat, especially when he saw Bevan's gaze dwell there. "You must sit at our table and welcome."

Sir Ned's gaze flickered back to meet his and he inclined his head. "That is generous, Wycliffe, thank you."

James swept past him, escorting Gunnilde into the hall. It did not take him long to spot his brother-in-law, for Hal was holding forth to a table full of his cronies. Not only were Kit and Cuthbert sat in attendance, but also Hadrian Kellingford, Cosgrave, and the boy with the snub nose whose name he had forgotten, if he'd ever known it.

Grimly, James made his way past the other tables to join them. He would rather not have been besieged on all sides by noisy lads, but it seemed he had little choice in the matter. Then he noticed the sour expression on Sir Ned's face as he lowered himself onto a bench opposite them. He was even less happy about finding himself surrounded by squires.

James's mood brightened perceptibly, especially when the boys began accosting Bevan, and he was forced to give them his attention while James saw Gunnilde seated. Hal leaned across the table. "Where's Neville?" he asked above the din. "Thought he'd join us here tonight."

James threw a glance about the hall. "He must be dining with friends."

"Maybe the Ashdowns," suggested Kit wistfully. "I expect they lay on a pretty good supper spread. Lucky devil. He might have included us."

"You've met the Ashdowns?" James asked in surprise, thinking of the elderly sisters across the corridor.

"Aye for Neville introduced us," Cuthbert explained. "They promised to come and watch us compete in the Revels." As both sisters were in their seventies, James was a little surprised to hear this.

"Mistress Ruth said she might lay a wager on my winning the wrestling," Hal said with a failed attempt to look modest.

"Only after you invited her to feel your arm muscles," Kit interjected witheringly.

James turned to Gunnilde, who sat quietly at his side. Noticing his querying look, she said, "Did you know I have not yet met the Ashdowns." She sounded rather sad about this fact.

"I will have to introduce you," he said, realizing he had been remiss in this quarter.

She nodded, then squared her shoulders and turned to face Sir Ned. "How are you finding your visit to court, Sir Edward?" she asked loudly, in order to make herself heard above the general din.

Bevan looked up, a hunted look on his face. "Busy," he answered, casting a jaundiced eye over the boys laughing and jostling each other around him.

"You have found yourself much involved with the Squires' Revels?" James asked. "Curious, I have not seen a single knight attached to their number since they arrived." Bevan's eyebrows snapped together, and he opened his mouth on some swift rejoinder when Gunnilde forestalled him.

"Yes, I must agree, husband," she said swiftly. "They have all been running riot for the past week. Indeed, James was forced to step in and

255

break up a scuffle that broke out here the other day. It was all very shocking and no knights in sight to restore order."

Bevan had the grace to look discomforted. "I, uh, have had…some other business to attend to." He coughed. "Some trifling ailment to contend with, nothing serious, but I will own it has preoccupied me of late." James wondered that he should look so bashful about it. Mayhap it was something embarrassing that no knight would wish to own to. Like a bunion from wearing too-tight shoes.

"Is that why that witch has been visiting you in your rooms?" Cuthbert asked with interest. The boys promptly all stopped talking and turned to look at Bevan, who turned quite red.

"She has only visited me here once!" he snapped. "Besides, it's none of your damned business, Ames!" Cuthbert shrugged, having apparently taken no offence. The other boys scuffed their feet and shot surreptitious looks at each other, whispering behind their hands. Cosgrave gave a suppressed snort of laughter and almost got shoved off the bench. James affected not to notice their horseplay.

"I trust your friend's health continues to improve," Gunnilde said politely after the heavy pause. Sir Ned looked blank. "We heard that Sir James Attley broke his arm."

"Oh, Attley. I'm not so sure. I had the strangest letter from him yest'reen. I'm wondering if he might have been in the grip of a fever when he wrote it."

Cuthbert looked up with interest. "Was it about Ancel?" he asked.

Sir Ned's knife clattered on his plate. "Now, how the hells did you know that?" he demanded, looking thunderstruck.

Cuthbert shrugged. "Just a guess," he said evasively.

256

Sir Ned spluttered and James wondered what on earth Cuthbert was talking about now. The boy was incredibly cryptic at times.

"Why, what do you suspect him of now?" Kit asked.

"Oh, just his usual tricks," Cuthbert answered absently. "You know how he is."

The others, it seemed, did know how Ancel was and left the topic alone, though Sir Ned still looked annoyed and sat there with a face like thunder.

Really, the fellow brought very little to the table in James's estimation. The rest of the meal went fairly smoothly, though Hal was forced to slap Hadrian's back a good many times to dislodge something he had "swallowed down the wrong way," and Cosgrave had a lively dispute with Kit about the wearing of cross garters during a vigil. When appealed to, James professed he had always worn full armor to his but doubtless things had changed.

"You ought to try cross gartering," Kit told him loftily. "You'll never look back. The trick is to wear one above and one below the knee and then cross them. I like to wear black ones as they contrast the most with the color of your stocking."

James thought Gunnilde perked up at this discussion, and she leaned forward to take a look when Kit held up one leg to display his garter technique.

"I always get the most compliments when I wear red ones," Hal argued. "All the ladies like a red garter in my experience." Cosgrave and Hadrian scoffed at the idea of wearing red garters. "You're just too cowardly to wear 'em," Hal commented serenely. "Besides, your legs are too scrawny, Cosgrave."

"At least they're not great meaty ham bones like yours!" Hal preened himself as though receiving a compliment.

"You couldn't wear red garters to a vigil," Cuthbert put in piously. "It wouldn't be right!"

"I never said to wear 'em to a vigil!" Hal retorted. "I'm talking about wearing 'em when you're at your wooing."

James wondered if all his opinions had been so strong at that age or whether Hal and his contemporaries were just particularly fierce when it came to expressing themselves.

He glanced across at Ned Bevan, who was regarding Gunnilde with a dejected air. James guessed he wanted to unburden himself and apologize for what had happened but had no idea how to go about it. After seeing him, James was more convinced than ever that this knight was the one who had so wounded Gunnilde with his casually hurtful words.

In any case, Gunnilde was affecting not to notice his frequent glances. Instead, she applied herself to her meal and addressed the rest of her comments predominantly to James or the boys. At the close of the meal an hour or so later, James half expected Sir Ned to request some private conversation with her. In the end, he dropped his gaze after wishing them a gruff good night and slunk from the Great Hall.

"Sir Ned seemed somewhat taciturn," he commented as they made their way back to their rooms.

She looked a little surprised by his words. "That is not his reputation. Though he said he had some woes of late, did he not?" she added vaguely.

"Some health issue," James agreed, wondering if she was really as unconcerned as she seemed about Sir Ned.

"Yes." She paused. "He did not seem very bothered about his close friend's injury though, did he?" Her tone was critical.

"No doubt they are always breaking bones on the tourney circuit."

"Yes, I expect so," she murmured, but her heart clearly was not in it, which surprised him, for was she not a keen follower of the lists? When she had spoken of them the night before she had sounded so enthusiastic, she had almost swept him up in her tales. In fact, he had wondered if a piece of music could not be composed around some of them. They were certainly dramatic enough.

"Did you notice how the boys addressed most of their questions to you this evening?" Gunnilde asked. "Expecting you to adjudicate in their disagreements."

The abrupt change in subject took him aback. "I...suppose they did," James said, though in truth he thought that might be due to Sir Ned's moroseness.

"I thought it rather telling. They have certainly accepted you and Neville into their circle."

"Yes," he agreed, feeling a little baffled about this himself. They reached the door to their rooms, and he paused with his hand on the door latch. "Gunnilde," he said impulsively. "Can you tell me that story again?"

"Which story?"

"The one about the lady left stranded in the castle on the moors."

"The lady—?" She gazed back at him in surprise.

"The one whose home was falling into ruin around her."

259

It took her a few moments before the light of comprehension sprang into her eyes. "You mean, Mistress Bartree's tale!"

Had it really been about her? James had not remembered. "Yes."

"Yes, of course!" She looked gratified by his request. "It can be your after-dinner tale," she told him indulgently.

He pushed the door open. "And then you can perhaps retell me the one about the knight who spurned his wife for being too lowly."

"When did I…?"

"Only to end up being brought to his knees for love of her."

"Ohhh! You mean Jeffree de Crecy and his wife."

"Was it them?" He frowned. "Yes, I think it must have been. Their names don't really matter though. It's the substance of the tale I want."

Gunnilde clapped her hands together. "Are you going to write a ballad around them?" she gasped, eyes shining.

"No."

"Oh." Her shoulders drooped with disappointment.

"My talent does not really run to such a thing as ballads," he admitted. "In truth, I am not good with words."

"You never know, the tales might inspire you," she said hopefully.

Which was his intention, but not for ballad writing. "Perhaps," he said slowly, and Gunnilde's face flushed with pleasure.

"Wait, let me first change into something more comfortable," she said, heading toward the bedchamber. Suddenly she stopped, turning on her heel to look at him. "Or, perhaps…"

"Perhaps what?"

She flushed. "Perhaps we could simply ready ourselves for bed," she suggested. "And I could tell you your stories there."

23

Gunnilde lay on her side facing James in the dimly lit room. She had told him first the tale of Magnatrude Bartree's lonely existence in her ruined family estate. Then she had described the tournament where Lord Kentigern had ignored his own beauteous wife in the stands to bestow the tourney crown on another.

At the close, James had asked her to repeat both stories only this time omitting all names or mentions of specific places. She wondered if he would replace their names with Sweet William and Fair Janet or some other variation. Maybe Sir William, she thought, as the hero would be a knight.

She hoped she had inspired him. Only imagine if he wrote some epic ballads inspired by such events, how proud she would be. He had not spoken for several moments, and Gunnilde eyed his perfect profile admiringly. "Have you ever been painted, James?" she asked softly.

"What?" He turned his head to look at her.

"I would love a miniature," she said without thinking.

"Of me?" She nodded. "What would you do with it?" he asked, a pucker between his brows.

"I don't know. Carry it around. Look at it whenever I felt doubt that I could possibly possess such a handsome husband," she joked feebly.

"I won't let you forget," he answered. "I won't give you the chance to let me slip your mind."

Gunnilde's heart gave a leap in her breast. "Are you saying—" that you don't want to be parted with me? she thought, but did not quite have the nerve to say. "—that you won't ever send me down to Wycliffe Hall without you?" she concluded instead.

"Not if I can help it." He cast a furtive look at her beneath his lashes. "You would not like it there without me in any case, would you?"

"No, I don't expect I would," she admitted. His shoulders relaxed. Was he gratified by that admission? And why did she want to please him so much these days? Gunnilde shied away from the reason, for it was a hopeless one.

"As married courtiers I daresay we will spend the majority of our time together," she continued lightly. "I know you have to do your thirty days a year for King and country—"

"Forty," he corrected her.

"But other than that, is there any reason we should have to be apart?" She caught her breath as she waited for his reply.

"None that I know of," he answered after a few heartbeats. "Does that please you?" His eyes did not quite meet hers.

"Quite well," she replied breezily. "After all, there is no one else here presently that I like so well as you." No sooner had she said it than she felt a flutter of anxiety. She ought not to have admitted that so soon. He would no doubt think her foolish in the extreme.

"Really?" he asked.

"Hal does not count," she said quickly, "for he is family."

He opened his mouth and suddenly, Gunnilde knew she had to prevent him from telling her that she did not rank so highly in his estimations. If he said that out loud it would hurt. It would hurt a lot. "I know you don't feel the same way," she gabbled, "but with time mayhap—"

263

"I already like you better than anyone else," he corrected her. Gunnilde stared at him. "I do not…put myself out to please others or bestow my confidences lightly. However surprising it may be, it turns out I prefer your company above all others."

"S-surprising?" Gunnilde stammered as she reeled over this confession.

"Yes, for I did not intend to like you. My initial impression of you was poor."

Gunnilde's heart sank, and she swallowed painfully. "Oh," she whispered. Doubtless it was her dumpy figure and too-large teeth that were to blame.

He twisted against the cushions to face her fully. "Why do you look like that? When you know full well you felt the same way about me!"

"No, for I always thought you were beautiful," she said defensively. She wished she had never started this conversation.

"We were not speaking of looks," James said impatiently. "But if we were—"

"Yes?" Gunnilde lifted her chin.

"If we were then I would have to admit that I—I noticed your…personal charms long before anything else about you," he said, turning bright red.

She ought to take exception to his disapproval on sight but shamefully Gunnilde found she did not care about that right now. "Which personal charms?" she demanded with bated breath.

James huffed out a breath. "Gunnilde…"

"Tell me! Please," she added in appeal.

He met her eyes fleetingly. "Your…person," he admitted in strangled tones. "Before I did not know…that is, I had no idea that I was attracted to…buxom women." He closed his eyes as though mortified by such a confession. "It disturbed me at first, how strongly attracted I was to you, for I thought your character was, well…"

"Never mind my character," Gunnilde urged him, sitting up. "You were attracted to my person? From the outset?"

"To a disturbing degree," he replied in clipped tones. "I spoke of you to Neville one time, he defended you, of course." He shook his head. "I think he found me out at once."

"What did you say of me?"

"I scarcely remember. Something about your manner of dress being improper." He sent an apologetic glance her way. "Then he told me what the bishop had said about women with horned hairstyles, tempting men from the path of virtue. I told him I could well imagine you did."

"Tempt men?" Gunnilde asked in disbelief.

"Yes, for you tempted me."

Gunnilde gasped. "James," she breathed. It was the single most astonishing and flattering thing anyone had ever said about her. "Did you really say that?"

"I did. I surprised myself as much as Neville," he added. "Later, of course, I realized that you weren't just some flaunting siren—"

Gunnilde reached across to stop his lips. He peered over her fingers with surprise. "I'd quite like to sit with the idea of you thinking me a flaunting siren for a while, if you don't mind," she said.

When she let her hand fall away, James caught and held it fast, before lifting it slowly back to his lips, pressing a kiss to her fingers. Gunnilde stared at him.

"I said you weren't just a flaunting siren. I still think of you that way," he confessed. "I think of it a lot. Especially when we are here together."

"In our bedchamber?" she queried croakily.

He nodded. "Sometimes it takes me a long time before I can get to sleep, knowing you're lying next to me in the dark and feeling your warmth stealing over me. I feel like I'll never be truly cold again," he said on a shaky outward breath

Gunnilde gazed at him. "James…" she whispered, feeling quite overcome. He swallowed, and when he would not meet her eyes with his, she reached out to touch his face and turn it toward her own. He did not resist, and when their gazes met, Gunnilde was stunned by the expression in the depths of his own.

Feeling almost mesmerized, she closed the distance between them. "Kiss me, James," she uttered huskily, and their lips met in a gentle, lingering kiss which almost had Gunnilde swooning. If Arthur Conway had ever kissed her thus, she would surely have demanded he married her on the spot!

Her arms twining about James's neck, she melted against him with a blissful sigh, as they continued sipping sweetly at each other's lips. James's hands roamed over her back, clasping her to him with increasing urgency. Wanting more, Gunnilde parted her lips over his but he did not seemingly take the hint.

She would wait in vain for him to deepen the kiss, she realized. There had been the merest suggestion of tongue in their previous forays, and she was his first kiss. Screwing her courage to the sticking place, she touched the tip of her tongue to his bottom lip and teased him there. James went very still.

She was not sure whether the hammering heart she could feel was her own, or his or the both of theirs combined, for her breasts were pressed up against his chest and she could feel his every breath as though it were her own. The shocking intimacy of breathing so closely to one another's faces made her head swim.

She tried to draw back to ascertain whether he liked it or not, but his hand slid into her hair and held her in place with a firm grip. Guessing he must not hate it, she did it again, this time dragging her tongue fully across the fullness of his bottom lip. James gasped and boldly, she took the opportunity to slip her tongue inside his mouth to seek out his own.

James went wild. The next thing Gunnilde knew she was lying flat on her back, and he was fully atop her, their tongues tangling along with their limbs. She was acutely aware of his muscled thighs straining against hers, along with something else which pressed into her belly and thighs with increasing brazenness.

"Gunnilde," he gasped raggedly against her mouth, his eyes glazed, one hand still gripping her hair tight. He threw his head back to drag some air into his lungs. Gunnilde caressed his shoulders while he caught his breath; they were such nice shoulders, she thought dreamily. Gods, he was the most beautiful man. She could scarcely believe he was gazing down at her with such mingled reverence and, well, lust.

Absently, she ran her hand down to rub his chest. He did not have much by way of chest hair, just a light sprinkling of coppery swirls. She petted it absently, twitching it with her fingers. He gave a stifled groan. "May I…?" He was staring at her breasts, she realized, and small wonder for her shift was so pulled about and twisted that it gave precious little by way of coverage.

267

Impulsively she flung her arms above her head. "Help me to take this off," she murmured. Nothing loath, James seized hold of the filmy fabric and dragged it up and over her head, leaving her entirely naked beneath him. "You can touch me if you like," she offered a trifle shyly when he remained where he was staring down at her.

"If I like?" he repeated hoarsely. His breathing was very labored.

Gunnilde glanced down at her breasts. "You want to touch me here?" she suggested, remembering his words about "buxom women." He favored them apparently. She was still reeling from that confession, but it gave her confidence.

She smiled at him reassuringly, and he trailed one hand down her neck, down to her breasts, so slowly and carefully that Gunnilde found she was holding her breath. His gaze remained on her face until he reached the swell of her breasts and then transferred to her full bosom.

"Gods," he groaned, kneading first on one breast and then the other. "I knew they were bountiful but this…this is almost too much. They're so soft."

"Too much?" Gunnilde faltered. Was he saying they were too big?

"I doubt I could even fit them in my hands," he whispered. "Let me try."

Gunnilde squinted up at him. To her surprise, she found both breasts cupped firmly in his hands and squeezed with somewhat less reverence than she had expected. He groaned again. "I can scarcely contain them," he whispered. "They're spilling over." She regarded him with bemusement, but he was wholly caught up in his endeavor. "Let me try that again," he said thickly, adjusting his grasp.

This time his hands caught her nipples between his fingers, giving them a light pinch as he squeezed. Oh! To her surprise Gunnilde felt a

268

corresponding pinch between her legs. She moved against him, restlessly rubbing her body against his.

"James," she gasped.

"Hmmm?"

Too shy to put it into words, she reached up to catch his fingers there, pressing them closer together so they repeated the pinch. She gave a soft moan and bit her lip.

Again, he went very still. "You like that?" he asked. "Like this?" Experimentally he deliberately squeezed a rosy nipple between finger and thumb.

"Oh!" Gunnilde exclaimed, arching her back. James hissed his breath through his teeth as their bodies shifted and he slid between her hips. Gunnilde's heart thudded against her breast. At least, she thought it was her heart. It could have been his, so closely were their bodies aligned.

She drew her legs up to hold him more firmly in place where she wanted his weight. Where she wanted him. "James," she said tentatively. "Would you like to—to—"

"I'd like to kiss your breasts," he interrupted her throatily. "May I?"

"Oh." She had not anticipated this request. "Of course, if you like." She opened her mouth to reassure him further, but he had already lowered his head, and was greedily engulfing one nipple, making her gasp.

This was not really a kiss, she thought, wide-eyed, as he licked and sucked her there with wanton abandon. Or if it was a kiss, then it was not the innocent kind she had anticipated from him. This one made her squirm and wriggle in his grasp. James groaned around his mouthful, sending a reverberating sensation through her core.

Gunnilde caught hold of the hand resting beneath her breast and dragged it down her belly. As she ran his hand over the hair between her legs, he released her breast and looked down, panting hard.

"Touch me here," she blurted.

His eyes flashed. "How? Show me."

She slid two fingers over his own, guiding them into her cleft. Finding herself so wet already, Gunnilde blushed. Was he shocked? When she dared venture a look at his face, his gaze was riveted to the place where their combined fingers disappeared between her legs. He did not look shocked so much as awestruck.

He breathed in raggedly. "This is how you touch yourself?"

She cleared her throat. "Sometimes."

After the slightest hesitation, he mimicked the same circling motion as her own. "Tell me if that is right."

"A little harder."

Once he had the pressure right, Gunnilde withdrew her own fingers, trusting him to the task's completion and giving herself over entirely to sensation.

"This feels nice?" he rasped, his gaze very intense.

She nodded her head. "Yes. Oh yes," she breathed, her eyelids drifting shut. She didn't want to shut them. The most handsome man at court was currently looming over her with his fingers working between her legs. If Gunnilde closed her eyes she would find it hard to believe such a thing was happening to her.

He thought she was a seductive siren who tempted men from the straight and righteous path with her buxom person and ungodly hair arrangements. Gunnilde's eyes flew open, and she gasped. But no, it was real. James Wycliffe's expression was one of rapt concentration. He whispered her name in a sort of awe. The wave crested and she gave a choked cry.

James's fingers stilled at once as though he knew. Slowly he lowered his head to press a reverent kiss to her brow. He murmured something she did not quite catch, though strange to say, she thought he had thanked her.

"Now you show me," she requested once she had caught her breath. "Show me how you do it, James."

24

James settled back on his haunches and gazed at her as she propped herself up on her elbows. Gods, her breasts! He needed to stop staring but, oh gods, the way they bobbed and jiggled. He wanted to hold them while they did that. He would wager it felt extraordinary.

Gunnilde's expectant gaze drew him out of his reverie. Show me how you do it, James. She meant how he pleasured himself, he realized in sudden panic. "I can't," he admitted, blowing out a shaky breath. "If you were to touch me like that right now, I would burst."

Her eyes widened. Was that too frank? Gods, even the sight of her in this moment was enough to set him over the edge. He gave his head a quick shake. "I'm way too close."

"To your pinnacle?" Gunnilde enquired, glancing down at his manhood which was spilling out of his braies in a frankly indecent manner. It looked swollen and angry, so engorged was it. James was embarrassed she should have to see him like this. His aroused state was hardly pretty, as hers was. It must be jarring and rather off-putting. Mayhap he should draw a blanket round his waist to cover himself?

"I would not mind," she said frankly. "When you say burst…?" she started to query but then catching sight of the look on his face, she bit her lip, curling her fingers into her palms as though curbing an impulse to pet him. An astonishing notion occurred to him, that Gunnilde might actually want to touch him there.

It could not be true, he told himself, feeling light-headed. She could not voluntarily want to touch him right now. To pet it. His mouth turned dry. It had to be wishful thinking on his behalf. It was the only explanation. "It's very impressive, isn't it?" she said in a hushed whisper. There could be no mistaking the direction of her gaze.

James shut his eyes for an instant to draw strength. He might have known she would be encouraging. His cock throbbed so proudly, it felt like the damn thing had its own heartbeat by this point. His head swam. "You think so?" he asked in a choked voice.

"Oh yes," she agreed admiringly. "It's ever so big and has such ruddy coloring."

Was it possible to pass out from an abundance of lust? If so, he felt perilously close to it.

"Well, if you do not wish me to touch you…then"—she gave a small cough—"perhaps you would like to…to…" She seemed to cast about for the right phrasing. "Have a try at consummating our marriage?" she suggested politely.

"If I would like to…?" he repeated numbly. Consummating our marriage seemed like such a cold way to describe what he wanted to do with her. He felt like he was burning up with desire for her from the inside out.

Seeing the question in her eyes, he swallowed down his torturous thoughts and nodded his head. "Yes," he groaned. "Gods yes, I want to. If you…?"

She nodded and lay back down. "You need to take off your braies," she reminded him as he started to awkwardly clamber back up over her.

"Oh." He froze and then struggled to get the damn things off. Gunnilde giggled at his ridiculous haste and muttered curses. Strange to say, her mirth did soothe him a little. Once divested of the plaguey things, he flung them over the edge of the bed.

"Come here, James," she said, opening her arms.

His scramble to do so was inelegant. "Sorry," he groaned as he tried to settle between her legs in a respectful fashion, something very hard to do with his inflamed appendage jutting out toward her with no manners whatsoever.

"I don't mind," she answered, half reaching for him before remembering. "Does it hurt?" she whispered.

Small wonder with all his wincing and groaning, he thought. "Not really," he said. "If there is pain of sorts, then it is merely the pain of anticipated pleasure."

"Anticipated pleasure," she repeated, nodding slowly. "I have that too."

"You do?" he croaked, meeting her gaze squarely. "Only they do say…"

"That the first time is not good for women," she finished, "but it has already been good for me. Do not worry. Come and kiss me, James."

He did so, trembling all the while. Gunnilde's hands smoothed over his back, stroking and patting him there as though to reassure him.

Breaking the kiss, he asked, "Can I touch you?" She nodded but made an exclamation of surprise when he cupped her mound. "Is this not…?"

"Yes, of course it is," she said hurriedly.

He hesitated. "Only you looked a little startled."

"It's just…I imagined you would touch me somewhere else." She gave an apologetic laugh in answer to his look of query. "You do seem quite, well, fond of my breasts."

"Yes," he admitted on a shaky breath, "I am, but I need to, er, well…introduce my worm to your rose," he said, cringing inwardly at the metaphor. It hadn't sounded wonderful when Shadbolt had used it. It sounded even worse now.

Fortunately, Gunnilde was more than equal to the situation. She set about adjusting her position beneath him, sticking out her knee to make things easier for him. "Right, well…" She glanced down her body to where his manhood lay pressing into her belly. James saw just a trace of trepidation in her eyes before she hid it from him. "I am ready."

James hesitated. "May I…?"

"Please do," she answered politely. He slipped two fingers into her pretty quim. She was still deliciously wet and slippery, and he needed to be sure he knew what the hells he was doing. With the utmost care he traced her folds, making her out. "Tell me to stop if you need me to," he said gruffly, then sank his fingers slowly, so slowly into her tight, deep warmth.

Oh my gods. He bit back a groan. Gunnilde's eyes grew wide again, and James stared into their cornflower-blue depths. Her faint gasp recalled him to the situation at hand. "Is this…?"

"It's not uncomfortable," she assured him quickly.

"Good." His voice was gruff. "This is going to feel so good for me, Gunnilde. I only wish…"

"I'm glad," she interrupted him warmly. "I want you to feel good, James. You deserve to." She smiled at him, and James felt dazed. She was so fucking pretty and kind and, well, remarkable really. It could not just be him that saw it, surely? It shone from her, like a sort of inner radiance.

He withdrew his fingers and aligned their bodies. As he started to push inside, he watched her face carefully all the while. Gunnilde's expression wavered a couple of times and she tightened her grip on his upper arm at one point with a sharply indrawn breath but otherwise showed no sign of pain. He went slowly, almost unbearably so, but soon enough found himself fully sheathed, their bodies intimately joined.

He let out a long exhale as the clamoring thoughts in his head shut down, the wheels stopped turning, and time stood still. He was not sure how long he remained like that, unwilling to move, reveling in the sheer intimacy of their connection. Gunnilde's eyelids fluttered. "James?" she whispered.

His hips surged forward, as though he had been waiting for her say-so. Gunnilde's gasp spurred him on even further, like the flick of a whip. He thrust his hips, groaning at the sensation of her all around him, gripping him so tight. Her arms about his back, her knees pressing into his sides, and her sweet, tight cunny.

He just could not get enough of her, her scent in his nostrils, her hair in his fist, her body beneath him, all of it. Lowering his face to her neck, he buried it there, luxuriating in her soft cool skin as his body burned with a driving need that overset everything he had ever known about himself, or thought he had known.

He was not cold, aloof, or unaffectionate. Most astonishing of all, he realized what his pounding heart denoted. Not just the fact he was physically exerting himself in a most unaccustomed way right now, a most unaccustomed and pleasurable way.

No, he was in love. With his own wife, no less. He lifted his head to look at her, to really look at her as his breaking point hurtled closer. Gunnilde was watching him, a look on her face that he had not seen there before. He was not sure what it denoted, only that he had put it there.

His chest burned. "Gunnilde—" he gasped but he had left it too late for speech, and without more ado, he tipped over the edge and came so hard it stole the breath from his lungs, and the vision from his eyes. Her beautiful face shimmered and swam before him and James blacked out from the sheer overwhelming pleasure of it all.

25

"Oh my gods!" Gunnilde wailed. "I thought I had killed you!" She was stood beside the bed, entirely naked, holding a pitcher in her hands. Her eyes were huge and scared. James blinked up at her in confusion.

His euphoric haze had been cruelly dispelled, though the blood was still thrumming through his veins and a feeling of well-being lingered. He shivered violently. For some reason his face and shoulders were wet. "Did you throw water on me?" he asked in confusion.

"Yes, I did!" she burst out. "That is what they do at my father's tournament when someone is knocked unconscious."

"I was not knocked unconscious," he pointed out.

"Well, you sort of were," Gunnilde replied, worrying her lip anxiously. James peered up at her, then rose onto one elbow. Gunnilde set the empty jug upon the floor and straightened back up. "Do not exert yourself, husband, I beg of you," she extorted breathily.

Instantly he felt flooded with gratification, though whether it was her calling him husband or the tone of voice she used, he was not certain, for he found he liked them both. "Come back to bed," he exhorted, sitting up and pulling back the covers. "You must be freezing."

Gunnilde scarcely seemed to hear him, her hands were fluttering about his chest. "Your—your heart… It does not feel…irregular or weak?" she asked earnestly.

It was beating like a godsdamn drum, James reflected. The blood was singing in his veins. He had never felt so alive. "I feel entirely well," he told her truthfully. "Better than I ever have." He lifted his hand to touch her hair, smoothing it back from her face. It looked rather untidy now, no doubt at least partly due to his own mishandling of it.

"No," Gunnilde said, shaking her head and worrying her lip with her teeth. "That can't be right. You fainted."

"I did not faint," he assured her, catching her arm and drawing her back into the bed beside him.

"Yes, you did, James!" she said unevenly, then burst into tears. "You—you slumped over me like a dead man and then toppled sideways in a dead faint. I could not rouse you!"

He tutted, drawing the covers up around her shoulders. "Come here. Did I scare you? I'm sorry, sweeting," he fussed over her, kissing first her brow, then down her cheek, catching her chin and turning her face toward his. She allowed his coaxing, consoling kisses but gave an exclamation when he ran his tongue along her bottom lip.

"James! You can't possibly mean to—"

"Shhhh, let me reassure you," he whispered into the shell of her ear. "I need to make you feel better." He slid his hand under the neckline of her shift to gently cup her breast. Misinterpreting his gesture, Gunnilde lifted her own hand to rest it over his heart.

"You feel how strongly it beats?" he asked, stilling at once.

She nodded and he smiled down at her. "You see? My heart is fine."

"Then why did you—?"

"It was just…too good," he admitted, shrugging his shoulders and turning rather red. "I was overcome. I won't do it again. I promise."

279

"But what if you do?"

"Then you can throw cold water on me again."

"No," Gunnilde insisted. "I need reassurance that your health is not too delicate for—"

He drew back to look at her. "For what?"

"Copulation," she said, lifting her chin. He spluttered incoherently. "I want to consult a physician, James," she said, a stubborn look on her pretty face.

"A physician?" James was horrified.

"Yes. There must be several famous ones here at the palace."

"I am not seeing a physician, Gunnilde. I'm positively bursting with health and vigor!"

"Well, maybe now you are but moments ago you gave me the fright of my life!"

"And I apologize for that," he placated her, "and assure you that I won't do so again."

Gunnilde's palm planted in the center of his chest, pushing him firmly back.

"You cannot possibly ensure any such thing, James, and you know it. Your health is far too precious to me to overlook this."

Too precious? Her words affected him strangely. Against his will, he felt his resolve weakening. "I am not seeing a physician, Gunnilde, and definitely no one here at the palace."

"In that case, how would it be if we were to consult with Sir Ned's witch instead?" she asked, clasping her hands together.

His brows snapped together. "With whom?"

"You remember, Cuthbert mentioned her at supper. Sir Ned has been consulting her about his ailment. He said she had visited Sir Ned here in his rooms."

James frowned, not caring to be associated with anyone connected with Sir Ned Bevan. "I do not want—"

"I could easily ask Cuthbert to bring her to along to us next time she visits him," she cut in eagerly. "Please, James?" She turned a look of entreaty upon him that he felt entirely powerless to withstand.

"Oh, very well," he conceded with ill grace. "If it will put your mind at rest."

"It will, thank you," she said, turning in his arms and embracing him warmly.

He closed his arms about her at once, dragging her closer. His libidinous body perked right back up at finding the object of his desire in such gratifying proximity to him once again. Gunnilde made a stifled noise of protest as he kissed her neck.

"James, you need to lie quietly now for the rest of the night," she tutted.

"I feel entirely spry now. Remarkably so."

"I am not risking it!" she said, loosening his grip on her waist. "Not until we have consulted with Sir Ned's witch."

James scowled. "Don't call her that. It makes me want nothing to do with the woman."

"I do not know her given name," she pointed out sensibly. She settled on her side, facing away from him as he crowded against her back.

"Gunnilde…"

"Good night, James," she said firmly. "Think calming thoughts, please."

She could definitely feel his hardness against her buttocks. Sliding a hand over her hip, he sighed. The evening had not ended perfectly, though it had definitely scaled those heights earlier.

He could not really complain though, not when he was free to wrap himself about Gunnilde's pleasing form in the dark under the covers.

26

"Gunnilde told us what you were about last night, Wycliffe. Why don't you tell us all about it?"

James froze and turned to look at his brother-in-law. Hal could not possibly have said what he thought he had just said.

"Aye," Kit agreed cheerfully. "Gunnilde says you've the makings of a fine ballad maker and she's every faith in you."

James relaxed. Oh that. "Where is she anyway?" he asked, glancing about the sitting room. Hal, Kit, Cuthbert, and Hadrian Kellingford were sat up to the table feasting on heaped dishes of roasted fish and toasted bread which they were slathering in butter. James's stomach rumbled. He walked over to the table and sat down on the bench next to Kit, who moved up to make him room and passed him a plate and a knife.

"Neville's taken her over to meet the Ashdowns," Cuthbert explained, swallowing a mouthful of bread. He nudged the platter of roast fish closer to James. "She was feeling left out, not having met them yet."

"Oh." James helped himself to a large piece of bread and covered it generously with butter. For the life of him, he could not understand everyone's preoccupation with the Ashdowns. Still, if anyone was to perform that office, it should have been him, not his brother.

"Gunnilde told us all about her plans for you to become a famous ballad writer," Hal reiterated. "So come on then, don't leave us in suspense. Tell us about this ballad. I'm fond of a ballad myself so I'm a pretty fair judge," he said modestly.

James paused. "Er…" Four expectant faces turned toward him. "It's true, Gunnilde would like me to take up writing ballads," he admitted, scooping up some fish. "But in truth I do not think I am suited to the writing of such things. I'm far better at writing music than words."

"A few words shouldn't trouble you!" Hal scoffed. "We can help you, can't we, lads?" Cuthbert and Hadrian made noises of agreement.

"Right willingly," said Kit, who was apparently in a good mood today. "What is your hero's name?"

James cast about him without inspiration. "He should be false rather than sweet" was the only thing that sprang to mind.

"How about…False Billiam," Kit ventured.

"False Billiam?" Hal echoed, nodding his head. "Not bad. Has a sort of ring to it. He sounds a disreputable sort. Now, who's he courting?" He rubbed his hands together. "It has to be Fair someone. Mayhap Fair Eliza."

"There's to be no courtship," James answered firmly. "Instead of a romance I was thinking it could be a tragedy. False Billiam could…have some kind of ailment." He shrugged. Yes, that was it. An ailment. Ned Bevan had an ailment, not him though. He was in perfect health.

"What kind of ailment?" Hadrian asked, looking intrigued.

"A bad one. The kind where body parts drop off," James answered with decision.

The boys all sat up with interest. "You mean, so he loses a limb in every verse?" Kit queried.

"Inspired!" Hal decided.

"Yes," Cuthbert chimed in. "You could start out with small things like a finger or a thumb and then build up to larger limbs."

"You do not think that would alter the tone of the piece?" James asked with misgiving. It sounded more comical than tragic.

"Yes, it would make it better," Hal replied firmly.

"Only consider," Cuthbert suggested, "if you start all flowery at the beginning, everyone expects it to be one way, but then in the second half it turns funny, only think how surprised everyone will be!"

"And the last body part can be his twig and berries," Kit said eagerly. "But in every verse leading up to that one, the audience has to think will be his pizzle. Like, have a rhyming part to it, that ends up being something entirely innocent. You know the trick of it, I expect."

"I really don't," James responded.

"Like have him lose his fizzle, instead of his pizzle," explained Kit.

"What the hells is a fizzle?" Hal demanded.

"I couldn't think of anything that rhymed," Kit admitted.

"Then how is Wycliffe to?" Hal asked with disgust. "He already told us he's no wordsmith!"

"Very well, then," Kit responded with dignity. "Have him lose a lock, as in a bit of his hair, then in the next line, tumpty-tumpty-tumpty off fell his cock."

The boys all groaned. "That's terrible, Montmayne," Cuthbert said, speaking for the group.

"'Tis plain to see you're no poet!" Hadrian hooted.

"I never said I was!" Kit responded hotly. "Very well, let's hear your suggestions, if you're so superior at rhyming than I!"

"Ignore him," Cuthbert said, turning back to James. "It could definitely work. And then for the next ballad, you could make it really tragic. Have False Billiam get an ulcerated leg."

"But make it really foul smelling, puss filled, and oozing," Hadrian put in enthusiastically. James lowered his piece of toast.

"That does not sound romantic at all," Hal objected. "What you should do, instead of giving him an ulcerated leg, is have False Billiam thrown from the castle ramparts, or else dashed to death under some horse's hooves. Have him die some noble death like that."

"Why could he not plunge to his death whilst also possessing a rotting leg?" James asked, propping himself up on one elbow.

Hal sent him a stern look. "Now you're not taking it seriously."

James's lips twitched. It was true, he was not taking it seriously.

"Then he could come back and haunt the Fair Eliza for playing him false," Hadrian concluded with satisfaction. "You always find ghosts in ballads."

"There is no Fair Eliza," Kit reminded him. "Did you not hear Wycliffe say so?"

"In truth, I have no intention of writing this masterpiece," James admitted before another row broke out. "I am convinced I would make a very poor job of it."

"A pity," said Hal, shaking his head. "I'm half inclined to have a stab at writing it myself."

"Please do. I make you a present of my idea."

"Really?" Hal asked eagerly. "I will say that's handsome of you, Wycliffe. If I happen to make my fortune with it, I will give you a portion."

"What about me?" Kit demanded. "At least part of the idea is mine."

"Yes, the rubbish part," Hal said dampeningly.

Before a full-scale row broke out, the door opened and Gunnilde and Neville advanced into the room. James started to stand, before realizing no one else was so polite. Gunnilde met his eyes with her own and gave him a shy smile. James felt his color rise.

"Ah, here you are, James," Neville said, brightening. "I just took Gunnilde along to meet the Ashdowns."

"Sit ye down," Hal said. "Move up, lads, Neville needs a place at table. The food arrived while you were gone. No, don't worry about m'sister, she can sit on Wycliffe's lap."

"Hal!" Gunnilde murmured in reproach, though James found he was not unwilling. Somewhat imperiously, he held his hand out to her, and she rounded the table with downcast eyes. She squeezed onto the bench beside him, not quite on his lap but certainly pressed in close, for there was not much room. James did not mind, for it gave him an excuse to pass his arm about her. Hal sloshed ale for them into two cups and pushed them across the table.

"A couple of letters arrived this morn. One of the pages delivered them," Neville announced as a curl of butter dropped from his knife and

287

onto his sleeve. "Damnation! This is a new tunic," he muttered, scooping it back up with his knife.

Hadrian guffawed. "Clumsy oaf."

The boys joined in, judiciously abusing his brother's new tunic along with his clumsiness. James ignored them, for plainly this demonstrated Neville had been accepted as one of their number.

"What did you think of the Ashdowns?" James murmured in Gunnilde's ear, wanting private speech alone with her, no matter the subject.

"They seem entirely amiable," she answered, nibbling daintily on a piece of toast. "They were very welcoming and professed themselves vastly pleased to meet me."

"Who do you suppose the letters are from?" Neville asked. "I did not recognize the seals." James frowned at him, not caring much about any letters at present.

"They might be replies to our invitations to that supper we are hosting here in the small gallery," Gunnilde volunteered a little nervously.

"Have some fish," James urged her, seeing she had selected the smallest piece of bread on the platter.

"I'm not really hungry," Gunnilde replied in a small voice.

James frowned. "Not feeling ill, are you?"

"No, of course not!"

"Not like you to turn your nose up at good plain fare," Hal chimed in. "What ails you?"

Gunnilde opened her mouth as though to deny any such thing when her eyes lit up and she dropped her hand to squeeze James's thigh in warning. "As a matter of fact, I am feeling a little peaky this morning," she said, turning to Cuthbert. "I did wonder if you might be able to send that witch of Sir Ned's my way."

27

Gunnilde opened the letters after they ate, and found they were acceptance notes to the invitations she had sent out thus far at court. The Portstanleys, the Bardulfs, and the Gilchrists had all confirmed they would attend, as had Earl Vawdrey and his countess.

James read each note she passed him with a blank look on his face. She suspected he had forgotten all about their banquet by this point. "And finally, Lady Winifred Hawes says she will be pleased to attend," Gunnilde read out, opening the last.

"Is she a lady-in-waiting?" Hal asked. "I've not heard of her."

"No, she's a very serious-minded young lady who loves books and learning," Gunnilde responded. "And tippets," she added, glancing down at her own snowy white sleeve streamers. She had been highly gratified about that.

"I had better set off," James said after casting his eye dutifully over Winifred's reply. He passed it back to Gunnilde. "Her penmanship is good, though not as neat as your own."

To her embarrassment, Gunnilde found herself blushing at this tepid compliment. "Where are you going?" she asked, setting the acceptances down in a haphazard pile.

"To Master Gregory's. I want to spend the day working in the music room."

Gunnilde bit back a wild impulse to ask if she could accompany him. Probably the last thing he wanted was her cluttering up the place while he was trying to compose. "Did you say that Master Gregory lives with his daughter?" she asked as he set a hat upon his head.

"Yes, his daughter, Justina, keeps house for him."

"And is she married?" Suddenly it was imperative that Gunnilde knew this.

"She was married to a farrier at one point," James replied, crinkling his brow. "I do not remember seeing him in a good while though, and she goes by her father's family name so…" He shrugged.

"Oh." She did not know if she was reassured by that or not.

He approached her with a slightly self-conscious air and lifted her hand, kissing her wrist and holding it for just a little longer than was strictly necessary. Gunnilde's spirits rose. Words appeared to tremble on his lips. She held her breath. At this moment Kit cleared his throat and James seemed to snap out of it, releasing her and taking his leave without more ado.

Hal swiftly volunteered to accompany Gunnilde to the Queen's rooms that morning, and though she initially suspected it was because he wished to catch the eye of some lady or other, it soon became apparent he had another motivation.

"Had a letter from our father this morning," he started portentously once they had left the courtiers' quarters behind them. He winced. "He's cutting up rough, truth be told."

"Over my marriage?" Gunnilde's heart sank though she was not entirely surprised to hear this. Father could be difficult at times.

"Yes," Hal agreed. "His nose is properly out of joint. It's mostly bluster but he's saying the gates of Payne Manor are barred against you at present." He cast her a sympathetic look. "He'll likely be over it in a couple of months, you know what he is like."

Gunnilde huffed. "You would think he would be glad of the fact I've a husband now. He certainly did precious little to bring my married state about!"

"I know," Hal agreed. "And it's not as though Wycliffe is a poor prospect. He's pretty decent, all told."

Gunnilde felt the color creeping into her cheeks. "You approve of him for a brother-in-law?" she asked in a carefully casual tone.

"Aye, I do," Hal agreed absently. "He's not who I would have chosen for you, mind, but you could have done a lot worse."

As Hal had already told her of his own candidates for the role, Gunnilde disregarded this as a valid criticism. "I myself was not initially convinced we were ideally suited, but since then, we have rubbed along quite admirably together."

Her tone sounded stifled to her own ears, for she did not want Hal to know the fresh turn her feelings had taken. He might think her fickle or simply dazzled by the male beauty of James's face and form. She cast a sidelong look at his face, but her brother did not look unduly critical of her words.

"Aye, you've both been sensible and made the best of it," he agreed readily enough.

Strangely, his words did not please her. She would have preferred a ringing endorsement of their compatibility but perhaps that was too much to hope for. "Yes," she agreed flatly.

"Conway would likely not have made you much of a husband, in truth," Hal continued consideringly. "His mother and sister have the sway of him, and you would have had a battle on your hands to rank higher with him than them. I know you and Mildred were always friends but…"

"Muriel," Gunnilde corrected him. "His sister's name was Muriel."

"But she always liked to have the upper hand of things, did she not?"

Hal was strangely perceptive at times. Muriel had indeed always been the leader and Gunnilde her follower. "It's been an age since I spent any time with her," she sighed. "Those girlhood days seem ages ago. Since her marriage she has not bothered to correspond with me at all. I invited her and Sir Christopher to my banquet, but I doubt whether they will attend. They are not much at court it seems."

"You have other friends now, in any case," Hal said dismissively. Did she? Gunnilde considered this. She wished Eden was at court. "You will invite your fellow ladies-in-waiting I expect."

"Oh, them." She could not muster much by way of enthusiasm.

"Estrilda would certainly attend," he said airily. "And perhaps Emma Thackeray."

Emma Thackeray? Gunnilde looked at him out of the corner of her eye. Was this a new favorite of his? "Oh yes? I will have to invite them, then. What say you to Mistress Stanhope?"

"A most amiable girl," he replied at once. "But I say you should ask 'em all! Why not? The more the merrier, I say."

Gunnilde gave a laugh. "I can see why you're so popular, Hal."

"That's better," he said approvingly. "Now you look like your old self. You were too quiet at table. Not really ill, are you?"

"No, I just don't feel very excited about the banquet anymore. I hope the Conways don't come," she admitted in a rush. "I don't really care about seeing them again, even if the Queen does desire it."

293

Hal looked surprised by this, but when he opened his mouth it was not to question the Queen's motivations but to ask if Sir Ned would receive an invite.

"Sir Ned?" Gunnilde prevaricated, as though she could scarcely recall him to mind.

"You did not seem terribly friendly toward him last night at supper. It was not just I that noticed it."

Gunnilde was startled. "Really? I had no idea that I might seem unfriendly!"

Hal cleared his throat, "Well…" he said feebly.

"I have been nothing but polite to Sir Ned!"

"Icily polite."

"We are not on such terms that I should be warmer," she responded coolly.

"But you're nice to everyone," Hal pointed out. "So, it looks most particular when you're so cool with him." He took a deep breath. "Is there anything that I should know about? Only, Kit thought I should ask you in case he has ever overstepped or done aught amiss."

"Nothing of the kind!" she protested, turning bright red. Unfortunately, she could see her reaction had stoked rather than quieted Hal's vague suspicions.

"Because if he has ever acted in any way untoward, then I should know about it," Hal said direly.

"It is just…I happened one time to overhear some less-than-complimentary remarks he made about me," Gunnilde confessed.

"Remarks?" Hal paused, his eye kindling. "What kind of remarks?"

Gunnilde was alarmed to see his reaction. She did not want Hal brawling with a fully grown knight! "Oh, it was naught, really," she assured him. "Merely Sir Ned felt that Eden was deliberately throwing me into his path at Vawdrey Keep and he found it a little wearing."

"Oh." Hal paused. "And was she?"

Gunnilde felt her face get hot. "Yes, perhaps," she admitted in a small voice.

"Ah." Hal relaxed. "I suppose I can hardly take exception in that case."

"No indeed," she agreed faintly, avoiding his eye.

"It's only because I am currently acting as his squire that I speak to you about this, Gunnilde," he said. "Otherwise, I would not care if you consigned the fellow to the pits of hell."

Gunnilde pondered this and saw her brother's point. "I did not mean to make things awkward for you, Hal," she said truthfully. "I will…try and be more civil to Sir Ned."

"Lord, don't do that!" Hal begged. "You're already terrifyingly civil. Instead, why don't you aim to be a little easier in his company."

Gunnilde fought down her instinctive response. "Very well, brother," she said instead.

"There's a good girl." Hal clapped her on the back. "I'll leave you now," he said, for they had reached the Queen's apartments.

295

28

No sooner had Gunnilde entered the Queen's chambers than she was accosted by Viscount Bardulf.

"Ah, Lady Wycliffe. Thank the gods. I was preparing for unmitigated boredom for the next hour. Come and sit with me."

He was dressed today in a bright green tunic trimmed with gray fur. Gunnilde especially admired his dark orange hose, and a very flashy gold chain he wore from shoulder to shoulder all set with large green stones. They surely could not be emeralds, could they? She sank down onto the cushioned bench next to him.

"Now, tell me what you have been about," he said, propping himself on one elbow. "For it is very dull here this morning. The Queen is yet to make an appearance." He shot her a sideways glance. "These days if she is not sequestered with the King in his apartments then she is shut away with The Bartree. It is too bad, really, none of her other ladies are given the opportunity to distinguish themselves. No doubt she will emerge when she is ready."

"Yes," Gunnilde agreed wistfully. "There was some mention of my being made a woman of the bedchamber when I first became one of her ladies-in-waiting, but I have not dared to try and muscle my way in there for fear Mistress Magnatrude would surely give me short shrift indeed."

"You should try," he told her promptly. "Just march in there and start folding the Queen's stockings. What, pray, could Mistress Bartree do about it?"

"March me right back out again with my earlobe pinched between finger and thumb," Gunnilde responded promptly.

He laughed. "You could be right. But really, faint heart never won fair maiden. Speaking of which, how goes your wooing? Apace I hope."

Gunnilde gave a start. "What do you mean?" To her embarrassment she felt her face flame bright red.

His eyebrows shot up. "Are you not an acknowledged champion of lovers? I quite understood you espoused the cause of the lovelorn in the palace."

"Oh." Gunnilde relaxed. For one horrible moment, she had thought he was asking if she had managed to secure her own husband's affections. "I had to give all that up when I married," she explained. "James did not think it fitting that his wife should be instrumental in such a role."

"Beneath his dignity, was it?" he asked dryly. Gunnilde shrugged. "And how is Sir James navigating married life?"

Gunnilde thought fleetingly of James passed out cold the night before and shivered. The whole thing had given her the most awful shock. "He is coping remarkably well," she said, lifting her chin.

Viscount Bardulf's eyes gleamed. "Is that so? I thought I caught a glimpse of him in a common tavern the other evening but perhaps I was mistaken. It certainly does not sound like something Sir James would partake in."

Gunnilde's eyes widened. "Did you not notice his companion?" she asked.

A smile played about his mouth. "I hope I am not so indiscreet as to speculate on her identity."

"It was me," she said bluntly, in case he had thought James had been consorting with some other woman. He laughed. "I am not remotely discreet," Gunnilde admitted. "I think that is why the Queen likes me."

He looked thoughtful. "You could be right."

Gunnilde frowned. "I wonder that you did not introduce yourself."

"I did not think you would appreciate me interrupting the two of you in that moment. You seemed very…occupied with one another." His eyes held a distinct gleam, and it occurred to Gunnilde that he might have seen James fondling her feet. She cleared her throat. "I take it that Lady Bardulf was not with you."

He shook his head. "My Jane would not care for such an establishment. She is a jewel which shines brightest in the right setting."

Gunnilde considered this. "Lady Bardulf is very lovely."

"She is," he responded at once. "She is my greatest treasure."

The soft way he said it almost took Gunnilde's breath away. "How did she win your love?" she heard herself ask before she could stop herself. "I ask for academic reasons, you understand," she added quickly. "Though I no longer dabble in affairs of the heart for others, I confess it is still an arena that interests me." Stop talking, Gunnilde, she upbraided herself.

He tipped his head to one side. "In truth, Jane stole my heart before I was even aware of its existence. It was quite disconcerting at the time. But she sustains its survival outside of my chest through a hundred daily gestures."

"Such as?" Gunnilde asked, clasping her hands together.

He gave her a considering look. "You are fond of apparel, are you not? Why don't you try getting a gown made up with some device from your husband's coat of arms," he said, surprising her greatly. "Jane surprised me once by having serpentine devices beaded into her bodice."

298

The memory seemed to carry him away for a moment and he smiled dreamily to himself before coming back down to earth. "It was most efficacious. Now, tell me, what beast does your husband's family adopt for their crest? Some domestic animal perhaps with dull plumage and an uninspired appearance."

Gunnilde eyed him sternly. "You are quite wrong, my lord, for the chivalric beast of the Wycliffes is a unicorn."

"A unicorn, no less!" he exclaimed, looking impressed. "That is certainly far more imaginative than I should have supposed. Well, henceforth, Lady Wycliffe, you must have your mittens embroidered with unicorns, your slippers emblazoned with unicorns, your buttons engraved with unicorns, your..." He paused as though struck by some notion. "I have it! You must affect a unicorn's horn as part of your hair arrangement! Only think how striking it would be! And you are particularly known for your horns, are you not?"

"A unicorn's horn?" Gunnilde repeated skeptically. "How do you imagine I would go about affecting such a thing?"

"I have not the smallest notion, but you are a resourceful woman and could doubtless come up with something."

"I think I prefer the idea of unicorn mittens and slippers," she confessed. "Perhaps I could get some embroidered on my sleeves or bodice."

"What about these things?" Viscount Bardulf suggested, flipping one of her snowy white tippets. "Could they not be adorned?"

"My tippets?"

"Is that what they are called?"

She looked at him in surprise. "Do you not know? But…how funny! They originated here in Aphrany with you, did they not?"

"With me?"

"Yes, for I saw you in some when I first came to court. You wore red ones over a black tunic, and I made sure to ask what they were called, for I thought them very striking. I was told they originated in Vlandivar and you were the first to wear them here at court."

Lord Bardulf looked pleased. "I like to trial such fashions," he said modestly, "but I often discard them just as quickly. It has been said of me, I believe, that I am such a leader of fashion that by the time the rest of court has caught up with me, I have long moved on."

"But it was me that said that!" Gunnilde exclaimed, feeling gratified.

"Yes, I know," he said, sketching her a bow. "A vastly pretty compliment, I thank you."

"But how did you know?"

He tutted, "You must realize how things get overheard and passed along, my dear Lady Wycliffe. Court is positively rife with such whisperings. Besides, a very impudent young squire approached me and asked if I was the Lord Bardulf he had heard so much about. He quoted you as igniting his interest and asked for the name of my tailor."

Gunnilde had just opened her mouth to find out which of Hal's friends that must have been when a small cough sounded at her elbow. Turning, she found Mistress Bartree's page, Unwin, stood there. His hair was a good deal tidier than the last time she had seen him, he must have had a trim.

"My mistress sends her regards to Lady Wycliffe and requests her presence in the Queen's bedchamber," he announced with a bow.

"Well, aren't you honored," Lord Bardulf drawled.

Gunnilde blinked. "I will come at once," she said, getting to her feet. She turned to Lord Bardulf and bade him a good morning before hurrying after the boy's slender figure. She checked her appearance in the doorway, ensuring her coiled puffs were still tidily pinned at her brow, and that her ruby brooch was on straight.

On entering the Queen's bedchamber she found only Mistress Bartree present. The older woman looked up from where she was tidying a box of jeweled pendants. "Lady Wycliffe," she said curtly. "Sit you down. The Queen will be out presently."

Gunnilde could only surmise that Queen Armenal was in her garderobe. She sank down onto a low seat and folded her hands to wait. "Is there nothing I can do to help? Perhaps I could—?"

"No," the other woman responded shortly. "The Queen likes you because your prattle amuses her. Leave the tidying away and care of her to me. Some of us do not have your pretty ways. Let me serve her in the ways I can." Her words came out half choked in their vehemence.

"You do not like me," Gunnilde said matter-of-factly, "but I, too, must be allowed to wait on Queen Armenal."

Mistress Bartree pursed her lips. "I realize that and have said my piece."

Gunnilde suppressed a sigh. "I never thanked you for providing a ring for my wedding ceremony. It was kind of you. I will be able to let you have it back soon, for my husband has promised to procure me another."

Mistress Bartree did not look up from her task. "I don't want it back," she said without emotion. "I no longer have use for it."

Gunnilde glanced down at the ring which currently adorned her finger. "I assumed it must be a family piece," she said.

"No." The older woman averted her eyes. "Not my family anyway."

So…it was given to her by another, Gunnilde surmised. A man? She eyed Mistress Bartree with interest. "It was given you by way of a love token?" she guessed boldly.

Mistress Bartree threw a challenging look her way. "No doubt you find such a thing hard to believe."

"Not at all."

"I was young once."

"You are an attractive woman still, Mistress Bartree, and not so very old." She could not be more than five and forty, Gunnilde estimated, though she wore such ugly headdresses.

Mistress Bartree's lips flattened to a thin line. "I was not looking for flattery," she said harshly. "Save your flummery for the Queen."

At this point they heard a step, and both stood up as the Queen entered the room. Gunnilde was shocked to see Armenal's wan and listless appearance. She looked sallow and strangely shaken.

"Come and sit down, Your Majesty," Mistress Bartree urged, rearranging cushions on a comfortable-looking seat.

"I must make an appearance soon, lest tongues start to wag," the Queen said tiredly, but she dropped into the seat all the same. "Have Unwin fetch me a posset, Magnatrude, for that unpleasant taste I told you of lingers still on my tongue. You know the one which settles the stomach." She pressed her hand to her midsection and Gunnilde saw her wince. Was the Queen ill?

302

"Yes, Your Majesty." Mistress Bartree hurried from the room to summon her page.

"You are not well, Your Majesty," Gunnilde ventured. "Must you make a public appearance today? The King would wish you to conserve your strength, I am sure."

The Queen smiled grimly. "I am not ill, rest assured, my good Gunnilde. I am merely afflicted with the condition that often afflicts wives sooner or later." She sighed. "Rather later in my case."

Gunnilde sat back in her chair. Was the Queen saying…?

"But yes," Queen Armenal said, nodding gently, "It appears I am with child."

Gunnilde's mouth dropped open. "C-congratulations, Your Majesty!"

"Thank you." Her tone was rather dry.

Mistress Bartree bustled back in. "You will refrain from discussing this matter before others until it is formally announced," she said, glaring at Gunnilde.

"Oh, of course," she agreed quickly.

"I hope you are fully aware of the honor done to you!" she continued fiercely. "Thus far, only a very select few have been informed. Scarcely anyone besides the King and the royal physicians."

"Is that why the Queen has been spending time with her married ladies of late?" Gunnilde blurted, thinking of her previous conversation with James.

Mistress Bartree looked immediately affronted but Queen Armenal gave a wry laugh. "You see, Magnatrude. The rumors have likely already started. Yes, that is why," she said. "I have needed advice from my ladies who have been through the same ordeal. Countess Vawdrey has been invaluable, I will admit, though I am not at all fond of her husband. After the Solstice I shall insist that my good Linnet comes to court again, and the little Mathilde. They have contended with several confinements and seem none the worse for the ordeal."

Gunnilde saw this did not please Mistress Bartree and felt strangely sympathetic. It must be hard for her to fall from favor due to her own lack of experience in such matters.

"And now," the Queen said, rousing herself, "you must talk to me, Gunnilde, and enliven me with your chatter, for I am sorely in need of a tonic to pick me up before I must face the others. Tell me how your banquet it is taking shape."

Gunnilde explained that she had started to receive replies to her invitations, reeling off the confirmed attendees. "I still need to send out more invitations," she admitted, turning to Mistress Bartree. "I will start with you and Unwin. I mean to invite all of my fellow ladies-in-waiting." Before the stunned woman could respond, the Queen cut in.

"Yes, quite right," the Queen agreed, "but never mind about that, I wish to know if you have heard back from your erstwhile suitor and his family."

"Not yet, Your Majesty. In truth, I had no idea of the direction to send Sir Arthur's invite, so I simply included it with his sister's. I was informed the Lellands are not currently at court and was instructed to send it to their place in Fulford. I did so accordingly."

"Fulford is not so very far away," the Queen asserted. "But certainly, they must come. It is nonsense to think otherwise. Did you inform them there will be a royal presence?"

"I did, I said Your Majesty had graciously consented to attend."

The Queen looked appeased. "Well, in that case they can have no excuse."

Gunnilde folded her lips. Wordlessly her eyes met Mistress Bartree's. Was it her imagination or did the other woman's hold just the faintest hint of sympathy in their depths?

"And what of the menu? Have you consulted with the royal kitchens yet?" the Queen asked imperiously.

"I have not," Gunnilde admitted, and the Queen tutted.

"We must put our heads together. The fare must be very grand and opulent if we are to impress on them the eminence of your elevation. Perhaps swan or peacock for the main course. They must be dressed with feathers and presented very fine."

"Yes," Gunnilde agreed dutifully while privately hoping that James's purse could extend to such exotic birds. Perhaps she would not send out many more invites after all. She would not wish feed more than fifty guests with such sumptuous dishes.

"My burgundy velvet, I think," the Queen said, addressing Mistress Bartree, who was holding two gowns aloft for her selection. "And for your dress?" she asked, turning back to Gunnilde. "Have you had any thoughts as to your banquet attire?"

Gunnilde perked up. "Ah yes indeed, Your Majesty," she said, silently thanking Lord Bardulf for his recommendation earlier. She settled back in her chair, preparing to hold forth enthusiastically about the unicorn motif.

29

After hurriedly visiting a jeweler and making arrangements for a tailor to visit them the next morn, James spent the rest of the day locked in the room he rented at Master Gregory's town house, immersed in his work. He had spent a productive day filled with inspiration and managed to lay down the score for a good deal of his ideas on paper.

The piece he was working on was a haunting composition which put him in mind of moldering ruins and broken dreams. At one point he even went to fetch Master Gregory, who sat nodding his fluffy head in appreciation as James poured out his vision, playing bits and pieces on the various instruments he had stashed about the room.

"It sounds well, James, very well," his old music master concurred. "I especially like this part." He plucked out part of the melody on a lute which was propped against his chair. The old man only had to hear a piece of music once and he could emulate it. "The way the music swoops and soars in this part is very fine."

They went on to discuss the manifold possibilities for the next movement, while James scribbled notes furiously on pieces of parchment. Emerging from the house around half past four into the busy street, James found he had to shake his head a few times to dispel the creative fog that clung about him.

Justina, Master Gregory's daughter, had been surprised he was returning to the palace for there was a cot in one corner of his room that he often dossed down on when in the grip of a creative spell.

"That wife of yours must be instilling good habits in you," she'd decided, leaning against her broom. "I declare the way you and Father carry on for hours with your music, neither eating nor drinking and losing track of time just isn't decent! It's about time you had someone to impose some sort of order into your life." She gave him a farewell nod and James started off down the street.

The truth was, he had not even considered sleeping over at the Gregorys', however often he might have done so in the past. Despite his immersion in his work, he was still very aware of the fact he had a wife installed in his bed and that he very much wished to return to it and join her there. If only he could persuade her that naught ailed him.

On reaching the palace, he hastened to their rooms and was surprised to hear an unfamiliar voice conversing with Gunnilde's from the sitting room. Pushing the door open, he found Gunnilde sat chatting to a woman in a green wool dress and nibbling on twice-baked biscuits. "You don't say!" she was exclaiming excitedly. "And how pray is he supposed to free himself of this curse?"

Both women jumped guiltily on seeing him stood in the doorway. "Ah, here is my husband now," Gunnilde announced brightly. "James, this is Mistress Fern. She is Sir Ned's witch." The witch turned to look at James with interest. She did not seem to object to Gunnilde's describing her as such, though James would not have been surprised if she had.

Mistress Fern seemed at pains to present herself as older than she was. Her dress was plain and hung off her in an ill-fitting manner. She wore her hair severely scraped back and wore precious little by way of adornment save for a cord around her neck from which clinking amulets hung. It was hard to gauge her true age, though James would not be surprised if she had not yet reached thirty. Her skin was smooth, however much she frowned, and if she wore her hair loose around her shoulders as maidens did, James fancied she would look a good deal younger than she did right now. Her narrowed eyes surveyed him with dispassionate interest, and it occurred to him that she was sizing him up in return.

"Well, he looks healthy enough," she said to Gunnilde as though discussing a pig in the marketplace. "Would you object if I take a look at his teeth and ears?"

"Please do," Gunnilde responded before James could answer. Jumping out of her seat, she crossed the room to take James's arm, steering him firmly toward the witch. When James made as though to object, she gave him one of her encouraging smiles. "We are very fortunate that Mistress Fern was due to see Sir Ned at the palace this afternoon, so Cuthbert was able to bring her over directly after his consultation."

"Fortunate indeed," James answered, bracing himself. This was still better than seeing a physician, he consoled himself.

The witch stood up and peered into his face and ears. "His color is good," she murmured, then tapped his chin. "Open wide. Hmm. Teeth look in excellent condition." She pulled down on his lower eyelid and peered into his eyes. "Extend your wrist," she said, holding out a hand. James did so and she felt for his pulse, with her head tipped to one side.

"Any open sores, lumps, or bumps I should know about?"

James winced. "No, thank gods."

"Do you feel weak or nauseous after the act? Like you want to vomit?"

"The act?" James queried.

She hesitated as though selecting the correct phrasing. "The act of physical love," she said after a heavy pause.

"No. Quite the opposite in fact."

She released his wrist. "Did you take sustenance before the act? Food? Drink?" She looked over at Gunnilde. "You've got to feed a beast before you set him to work."

308

"He had not long eaten," Gunnilde replied earnestly as James reeled at being thus discussed. "Tell me, could it really be some entirely harmless reason that caused him to keel over like that?" she asked anxiously.

"Depends," the witch said, casting a speculative eye over James. "You are not long wed, you said. Is't possible you had overdone things a bit? Forgotten how long you'd been shut up in your bedchamber together?"

"Oh no," Gunnilde assured her. "This was the very first time."

"The first time?" The witch's eyebrows shot up. She looked from one to the other. James felt like his face was on fire. "When you say the first time, d'ye mean together or…?"

"For both of us," he interrupted. "Neither of us had ever committed 'the act' before."

Mistress Fern nodded thoughtfully and sat back down in her seat. "Ever get any shortness of breath or a pounding in your chest by way of normal everyday life?" she rattled off.

"Never."

"What about when riding or when rushing about your business?"

"No."

"You have any trouble getting hard or taking a piss?"

"No!"

"Did you feel any pain at any point when you were getting the job done?"

"No, I did not."

309

The witch cast her eyes up to the ceiling and rocked back onto two legs of her chair. "Hmmm," she said thoughtfully, then came crashing back down again onto four. "Is't possible, my lad, that you forgot to breathe when you were so caught up in the act?" she demanded forthrightly.

"I'm sure that can't be it," Gunnilde said with a frown.

"Yes," said James.

"Yes, it's possible?" the witch enquired, pouncing on his reply.

"Yes," he agreed. "My breath was coming faster and faster as we...went. It got to the point where I could scarcely draw it. I was too...distracted." He cast a furtive glance at Gunnilde. "My focus was elsewhere."

"Well, there you have it," said the witch, slapping a hand down on the tabletop. "If you only breathe out and don't breathe in, folks pass out. It stands to reason."

Gunnilde's open mouth snapped shut. "That can't be it!"

"I expect it was," said the witch. "You put his head in a spin, and he forgot how to function. It's more common than you'd think. They're simple creatures at the best of times. You need to remind him next time."

"Remind him to breathe?" Gunnilde sounded incredulous.

The witch nodded. "To fill his lungs, calm down a bit, and pace himself."

James knew he should feel annoyed, but instead he merely felt relieved he wasn't going to have to eat powdered frog spawn, or something equally foul.

"So…you do not think it is something we need to be unduly worried about?" Gunnilde persisted.

"Not at all," the witch assured her off-handedly. "It's a bit unusual but some are like that. A surfeit of lust, that's all he suffers from, and you've cured him of that already."

Mistress Fern's turn of phrase seemed to alternate wildly between coarse and polite, James thought. Suddenly it occurred to him that she might well be doing an impression of an older and less polite woman. Mayhap she was merely an apprentice witch.

"A surfeit of…?" Gunnilde repeated faintly.

"He got a bit too worked up, that's all. He'll be fine once you're both accustomed to the way of married life. If you do it enough times, he will build up a resistance and be able to withstand the pleasure in future."

James brightened. Perhaps the witch knew what she was talking about after all.

"And you don't think we should trouble to consult a physician just to be doubly sure?" Gunnilde asked conscientiously.

Mistress Fern snorted. "By all means, if you want him to blather on about balancing humors. All a physician is going to tell you is that unwarranted abstinence is to blame and that the excess seed has built up and weakened his heart." Gunnilde turned pale and the witch waved a dismissive hand. "Pay no regard to their foolish ways. I can tell you now his heart is strong and healthy as a horse."

"Well, that is a relief," James decided. "And I have no intention of consulting a physician to be told celibacy is to blame for weakening my constitution."

"Very sensible," Mistress Fern agreed. "Besides, you're not celibate anymore, are you?"

"No," he agreed. "Decidedly not. Now, as to payment…" He reached for his pouch and tipped out some coin into the woman's palm.

"Very generous," the witch said cheerfully, reaching for her cloak which was draped over a nearby chair. "I'll leave you to it. I wish you joy of each other." She gave him a nod, shook Gunnilde's hand, and swept from the room without more ado.

"I don't think I've ever met a witch before," James observed.

"What, never?" Gunnilde looked stunned. "Not even in the country?"

He shook his head. "My mother does not hold with old-fashioned ways. Would you say she was fairly typical of the type?" he asked, suddenly curious. "Do witches never curtsey?"

"No," Gunnilde answered. "Not in my experience. They don't acknowledge man-made hierarchies. I've only ever seen one curtsey to magpies."

"I see," he pondered. "Curious."

"I rather liked her. I do hope she is right about your heart, James."

"Well, there is only one way to find out," he replied swiftly. He extended his hand to her. "Shall we, Lady Wycliffe?"

30

James rushed her into bed once he had helped her with her fastenings. After unpinning her veil, he urged her to simply leave her hair as it was.

"I rather think you like my scandalous hair arrangements these days, husband," she ventured, sliding under the sheets in her thin shift.

"Oh, I do," he murmured without shame as he stripped down to his braies.

"What would you say to one horn, if it was central to my head, instead of one at each side?" she enquired doubtfully. "Only, personally I think it might look a little odd."

"I am not good at picturing such things," he admitted. "But if you thought it looked well, then I am sure I would agree." He plunged his hands into the basin of cold water and set about washing at a brisk pace.

"I suppose it would not look much stranger than a steeple hennin," she mused. "Still, I think embroidering unicorns on garments would be a good deal easier."

"Embroidering unicorns?" he echoed, casting aside the soap flakes and snatching up a drying cloth.

"For my outfit for the banquet," she explained. "Only fancy, the Queen ever so kindly decided to make me a present of a new gown for the occasion. I was telling her my ideas and she insisted her seamstresses were the only ones who could fulfil such an order at such short notice."

"And what will this gown be like?" James asked, crossing the room to join her.

"Purple velvet over an undergown of cloth of gold," Gunnilde responded in an awed voice. "Does it not sound very grand?"

"And will you have slashes in the velvet to reveal the gold cloth beneath?" he asked.

"That would be my preference, but I do not know if the Queen's dressmakers are familiar with such new techniques."

"When do you meet with them?"

"The day after tomorrow. Can I borrow one of your family crests to lend to them?"

He nodded. "Maybe we should arrange for my outfit to match yours," he said, climbing under the covers and taking her in his arms. He sighed against her hair. "I arranged for a tailor to come to our rooms tomorrow morn at nine."

"Did you really?" She sounded pleased. "He must certainly get to work on a new doublet for you. Purple would look well on you, trimmed with gold. But then, everything looks good on you," she sighed.

"Do you think so?" He did not care what he wore, so long as she was satisfied with it.

"Yes, it used to vex me, but now I take pride in the fact you are the handsomest man at court. Estrilda recommended a needlewoman to me this afternoon and I am to give her a pair of my tippets tomorrow for her to adorn. She was not sure about embroidering slippers as they must use much smaller needles for shoe leather."

"We will likely have to visit a cordwainer for that level of expertise," he said dubiously. "Do you recall the name of the one who made your favorite slippers?"

"Yes, but there is not time to get a whole new pair of shoes made up. The banquet is only just over a week away. In truth, I have been very remiss over the arrangements," she said, sounding remorseful.

"Well, we have been busy," he pointed out. "A lot has happened over the past couple of weeks."

"True," she agreed, resting her cheek against his shoulder.

"I also visited a jeweler this morning to order you a new posy ring."

"Did you?" Gunnilde sounded pleased, then her face fell. "Oh, but Mistress Bartree told me today that she does not care to have her ring returned after all." She lifted her hand to gaze at the gold band. "It seems it holds no positive association for her. She said I can keep it and welcome."

James shrugged. "There is nothing to prevent you from wearing two rings. After all…" He reached across to take her hand and turn it so he could contemplate the ring. "This was the one used at our ceremony. I cannot show the love I owe," he read aloud. "The inscription is on the outside of the ring." He frowned.

"Yes," she agreed.

"For some reason, I thought it was on the inside. The one I commissioned for you has the writing inside."

"Oh, well, that sounds nice. Like a secret betwixt the two of us. Did you have the same thing inscribed?" she asked curiously.

"No." He flushed. "In truth I do not know if you will care for the inscription I went with," he admitted uneasily. "It was an impulsive choice."

"As long as it is not 'Daughter to Sir Aubron Payne of Payne Manor' I will be content," she told him dryly.

"When did I...?" Oh, that first letter he had written home after their marriage. He colored faintly, thinking of his former ineptness. "I hope I have improved somewhat in recent days."

"Oh, you have," she assured him, patting his chest. "I am sure I will like it, whatever words you chose. I am just heartily sorry that you will have to face so many expenses all at once." She sounded guilty. "The Queen insists we must serve peacock and swan at our banquet. I am sure it will be very costly."

"I'm working on a piece of music I think will sell," James told her. "So, we need not worry overmuch about getting into debt."

"Really?" she said swiftly, looking intrigued.

"It is not a ballad," he said before she could ask. "But it was inspired by that first tale you told me. The one of the lady left to molder among the ruins of her childhood home."

"Mistress Bartree's tale? I hope you include her triumphant rise to fame and fortune at the end," she said.

"Not in this piece, but perhaps in the next," he said vaguely. "It could have companion pieces."

"Have you titled it yet? Only, I have just had an idea. Do you know what I think you should call it, James?" she asked with sudden enthusiasm.

"No, what?"

"'I Cannot Show the Love I Owe,'" she said, lifting her head. "Would that not be the perfect title?"

He considered this. "It is a good title, certainly."

"So, will you call it that?" she persisted excitedly. He nodded as she rose up onto her elbow, affording him a view of her abundant charms.

"Yes," he replied. "Whatever you will it shall be."

"Really?" She looked flattered.

"It also occurred to me today that I should approach the Bishop of Badsbury with the last two pieces I composed." He shrugged. "It would not hurt to seek an interview with him. I could even write to the Bishop of Hudde asking him for a letter of recommendation. If I do not seek out these opportunities, they will not land in my lap."

Gunnilde nodded. "Yes, that is a good notion. Well done, husband." Her eyes roamed over his face. "You will never guess what Mistress Fern told me before you arrived home. I can tell you, as you're my husband," she said quickly, "and because I know you will not tell anyone else."

"What was it?" James asked uneasily.

"That Sir Ned is laboring under a curse!" she said, dropping her voice. "Apparently, he crossed some old crone who cursed him soundly and told him until he made reparation for his past mistreatment of the fairer sex, then he would never lie with a woman again!" She drew back to look at him. "What say you to that?"

"How could she prevent him?" James asked, spotting the flaw at once.

"Well, apparently, he approached Mistress Fern because ever since this old woman screeched in his face, he cannot well…" She dropped her gaze demurely. "A certain part of him is not functioning as it should. That was part of the reason why she agreed to come and see us yesterday. When she got him to list the women he had wronged, he could only think of me and this old woman he apparently collided with

317

in the marketplace. At first, Fern said she was disposed to disbelieve him, but now she's not so sure."

James's eyebrows rose. "So, the knight you overheard that time…" he said, voicing his long-held suspicion aloud.

"Yes, it was he," she admitted frankly.

"And has he yet apologized?" James could not keep a certain chilliness from his voice.

"Not really. Fern says he is lamentably poor with words, especially when he is ashamed. Apparently, he was too embarrassed to approach me about it at the time and when he had finally worked up the courage, he found I had left for the winter capital already."

"Oh yes. Bashful is he?" James found himself harboring harsh feelings toward the knight still. "Well, I suppose he will just have to suffer until he can bring himself to do the right thing."

"Presumably he will approach me with an apology at some point," Gunnilde said impassively. James found himself bristling at the thought, even though she did not sound excited at the prospect. "I have another secret too, but it's the Queen's," she admitted in a rush. "Shall I tell it to you?"

"Is it anything to do with us?"

"No."

"Then keep her confidence."

Her shoulders relaxed and she smiled at him. "Are we going down to supper after this?" she asked, giving his chest a tentative stroke. James sucked in a breath to stave off his immediate reaction. He was suddenly devoutly glad that he had not been similarly cursed. Perhaps he had some small sympathy for Bevan after all. "Only, the hour is a little early for us to sleep, though it is pleasant to lie here together discussing our day." She tipped forward to drop a kiss on his cheek.

"I was not really intending for us to sleep," he confessed.

"What, then?"

He wrapped his arms around her, kissing her shoulder to her neck. "I thought we could practice building up my resistance to pleasure," he whispered into her ear.

"I see…"

"I want you to do your best to render me entirely senseless again," he admitted huskily.

"James!"

"But this time I'll resist, by remembering to breathe."

"But what if you forget?"

"Then you can remind me."

James's hands settled either side of her waist as he rolled her more firmly atop himself. She tried to pull back, no doubt to ask him if she was not too heavy, but his lips chased hers, unwilling to part.

"Stay where you are," he begged when their kiss broke. "Just as you are."

"Above you? Like this?" Gunnilde asked with surprise.

"Yes," he breathed. "No. I want you to take off your shift."

Gunnilde straightened up and pulled her shift up over her head, discarding it over the side of the bed. "Is this better?" she asked archly, covering her breasts with her hands. Well, the nipples at least. Her breasts were too large to be confined by her palms. The sight had his cock straining against his braies.

"Come back here," he entreated. "I want to feel you in my arms again."

Carefully, she lowered herself back on top of him, and he drew the blankets up around her at once, caressing her back. "It's a shame to obscure the view," he murmured, "but I should not want you to grow cold."

"James, if I squash the breath out of you, you must tell me," she fretted.

"Trust me, I'm a good deal stronger than you imagine," he soothed her, his hands sliding forward to cup and fondle her heavy breasts. "Gods. Your breasts, Gunnilde."

"Yes?"

"They are so wondrously abundant."

"Hmmm."

"You have no notion how they tortured me in the early days of our marriage!" he admitted raggedly as he plumped and made out their shape.

"Tortured?" She sounded startled.

"Aye, for every time you undressed for bed, I could see their outline in your shift."

"Ohhh," she whimpered faintly as he pinched and rolled her nipples. "Did you wish to make free with them, as you do now?" she whispered.

"Gods, I could scarcely imagine such a state of affairs where I could be so fortunate. That I could be so privileged…" He shook his head. "I would ne'er have believed it possible."

"What did you imagine, then?" she enquired breathlessly, pushing her breasts further into his hands. He made a noise of appreciation deep in his throat.

"You brushing them against me in the night," he admitted hoarsely, glad it was dark. "And my spilling in my braies at the barest, featherlight touch…" He swallowed. "I could have, you know."

"James," she whispered. "Would you like to touch me somewhere else?" The words hung for a moment between them as James sucked in his breath.

"Gods, yes." Swiftly he rolled her onto her back. Gunnilde made a sound of protest to surrender the uppermost position, but as soon as he had his fingers between her legs, she gasped and widened her thighs to give him access. "You're so wet," he told her gruffly. "Gods, Gunnilde."

"Oh James." She gave a little sob, arching into his hand.

James felt his chest pound. Breathe, he reminded himself as he petted and rubbed her glistening folds. "There?" He circled the little nub of flesh. "Tell me, sweeting, so I know what pleases you."

She inhaled sharply. "Yes, James! Oh yes!" His heart swelled as her legs tensed and shook before she collapsed with a cry, limp and sated against the mattress. He crowded closer to kiss her brow, her cheeks, her pretty mouth. "Was that nice?" Suddenly it was imperative that he heard her say so. He felt her lips curve into a smile, even as he kissed the corners.

"Oh yes," she murmured languorously. "And now 'tis your turn." She let her thighs fall apart to accommodate him. "You will remember to breathe though, won't you?" He nodded. "Promise?"

"I promise," he said, stripping off his braies. Gods, he'd have to concentrate though… The sight and feel of her, even in the shadowy bedchamber. She was all warm to his touch, no doubt flushed and rosy. He had not thought to bring candles into the bedchamber as there had been light enough when they had entered. Now though, he wished he'd had the forethought. Darkness fell thick and fast at this time of year.

"James?"

"Mmm?"

"Come here." Apparently, he was not moving fast enough. He lowered himself into her open arms. "Can I kiss you?"

His heart stuttered. "Yes, of course."

"You're not too close?"

"No," he asserted, for it turned out the witch was right. Practice was helping him build up a resistance to pleasure. His lips found hers, and they exchanged kisses, which started out wet and lingering and then turned increasingly frantic, at least on his behalf. He tore his mouth from hers. "Gunnilde—"

"Yes, yes, all is well," she urged him on. "Do not delay. Not on my account."

Thankfully, he reached down to set his cockhead at her glistening entrance and without more ado, started the slide home. Gunnilde's breath hitched, and he felt her palm come to rest over his heart. Its pounding must reassure her, he thought as he pushed his way inside her, by exquisite increments until, finally, he was fully sheathed in her welcoming depths.

He let out a shaky groan and filled his lungs with air. "Gunnilde," he breathed, closing his eyes.

"Do not pass out, I beg you."

"Pass out?" He gave a shaky laugh. "Nay, I could not bear to miss a single instant spent in the paradise of this body."

Gunnilde gasped beneath him as he started to move, though whether it was from his words alone or his actions, he could not say.

"James," she whimpered moments later as the momentum built.

"I'm breathing," he promised through clenched teeth. "I'm pacing myself."

"Oh!" Her hands flew to clasp his sides. The bed jolted as she started moving beneath him, lifting her hips to meet his thrusts.

"Fuck," he wheezed.

"James, don't you dare!" she shrilled. "Oh, don't you dare to stop now!"

Stop? Why the hells would he stop? The whining noises she was making were making him quite frantic. She clutched his arse, dragging his body closer still, urging him on. He grabbed the back of her knee, shoving it out, pressing it into the mattress, so he could get closer, deeper, he could not get enough of her.

"Oh, James!" she cried out, and he felt her body's tight clasp of him clench and convulse, precipitating his own violent release. This time though, he did not black out. Just held on for dear life and rode out the wave of almost unbearable rapture that broke over him.

He slumped over Gunnilde, breathing hard. "Are you—?"

"Yes," she sobbed. "Yes."

Gathering her in his arms, he pressed ardent kisses to her neck and shoulder, more words quite frankly beyond him at this point.

31

James awoke to Gunnilde hanging over him with a solicitous expression on her face. He closed his arms about her at once, pulling her in close.

"What are you about?" he murmured against her brow. "Checking that I'm still breathing?" He kissed her cheek, but when he sought her lips she drew back.

"Is it any wonder, after the shock you gave me the time before last?" She had a slightly self-conscious look on her face, James noticed, wondering why. They had not emerged from the bedchamber the previous evening and went without supper.

The lack of victuals had not slowed them down in any way, indeed they had sought each other out a further three times before dawn. The last time had been a lot more leisurely and less intense, and James had been able to savor the experience.

Mayhap she was feeling a little shy after being so free with him the night before, he thought, seeing the way she dropped her gaze, avoiding her eyes from meeting his. "I'm a perfectly healthy man in the prime of his life," he assured her. "Nothing ails me, wife."

"Indeed, I am beginning to think so," she agreed, stilling his roaming hands with her own. "Stop that, James, it is not as early as you think. We have overslept and the tailor is due to visit us at nine, you said."

"It cannot be that late."

"It is already past eight and we need to up and dress! Bennett has brought the washing water and lit the fires."

He groaned when she slipped from his arms and hopped out of the bed. "Curse the tailor," he complained, going up on one elbow to watch her snatch up her woolen mantle and then cross the room to begin her ablutions. "You could rest abed a while longer, wife. Do not forget it is the royal seamstresses who are making your gown."

"I have not forgotten the fact," she assured him. "But I wish to oversee your own outfit and ensure it is, well, sufficiently impressive."

James felt a twinge of misgiving but shrugged it off. After all, so long as she was happy with it, what difference did it make to him? He scarcely cared about such things, and he supposed after all the care she put into her own appearance it was only right that he should be led by her in such matters.

"You have some ideas already?" he asked, feeling resigned to his fate.

"Yes indeed!" She turned to look at him over one shapely bared shoulder. "I was thinking one of the new shorter doublets would look very well on you. Perhaps with slashed sleeves down to your elbows, to show the gold cloth underneath."

"Hmmm." He found himself devoutly wishing Mr. Hughes the tailor was not due until the afternoon. He supposed Gunnilde would be in need of sustenance, but for his part, he felt bursting with health and vigor and remarkably inclined to drag her back under the covers.

Setting down her washcloth, Gunnilde flitted over to her trunk and retrieved a pen and ink drawing. "See here," she said, approaching the bed. "Something like the cut of this one."

With great reluctance, James dragged his gaze from her face to peer at it. "It looks rather short." He frowned. "Where did you get that drawing?"

326

She avoided his eye. "A friend kindly drew it for me," she said, sliding the drawing into the leaves of a book and returning to the washstand before he could make a grab for her.

"Viscount Bardulf," he guessed, rolling his eyes.

"He is always so beautifully turned out and indeed, it was terribly kind of him for he told me himself that he jealously guards his tailor's secrets against potential rivals. He said he only drew this for me as a particular favor and could think of none other that he would extend such a courtesy to."

James pulled a face but made no comment. Gunnilde cleared her throat. "Come now and wash, James," she said, setting her own cloth aside. "I will throw this water away and pour you out fresh."

Suppressing a sigh, James climbed from the bed and started his own ablutions as Gunnilde hurriedly dressed and arranged her hair. She could wrap and pin those horns at her brow in next to no time these days, so used had she grown to fashioning them. He watched her out of the corner of his eye as he pulled on his clothes.

Once she had pinned her veil in place, she hurried into the adjoining room. James followed close on her heels and found Bennett setting a plate of bread and roasted fish upon the table. "Didn't know if you was expecting the young gentlemen this morning," the servant murmured defensively, seeing James's raised brows at the quantity of food. Had Bennett noticed that he had deprived Gunnilde of her supper the night before?

"That's very thoughtful of you, Bennett, and does you credit," Gunnilde assured him. Mollified, Bennett withdrew and Gunnilde poured ale into two cups, glancing around as though to check if Neville had made an appearance.

327

James dropped down on the bench next to her and she gave him a distracted smile. "Have you seen there is a letter here on the table addressed to you?" she asked.

James glanced at it. "It's from home," he said dismissively.

"Hal received a letter from our father yesterday," she admitted, lowering her eyes. "He did not write to me."

James scanned her face. "Your father was displeased by our recent tidings," he guessed. "What did Hal say? Sir Aubron made mention of our marriage in his letter?"

"He is displeased," she admitted with an awkward laugh. "Apparently I am persona non grata at Payne Manor at present."

James hesitated before wrapping an arm about her waist. "He will come around," he predicted, squeezing his pleasing armful.

"I know," she said, touching her hand to his. "He is sure to, when he actually meets you," she spoke with a confidence that quite touched him.

"You think so?"

"Oh, but certainly, how could he fail to be impressed by you? I am sure everyone must be who meets you."

James thought fleetingly of the few facts he knew about Sir Aubron Payne. His father-in-law was known to be an admirer of knightly feats and held a tournament for them once a year at great personal expense and pother. James felt a conviction that the son-in-law Sir Aubron would have liked most of all would have been selected from among their number, not from court.

328

"After all, Hal and his friends have accepted you with open arms," she reminded him lightly.

This was surprisingly true, James reflected. Gunnilde jumped up on hearing a knock on the outer door. James turned and rose to his feet hearing Bennett announce the tailor had arrived.

The next hour passed with a flurry of chatter and activity between Master Hughes and Gunnilde. He had brought along some sample cloth and a few drawings of his own which he was swift to modify on consultation.

"Something more along the lines of this, milady?" he asked, showing his amended sketch to Gunnilde. He had long ceased consulting James, who merely looked to his wife every time he was asked for an opinion.

"Oh yes," she said, clapping her hands together. "That is the very thing! Oh well done, Master Hughes. I think we are now in perfect accord with one another."

The tailor mopped his brow, looking relieved. James thought he might previously have been one of Master Hughes's less exacting customers. Those days were clearly over.

"And you have need of this outfit by Tuesday?" the tailor said nervously. "I will need to prioritize the order above all other work."

"You will," Gunnilde agreed. "We will of course make reparation for such consideration." A sum was agreed which made James wince, but after all, it was now a matter of urgency.

"Sir James will need to call into Roper Street every day until then," Master Hughes warned, referring to his establishment. "We must have daily fittings." James nodded, resigned to his fate.

Neville had drifted in at one point, eaten a good deal of toasted bread and fish and shown a lively interest in his brother's new suit of clothes. Master Hughes had been invited to partake of the fare, for mercifully none of the squires had shown up that morning.

The tailor had joined them gratefully and listened as Gunnilde and Neville had debated the height of collars, the length of cuffs, and what best displayed a man's legs to advantage, giving his own opinions cautiously when appealed to.

All the while James contented himself with watching his wife. What was it about her that made her stand out so much from everyone else? he puzzled. It was not merely her looks, or the willful peculiarity of her manner of dress. It was something else, something more elusive and infinitely more valuable.

The closest he could get to it was that she was always the only person in the room who did not trouble to attempt to hide her excitement or pleasure in things. All about the palace, the courtiers swanned about wearing practiced looks of sophistication or boredom.

They smothered yawns or complained about the crowds, even as they showed up and queued to attend every event. Even the scholastic, enlightened members of court pretended to a certain aloofness or detached indifference to their elevated status.

Yet, Gunnilde gazed about her with eager appreciation. She embraced every new experience with open enthusiasm. She was utterly unlike anyone he had ever known.

"Good fellow, that," Neville said, breaking into James's thoughts moments after the tailor bade his farewells.

"Who?" James asked.

"Hughes, the tailor. I'm tempted to throw some business of my own his way. When I next get my allowance, that is," he said, casting a meaningful look at James. James ignored him. He had enough expenses at present, and it had not been so very long since he had last given his brother funds.

Neville's eyes fell to the letter left neglected on the table. "Hie, what's this?" He picked it up and turned it over. "It's in our mother's hand."

James nodded. "I recognized the seal."

"Yet, you have not broken it."

"No, for I am not overanxious to hear news of home," he admitted. "You may read it, if you are so keen."

Neville speedily dropped it with a moue of distaste.

"Do you think your mother will be similarly affected as my father?" Gunnilde asked. She had finished her meal and was dabbing a napkin to her lips, which were shiny with butter. She had eminently kissable lips, James thought, then realized his wife and brother were waiting for his reply.

Speedily reviewing her words, James shrugged. "It little matters. What's done is done."

He did not know it yet, but in that sanguine belief, he was quite wrong.

32

Gunnilde went along to the Queen's rooms that afternoon, feeling somewhat mixed emotions. She knew she and James had their own paths to follow. She had to hand out invitations to their banquet and also, hopefully, to wait on the Queen. James had to go off into Aphrany to spend the rest of his day working on his music.

Still, she did feel somewhat loath to part with him so soon, despite her skittishness around him all morning. Gratifyingly, she knew she was not the only one feeling that way. James had been remarkably inclined to tarry over their farewells. She also now knew there was nothing remotely wrong with his heart. Mistress Fern had been entirely right in her supposings.

Gunnilde wandered about the Queen's presence chamber for a while, handing out her invitations to her fellow ladies-in-waiting. Some were gracious on receiving them, like Margaret Pryor and Frances Lessimore, who expressed their thanks and promised to attend.

Others, like Lucy Melvin, were more aloof, demanding to know who their fellow guests would be, should they deign to come. They soon thawed on hearing the likes of the Vawdreys, the Bardulfs, and even the Queen would be in attendance, but privately Gunnilde knew she would not forget their initial reactions in a hurry.

"Someone is trying to catch your attention, Gunnilde," Emma Thackeray giggled, nudging her in the ribs. Emma had been a good deal friendlier lately and Gunnilde suspected this was due to her newfound friendship with Hal. "Is that not Lady Harriet Portstanley and that little friend of hers?" she asked. "The bookish one."

"Dear me," Lucy Melvin said loudly. "I thought Lady Harriet was meant to be the shy, retiring sort. It looks most ill-bred of her to be jumping up and down like that, practically waving her arms about. I suppose she has little choice but to act in such a vulgar manner, seeing as she is not free to simply walk into the Queen's private rooms as we are."

Gunnilde looked around and found they were gazing in the direction of the double doors leading out to the wider receiving chamber. "Harriet is a particular friend of mine," she retorted, "and as such we do not stand on ceremony with one another."

Giving the briefest of curtseys, Gunnilde exited the more exclusive room and hurried out toward Harriet, who she found stood with her friend Winifred Hawes. "There you are!" she exclaimed, holding her hands out to them. They were clasped warmly. "I am so glad you are both able to come to our banquet," she said. "Winifred, what lovely tippets! I vow they are even whiter than mine!"

Winifred flushed, glancing down with pride at her sleeves. "I have three pairs now and keep them in constant rotation!" she declared. "I have received many compliments, and my cousin has recently espoused the wearing of them too!"

"I'm so pleased!" Gunnilde said, flushing with pleasure.

"Mother has promised that I may order some when next we see the tailor," Harriet put in hurriedly. "Only I want a light blue pair for myself and a pair of palest green. All my gowns are varying shades of either blue or green. I was once told that those colors suit me best of all."

Gunnilde was much impressed with this. "Is that so? Those colors do assuredly become you well, Harriet, and suit your eye color and that particular shade of brown hair."

"I only wish that I could wear more adventurous hair arrangements," Harriet sighed. "But alas, my hair is straight and lank and will not puff out as yours does, no matter how I try to wrap it."

"Have you tried to supplement it?" Winifred asked, lowering her voice. She cast a quick look about. "Only, I have heard that some ladies do."

Gunnilde dimly remembered her wedding night when her fellow ladies-in-waiting had put her to bed. Someone had intimated as much then. "Yes, I have heard that rumor too, only I do not know how it works, for my own hair is very fulsome and I have never had need of it."

"Yes, you are lucky and naturally blessed," Winifred sighed.

"I will have to make discreet enquiries," Harriet said thoughtfully. "I expect Lady Schaeffer would know. She is very knowledgeable."

"Lady Schaeffer?" Gunnilde said quickly, thinking of that sophisticated lady. "Oh, I adore her headdresses. You must introduce me sometime, Harriet. I would dearly love to ask her about them."

"Oh, most gladly," Harriet promised. "She has asked me about you too. She said you seem a most interesting girl. She calls us all girls," she said apologetically. "She does not mean any offense by it, but you know, she is rather older so…"

"Oh, no offense taken," Gunnilde assured her. "None whatsoever."

"Will there be dancing at your banquet, Gunnilde?" Winifred asked. She looked rather anxious. "Only, I am not the most proficient dancer."

"Oh, assuredly! James knows many musicians and has promised to engage at least four. You will not be compelled to stand up though, Winifred, if you do not care to dance."

Gunnilde was just telling them about the tippets she was having specially embroidered when Winifred's eyes opened very wide and fixed over Gunnilde's shoulder.

"Oh, Gunnilde!" whispered Harriet. "Mistress Bartree approaches! You must be wanted within."

Gunnilde turned with surprise to find Mistress Bartree stood at her elbow wearing a disgruntled expression on her face. Who was keeping the Queen company in her privy chamber, seeing as her favorite had been cut loose from her tether?

"Good afternoon, Mistress Bartree," she said, bobbing a curtsey. "Pray allow me to introduce my particular friends Lady Harriet Portstanley and Lady Winifred Hawes."

Curtseys were exchanged, and Mistress Bartree unbent sufficiently to bestow chilly smiles upon Gunnilde's companions before turning back to her and telling her they were needed in the Queen's privy chamber.

"They look like reasonably sensible girls," the older woman observed as they made their way through the presence chamber. "Surely they are not expecting you to find them husbands?"

"Oh, I do not actually do that anymore. James did not think it fitting." As she said it, she suddenly thought of Neville. Would not someone like Harriet or Winifred make him a good match? Both were heiresses and exceedingly worthy young women of education. Just the sort of partner that Neville would need. She wondered if James would agree.

"Where were you this morning?" Mistress Bartree demanded, cutting across her thoughts. "We expected you in the Queen's chambers."

Gunnilde was startled. "Her Majesty did not mention—"

"Were you anticipating a written invitation?" the other snapped. "If you wish to attend the Queen, you must first show willingness by turning up promptly to partake of those duties."

Gunnilde considered this a moment. "That is interesting advice."
Mistress Bartree inclined her head coldly. "I hesitate to point this out,
but there are dozens of ladies who show up day in and day out to the
Queen's chambers and receive scant attention from Her Majesty."

Mistress Bartree's lip curled. "This current crop are not worthy of her
attention. I hope you do not pretend to be in ignorance of the many
ways the Queen has condescended to give you her gracious attention
and mark you out for favor."

"I do not," Gunnilde answered swiftly. "And I am very grateful to Her
Majesty. But with all due respect, I can scarcely show up to help the
Queen dress when I am not permitted to lift so much as a pair of royal
stockings."

They had entered the privy chamber now, with even fewer inhabitants.
Gunnilde noticed Lady Wymarka Kloch and Millicent Everidge sat
embroidering together in the window seat. Next to the door that led to
the Queen's bedchamber, two of the King's royal guards stood to
attention.

Mistress Bartree rounded on Gunnilde. "I have already explained—"
she started hotly.

"You expect me to sit around and fill the room with empty chatter while
you perform all the useful offices," Gunnilde supplied. "But I am not so
presumptuous as to turn up in the Queen's presence without even the
flimsiest pretense of usefulness. You must perceive how awkward it
would be, Mistress Bartree, if you only gave yourself pause to consider
it from my own point of view."

The other woman stiffened but did not argue. Two spots of bright color
appeared on her cheeks. "You—" she began in a choked voice, before
breaking off abruptly.

336

Gunnilde gazed about them. "We are causing quite a stir," she said, noticing the glances thrown their way. "The other ladies are all whispering that we are at odds."

"You flatter yourself," Mistress Bartree said with a twist of her lips. "They are more likely gossiping about the King."

"The King?"

"That is who is currently with her," Mistress Bartree answered crossly. "He is always encroaching on her these days."

Gunnilde's eyes widened. "You mean…"

"Do not be indiscreet, Lady Wycliffe, I beg you!" the other said quickly. Gunnilde guessed she was terrified she would let something slip about the pregnancy.

"He is her husband," Gunnilde answered mildly. "Is it not to be expected that he should be entitled to a share of her time?"

"Husbands have a time and a place," Mistress Bartree said sourly. "Besides, he will have the young prince to take up his attention very soon, will he not? Why must he continue to persecute Queen Armenal with his presence!"

Gunnilde glanced about. "Is that common knowledge now?" she asked, lowering her voice. "I understood it was still quite a secret."

Mistress Bartree shrugged an irritable shoulder. "All of court is now awash with whispers of the royal whelp's visit," she said contemptuously.

Ringing footsteps had them all turning as the King emerged from the Queen's bedchamber. Around them, everyone sank down into a sea of curtseys.

337

"Come!" Mistress Bartree said with a quick hand gesture. "We will be wanted."

Gunnilde fell in step with her as they made their way toward the door to Aremenal's room.

"Ah, Hilde!" the King said, catching sight of her and beckoning. "Met that brother of yours yesterday."

"Did you, sire?" Gunnilde bobbed another curtsey, acutely aware of Mistress Bartree stood at her side, cold and disapproving.

"Seems a likely lad, if ever I met one. I had him sounded out by my man Vawdrey and made a part of my son's retinue for his impending visit."

"But what an honor, Your Majesty! I am sure Hal will be fully sensible of it and most grateful for the opportunity to distinguish himself with the prince."

"Aye." The King nodded. "The boy expressed himself well. I expect great things from him. They tell me he cannot be beaten with the staff or at wrestling."

"Such is his reputation, Your Highness."

"Hmmm." The King looked impressed. "I mean to watch some of these Squires' Revels. I have not done so before but this year I find myself somewhat intrigued."

"The boys will be beside themselves with excitement, Your Majesty, I have no doubt."

The King's gaze strayed over her head to dwell on the door behind them to Queen Armenal's apartments. His eyes looked troubled. "You

338

must attend the Queen with all diligence, Hilde. She will have need of your support at this trying time."

Did he mean with her pregnancy, or with the impending visit of her stepson? "Of course, Your Majesty," she said aloud. "It has long been my greatest ambition to serve the Queen."

Mistress Bartree inhaled sharply beside her, but King Wymer did not seem to find anything amiss in her words. "Very good, Hilde. Carry on." He nodded toward Mistress Bartree, who curtseyed again and then moved forward.

They found the Queen sat before the fire, a distracted look upon her face. "Your Highness," Mistress Magnatrude said, rushing forward. "Shall I fetch you—?"

"Do not fuss, my good Magnatrude," the Queen told her fondly but firmly. "Please. The King has done enough fussing and fretting to last me a whole calendar month. This baby distresses him. He has no need of an heir, but these days he finds he has need of me."

She gave a small laugh. "After all this time I have finally become indispensable to this King of Karadok. He worries, oh how he worries that he will lose me. You would not believe how exhausting it is to put on the brave face for him all the time. I cannot ever be weary or lackluster in front of him. The King must never see me lacking in vitality. It alarms him."

The Queen's shoulders drooped for a moment. "Here, take this and add it to my jewel case." She passed over a sapphire and pearl necklace, which Gunnilde guessed the King must have gifted her just now. "Lovely, isn't it?" she commented when even Mistress Bartree could not pass up the opportunity to admire it. "Poor Wymer does not wish me to feel neglected while he entertains his son the prince." Her tone was rather dry, but Gunnilde did not think she sounded unduly put out.

"Have you met Prince Raedan before, Your Majesty?" she asked.

Queen Armenal nodded. "A mere handful of times," she answered. "He is a stiff, cold little boy. Nothing like his father. I wonder what all these courtiers who clamor for the glimpse of him will make of him. They will be disappointed, I think." She sighed.

"Gunnilde, be seated next to the table and pour us some drinks from the tray." Gunnilde set about filling the three goblets as Mistress Bartree tidied away the jewel case. "Tell me the day's news, for I have need of distraction."

"The details of the prince's visit seem to be the subject on most tongues," Gunnilde replied truthfully. "My brother is to be part of an official party of squires to welcome him. The Squires' Revels are to form part of the entertainment for the prince, it seems."

The Queen nodded. "That was one of Lord Vawdrey's little ideas," she commented. "My husband always relies on him for inspiration."

"It seems Lord Vawdrey selected the squires for the prince's welcoming party too."

"No doubt," Armenal replied shortly. "Who else is to feature therein, do you know?"

"Cuthbert Ames, who is squire to Sir Roland Vawdrey," Gunnilde told her at once excitedly. "Kit Montmayne, squire to Sir Garman Orde—"

"He is known by a much-venerated northern title nowadays," Mistress Bartree corrected her, seating herself nearby. "And called Earl of Twyford."

"Oh yes, I always forget. He competed so many years at my father's tournament that I always think of him as Sir Garman. If it comes to that, Sir Roland is now hailed as Viscount Vawdrey," she added guiltily. "I do not know why but it always takes me a while to remember new titles."

The Queen pulled a face. "My brother Wilhelm does not award titles as frequently as they do here in Karadok. I am pleased for Eden, of course, but otherwise I do not see why the Vawdreys should have found such favor. In Lascony they would not have risen to such prominence, I can assure you."

Gunnilde fidgeted in her seat. It would be tactless indeed to point out that Sir Mason, or the Duke of Cadwallader as he was now known, had been a general in the late war, and had risen from the ranks for crushing northerners under his booted foot. Mistress Bartree was one such northerner, whose family had lost everything.

As for Earl Vawdrey, 'twas clear the Queen resented his great influence upon the King. She could only suppose that Sir Roland had offended by stealing Eden away from the Queen. Either for that transgression or because he was a brutish knight, which the Queen also looked down upon.

"I had a letter this morn," the Queen said in a swift change of subject. She gazed pointedly at Gunnilde. "From your new mother-in-law."

Gunnilde felt the color rush to her face. "You did? James had a letter too. She must have sent them at the same time."

"Did he tell you the contents of his letter?" Gunnilde shook her head. "Probably he is wise to keep his own counsel," the Queen admitted. "His mother, she was most displeased to have lost the prospect of the Lady Constance for a daughter-in-law."

Gunnilde's heart plummeted. "Oh," she whispered, wondering if his mother had said as much in her letter to James.

Surprisingly, Mistress Bartree spoke up at this point. "I doubt she had heard of the Lady Constance's elopement when she wrote that letter," she said in disapproving tones. "If she had, she could hardly regret the loss of such a woman for her daughter-in-law."

The Queen shrugged. "Well, if she had heard tell of it, she did not own as much."

Gunnilde darted a grateful look at Mistress Bartree, though she did not really know if she had spoken in defense of her or just a generalized hostility toward all other ladies at court.

"It might perhaps be politick of Sir James to take you to visit his mother at Wycliffe Hall and appease her," the Queen mused. "The Solstice is after all a time for families. It may soften her heart toward you."

"Oh no," Gunnilde said in horror. "We settled it very early on that we would not visit his home before next spring. Neither of us wished for it, you see."

The Queen's eyebrows shot up. "I see."

"And with the Squires' Revels and our upcoming banquet it really does not seem like the ideal time to leave court, does it?" Gunnilde said desperately.

"Well, I am sure you must know best," the Queen said, still looking vaguely disapproving. "Wymer's parents were both dead when I was married, so I have no experience of my own in such matters."

Gunnilde pressed her lips together and tried not to worry. The Queen was just out of humor, that was all. It was nothing to do with herself or James. Nothing at all.

33

On returning to their rooms that evening, Gunnilde found only Neville in residence.

"James isn't back yet," he said, looking up from the letter he was reading. Gunnilde recognized it as the letter that had arrived that morning.

"He said he was going into town to work on his music this afternoon," she said, crossing the room to pour herself a cup of ale. She watched him set the letter down on the arm of his chair, frown, pick it back up again, and stuff it into his tunic. He cast a furtive look in her direction.

"Can I help you to some refreshment?" she asked, lifting the jug.

"Oh, no thank you."

She thought he looked rather uneasy. "Did you spend a pleasant day?"

Neville seemed to cast about him as though trying to remember how he had passed his time. "Er, I went to watch the lance throwing this afternoon," he said, brightening. "Cosgrave has a surprisingly good arm, you know."

"Did any of our own pet squires advance to the final?" she asked with interest.

"Oh, all of them, your brother, Ames, Montmayne, Cosgrave."

"What about Hadrian Kellingford?"

Neville shook his head. "He was being forced to run laps about the field dressed in full armor as the result of some misdemeanor or other."

Gunnilde sighed. "If it's not one of them, it's another. Can they never stay out of trouble?"

Neville grinned. "There's always something afoot with that company," he said with relish.

"I am sure you and James must have been far better behaved when you were squires."

"Yes," Neville agreed forthrightly, "but I don't think we enjoyed the experience half so much."

Gunnilde smiled. "I suppose that must count for something."

"I would say so." Neville gestured to the seat next to his. "Won't you come and sit here before the fire awhile?" He glanced toward the window. "I wondered if we might see snow before the day was out. The sky looked so white and there was such a bitter chill in the air."

"I feel it may be too cold currently to snow," Gunnilde commented, moving to collect a folded blanket off the bench before she seated herself in the chair beside his own. She arranged the blanket around her shoulders like a shawl and settled back comfortably. "At least Bennett is keeping the logs piled nice and high for our fires."

"These days he is!" Neville said darkly. "But in past days it was cold as the grave in here with precious little cheer! It has been a good deal more pleasant living in these rooms since you moved in, sister."

"Really?" Gunnilde turned to look at him.

"Oh, decidedly! I scarcely recognize my brother so amiable is he becoming!"

344

Gunnilde was pleased. "I'm sure it is at least partly because I have encouraged him to partake in regular meals," she said earnestly. "You must have noticed how he breaks his fast now. It seemed to me, when first we were married, that his irritability might be down to the infrequency of his meals causing digestive problems."

Neville gazed back at her with an arrested expression on his face. "Really?" he asked in strangled tones.

"It is often the way with artistic types, I understand," Gunnilde explained. "They get caught up in their creative work and forget to eat."

Neville gave an explosive cough, then begged her pardon. "It is certainly true that he seems a good deal calmer these days," he ventured cautiously. "But I would attribute it less to his stomach and more to another organ." Gunnilde's eyes widened. "I mean his heart, of course," he said hastily. "He seems much lighter of heart, and I attribute that entirely to you, Gunnilde."

"To me?"

He nodded and cleared his throat. "It's very noticeable, to someone who knows him of old."

"Like yourself?"

"Like myself," he concurred. "You see," he said, leaning forward in his seat, "James has always had a lot of worries heaped onto his shoulders by our family. A lot of expectations. He was never carefree, not even as a child. Our father, you know, was always entirely useless. My mother decided James was to be our salvation and simply burdened him with the responsibility of our family fortunes."

"I see," Gunnilde murmured. She had suspected as much.

345

"Father resents the fact we all treat James as the head of the family, that we have to apply to him for funds. He calls James a tyrant because he is the one controlling the purse strings. Mother is always taking offence over something or other, her feelings are constantly hurt. Father always has an injured air. Even I try to guilt James whenever I run out of funds," Neville admitted, scratching his neck.

"We all point out his faults while simultaneously holding him to the highest standards. Our parents bemoan his lack of family feeling in private, whilst also lauding him to the skies to all and sundry as an exemplary son. Is it any wonder that James rarely wants to go home where everyone depends on him and makes constant demands on him? Or that he often has no patience for us?"

"No, perhaps not," Gunnilde sighed.

"It's different with you though," he said, giving her a frank look. "He does not try to run away from you. Quite the opposite in fact. His eyes seek you out, you know, across a crowded room. For guidance, I mean," Neville said cryptically. "Or perhaps I should say solace. Whenever he sees you're there, he just…"

"What?" Gunnilde prompted when he fell silent as though searching for the right word.

"Unwinds," he concluded. "His tension seems to dissipate. I've noticed it many times. I believe your presence reassures him somehow." Gunnilde considered this, whilst gazing at the fire. "I always thought he must sleep with a frown on his face, grinding his teeth," Neville continued. "I'm guessing that's changed." He shot her a piercing look. "He used to get up in the night too and pace about for hours. Used to get a lot of headaches too."

Gunnilde considered how soundly James slept, wrapped around her. "Well, I can see why," she said slowly. "When he has had so many worries in his life to contend with."

346

"Yes, it's a good thing that his choice of wife does not add to them. I just wish everyone could see that."

"Everyone?" Gunnilde echoed, hearing the frustration in his voice.

"Oh, the naysayers," he said uneasily. "You know how there's always someone to throw a spoke in any wheel." There was a faint bitterness to his voice that concerned her. Did he count his mother among these naysayers? Had her letter indicated as such?

"He would have avoided Constance like the plague too, if he had ever married her," Neville added distractedly. "Installed her at Wycliffe Hall and simply left her there. I cannot for the life of me see why Mother cannot fathom that! The whole time they were courting he looked as though he would as soon face an execution! But there, Mother does not care a rush for James's happiness. Everything is about prestige and appearance and…and status with her."

Gunnilde shifted uneasily in her seat. She was sure her lack of a dowry must be adding insult to injury when it came to his parents. If only her father was not being so plaguey difficult about things. Ought she to write to him again and explain how well things were going with her marriage? She was just debating the matter when the door opened, and James came through it.

His eyes lit up when he saw her, and he walked right across the room without shedding his hat and cloak. "Here," he said, thrusting a pouch into her hand. "I collected it on the way back from Master Gregory's."

"Is it my ring?" Gunnilde asked, pulling excitedly at the strings until she had opened it and extracted the gleaming gold posy ring. She held it up and turned it in her fingers to read the inscription on the inside of the band. "To my beautiful rose, from your undeserving worm," she read aloud. "Why James!" she gasped. "How positively scandalous!"

He laughed and held his hand out to her. She took it and he pulled her to her feet. "Give it to me." She dropped the ring into his palm, and he reached for her other hand.

"Wait, let me move the other to my right hand first." She transferred Mistress Bartree's ring and then held out her left hand. James slipped the ring onto her third finger and they both looked down at it.

"What do you think?" James murmured.

"Oh, I absolutely love it."

He caught her up in his arms and only broke their embrace when Neville coughed. James turned his head to look at his brother. "When did you get here?" he asked with surprise.

"I was here all along! Not that you noticed!"

"How was your afternoon?" Gunnilde asked quickly, reaching for the fastenings to James's cloak. "Let's get you out of these things."

James looked down in seeming surprise to find himself still clad in his outdoor wear. "It was good," he said with a slow smile. "Really good. I think this latest piece is one of the best I've ever written."

"Really?" Gunnilde draped his cloak over the back of her chair and reached up to take his hat. "But that's wonderful, James."

"Yes," he agreed.

"Who have you written it for?" Neville asked with interest.

"No one," James admitted. "Though Lady Schaeffer did approach me the other day about writing something to commemorate her husband's fortieth year in office."

"You would not give him Mistress Bartree's piece of music though!" Gunnilde protested swiftly.

"No, but I have at least three others that I wrote this year that I could repurpose," James answered, his expression reflecting only the faintest twinge of guilt at this proposal.

"We'll make a man of business of you yet!" Neville said approvingly. "But why do you say this latest piece is Mistress Bartree's?" He looked intrigued.

"It is inspired by her personal history," Gunnilde told him.

James looked uncomfortable. "Gunnilde…"

"It is though, and I really want to hear it."

"Do you? It is not entirely finished yet, though I have a few musicians meeting me at Barnabus Hall tomorrow to play a run-through of what I have arranged so far. We had an impromptu rehearsal this afternoon and it was…promising. I want to hear it in a building with a raised roof."

"Really?" A request to join him trembled on her lips.

"Do you want to come along with me and hear it?" he asked tentatively.

"Could I?"

"Hold fast," Neville interrupted. "Have you not heard? Prince Raedan arrives at court tomorrow. I hardly think you will want to miss that event, now, will you?"

James's face fell. "Oh, well, another time perhaps."

"No!" Gunnilde blurted, clutching at his tunic. "I mean, I want to come with you tomorrow! The prince will be at court for a while, so it will not signify. No doubt I will see him sooner or later, most likely at the Revels."

Neville looked shocked, but a slow smile spread over James's face. "You would rather accompany me, Gunnilde?" he asked.

She nodded. "Oh yes."

"Good," he said simply.

34

James dropped a kiss on her plump shoulder. "You really do not care about catching a glimpse of the prince tomorrow," he marveled later as they lay in bed together wrapped in bedsheets. At one time he was sure such a thing would have been her priority. A smile curved his lips. It pleased him to think her priorities might have changed. That he might take precedent over some court event.

He felt dopey from pleasure, boneless and tranquil as he lay with his wife in his arms. They had eaten, made love, and bathed together. Today had been a good day. A very good day.

"No, I don't mind missing Prince Raedan's arrival," she confirmed, smothering a yawn. "I would much rather spend the day with you."

A general sense of well-being spread about James's body right down to his fingers and toes. "Did you see the royal tailor today?"

She nodded. "I did."

Something in her tone had him paying close attention to her words. "It did not go well?" he queried.

"No, no," she was quick to reassure him. "Signor Castellar had the most luxurious fabrics and trims, all of which he made fully available to me. It is just…he is somewhat traditional in his outlook."

"He does not believe in slashing sleeves and pinking bodices?" he guessed.

She turned her head to squint up at him. "How ever did you know that?"

"Just a guess. The royal tailor is likely to be well established in his trade, is he not? And as such, not the most innovative."

"Well, yes," she agreed dolefully. "He thinks he knows best about every decision and purses his lips the moment I suggest a deviation from his established pattern." She sighed. "I can hardly offend him though, not when the gown is a gift from the Queen."

"No," he agreed. "You will have to content yourself with full artistic control over my outfit."

"You really would not mind?"

"No. You can do whatever you want with me these days."

She gave a chuckle at that. "You should not tempt me. Are you not scared I would turn you into a…what was it you said before? A popinjay?" she teased.

He shrugged. "Not especially. Maybe hearing your brother and his friends talk about cross garters and red hose has broadened my outlook. If you like it, that's all that matters as far as I'm concerned."

"Really?"

"I am entirely serious," he assured her.

She gave him a considering look. "I do believe you are," she said slowly.

He shifted his hand to squeeze her hip. "Believe it," he said. "My only request in return is that you procure more pairs of colorful stockings. I like those on you."

"Colorful stockings?

"The brighter the better," he murmured, kissing the tip of her ear.

She gave a gurgle of laughter. "I believe I can manage that." She placed her hands on either side of his face, a more serious look stealing over her features before she lightly kissed his nose.

"Something troubles you this eve?" he asked lightly.

"Oh no," she said unconvincingly. "'Tis only some matter that weighs on my mind. Nothing of import, I assure you."

"What is it?"

She took a deep breath. "Tell me, did you read your mother's letter in the end?"

He sighed at the recollection of the only rain cloud on the horizon. "I cast my eye over it after supper at Neville's urging."

"And?" She drew back to look at his face.

"And what?" he asked, frowning at the distance she had put between them.

"Was she upset? About our wedding?"

He shrugged. "Once you know her, you will find Mother is always upset about something. She's rarely pleased at any outcome, even those of her own making. Do not trouble yourself about it."

"Did you tell her we married at the Queen's behest?" Her question struck a discordant note, though he was not really sure why. Before he could reply, she added, "Because she has written to her."

"Who? What do you mean?"

353

"The Queen. Your mother wrote to her," she clarified.

James felt a stab of annoyance run through him. "To say what?"

"I do not know. Queen Armenal suggested that we might go to Wycliffe Hall to try and set her mind at rest, but I explained we had no plans to travel there until the spring." She bit her lip, peeping up at him. "She did not seem to think that very filial of us."

"Damn the woman," he said, enfolding Gunnilde close again. "What does she mean by interfering in our business?"

"The Queen or your mother?" Gunnilde enquired in muffled tones from the vicinity of his chest.

"Either one of them!" he said roundly. "And I had not really thought of going to Wycliffe Hall before the summer, truth be told!"

"Really?" She tipped back her head.

"Yes really. Truthfully, I would far rather set about appeasing your father than my mother. Though at this precise moment, we are both embroiled in our own endeavors and could do without the distraction."

"Our own endeavors?" Gunnilde repeated uncertainly.

"Well, I have my music to work on," he reminded her, "and you have your duties to the Queen and the upcoming banquet. Also, we are supporting your brother and his friends at the Revels, are we not?"

"Oh yes, of course," she agreed absently, as though her mind were pondering other matters. "Do you really think you could repurpose one of your previous compositions for Lady Schaeffer?" she asked suddenly.

"Quite easily," he admitted, "though I have never thought to do such a thing before. And quite honestly, I would rather continue work on this latest piece than look at tinkering with an older one. Still, we need the money."

"No, but…it will not compromise your personal integrity, I mean?" She looked anxious.

"Well…" He shifted awkwardly. "Some pieces you feel stronger about than others. This latest one for instance. I would not like to lie about its origins."

"About its inspiration, you mean," she asked.

He hesitated. "Yes."

"Even though Mistress Bartree is unlikely to ever commission such a piece?"

"Even then," he agreed.

She lapsed into silence, considering this. "Perhaps we could obscure the subject matter somewhat?" she suggested. "Say it is based on the story of a lady left to molder in ruins. We need not necessarily state it is Mistress Bartree's story."

He mulled this over. "Yes, I was thinking the same thing. It would not seem right to, well, broadcast that lady's tale unsanctioned." She gave a small smile by way of reply. "What? Why are you smiling?"

"It is just…you are very nice in your notions. You are considerate. I like that about you."

"You do?" He paused. "You do not…think me somewhat stuffy and uptight?"

"A little," she admitted, "and…I think I like that too. It makes me feel quite adventurous and bold by way of comparison." He spluttered. "I like how I feel when I am with you," she said in a strange voice. "How I feel about myself, I mean. You make me feel like I have a strong and distinctive personality. Like I am not at all forgettable."

"Forgettable?" he echoed in surprise. She had voiced that thought once before, though he could not remember when. Oh yes, that was it. She had overheard Bevan say it about her that time at Vawdrey Keep.

"Yes." She gave an embarrassed-sounding laugh. "Like I am not some entirely forgettable girl."

"Gunnilde," he said, catching her chin and looking straight into her eyes. "You are far, far from that. The furthest I could imagine. You are not remotely forgettable," he told her firmly.

Her eyes when they finally met his own were shy, uncertain. "You mean that, James?" she asked in a hushed voice.

"I do. Anyone who has ever given you that impression must be the veriest fool. You are remarkable," he breathed and pressed a firm kiss upon her mouth. "The most remarkable girl I have ever met."

Gunnilde's cornflower-blue eyes went very wide. "James… Even if you are just saying that to make me happy—" she began in a shaken voice but could not continue.

"I'm not," he said gruffly, kissing the tears from her eyes. "I mean every word. Every word of it." Then he set about convincing her of it with his eager body.

35

It was a bustling day in Aphrany. Gunnilde looked about with interest as they exited the tailor's premises. Master Hughes had been assiduous with his attention to detail, and James had dutifully stood about while pieces of cloth were pinned to him, then swiftly removed for other pieces to take their place. She had been most impressed by his patience, for she knew full well that matters of dress were not a passion of his, as they were for her.

"Where next?" she asked. "Which direction is Master Gregory's house?"

"This way." James took her hand in his and led her down a side street to a tall, crooked building which seemed to be divided into three different residences. He rapped smartly on the door, which was duly opened by a sensible-looking woman hefting a broom. "Oh, so it's you, Sir James. And this your lady wife, I take it?" she said, turning to Gunnilde.

"Yes, this is my wife, Lady Wycliffe," James said, helping her to lower her hood. "Gunnilde, this is Justina Gregory, Master Gregory's daughter. She keeps house for him."

"I am very happy to make your acquaintance, Mistress Gregory." Gunnilde smiled, removing her mittens.

Justina Gregory bobbed a curtsey, looking her up and down, her eyes widening as she took in her red leather boots and unusual hairstyle. "Likewise, Lady Wycliffe. I'm glad to see someone has the managing of him. I've seen a marked improvement of late in his habits. No more dossing down on that mattress while he scribbles down tunes and forgets to take his meals or keep track of his days like a decent man should!"

James cleared his throat, looking faintly annoyed, but Gunnilde was most curious to hear how he used to disport himself as a single man. "How very irregular," she commented, giving him a sidelong look. "I certainly should not tolerate such behavior from a spouse!"

"No more you should!" Justina Gregory agreed. "I put up with a lot from my last husband but sleeping under another roof I would not abide. That were the final straw and so I made it known! Showed him the door quick smart. Not that your man was keeping indecent company like mine," she conceded. "I wouldn't stand for any harlotry under this roof, not for twice the rent we charge him for that attic room. Not for any price!"

"Such sentiment does you credit," Gunnilde assured her.

Mistress Gregory sniffed. "He'll be showing you up there now, I suppose. I keep it clean and cobweb free, but I can't be held accountable for the piles of books and papers strewn about. And the instruments cluttering up the place! I never knew the like! Even Father was never that bad!"

"Well, I am sure I am grateful that they are stored in your attic rather than our rooms at the palace. Courtiers' quarters are notoriously small and poky, and I doubt they would all fit comfortably."

"Is that so?" Mistress Gregory looked intrigued by the mention of the palace. "Your husband doesn't talk much of royal matters when I can get a bit of conversation out of him," she admitted. "He's a bit of a dark horse is Sir James."

James shifted from one foot to another. 'Twas plain he was keen to escape to his music room.

"I will be glad to discuss such matters with you, Mistress Gregory, if you are so inclined as to listen," Gunnilde assured her. "Perhaps next time we visit?" She glanced at James, who nodded his willingness.

358

"That would be very agreeable, Lady Wycliffe," Justina Gregory said, looking pleased. "Very handsome of you, I'm sure."

Without more ado James ushered her up a narrow staircase which took them past three whole floors, until they reached a large attic room up in the eaves. Gunnilde gazed about in some surprise. "Surely this attic is far bigger than the rooms below!" she exclaimed, turning in a circle to take in the spaciousness.

"Yes," James replied, "for in this style of residence each floor overhangs the previous one and increases in floor size."

"It's huge! You could house a whole family in here!"

"I am sure that others on this street do," he said. "Come and look out of this window."

Gunnilde accompanied him to the mullioned window and gazed out at the cobbled street below. "It's a fine view," she commented. "Though somewhat different to the ones we are afforded at the palace." Here there were no carefully laid out knot gardens, no picturesque walkways and avenues. Everywhere was teeming with life.

"Yes, indeed," he agreed. "Will you be content to sit here?" He moved a stack of papers to reveal a straight back wooden settle. "There are some cushions somewhere." He cast about until he found a pile of faded cushions which had been set on the mattress tucked away in the corner. He fetched them for her and arranged them on the seat.

"Yes, this will suit me very well," she assured him, sitting herself down and folding her hands in her lap.

"I just need to jot a few last-minute thoughts and ideas down before we leave for Barnabus Hall in an hour's time. I hope you will not find it too dull."

"Oh, not at all," she assured him.

"A few fellow musicians should start arriving soon. Sanders and Horsham said they will meet us there, but doubtless Chamberlain and Billingsley will come here first for they have not yet seen my notations."

"I see." Glancing down at another stack of ink-covered parchments, Gunnilde saw that his notations appeared to be a series of scribbled notes and strange symbols that she guessed must denote various musical instructions. It looked like another language to her. At this point, a short man in a shabby tunic shuffled sideways into the room. He had pale dreamy eyes and wore a close-fitting cap upon his bald head. On catching sight of Gunnilde, a look of confusion crossed his face before being replaced by one of delight. "My dear James," he exclaimed in astonishment. "Is't possible you have brought your lady wife to my humble abode?"

James straightened up at once from the paper he was poring over. "Master Gregory, please come and meet my wife, Gunnilde," he said, crossing to take the old man's arm and lead him to Gunnilde's side. She surmised he was a little unsteady on his legs and was impressed he had found his way up the rickety stairs.

The old man took her hand in his and bowed over it. "I am honored, honored, my dear," he mumbled. "Most gracious."

"I am very happy to make your acquaintance, Master Gregory," she responded warmly. "I know how important you are to James, and I hope we, too, will become good friends."

His rheumy eyes filled with tears, and he pressed her hand. "You are kind, very kind."

"Not at all, I hope I know what deference is due to James's mentor and closest friend."

Feeling James's eyes upon her, she turned to check all was well and found a small smile playing about his mouth. "I might have known you would put him at his ease," he observed. "Sit you down here with Gunnilde, while I put the finishing touches to my manuscript," he told his friend. "She will keep you entertained until it is time for us to leave."

Master Gregory seemed nothing loath and he and Gunnilde enjoyed a cozy chat while James scribbled furiously with quill and ink.

"Has he played it for you?" Master Gregory whispered, motioning toward James's latest piece of work.

"No, he has not," Gunnilde admitted, not liking to make it known that she had thus far heard none of James's music. "I am very much looking forward to a run-through of it at Barnabus Hall later on today."

"Ah yes," Master Gregory said, holding up one finger. "I, too, look forward to hearing it played with musicians that can truly do it justice." At Gunnilde's mystified expression, he explained with a twinkle in his eye. "Thus far, only James and myself have plucked out the various strains on different instruments and never with all of them playing in harmony and perfect synchronization at once."

Her confusion lifted. "Oh, I see."

"Though, of course, it will take many attempts and practices before it is ready to be heard by a full audience."

Gunnilde nodded. "You and James know many different musician friends?"

"Oh yes." Master Gregory nodded. "Though, for my part, rather less than I was used to." He sighed. "A lot of my own contemporaries did not make old bones. They did not all have dutiful daughters to look after them," he added ruefully.

"Mistress Justina seems a very capable woman," Gunnilde concurred.

"Oh, she is that," he agreed with a chuckle. "She makes sure I join her at table and clear my plate at mealtimes! I am very fortunate to have two young people who care for me." His eyes traveled fondly over James, then he seemed to remember present company and turned back to her. "And your, er, own situation, my dear? Your father is…?"

"My father has a young wife to take care of him," Gunnilde said cheerfully. "He has no need of a daughter to keep him in good health."

"I see, I see." He nodded. "And you have, er, brothers and sisters?"

"I have a brother, Hal. We look out for each other. He is at the palace now as a matter of fact. Fortunately, he and James seem to deal fairly well with one another."

"That is important," Master Gregory said fervently. "Marion and I often wished we had been blessed with more than one child but alas, it was not meant to be."

"Marion was your wife?"

"Yes, indeed." His eyes grew even more watery. "She was a good woman. Down to earth, like Justina, but a man like myself needed a good practical wife to keep my feet on the ground. She kept the hearth swept and the rent paid. Without her, I would have been quite lost."

"I hope with time, I may become invaluable to James," she admitted wistfully.

"Oh, I am sure you already occupy a place of great significance, my dear. Why, James told me himself what a clever and educated young lady he was betrothed to."

An unpleasant jolt ran through her as she realized he must have been describing Constance. He would hardly have described her in such terms. She cleared her throat. A swift change of subject seemed the best stratagem. "You must have met James's parents many times over the years, I think," she said with a brittle smile.

The older man frowned. "Not as often as you might think. When James was a young boy, I visited Wycliffe Hall for his lessons. After that he came to my abode in Caer Lyoness. His mother would write to me to check on his progress as a student, but rare was the occasion we actually met. I daresay I have never met his father above twice in my life."

"I see," she answered thoughtfully. "And how many years have you lived now in Aphrany?"

"Oh, it must be above some six or seven years now," he decided. "My daughter married, and I moved here with her. Happily, James winters in Aphrany with the royal court, so I still see plenty of him." He beamed good-naturedly. "I have been fortunate indeed."

They spent the next hour pleasantly enough. Master Gregory meandered through the room retrieving various instruments and returning to the settle to demonstrate how they were played. A good few of them it seemed were his own, though he thought of them as much James's these days.

"My fingers are so stiff some days, I can scarce manipulate the strings. Besides, Justina prefers them to be confined to the attic. She says I have a tendency to let my paraphernalia trickle down the staircase." He pulled a contrite face. "I've always needed a lot of organizing," he confessed, making Gunnilde laugh. For a moment there had been something of the scolded boy about him, despite his wrinkles.

Soon after, two of James's musician friends arrived, a short, friendly individual called Arthur Billingsley and a tall, quiet fellow named

William Chamberlain. They carried instruments of their own over their shoulders and spent a couple of hours learning the piece with James before he declared it was time to set off for Barnabus Hall.

They had only a twenty-minute walk, which would have been more like ten if they had not been accompanied by Master Gregory, still no one seemed to mind. The musicians all carried two instruments apiece, and Gunnilde took Master Gregory's arm, more to steady him than for an escort.

They made quite a merry party as they started down the street. Gunnilde looked about with interest for though she had visited Aphrany a few times since her arrival in the capital, she did not know it well. The quarter they were frequenting today appeared to be filled with workshops, producing pottery and textile goods.

On reaching Barnabus Hall they found a raggle-taggle bunch of musicians awaiting them on the threshold, stamping their feet and blowing on their fingers to keep out the cold. James introduced her to two of their number, Jim Horsham and Thomas Sanders.

It appeared the others had tagged along with them and James needed an introduction as well as she, although a couple of them he appeared to know by sight or reputation. They did not tarry long outside the hall, for it was cold without and the air was damp.

Inside, Gunnilde sat quietly on a wooden bench, as the others moved up the front to set up. She kept her gloves and cloak on, for there was no fire and the dark wood interior of the building was not terribly warm.

By this point she was familiar with the haunting refrain of the piece, for she had heard James, Arthur, and William practicing snatches of it back at Master Gregory's. Now, she got to hear several of the disjointed parts played together by a variety of different instruments. It did not take long before she got swept up in the music.

Every time they stopped to go over some passage that did not sound to James's liking, she had to bite back her protest. It sounded divine! More than anything she wanted to hear it played all the way through!

Having said that, listening to Arthur Billingsley piping out a lilting melody by himself had her sitting up straight in her seat to hear him. He was certainly a very accomplished musician. After his solo, they all stood up in turn and played their parts separately. James pulled a couple of them aside, correcting them on certain notes and making them go over it again. Finally, he had them play certain sections in unison. Gunnilde found herself craning forward and clutching her mittens together tightly. If only poetry was as enthralling, she thought breathlessly. Then she would understand why it was so popular!

Finally, after many false starts, they played continuously for several minutes without interruption, and at the close of it, Gunnilde found her face wet with tears. How beautiful and heart-breakingly tragic and truly wonderful it was, she thought, using her mitten to mop up her tears.

As the splendor of the music faded, she felt suspended for a moment in a sublime reverie where all hopes and cares of the real world had faded away, leaving her quite at peace. She was not sure how long she sat there feeling strangely moved. Only that as the feeling faded, other less blissful thoughts intruded.

Along with her realization that James was incredibly talented, an uncomfortable awareness stole over her of her own stupidity. How utterly ridiculous she had been thinking that she could help James direct his gift into more appropriate channels. She cringed to think of her avowals to secure him more success, of her efforts to make him write instead a ballad.

Her cheeks flushed hot to remember how she had assured him that she would aid him with his career at court. What a little fool he must have thought her! No wonder he had not taken her seriously. How she must have embarrassed him with such talk. Biting her lip, Gunnilde resolved never to mention such a stupid thing again.

She sat there, dazed, as his music still rang in her ears. To think that she had imagined she could ever be a useful wife to James, well-placed to promote and encourage him. She had known nothing about the qualities a wife of his ought to possess. Nothing at all.

36

Five Days Later

"I don't mean to overstep but is everything well with my sister?" Hal asked. James paused in the act of removing his cloak. "Only she's been quiet these past few days and it's not just me that's noticed it," Hal continued. "Your brother agrees with me, isn't that right, Neville?" He shot a look at James's brother, who was seated opposite him petting the little dog, Dustin.

Neville cleared his throat. "Yes," he agreed. "She seems…subdued. Not her usual self at all."

James glanced about the room to check if any more of his brother-in-law's friends were lurking hereabouts. They had not been around so much lately as their duties with the young prince took up a lot of their free time. Mercifully, it seemed it was just family tonight.

"She's been damnably busy of late," James reminded them both, coming into the room. "And so have I. This wretched banquet has been taking up all her time. The cooks, the tailors, the decorations, the borrowing of the silver plate," he listed. "There's a lot to organize and rather more to these affairs than you would think."

"Yes, but you would think she would enjoy that," Hal said critically. "She always liked it when we held feasts at Payne Manor. There she would be bustling about, fetching and carrying, bright-eyed and joyful but here…"

"Here, what?" James asked with a frown, throwing his cloak over the back of a chair and pouring himself a goblet of ale.

"Here she goes about all pale of cheek, eyes downcast, brooding, and when she does talk it's in fits and starts. It's not like her, I tell you. Something's amiss."

James took a swig of his ale while he considered his answer. In truth, he had noticed Gunnilde's change in behavior himself and had asked several times if anything ailed her. All she ever did was assure him that naught was wrong, nothing at all.

She certainly had not been rejecting his advances in the bedchamber. There, she was as enthusiastic as ever. He should not have taken that for assurance, however. That had been remiss of him. Most remiss. He threw himself down on the bench next to Neville.

"Steady on, you'll startle Dustin!" his brother reproached him. Sure enough the dog let out a shrill little bark. "He's a great oaf, isn't he, boy?"

James murmured his apologies and reached across to scratch behind Dustin's overlarge ears. "I have spoken to Gunnilde as a matter of fact. She tells me she is simply much occupied. As well as everything else, she's still working hard to ingratiate herself with the Queen and her fellow ladies, do not forget."

"Aye, but is she?" Hal demanded at once. "From what I've heard, she's been running around court with those two mousey friends of hers of late and attending dry old lectures like she's a regular outcast instead of one of the Queen's favorites!"

"Lectures?" James echoed, sitting up. What mousey friends? "But why?"

"Hanged if I know! Patience tells me they've scarcely seen her in the Queen's chambers this past week!"

"Scarcely seen her?" James echoed. "But she goes along there every day!"

The other two looked uncomfortable. "Well," Hal responded lamely, "possibly she shows her face, then ducks out soon after. Your guess is as good as mine."

"Possibly Mistress Rheinholdt exaggerates," Neville put in hurriedly. "I daresay Gunnilde divides her time between the Queen and her new friends quite equitably, 'tis only that she has divided loyalties of late."

James put down his drink. "If they are the ones I am thinking of," he said slowly, "then they are not new friends at all. Quite the opposite."

Hal and Neville exchanged looks. "What d'ye mean?" Hal demanded.

"Well, when your sister first came to court last September she spent all her time with Lady Harriet Portstanley and her scholarly friends. Countess Vawdrey introduced her to their circle."

"Well, that doesn't sound like Gunnilde's sort of thing at all," Hal said dismissively. "No wonder she moved on."

"No, it did not suit her," James agreed. Gunnilde had said something at one point about intending to stand a good friend to Harriet. Could this all be part and parcel of that endeavor? Surely, though, she would not prioritize such a thing over her own personal ambition?

"She has not mentioned any change in her friendships recently? Any quarrels?" Neville queried.

James shifted uneasily in his seat. "Truth be told, she has no close friendships among the Queen's ladies. They have not exactly welcomed her with open arms."

"Well, my friend Emma Thackeray—" Hal began only to be cut off by Neville.

"It is the curse of being a royal favorite," James's brother opined. "Neither Eden Montmayne nor Jane Cecil was exactly overburdened with close personal acquaintance when they occupied that position, and Mistress Bartree assuredly is not!"

The door opened at that moment and Gunnilde entered carrying a small pile of books. "Evening all," she greeted them, closing it behind her. James scrutinized her face keenly, but she gave nothing away, smiling politely all round and making her way into the room.

Suddenly, he recalled her indignant account of how Mistress Bartree would not share her duties. Gunnilde had been so spirited and open in the retelling. He missed those days. She had not spoken with such animation in a while. "How is Mistress Bartree?" he asked as Gunnilde sank onto a seat next to her brother and placed the books in a neat pile at her feet.

"She is much the same as she always is." She shrugged. "Perhaps a little sourer, as the Queen was conferring with Viscountess Bardulf all morning, so she was left out in the cold like the rest of us."

"In the Queen's privy chamber, was she?" Hal asked casually.

"Yes," she replied, picking the top book off the pile and opening it.

"How about this afternoon?" Hal persisted. "Was the Queen still favoring the viscountess?"

Gunnilde hesitated. "I, er, well, I did not go to the Queen's chambers this afternoon," she admitted, keeping her eyes firmly trained on her book. "I was invited to attend a function in the lower gallery with some friends and went to that instead."

Hal opened his mouth to interrogate her about which friends but as James already knew this, he forestalled him. "Perhaps you should tell Mistress Bartree about 'I Cannot Show the Love I Owe,'" he suggested. "You could tell her it will be performed at our banquet in her honor."

Gunnilde almost dropped her book. "Really?" she gasped, snapping it shut. He nodded, glad to get a strong reaction out of her. She flushed and bit her lip. "How do you think she will feel about it?"

James shrugged. "I hardly know. She may even be wildly offended."

"Offended?" she repeated indignantly. "Once she has heard it, she could not be!"

"What the devil is it?" asked Hal. "A poem?"

"A piece of music," his sister corrected him. "The most wonderful piece of music you ever heard! James wrote it."

James was surprised and gratified by her vehemence. Had she really liked it that much?

"I did not realize you were going to perform it at our banquet," she exclaimed. Which, as he had only just decided on it, was hardly surprising. "I know Arthur Billingsley and Master Chamberlain are playing for us, but will you invite the other musicians to come too?"

"Yes," he confirmed, "but if they cannot attend it hardly signifies. I can arrange a pared-down version for our guests."

"Oh no!" she said, shaking her head. "If Mistress Bartree is to hear it for the first time, then it must be in its full magnificence!"

As Gunnilde had only heard it played in its early stages, James did not think even she had heard that. They had been practicing every day since then and he had tweaked and fine-tuned a good deal of it, as well as brought three more musicians on board.

"Why did you want to go and write a piece of music about The Bartree?" Neville asked with disgust. "I daresay she will not send so much as a penny piece your way in patronage!"

"Yes, and what happened to False Billiam?" Hal asked sternly.

Gunnilde rounded on them at once. "Because her story inspired James, of course!" she said heatedly. "It gave him the creative spark." She looked suddenly self-conscious. "I was hearing all about such things in my lecture this afternoon by Master Aldwick."

James sat up in his seat. "And who, pray, is Master Aldwick?"

"Oh, have you not heard of him? He is a poet that Winifred admires very much. She says he is sure to become one of the greats, given time."

Ah, thought James, Lady Winifred Hawes. This confirmed his suspicions. "But why are you listening to poets when you do not care for poetry?"

"Oh, well…" She glanced down, pleating her skirts. "I thought I should likely give it another try. Besides, it only lasted an hour. After that, I accompanied Harriet to her tailor's appointment."

"Wanted your opinion on a new gown, did she?" Hal asked. "I'm not surprised. She's one of those quietly pretty girls. She needs something to make her stand out from the crowd. Maybe a nice scarlet brocade."

"Lady Harriet?" Neville said, frowning. "I'm surprised you even know her, Payne." Vaguely, James noted his brother sounded put out by this, though he had no idea why.

"Oh, I'm on my way to racking up a fair acquaintance about court now," Hal said comfortably.

"Especially among the ladies," James said dryly. Hal nodded in agreement, quite unabashed.

"In fact, Harriet wanted me to explain tippets," Gunnilde clarified. "For Master Forrester had never heard of them, and Lady Portstanley won't let her engage a more up-to-date tailor."

Hal tutted. "That's too bad. Her current one doesn't do her justice."

Neville huffed. "Lady Harriet has an understated grace that needs no refinement," he said coldly.

"In any case," Gunnilde said with satisfaction, "he took a look at the construction of my own and Winifred's tippets and assured Harriet he could produce something along similar lines."

"What of the banquet preparations?" James asked. "Have you heard any more from that quarter?"

A somewhat harassed look entered her eye. "The palace kitchens have assured me all is now in order," she replied. "Monsieur Roche says the dishes will be dressed most elaborately and the palace steward has agreed to lend us the silver plate for the evening."

"And what about Signor Castellar?" he enquired, naming the Queen's tailor.

Her shoulders relaxed. "I will own that the gown is looking very well indeed," she conceded. "I do not think anyone will find fault with me on that score."

James frowned at her turn of phrase. Of course no one would find fault with her, the idea was absurd.

She turned toward him. "How many musicians must we now accommodate? I wonder if I should ask for a larger room to fit us all in?"

"At least eight," he answered. "Possibly as many as ten."

Gunnilde's eyes widened. "It is difficult to anticipate when I do not know precisely how many guests will turn up. Many of the ladies' attendance seems to depend on their whim of the evening."

"Hah!" said Neville. "If the Queen will be there, so will they, never fear. They are merely pretending indifference."

"Have you heard back from the Conways?" asked Hal. "I mean the Lellands or whatever they are called nowadays."

"No," Gunnilde admitted, worrying her lip. "But the letter might not have reached them in a timely fashion considering the time of year and the state of the roads. They may still appear on the day."

James could not tell if this prospect appealed to her or not and the fact annoyed him. He should know, because Gunnilde should have told him. She used to tell him things all the time. Why the hells didn't she anymore?

37

The door opened as Gunnilde lay in the round wooden bathtub, soaking in the herbed water. She always liked to wallow for as long as possible and that was even more true at present. Cocooned in the white sheets and warm, fragrant water, she could try to forget all about her manifold worries. Twitching the modesty curtains aside, she checked to see who had entered the room.

"It's me," James said shortly and crossed the room toward the bed. Hearing the mattress rustle and dip, she guessed he had lain down, as the curtains obscured her view of that part of the room.

Silence reigned for all of a minute as she furiously considered various topics she could raise, only to dismiss them as unworthy and beneath his consideration. The banquet preparations were too dull, her concerns over his mother's letter, too contentious. Everything was so difficult now she had realized her own feelings and how ill-suited they were. If only she could have continued in blissful ignorance of the fact!

He cleared his throat and Gunnilde stilled. "Do you ever find yourself missing your…your former matchmaking endeavors?" he asked, startling her greatly.

"Sometimes," she admitted truthfully, then wondered if she should have lied. But after all, what would be the point in denying it? James must have realized their incompatibility long before she had.

"When I said what I said—" He broke off with a frustrated huff.

Gunnilde propped her elbow on the side of the tub. "When you said what?" she asked curiously. It was somehow easier to ask when she could not see him, only the plain white sheets hanging down from the ceiling.

"That it was not fitting that my wife should be involved in such things," he supplied in a rush.

"I have not done it since, James. Not once," she assured him.

"I know. But what I mean to say is I should not have dismissed your interests so out of hand. It was inconsiderate of me." He paused. "Arrogant, even."

Gunnilde blinked. "Oh," she said. "Well…"

"And you have you missed it," he said ruefully.

"A little, yes. Did you—?"

"Why have you—?" They both spoke at the same time, stopped, and then halted. "You speak first," James said.

She gave an awkward little laugh. "I was just going to ask if you noticed how prickly Neville became over Harriet earlier? When Hal was critical of her manner of dress."

"I did notice," he acknowledged, surprising her. "Do you think it indicative of something?"

"I just wondered, that's all."

"You think he might admire her?" She could hear the frown in his voice.

"Possibly. What do you think?"

"I would have thought it just as likely that your own brother admired her."

"Yes, but Hal admires dozens of women. By contrast, I've never heard Neville speak of any young, marriageable women."

"No," James agreed. "Usually, he is the pet of much older women like the Ashdowns."

"Hmmm," Gunnilde mused. "It is certainly interesting, is it not? What kind of wife do you think would suit Neville? For my part, I think a quiet and studious wife like Harriet might bring out his protective and considerate side."

"I think he is yet too young for marriage. Neville cannot even support himself at present!" James replied scathingly.

"But if he married a rich wife then that need not be such a consideration."

James was silent for a moment. "I was not referring to money alone," he said at last. "There is rather more to supporting a spouse than that."

"Yes," she agreed quietly. "That is true."

"Do you feel supported?" he asked suddenly. "By me?"

Gunnilde breathed out. "Yes. I just wish…"

"What do you wish?"

"That I could support you better." Her words came out rather choked. "You must sometimes reflect that—" She could not bring herself to continue. That Constance would have made you a better wife, she thought, closing her eyes. Constance Northcott, who was so well-connected, wealthy, and much admired. No wonder her mother-in-law was writing letters of complaint to the Queen. Perhaps it had even been a letter of petition, she thought dolefully.

"What did you say?" The curtain was swept aside, and James appeared beside the tub. He dropped down so that he was crouching on eye level with her. "I did not catch what you said."

She sank down under the herb-strewn water, covering herself with her hands. "I-it was nothing. Why are you asking anyway? About the matchmaking, I mean. That was all ages ago."

"Well, I heard you had taken up with the friends Viscountess Vawdrey selected for you again," he said, keeping his eyes respectfully on her face. "And my understanding was that you had originally dropped them to pursue the more interesting role of lover's confidante."

"You are right, that is what I did," she admitted quietly. "And now I heartily wish that I had not. I wish now that I had tried harder to fill the role Eden had envisaged for me. The one I was too foolish to appreciate."

"What are you talking about?" he demanded. "Did you not successfully pair up many couples who went on to marry?"

She hesitated. "Well, yes. Four of them."

"Is that counting Sir Douglas and Constance?" he asked, completely robbing her of breath.

She could not answer his sly smile. "James!" she uttered instead, half alarmed, half disbelieving.

"What?"

"Of course not! I would hardly count that pairing as a success, not when—" She could not meet his eyes.

"When what?" he asked.

"When it got me—us—into so much trouble." She bit her lip.

He slid his hand down the side of the tub into the bathwater, picking up the sponge lying on the bottom of the tub. "Maybe I do not view it the same way as you do," he said, lifting the sponge to run it lightly over her shoulder. "Why don't you turn around and let me wash your back."

Turning bright red but feeling loath to refuse him, Gunnilde turned around, presenting her back to him. She had to gather her wet hair over one shoulder to move it out of the way. There was a heavy pause, while she harbored the awful suspicion he might be ogling her over-large bottom. Then she felt the sponge squeezed against her shoulder blades.

"You have the loveliest body, Gunnilde," he said throatily.

Did he really think that? "Thank you."

"Tell me about your friend Lady Winifred's prospects," he said, surprising her again. "Have you anyone in mind for her yet?"

"I promise you faithfully, James, I have not been matchmaking," she said, looking back at him over her shoulder.

He rubbed the sponge over her back in a circular motion. "No, but if you were."

"Well…" She thought about it. "Winifred is so exceedingly clever as well as being of good family. I think any family would be proud to admit her as a daughter-in-law."

"Hmmm. Is that so? Yet she looks to you for guidance when it comes to dress," he pointed out.

"Yes, that is true." Gunnilde's heart swelled with pride. "I really like her and Harriet. I want them to be happy and successful here at court."

"Do their lectures and meetings not make them happy?" he asked, rubbing soap leaves up and down her spine.

"Yes. I only wish I could enjoy such worthy occupations as much," she admitted. "Perhaps with time I will learn to."

"Why should you? Other things make you happy, do they not? You could still be friends with Harriet and Winifred without adopting all their pursuits and endeavors as your own."

Gunnilde thought about this. "You do not think that in order to foster good relations with another, one needs to share mutual interests to keep that bond alive and strong?" Even to her own ears her voice sounded stifled, almost scared.

His hands paused momentarily. "I think," he said, running his hands up and down her soapy sides, "that if the bond is real, you will find other points of mutual connection."

"Such as?" she asked, holding her breath.

He cleared his throat. "Well, they both clearly value your opinion on matters of fashion." Gunnilde's heart sank like a stone, for she realized she had not been thinking of her friends at all when she asked that question. She had been thinking about James. And James did not care about fashion at all.

"Yes," she said, fighting back tears. "That is true."

"You have washed your hair already?" he asked, running a hand over her damp hair.

"Yes. I do that first, for it takes an age."

"I'm not surprised. There's so much of it." His tone was openly admiring.

"You like my hair?" She would take anything at this point, and her hair was the one thing she had always been able to take pride in. Likely he did genuinely admire that at least.

"I do. I like everything about the way you look."

Gunnilde almost gasped. She had nearly forgotten. He did like buxom women. She had helped him discover that fact. Still, everything? That had to be an exaggeration. "What about…my teeth," she asked tentatively.

"What about them?"

"It has been observed that they are somewhat over-large."

"Observed by who?" He sounded annoyed. "Who the devil said that?"

"I forget," Gunnilde lied lightly. "Doubtless some long-forgotten friend of my youth."

"Well, they were clearly jealous of you," James answered testily. "Doubtless their own were pitifully undersized and decayed while yours are large and healthy."

Large and healthy, Gunnilde thought dolefully. Yes, that described her perfectly. Gunnilde Payne, large and healthy daughter of Sir Aubron. She supposed she should be grateful James had not described her thus in his letter to his parents.

No, stop that, Gunnilde, she told herself crossly. He likes your large and healthy body. When it came to James, his physical attraction to her was her only advantage, for she had precious little else to offer him. Taking a deep breath, she turned about in the tub to face him. "James," she said, "why don't you join me now?"

He blinked. "Join you…?"

381

"In the tub," she elaborated, patting the water invitingly as though it were a mattress. She forgot it would splash. Shaking the water droplets out of her eyes, she gave a rueful laugh. "Though you might want to ask Bennett first for another two buckets of hot water to top it up. It is not as hot as it was."

But James was already stripping off his clothes. "I don't care about that," he said, flinging off his tunic. "During my days of King's service, I've often bathed in cold-water streams. Unless you want more hot water? In which case, I can easily fetch more," he said, pausing in the act of unlacing his crotch.

"No, no, I am content," she assured him. "Do not go on my account."

With a flattering haste, he finished undressing his gorgeous body. No matter how often she feasted her eyes on him, Gunnilde was sure she would never get used to his masculine beauty. It was astonishing how good-looking he was. She felt quite dazzled by it at times.

In no time at all, James slid into the water beside her, his long, well-formed limbs brushing up against her own shorter, chubby ones. Even if she were not trying to seduce him, there was no way Gunnilde could have arranged herself so their bodies would not be pressed against one another.

"You're so tall and well favored," she told him admiringly, stroking his thighs.

He made an involuntary noise in his throat. "Gunnilde," he said huskily.

"Have you enough room?" she asked, pretending she had not noticed his hard cock and flushed face. She drew her knees up, wrapping her arms about them and obscuring his view of her breasts. Well, most of them, anyway. They were not so easily hidden.

382

"It's not room that I crave," he answered, meeting her eyes, his hair falling over his one eye. Gunnilde's heart squeezed. Remember what you are about, she admonished herself. You are the one that is supposed to be doing the seducing here, not him!

"What, then?" Gunnilde asked, a small smile playing about her lips.

"Closeness," he answered.

"Is this not close enough?" she asked coyly. He shook his head. "No? I hardly know how we could be closer still. Unless I come and sit in your lap?"

His nostrils flared. "Yes," he answered, his voice deeper than usual. "Like you did at our wedding banquet when you rescued me."

"Rescued you?" she queried as she clambered up onto her knees. There was no dignified way she could do this, she thought as she scrambled inelegantly over him. She was not lithe enough to do it with grace. Not that James seemed to mind. His hands were at her waist, on her hips, urging her closer, groaning loudly as she settled her plump body atop of his.

"How did I rescue you?" she asked breathlessly, feeling the press of his thick, heavy cock against her soft belly.

"From that jester," he whispered. "Do not tell me you have forgotten. It is burned on my memory like a brand."

Gunnilde gazed down at him in puzzlement. "You mean—?"

"When first you kissed me," he said in a gravelly voice.

"Well, in fact our first kiss was after we exchanged vows," she reminded him.

"No," he rumbled, his eyes trained on her mouth. "No, that was when I first kissed you, which was naught but a pathetic peck. Yours was much better."

Was it? Gunnilde cast back in her mind, but surely hers had been just as close-mouthed an effort, scarcely even qualifying as a kiss? She looked back at James, but he gazed back at her so intently that she found she had to believe him. What had she done that had affected him so?

"You mean, when I did this?" she asked, slowly placing her hands on either side of his face.

He caught his breath. "Yes," he hissed.

Oh. So, it had been her seizing the initiative. "You like for me to have the upper hand, James?" she asked, making him whimper. Goodness, he did like it, she thought with dawning realization. He liked it a lot.

"And this?" she asked, lowering her face to his and sealing her lips to his mouth. In fact, this was quite, quite different, she acknowledged, as she ran her tongue against the seam of his mouth. She wouldn't have dreamed of kissing him thus at their wedding feast. Part of her wondered if he would not have shoved her off his lap if she had done such a thing!

Well, he certainly was not pushing her away now, she acknowledged as he sucked her tongue into his mouth with a needy groan. Gunnilde only allowed him the briefest stroke of her tongue against his own before she withdrew, making him gasp with dissatisfaction.

"We did not kiss in front of all our wedding guests like this," she reminded him, tutting. "Such a thing would have been most improper."

"Nay, you kissed me longer," he insisted. "Much longer. Until the jester fully passed us by."

"Did I?" she asked, frowning as though with the effort of recall.

"Yes," he growled. "Do it right."

She had to hide a smile. Do it right, indeed! If she did it right, it would be naught but a simple pressing of her face against his own! "Oh, very well," she said, tossing her head. It did not have quite the effect she desired, for her hair was wet and plastered down her back. Still, James seemed to appreciate the gesture, his eyes roaming greedily over her face and neck.

To reward his patience, Gunnilde lowered her lips once more to his, this time she sipped sweetly awhile before teasing the tip of his tongue with her own. James gasped against her mouth, his hands landing on her waist, grabbing her there and squeezing in an encouraging fashion.

Gunnilde stroked her thumbs over his cheekbones, slanting her mouth over his and deepening their kiss until James's tongue tangled enthusiastically with her own. His hands slid down her hips, cupping her bottom as if to pull her closer still, as if she was not already on top of him.

Dimly, it occurred to her that there was one way their bodies could be closer. If he was inside of her. Was that a thing they could do right now? Pulling back her face, she gazed down at James, letting her eyes travel over his flushed face.

"James?" she whispered. He did not answer, just gazed at her, his breathing ragged, his eyes unfocussed. How should she propose such a thing? She took a deep breath. "I want you inside of me. Right now."

He shivered, then heaved up onto his haunches. "James!" Gunnilde squawked, finding herself suddenly hefted up out of the water. What was he doing? She gaped down at him, amazed that he could bear her weight as he settled on the edge of the tub, with her still clinging onto him, perched precariously on his thighs. "You—you're getting water all over the floor!"

He was panting hard and did not answer, his attention focused between her legs as he parted her cleft and started gently rubbing her there. "I want you to be wet for me, not just from the bathwater," he said tersely.

Oh. Gunnilde touched her forehead to his and reached down to guide his thumb. "Touch me here," she told him bossily. After all, he liked her bossy. With a nod, he started circling the pad of his thumb just the way that she liked. "That's good, James," she told him in honeyed tones. "Very good."

He gave murmur of agreement, then slipped a finger up inside of her. Gunnilde's breathing hitched. "Oh!" she whimpered, shifting restlessly against him. She was definitely wet from his ministrations now. Very wet. "Another," she requested. He grunted and added another finger, stretching her to make her ready.

Suddenly, every glide of his fingers, every touch of his thumb thrilled her to her very core. She pointed her toes, arched her back, and cried out at the sheer pleasure of it all. James seized hold of her buttocks, tugging her forward, so she slid down his wet, muscular thighs toward his throbbing cock which jutted out toward her. Unable to withstand the temptation, she wrapped her fingers around it, squeezing gently.

"Gods!" James uttered in a guttural voice. He thrust himself more firmly into her hold, closing his eyes, chest heaving. "Fuck, Gunnilde," he panted. "I can't—"

"Oh yes, you can, James," she insisted sweetly. "You can do it now. Come inside me. I want you to." She leaned back, widening her legs and positioning him right where he needed to be.

James thrust up with his hips. "Oh!" Her eyes watered to find him so firmly lodged inside of her. He stilled at once, his eyes searching her

386

face in query. Gunnilde wriggled a moment to check all was well. She breathed out in relief.

"Yes?" he asked, a tense look on his face.

"Yes," she agreed. "More."

He breathed out shakily and bucked his hips again, once more, twice more, his fingers digging into the flesh of her hips until he was fully sheathed. Then he gave a low groan of relief, his mouth seeking hers again. Gunnilde kissed him back with all the wild longing she felt.

Feeling a warmth steal once more over her limbs, she realized that James was sliding back down the side of the tub, until they were half submerged in the water. Tearing her lips from his, she sat up to take stock of the situation. James's head was tipped back, and he was watching her through desire-glazed eyes.

"You're incredible," he said.

Gunnilde hesitated. Stupid to ask for clarification. He meant her body, of course. Still, she could not help herself. "Do you really think so?" she whispered.

He nodded and she felt a pang in her chest. How could he look so terribly sincere? He also looked calmer now he was inside her, which was unfair, as Gunnilde was feeling anything but. She wriggled against him and gasped at the sensation of fullness. "James," she whined.

"Let's stay like this awhile."

"Like this?" He nodded. "I don't know if I can. I need..." She bit her lip.

"What?" he asked throatily. "Tell me."

"To move."

"Move, then," he said it almost like a challenge. "Move on me."

Gunnilde released his shoulders to reach up behind him and grip the edge of the tub, then she shifted herself over him, making him grunt. She undulated, which felt nice, so nice, but wasn't enough. She needed more. More friction. She ground herself down on him, forward, then back, making him gasp and draw his knees up behind her, feeling him deep.

"Yes," he hissed. "Don't stop."

All the while, she felt the heat of James's gaze on her as she took her pleasure. His hands slid down from caressing her breasts to clasp her hips tight, urging her movements to become brisker and brisker, until it was more of a bounce. His eyes roamed greedily over her jolting breasts.

She rose up on her knees, only for James to growl and slam her back down onto his cock. She cried out at the sensation.

"Again," he urged thickly. "Do that again."

She did so, panting and sobbing and clutching the edge of the tub for dear life. The water churned around them, slopping over the sides. "J-James," she moaned brokenly.

"Don't stop," he rasped, his hips now moving furiously beneath her own. She whined as it all grew too much, tightening her thighs about him, her inner muscles, and throwing back her head.

James shouted aloud, surging forward to press a hot, breathless kiss to her throat. Feeling the scrape of his teeth there, she exploded in a shower of stars and felt him join her with a ragged groan of deep satisfaction.

388

38

It was two days later as Gunnilde hurried along the corridor from her final fitting with Signor Castellar that she ran full tilt into the solid form of a burly knight. He reached out to steady her, and Gunnilde recoiled as though bitten by a snake, for it was Sir Ned.

"Oh! Your pardon—" she blurted, seeing the stricken look on his face. Forcing herself to take a steadying breath, she plastered an insincere smile to her face. "That was my fault entirely, do forgive me."

"Gunnilde—" He faltered, addressing her quite incorrectly. Where once such familiarity would have gladdened her, she now felt herself bristle. "Can we not—?"

She met the look of anguished appeal in his eyes with one of cool politeness. "There is something I can help you with, Sir Edward?" she enquired.

He sighed and scrubbed his eyes. He did look tired, she noticed without much sympathy. "I—that is, could I beg the favor of a few moments speech with you, Lady Wycliffe?" he asked with an attempt to match her own politeness.

She inclined her head. "There appears to be no one else around at present," she said, glancing about them at the empty corridor. "I trust this spot is a convenient one."

Sir Ned hesitated, throwing a harried glance down the corridor. "Not for long I'll warrant," he answered with dissatisfaction. "This palace is crawling with courtiers."

"And I am one of them," she answered in clipped tones. "Perhaps you could come to the point. I am on my way to meet friends and have little time to spare this morn."

His face fell. "You must know why I—with how much regret I think of—" He threw another look of appeal her way. "I am not good at this."

"I cannot possibly comment on that, not knowing what 'this' is."

"An apology, of course!" he burst out.

"Is it?" She crossed her arms. "Traditionally an apology begins quite differently to your own effort." Seeing his look of blank incomprehension, she started tapping one foot against the flagstone floor. Really, no wonder the Queen thought knights dissatisfactory, she reflected; they certainly had their shortcomings.

"I'm sorry!" he blurted at last, the phrase finally dawning on him. "You must surely know that."

"Must I?" Gunnilde mused. "Oh, you mean because Mistress Fern explained your current predicament."

He turned bright red. "Oh, I just I bet she did, the little wretch. But no, that is not what I meant," he said vehemently. "My current predicament has naught to do with the fact that I bitterly regretted my words that day, as soon as I saw they had wounded you."

Gunnilde narrowed her eyes at him. "Oh, did you indeed?"

"I did. They have haunted me, and I don't just mean because of, well, you know, the curse," he said, scratching the back of his neck and looking uncomfortable. "Long before that, I felt quite sick to think of what I said. Those words drift into my mind at the most inconvenient of times and make my whole body itch with shame at their remembrance. I only wish to gods that I could scrub them from my own memory and yours."

He looked so shamefaced that Gunnilde found to her surprise that she believed him. "I must confess I had not the smallest expectation that you would feel thus," she said frankly. "I expected you to shove it to the back of your mind, and little think of it again until the awkwardness of our next encounter."

"Then you thought wrong! I swear to you, I felt this sense of scalding shame even before that hag's curse. I felt like the worst kind of… It is not my habit to… I had no idea you would overhear any of it!" he concluded incoherently. "I only wish you would believe me."

Gunnilde gazed at his miserable expression and gave a nod. "Oh, very well," she said.

A look of hope dawned on Ned Bevan's face. "You mean it?" he asked in a choked voice. "You really mean it?"

She nodded again. "Just try and be more considerate of the feelings of others in future," she said curtly.

"I can promise you that with confidence, for I have learned my lesson," he said, his words coming out in a relieved rush. "I've felt like the worst kind of knave ever since you whipped back that curtain and put me in my place. That took real fortitude to do that, you know. I've thought of it often since then with"—he hesitated—"much regret. You were so forthright, and I behaved like a complete whoreson."

He winced, though whether at his own language or his previous conduct she was not sure. "Then I was too cowardly to speak to you for days afterward, avoiding you," he admitted, swallowing. "And when I finally mustered the courage to face you, I found you'd run off to court and felt even worse!"

"You must really have suffered!" Gunnilde said blandly.

He flashed her an uncertain look. "No, I did not mean—! That is—" He took a deep breath. "Will you accept my sincerest apology, Lady Wycliffe? I swear I extend it in a truly chastened spirit. In truth, I've never felt so bad about anything before in my life. Not even when I knocked my first cousin's two front teeth out."

He looked so wholly contrite that Gunnilde found herself softening in spite of herself. "I forgive you, Sir Ned," she decided impulsively, extending her hand.

His face brightened. "Really?" Carefully he took her hand in his.

"Yes." She smiled at him and Sir Ned gulped. Before he could raise her hand to his lips, James appeared beside them and somehow Gunnilde found he was now holding it, while Bevan looked down at his own empty hand in bemusement.

"James!" she exclaimed in surprise, turning toward him.

He tucked her hand under his arm. "I'm afraid I must remove my wife from hence," he said to Sir Ned coldly. "I trust this conversation is concluded."

"Oh yes," Gunnilde agreed happily. "We are quite reconciled, is that not so, Sir Ned?"

Sir Ned cleared his throat. "Quite so," he said, looking from Gunnilde to James. Whatever he saw in James's expression seemed to cause him to take a step back.

"I hope you will attend our banquet on the morrow," Gunnilde reminded him. "Hal said he had extended you an invitation."

"Oh, er, thank you, yes," Ned answered awkwardly.

"Perhaps you could bring your witch along with you," James suggested, a decided edge to his words.

Ned flushed. "She would not come even if I begged her," he retorted, making Gunnilde's eyebrows rise. He took his leave of them and beat a hasty retreat.

"Did you notice he did not disclaim any ownership of Mistress Fern?" Gunnilde whispered. "I thought that interesting."

James did not reply, and when she glanced up at him, he appeared to be struggling with some unexpressed emotion.

"Not that I am attempting to make a match between them," she said hastily. That distracted him alright.

"Between Mistress Fern and Bevan?" he said disbelievingly.

"Yes, why not?" She squeezed his arm. "Anyway, what are you doing here in the palace this morn? I thought you were rehearsing today at Master Gregory's."

"I was. I nipped back. We're not meeting at Barnabus Hall until the clock strikes two, so I have time."

"Time for what?"

"To see if you wanted to take your midday repast with me."

"Oh." She smiled at him. "You will not mind us sharing a table with Harriet and Winifred, I hope. Only I promised to meet with them in the Great Hall."

"It is I who is the interloper," he acknowledged handsomely, "so I can hardly object to sharing you."

What lovely manners James had, she reflected over the next hour as he conversed politely with her friends. To think she had once thought him rude and unapproachable. She had been quite wrong in her assessment of his character. James was considerate, she decided, in the truest sense of the word.

He would not dream of describing either Winifred's or Harriet's appearances in a detrimental fashion to his friends. Of course, he did not really have much by way of friends. Master Gregory was a sweet, unworldly sort. She suspected he would be quite bewildered if James started discussing women's appearances with him.

Of course, he had discussed her appearance with Neville, by his own admission. She tried to remember what he told her he had said. Something about her manner of dress being very shocking, she remembered and had to hide her smile. He had been flustered even in the retelling.

She was glad she had not married a tournament knight, she realized with some surprise. She did not dislike Sir Ned anymore and she was thankful for that fact. It felt rather like a barb had been drawn out of her flesh, leaving her feeling whole once more, and freed from its torment. But the absence of pain did not mean that her former admiration came flooding back. In truth she felt…rather indifferent toward him and indeed the whole parcel of them.

While her resentment had blazed, a new ideal had taken root in her affections. She, like Winifred, Harriet, and Eden, now admired the artist above all others, she decided, for James was a true artist. That afternoon she had spent watching and listening in Barnabus Hall had opened her eyes to something truly sublime and she would never feel quite the same again.

Gunnilde was sure she would still enjoy a tourney should the occasion arise, especially if her brother should happen to be competing. If the doors of Payne Manor were ever opened to her again, she would happily sit through her father's tournament with a smile on her face, but she would no longer be filled with trembling excitement at the mere prospect.

No, that state of anticipation would be reserved in the future for James's wonderful compositions, she thought. They awed and enthralled her. Since "I Cannot Show the Love I Owe," she had heard another of his pieces performed, the one he had sold to Lady Schaeffer as a present for her husband.

That piece had been a good deal shorter and not as dramatic as Mistress Bartree's, and she had not heard it performed by four musicians as it should have been played. Instead, James had played the melody for her on Hal's lute. Still, it had taken her breath away, and at its conclusion, she had been moved to beg him to play it through once again so that she might savor the experience.

"What is it titled?" she had asked at the close.

James had looked a little discomforted. "'A Conscientious Man, Faithful of Duty,' he had said, clearing his throat. "Lady Schaeffer chose the title."

"And what was it called before you rededicated it?"

"It was just numbered thirty-eight."

"As in your thirty-eighth composition?" she had asked. He had nodded. "I hope one day I can hear all thirty-eight," she had said wistfully.

The next day James had brought one of his lutes back with him so that he could play her a private rendition whenever the mood took him. She especially liked his very early compositions, for their simplicity pleased her and his tender age when writing them touched her greatly. Numbers three and seven were particular favorites of hers, written when he was only ten years old. She had bade him perform them for Hal and his friends, who had made a surprisingly enthusiastic audience.

"Not bad, Wycliffe," Kit had commented. "If you would just put a little effort into stringing some words together, you could have the makings of a first-class ballad writer, I am convinced of it."

"He does not need to—" Gunnilde had started to expostulate when James had slipped an arm about her waist, distracting her.

"Tell me about False Billiam," he had interrupted. "How goes it with his story?"

"Not well," Cuthbert had snorted. "Hal can't get past the first couple of lines, though he did decide that Fair Margaret should get a new suitor after Billiam's tragic end."

"You mean after all his limbs drop off?" James asked dryly.

"After he plunges to his death from the castle ramparts," Hal corrected him.

"And his name," Kit had volunteered, "is Trusty John. Trusty John will be everything that False Billiam is not."

"I am very glad to hear it."

"Who in the world is False Billiam?" Gunnilde had asked in bewilderment. The boys had then launched into a confused account of the ballad they had taken over from James. "It sounds awful!" she had decided roundly, much to her brother's chagrin. "I for one am heartily glad that James did not decide his future lay in ballads if this is an indication of their quality!"

James had laughed. "I will stick to what I know," he had promised and kissed her hand.

39

Gunnilde's feet paced once more the length of their designated function room to check everything was in place and looking as it should. The second largest dining hall had been the one allocated for their use in the end, as the lower gallery was not deemed large enough to house all the musicians they now required.

Now space was no longer an issue, Gunnilde found herself apprehensive that they could fill the room. What if no guests turned up? She let her eye wander over the large fireplace which she had spent all afternoon festooning with holly and ivy. As far as Gunnilde knew, it was the first of the decorations put up in the palace, for they decorated very late in the season in royal residences.

Dozens of candles were lit and suspended all about to give the room a warm, inviting glow. The silver goblets glinted, reflecting their light, and the red and white berries glistened against the vivid greenery of their leaves.

It looked very well, she told herself. Everything looked as it should. No one could find fault with the provisions that had been arranged. Gods, she hoped enough people turned up to eat all the food and drink all the wine they had ordered in!

"Milady?"

Turning, she found their manservant hovering with a disapproving look on his face.

"Yes, Bennett?" The wonder of it was that he had decided to prioritize them for once instead of the Ashdowns. Bennett had made himself useful all afternoon, fetching and carrying for her and ably assisting with the draping of leaves. She had been quite impressed with him. "What is it?"

He drew himself up. "The musicians have arrived." His tone was much as though he was announcing the arrival of bailiffs. Bennett, it seemed, did not approve of musicians.

"Oh good! Please show them in. You know where we agreed they should set up."

He inclined his head and turned on his heel to admit them.

"Gunnilde!" It was James, coming in the opposite double doorway, a frown upon his handsome face. She caught her breath to see him in the splendor of his purple velvet and gold. She had never seen him displayed to such advantage! If he was to be painted, it should be wearing that, she thought dreamily. He looked an absolute vision!

"Are you listening to what I'm saying?" he asked abruptly, coming to a halt before her.

She started guiltily, throwing him a look of enquiry. "Sorry. What did you say?"

"Why did you not wait for me?" he asked.

"I wanted to ensure all was made ready," she explained apologetically. "I could not rest until I had. What do you think?" she asked, biting her lip.

His gaze flickered briefly around the room before coming back to dwell on her, specifically the low cut of her neckline. "I thought you said your gown wasn't a flaunting one."

"Flaunting?" She glanced down at her velvet and cloth of gold gown. "Do you think so? Signor Castellar called it 'regally commanding.' You do not like it?"

"I did not say that." He paused. "It certainly draws the eye, but then"—he shrugged—"you always draw my eye."

She held up her arms so that he could see the gold stitched detail on her tippets. "Do you see my Wycliffe unicorns?"

He gave a faint smile. "Yes."

"I must say, you look quite devastating," she said, taking in the cut of his purple doublet with the gold trim. The deep slashes in his sleeves displayed the sumptuous cloth of gold beneath. "Master Hughes has excelled himself. We must certainly employ his services again."

"You will kindly note my paneled hose, for was that not a complaint of yours in the early days of our marriage?" At her confused look, he added, "That I did not wear them."

"Oh. Well, I was quite right, for these look wonderful on you," she said, her admiring gaze sweeping down to his legs.

"What about yours?" he asked, lowering his voice. "Did you buy a new pair of fifteen-shilling stockings as instructed?"

"I did," she assured him.

"I suppose I am to take that on trust," he replied, a gleam in his eye.

Gunnilde hesitated, then caught her heavy velvet skirts in her two hands and lifted them to reveal her ankles. "How do you like them?" she asked.

"Very nice, though I am disappointed you did not have time to get your slippers embroidered."

"The next pair I will," she consoled him.

"Until then, I have this for you." He handed over a carved wooden box.

Gunnilde took it with a questioning look, then ran her fingers over the lid, which was carved with the image of a seated unicorn. "Oh, James, it's lovely! I could keep my brooch in it. The one the Queen gave me." Her hand flew to touch the jewel pinned to her bodice as though it was a talisman.

"It already has something in it," he replied.

"Oh?" Unlatching the lid, she found a pearl necklet nestled within the silk lining. "James!"

"It's just a short string," he said, lifting them out of the box. "But look here at the pendant."

Gunnilde peered closely and saw a round gold disc bearing the impression of a heraldic beast. "A unicorn," she exclaimed. "And are those my initials beneath it?"

"They are."

"I love it!" Her face fell. "But I did not think we were currently in funds," she said, lowering her voice. "However did you afford it?"

"I bought it with the proceeds from that piece I sold to Lady Schaeffer. Here, let me put it on you."

Gunnilde turned about, scooping up her hair and veil so that he could fasten it about her neck. She placed a hand on the pearls where they sat proudly at the base of her neck. "How do they look?"

"They are the perfect length for you."

"You mean because my neck is short," she said without rancor. "It is rather. I wish I had a swanlike neck like Frances Lessimore but my figure is not at all elegant."

"A swanlike neck on a woman would look patently absurd," James replied dismissively.

Gunnilde sighed. "At least your black eye has practically disappeared now," she said, reaching up to briefly touch his brow. He leaned down and, to her surprise, kissed her firmly on the lips.

"Look lively. Here comes your brother."

Glancing over her shoulder, she spied Hal on the threshold, resplendent in a bright green tunic decorated all over with white roses. Spotting them, he hurried over.

"Well, I must say you've done yourself proud, sister," he said, looking around with approval. "It all looks very well, very well indeed."

Gunnilde was gratified. "You will not be embarrassed to introduce the prince around, I hope."

"Gods, no! Not that I think he'll come. He's a taciturn little beast at the best of times. Never know what he's thinking."

Gunnilde's eyebrows rose. Over the past week Hal's, Cuthbert's, and Kit's enthusiasm had waned somewhat for their roles in Prince Raedan's retinue. "You did invite him though?" she asked anxiously. Hal nodded but clearly did not hold out any hope he would show.

Gunnilde had caught sight of Prince Raedan only twice since he had come to court. The first time had been during supper one night in the Great Hall, where she had craned her neck along with everyone else to catch a glimpse of him. They had all been rather disappointed, for the young prince was a stony-faced boy, with little by way of charm or wit to recommend him.

The prince had surveyed all around him with cold disinterest, while his father tried to bluster his way through supper, talking loudly and boisterously while young Raedan sat there like an effigy, unmoved and unfeeling, while everyone fell over themselves in an effort to ingratiate themselves.

The second time she had seen him, the prince was being escorted down the long gallery by Earl Vawdrey, who was giving him the palace tour. Excited whispers started as he approached the portrait of Marguerite of Lascony, a niece of Queen Armenal's who was rumored to be a front-runner in the field of prospective brides for the heir apparent.

Gunnilde had a fondness for Marguerite's painting, for she wore a pair of preposterously large jeweled sleeves which she admired very much, and moreover had wonderfully elegant hands. The prince halted a moment in front of her portrait, and everyone held their breath, wondering if he would say something pithy about his possible future bride.

In this, as in everything else, Prince Raedan disappointed them, for after passing his eyes over it, he moved along without comment. At this point everyone had decided that Prince Raedan was something of a lost cause.

"No, he doesn't give much away, does he?" Gunnilde said sadly. "Still, I wish he would come. It would be quite the coup for us, for he has snubbed every other courtier event, has he not?"

Hal snorted. "He can barely muster any enthusiasm for the events thrown in his honor by his own father, the King!"

"Has he attended much of the Revels so far?" James asked with a flicker of interest.

"Oh yes, but he shows precious little interest in proceedings. Cold-blooded, that's what he is. Less of an Argent lion and more of a codfish!" Hal glanced around. "Ah, here they are!" he said, hailing his friends. "Over here! Gads," he said in an aside, "they will be tripping over the points of those shoes before long, if they are not careful!"

Kit and Cuthbert entered the room in their finest arraignment. Kit looked a little self-conscious in a short doublet of bright blue, which he kept tugging down over his tights, while Cuthbert wore a tunic of sumptuous red velvet with white fur-lined sleeves all scalloped and cut around the edges. As Hal had pointed out, both boys wore the exaggeratedly long-toed shoes that were currently so fashionable.

"I'm so glad you've come early to set my nerves at rest," Gunnilde greeted them. "Now tell me, do you think there is anything amiss with the way the room is presented?"

Both boys assured her that all looked most splendid. "It does you credit, as does your own appearance, my lady," Kit told her graciously, bowing over her hand. He kissed her fingers with a flourish.

"Don't be impressed, he practices that gesture on a gauntlet," Cuthbert said dampeningly.

"Speaking of attire, what the devil have you done to your sleeves, Ames?" Hal enquired. "You got rats in your armoire?"

"My tailor informs me they are the latest thing," Cuthbert replied off-handedly. "The edges are dagged. Apparently, everyone will be wearing them this way by next spring."

403

Gunnilde's ears pricked up. "Is that so?" Obligingly Cuthbert held out his sleeve to her so she could examine the intricate cutting technique all along the edge.

He tipped his head to one side, looking at Hal's own elaborately decorated tunic. "White roses," he mused. "Who have you dressed to match, I wonder?"

Kit made an explosively derisive noise and Hal turned bright red. "Who says I have dressed to match anyone?" he asked belligerently. "I'll ask you to keep your baseless speculations to yourself!"

Cuthbert ducked his head to hide his grin, and Kit smirked, nudging James in the side.

"Shall I go and tell Bennett to start handing the drinks around?" James asked. "And tell the musicians to start playing?"

"Oh, would you?" Gunnilde cast him a grateful look as he took the empty jewelry case out of her hand.

"I'll put this somewhere safe," he said and went off in search of Bennett.

"I like his suit," Hal observed as all three boys turned to watch him walk away. "Your influence at work, I take it," he said, glancing at Gunnilde. Her bosom swelled with pride.

"He'd look good even in an old sack," Kit opined, promptly bringing her back down to earth.

"Maybe, but I believe he'll attract more patrons this way," Cuthbert said, meeting her eyes enigmatically. They watched as he gestured to the musicians and the music started up. Almost immediately the atmosphere seemed to take on a jaunty air. Servers filed into the room and started filling the goblets and handing them around.

"Ah, here's Neville now, with the Ashdowns," Hal observed as Neville walked in with an elderly damsel on each arm.

"Oh, how lovely!" Gunnilde cried, for both Mistress Ruth and Mistress Abigail Ashdown were beaming ear to ear and dressed in matching dresses of royal blue. James joined her once again, and they walked over to welcome them. Gunnilde told them all about how helpful Bennett had been all afternoon and complimented the sisters on their new matching gowns.

"Well, but you are also matching," Mistress Abigail said, looking her and James up and down. "You make a handsome couple, my dears."

"Speaking of handsome, where is that dashing brother of yours?" Mistress Ruth asked eagerly. "He promised to dance with me."

"Hal? Oh, he's here some whereabouts."

"Probably lying in wait for that Mistress Culmington he was telling me about, the young rogue!"

Mistress Culmington? Gunnilde's eyes widened. She had suspected for a while that Hal's affections had taken a turn from Estrilda toward Emma Thackeray, but she had not realized that Penelope was even in the running! Was there not some rumor circulating that she was in the midst of an affair du coeur with Sir Symond Chevenix? That was the trouble with spending most of her time with Harriet and Winifred, neither of them were ever abreast of palace gossip.

"Dear me, who is this?" Neville said, staring in the direction of the doorway. "What an unfortunate-looking headdress. It looks rather like she is balancing an anvil atop her head."

Gunnilde turned and spied her childhood friend Muriel Lelland stood just inside the doorway, looking decidedly ill at ease. Her headdress was somewhat cumbersome, though to Gunnilde's mind, it was the unbecoming chin strap that was mostly to blame.

"Who are they?" James asked as he took drinks from a passing attendant and handed them to the Ashdowns.

"It is my old friend Muriel," she said, "and her husb—" But it was not her husband, she realized belatedly, who hovered at Muriel's side. No, it was not Sir Christopher Lelland but Gunnilde's former affianced! "And—and her brother, Sir Arthur Conway," she finished unevenly.

James caught hold of her arm. "The Queen will be disappointed to miss this first encounter," he said. "Shall we go and greet them, wife?"

"Er…yes, let's," she replied, glancing up at him with some trepidation. Was it just her imagination or was James's manner somewhat preemptory? Together they made their way toward the unprepossessing couple. Arthur's moustache looked rather limp, Gunnilde thought. And why did he look so nervous?

Muriel practically let out a yelp as they came to a halt before her. "G-Gunnilde," she stammered. "Why, I scarcely recognized you! You look so grand." Her wide eyes took in Gunnilde's silk and velvet magnificence before she turned to James and her jaw positively dropped.

"Allow me to introduce my husband," Gunnilde said proudly. "Sir James Wycliffe. James, these are the friends of my childhood I told you about, Lady Lelland and Sir Arthur Conway."

As she spoke, Gunnilde turned toward Arthur, who was also staring open-mouthed at James. "Y-your servant, sir," he stammered, bowing at James, and then to Gunnilde's surprise, he turned to look at her, his expression equally dazzled. "My lady," he said in a choked voice, "it has been too long. You are looking quite uncommonly well."

James let out a hiss of air. "Your husband does not accompany you tonight, Lady Lelland?" he said, addressing Muriel, his voice cold and clipped.

"Alas no," Muriel answered, practically falling over herself to answer him. "Sir Christopher's health always suffers at this time of year. The damp, you know."

"It's doubtless his age," Arthur added. "It seeps into the bones, you know, and sets them to creaking."

James turned to her. "Gunnilde would not know about such things, for she has a young and vigorous husband," he observed, robbing her of breath. "Is that not so, my love?"

"Er, yes," she agreed, feeling rather flustered that he should address her thus. She shot him a sidelong glance. What was he doing?

"Though I suppose an older husband affords you certain freedoms that I would not permit my own wife," he continued. "For one, I would not allow Gunnilde to travel any great distance across country without me by her side."

"Fulford is not so very far away," Muriel protested before her brother cut in.

"Such sentiment does you credit, sir," Arthur replied hastily. "And I am sure I do not wonder that you feel that way." He bowed again gallantly in Gunnilde's direction. Both Muriel and James looked somewhat annoyed by his rejoinder.

"Sir Christopher knows that he can trust me to behave at all times with the utmost consideration of his honor," Muriel rallied, two high spots of color appearing on her cheeks.

"No doubt," James answered bluntly. "But my own feelings have nothing whatsoever to do with my wife's conduct. Rather they are concerned with others who would covet that which is mine and mine alone." He passed a possessive arm about Gunnilde's waist.

"Again," Sir Arthur said, bowing. "I fully comprehend your feeling, and I cannot wonder at them."

Over his shoulder, Gunnilde noticed the arrival of a gaggle of ladies-in-waiting. They glittered in the doorway in their jewel-colored gowns. She cleared her throat. "I am so glad you could both attend," she said brightly. "We hope—"

"The Queen arrives!" Piers Winstanley's confident voice rang out. "Make way for the Queen of all Karadok!" Everyone turned to look at his tall, commanding figure as he turned and swept an elegant bow. Queen Armenal sailed into the room accompanied by two royal guards who fell back to stand either side of the door.

The Queen shone with rubies tonight which flashed at her hair, her bodice, and her throat. She was gorgeously arrayed in a gown of gold and black silk, lavishly trimmed with fur. Muriel gasped and shrank back despite the fact there was ample room remaining.

"I cannot believe she has arrived so early," James murmured in Gunnilde's ear. "She must have really high hopes of being entertained tonight."

He and Gunnilde walked forward to present their bows and welcome Her Majesty to their gathering. The Queen smiled and nodded graciously. Then she paused, inspecting James with some surprise. "But you are quite striking tonight in your beauty, Sir James," she told him. "Even more so than usual. I think I see your wife's influence at hand in this new bolder style of dress."

He bowed again. "I give my wife free rein when it comes to such things."

"You are wise to do so," the Queen said, nodding. "Though I am not so sure that she is." She cast a quizzical look at Gunnilde. "The ladies, how they all stare! You must have noticed it, my dear Gunnilde."

"I have," Gunnilde acknowledged calmly. "And I am glad it should be so. Beauty is a thing that should be universally admired." She turned to look frankly at her husband. "Do you not think he would make the most remarkable portrait represented thus?"

The Queen looked much struck by this rejoinder. She turned to look at James once more. "He would indeed," she murmured. "Such rich colors represented against the auburn of his hair would make a striking image."

James cleared his throat. "My wife has nothing to fear by way of contrast or competition," he said, catching hold of her hand and squeezing it tight.

"Most handsomely put!" the Queen said approvingly. "I begin to think you have been hiding aspects of your character and even your talent from us, Sir James. Gunnilde tells me we are to hear some of your music this evening, inspired by the history of one of my own ladies."

"It was inspired by the tale my wife told me," he answered firmly. "The inspiration lay in the vividness of the retelling."

"Well," the Queen said thoughtfully, "my Magnatrude is not at all sure how to take the compliment. She will come tonight, I think, but more from duty than curiosity."

As if on cue, Mistress Bartree appeared in the doorway with her little page, Unwin. She was head to toe in black, unalleviated save for one jeweled bar brooch in the center of her bodice. Her expression was very dour.

"She cuts quite the figure, does she not?" the Queen mused. "A fitting subject for your music. Tell me, is it tragic in tone?"

"Oh yes, very," Gunnilde replied, eyes sparkling. "You will love it, Your Majesty. It quite moved me to tears when first I heard it."

"Indeed?" At this moment, a small stir arrived, for two more royal guards marched into the room. "But what is this?" cried Armenal in consternation. "Do not tell me that Wymer—?" Her words broke off as her stepson promptly walked into the room. "Oh!"

"He came!" breathed Gunnilde, looking around in excitement. Hal, Kit, and Cuthbert crossed the room to take charge of the situation, herding the crown prince in Gunnilde's direction.

Bows were performed and introductions made. "Royal Mother," the prince said, addressing the Queen. "I did not realize you would be in attendance this evening." He spoke the words blandly though politely.

The Queen smiled at him beneficently. "But yes. The good Gunnilde, she is a protégé of mine, and I take much interest in her progress. My attendance was assured from the outset. But you, my prince, you attend at the behest of Master Payne, I presume?" She turned to Hal. "You are the brother," she said, nodding to herself. "For me, I can see a strong family likeness. But who is this?"

Hal bowed. "This is my hound, Dustin, Your Majesty," he explained, lifting his arm to present the small white dog for royal observation.

"A hound?" Queen Armenal sounded doubtful. "This would not be considered a hound in my country."

"I dare assure you he is a hound," Hal answered mildly. "Whereso'er I goest, my faithful hound does follow."

"Usually tucked in his tunic or clinging to his arm," Prince Raedan supplied critically. "My father would not let me bring my own dog, Balto, to court, he—" But whatever he had been about to impart they were not to find out.

Dustin, realizing he was the topic of conversation, let out an excited bark and made a leap for the young prince. Surprised, Prince Raedan caught him and gave a startled laugh when Dustin's tongue shot out to lick his face.

"Down, sir!" Hal scolded without heat. "You are impertinent!" He stepped forward to disentangle Dustin from the prince's elaborate tunic, which was decorated all over with gold thread. "Ever heard of another animal that barks?" he asked the company at large with casual assurance.

An astonished silence prevailed. Everyone was far too shocked by Dustin's lack of etiquette to answer. "Then there you have it," he concluded with satisfaction. "He's a hound. No question about it."

"He fights anyone that disagrees," Kit interjected. "So, it's as well not to argue with him."

Queen Armenal blinked, and for a moment Gunnilde held her breath, worried that Hal had given unforgivable offence. "You are a handsome flower of youth," the Queen said, choosing to focus instead on Kit. "You are a Montmayne, are you not? And you," she said, turning to Cuthbert, "interest me very much for you are like the golden sun to his moon. The pair of you would grace any court, even my brother's court in fair Lascony. Come and tell me your prospects, for I find myself most interested in you."

411

Gunnilde breathed a sigh of relief as the Queen moved to one side with Cuthbert and Kit, a diverted look upon her face. She glanced at Hal, concerned her brother might feel left out of proceedings, but he seemed to have caught sight of some new arrivals and was haring off toward them.

"It's likely the arrival of Mistress Rheinholdt or is it Mistress Thackeray that is the current beloved," James muttered for her ears only.

They both turned to look at the new arrivals, but as a matter of fact it was Hadrian Kellingford and a bunch of other squires her brother had invited along.

"I'm not so sure Hal has not got a new love interest," Gunnilde answered. "Have you seen anyone wearing green and white this eve? Only Cuthbert intimated that Hal might have dressed to match his current lady love."

"There's a lady stood over by the fireplace," Prince Raedan spoke up, betraying the fact he had very sharp ears, "whose dress is embroidered all over with white roses."

"Indeed?" Gunnilde turned in that direction. "Oh dear," she fretted. It was Mistress Culmington. Hal had transferred his affections, she was sure of it, but when Hal strolled back into view moments later, he was escorting Patience Stanhope on his arm and listening most attentively to everything that lady had to say.

"Lord Vawdrey just arrived," the prince told her quietly.

"Oh!" Gunnilde grabbed James's sleeve, then hesitated turning back to the prince. "Would you like to come with us to greet them, Your Highness?" she asked, not liking to leave him unattended. He considered a moment before nodding and accompanied them as they

412

made their way to where Earl Vawdrey was stood with his plump, pretty countess.

Greetings were exchanged and Lord Vawdrey looked surprised yet pleased to see the young prince in attendance. "I see Master Payne has tempted you from your rooms this evening, Your Highness," he said with an approving smile. "No doubt, it is the lure of his sister's entertainments that drew you out."

"Well, he swore there would be no jesters present," Prince Raedan answered succinctly. "That was sufficient a draw for me."

James perked up at this. "You do not care for jesters, Your Highness?"

"No, I do not," the prince replied decisively. He and James immediately began trading stories of unpleasant encounters they had undergone with jesters over the years. "My father won't go anywhere without one!" Prince Raedan scowled.

Gunnilde's hands were seized by Countess Vawdrey. "You look so beautiful this evening, Gunnilde, quite radiant," Fenella declared, kissing her cheek. "I will not stand on ceremony with you, for we are traveling down to Vawdrey Keep on the morrow and I mean to tell Eden we are on the very best of terms. I hope you will not mind my exaggerating somewhat," she said apologetically.

"Oh, not at all!" Gunnilde assured her. "I only hope that Eden will forgive me for not informing her of all my news firsthand. I have a half-written letter to her in my rooms that I should have finished days ago, only I have been so busy, you see."

"I am not surprised, for there is always something afoot here at court. And tomorrow the Squires' Revels commence in earnest, so you will be attending those for the next three days."

413

"Oh, yes," Gunnilde agreed. She had scarcely even thought of the approaching Revels this past week.

"I only hope the young prince can be brought to enjoy himself there," Lord Vawdrey said in a low voice. "Your brother and his friends have done their best to interest him in proceedings but…" He pulled a face.

"They are boisterous, and he is reserved," Gunnilde observed.

"Yes, quite so. Still, I had hoped the Revels would interest him. After all, if he were not a crown prince, he would be of an age to enter squire hood himself. Alas, it seems knights and knighthood do not interest him remotely."

"Well, but there are different kinds of knights after all," Gunnilde said, remembering James's words on the subject. "Instead of regaling him with tales of Viscount Vawdrey or Lord Twyford," she said, proud she had remembered to use their new titles, "why do you not tell him instead of modest, unassuming Sir Renlow?"

"Sir Renlow d'Avenant?" Lord Vawdrey echoed.

"Yes, for he is a vastly different kind of champion, is he not? James trained with him, you know, and apparently, he was always quiet and kind."

Lord Vawdrey shot another look at James and Prince Raedan, who were now discussing the King's favorite jester, Robkin, with many scathing comments. "Do you know, that is not such a bad notion. You may be onto something there, Lady Wycliffe," he said thoughtfully.

"I think it sounds an excellent idea," his wife chimed in. "Eden always said you were clever, and I can quite see why." Clever? Her surprise must have shown on her face, for Fenella Vawdrey twinkled at her. "After all, there are different kinds of cleverness, are there not? It is not always derived from a book."

414

At this point, Gunnilde noticed that Harriet and her mother had arrived, and Winifred and her young cousin. Excusing herself from the Vawdreys, she made her way over to them. The room was fast filling now, so she was hailed several times, and returned many greetings before she reached them.

She was just complimenting Harriet on her new tippets when an altercation broke out over by the fireplace. They all turned in surprise to find Sir Symond Chevenix sprawled on the ground and Hal stood over him, flushed and indignant.

"You take that back, you unworthy dog!" Hal shouted furiously. "You sully this maid's fair name again in my hearing and I'll whip you like the craven cur you are!"

Gunnilde's mouth dropped open. "What the—?"

Pushing and shoving immediately started in the vicinity, along with a good deal of shrieking and screaming. Half the room surged toward the fracas, while the other half fled from it.

"Oh no!" Gunnilde turned toward the door to summon the royal guards, but they were already wading their way through the crowd. It was only after a moment that she realized they were not attempting to break up the fight, but rather to surround the Queen and the prince and protect them from any potential harm.

"James?" Gunnilde called, turning this way and that in vain, for she could not see her husband in the crush. Picking up her skirts, she pushed her way determinedly toward the front of the crowd to find her brother.

To her astonishment, she found James and Neville were already there in the thick of it with Cuthbert and Kit, surrounding a red-faced Hal, while Lord Vawdrey and Viscount Bardulf were restraining Sir Symond, who was now on his feet and seemingly furious. Gunnilde had not even seen the Bardulfs arrive!

"Get your hands off me, I say!" Sir Symond snarled, attempting to shake them off. Surprisingly, considering he was a decorated member of the King's guard, he could not loose himself from the two courtiers' grip. This fact seemed to enrage him even further.

"Now, now, don't get your breeches in a twist," Viscount Bardulf tutted. "What lamentable manners! Ah, but here is an arbiter, our hostess, to sort out this mess."

"What in the world has happened?" Gunnilde cried. When a sulky silence met her words, she turned to her brother. "Hal?"

Hal drew himself up. "Not a word will pass my lips. I would sooner die than repeat such foul—"

"Sir Symond insulted Mistress Culmington within Hal's hearing," Cuthbert interjected.

"I said naught that was not true!" Sir Symond spat out contemptuously.

"By gods I'll—!" James and Neville tightened their grip of her flailing brother.

"Calm down, Payne!" Lord Vawdrey said sharply. "That's quite enough!"

"Let me through!" the imperious voice of the Queen cut through the crowd. "If there should be an arbiter in this matter, it should be myself!" However, it seemed the guards were not amenable to this, much to the Queen's chagrin. Her angry voice could be heard muttering in the background.

416

Lord Vawdrey was speaking to Sir Symond in low tones, and whatever he was saying made the knight's face pale, then flame again. "Wycliffe?" Earl Vawdrey shouted. "Do you have that young brother-in-law of yours under control?"

"We have him, my lord," James responded grimly. Gunnilde breathed out a sigh of relief.

"Very well, then, I think apologies are in order. Sir Symond, you will start. First to your hostess."

Sir Symond shot a look of furious resentment in her direction. "I beg your pardon, Lady Wycliffe, Sir James," he muttered sullenly. "For bringing disquiet into your halls."

"And what of—?" Hal started but was duly jolted and elbowed by his captors.

"Quiet, you fool!" Kit seethed. "D'you want to be slung out on your ear?"

"And now you will apologize for the misunderstanding, Chevenix," Vawdrey continued in freezing tones. "As an honorable member of the King's guard, it is inconceivable that Sir Symond could have insulted one of the Queen's ladies thus. Therefore, he must have been misunderstood in this matter. Is that not so, Sir Symond?"

Sir Symond clenched his fists. His lip was swollen and bleeding, and his eyes bloodshot with fury. For a handsome man, the expression on his face could only be described as ugly. "I misspoke," he growled through clenched teeth. "I intended no insult to the lady."

"Handsomely said," Lord Vawdrey lied. "Lady Wycliffe, do you accept this apology?"

Gunnilde cleared her throat. "Right gladly," she responded.

417

Vawdrey nodded. "And now, Payne, your response?"

Now it was James's turn to whisper furiously in Hal's ear. "Well, but—
But what I say is this— Oh, well, if you insist" were Hal's huffed
responses. He lifted his voice. "I accept that I must have misheard Sir
Symond," Hal conceded with ill grace. "But if I ever hear—" Cuthbert
stamped on Hal's foot. "Ow!"

"Most handsomely accepted," Lord Vawdrey said before Hal could
recover. "And now, I believe the prince's guards must volunteer to
escort Sir Symond to the tower to take up immediate duties there for the
next five days. Alas, they are short of hands at present."

"Do as he says," the prince's voice rang out. "I will remain here with
Lord Vawdrey."

After some muttering, the guards appeared on either side of Sir
Symond, who shot a murderous look in Lord Vawdrey's direction
before being marched away.

"Dear me," said Viscount Bardulf, appearing at Gunnilde's side. "I was
not expecting this gathering to be quite so lively. I know you promised
to entertain us, my dear Lady Wycliffe, but this is almost too much."

The double doors closed behind the guard's ringing footsteps and the
room broke out in a babble of confusion.

40

The last of the notes died away and James lowered his shawm. He did not particularly care to perform in public but had filled in at the last minute when Wilford had failed to show. The silence of the room did not bother him, only Gunnilde's reaction, so his eyes sought her out at once. She was sat on the edge of her seat, hands clasped together, her eyes shining with unshed tears.

Was that good or bad? James was not sure, but he wanted to find out. He was already halfway across the room to her when the applause burst out, loud and jarring, jolting him out of his abstraction. Suddenly, everyone was standing up. Where was Gunnilde? She had been sitting front and center, but now the Queen was standing in front of her, impeding his view.

"Sir James!" the Queen hailed him insistently. "But this was masterly! Quite masterly! I must hear your firsthand account of such a remarkable work."

James frowned, peering around her. Ah, there was his wife! But who was that she embracing? A tall dark figure wearing a close-fitting cap. Belatedly, he realized it was Mistress Bartree, and relaxed.

"Sir James?" Queen Armenal prompted him sharply. She had sat back on the bench and was patting the spot beside her. "You must give me the benefit of your conversation for a while," she said ingratiatingly and smiled at him. "I am sure your wife can spare you."

Damnation. James spent what felt like the next hour being tortured by a lot of needless questions and seemingly artless exclamations from the Queen. He could scarcely follow what she was saying, so distracted was he.

Gunnilde could not seem to stay still in one place. One minute she was conversing with the Bardulfs, the next with the Vawdreys, and after that with the young prince again. Everywhere she went, she took Mistress Bartree with her in what James could not help thinking was his place.

Mistress Bartree appeared somewhat dazed, and rather flushed. She clutched Gunnilde's arm, and every so often, Gunnilde would touch her hand or rub her upper arm in an encouraging gesture. He must have become used to being the sole recipient of his wife's encouraging gestures, for James felt quite put out by it.

The Queen droned on in his ear like a buzzing gnat. "We must certainly see what we can do for you. I underestimated you, my dear Sir James, I see that quite clearly now."

Now Gunnilde was leading Mistress Bartree over to the musicians and introducing her to every one of them. Billingsley bowed low over Gunnilde's hand, and James practically gnawed on his own knuckle.

Apparently, Billingsley could not be trusted where women were concerned. He had some kind of irresistible charm, or so the others maintained. James himself had seen precious little evidence to support such a statement, though the fellow was a damn good vielle player.

"Gunnilde was quite wrong, I can see that now," the Queen observed, momentarily jolting him out of his jealous stewing.

"What do you mean, Gunnilde was wrong?" he demanded, returning his attention to the Queen.

Queen Armenal looked taken aback. "Well, about the role of royal musician, my good sir. The appointment should clearly be yours. You were born for it."

"Royal musician?" James stared at her. Was she in earnest? "I thought Master Palmore occupied that role."

420

The Queen waved this aside. "Master Palmore has held that role for fifty years or more and has not composed a note for over half that time, nor come to court. No, it is merely a courtesy role by this point. Wymer's father appointed him, and my husband, having no interest in the arts, has never replaced him."

She looked at James quizzically. "Did Gunnilde not tell you? There is a handsome allowance attached to the post and many attendant honors. I take it you would be interested?"

James sat up. After all, it would mean the end to all his monetary woes. "I would," he responded promptly.

Queen Armenal looked smug. "I shall speak to Wymer on the morrow, but rest assured he will not deny me in this request. I have many matters I would deem worthy subjects for your compositions," she said archly. "A whole list of them, in fact. Tell me, have you ever perused the tapestries produced by my Court of Love and Beauty? They are displayed in the upper solar."

James paused. In truth, he had glanced over them when they had first been hung, but they had left little to no impression on him. "I have not," he lied, thinking it prudent.

She looked somewhat disappointed by this. "Oh, well, I think you will find them an excellent source of inspiration for future works. I would like to discuss the matter in depth with you at some point, but perhaps we should wait until you have been officially appointed to the role, but as I say, the post is as good as yours. Congratulations, Sir James."

He gave her a perfunctory smile. "You are all that is gracious, Your Majesty."

A look of unease passed over her features. "And, perhaps that was not the only thing I have been wrong about," she said enigmatically, looking from James to Gunnilde and back again. "If I was mistaken…"

421

But James was already up off the bench and bowing. "You must excuse me, Your Highness, but my duties as host necessitate, I must now leave you."

"Oh, of course, Sir James, your consideration for your guests does you credit."

But it was not his duties as host that were at the forefront of his mind, but rather his privileges as a husband. Where the hells was his wife? James swept around the room in search of her, but the place was damnably full now with people milling around everywhere, showing no signs of leaving, despite the lavish supper and the entertainment being concluded.

"A nice flush hit, you have to give him that," he heard Neville opine.

"Oh, Hal's strong as an ox," Cuthbert agreed. "None of us can best him with a staff or at wrestling."

"He's burly, that's why," Kit observed. "Built for strength. Now if Sir Symond had turned tail and run, he never would have caught him. That's what I would have done in his shoes."

Neville snorted. "Well, you couldn't have done them in your own, or you would have tripped over them, my lad!"

James turned sharply in the other direction and practically collided with his cousin, Lady Gilchrist.

"Oh, James!" she said with some relief. "Here you are at last. I most particularly wanted to speak with you. I had a letter this morn—"

"Have you seen my wife?" James interrupted her. He had no intention of discussing his mother's feverish letter writing. He knew she was seriously displeased and could not care less about the fact.

"I think she was somewhere over yonder," she said, gesturing vaguely. "But I really think—"

Feigning deafness, James moved on. It suddenly occurred to him that Gunnilde might be speaking to those dull siblings from her home county. Stifling an exclamation of annoyance, he scanned the room for a blond moustache, or a large shapeless headdress.

Instead, he discovered Gunnilde stood in the distance in a small group comprising of Lady Portstanley, her daughter Harriet, her bookish friend Winifred, and Magnatrude Bartree. They all seemed to be having some earnest discussion.

Making his way in their direction, he found his brother-in-law surrounded by a group of twittering ladies-in-waiting.

"Oh, Master Payne," Mistress Culmington sighed in failing accents. "When I think of the ignominy of all I've suffered this evening, I feel quite wretchedly faint!"

Immediately Hal whipped a handkerchief out of his cuff and started fanning her face whilst slipping an arm about her waist to support her. The rest of the ladies stood around watching avidly and whispering. Estrilda Rheinholdt and Emma Thackeray stood a little away from the others, arm in arm and wearing matching expressions of disapproval.

"I would not be able to show my face from the shame of it, if I was her!" Emma whispered angrily. "After the way she has carried on with poor Sir Symond! And him with a betrothed stashed away in his home county!"

Estrilda tossed her head. "Some of us are quite dead to shame!" she declared dramatically.

Another of the ladies, James did not know her name, seized hold of Hal's other arm. "I, too, have come over all a-quiver!" She pouted. "It is so hot and overcrowded in here!"

"Hold fast to me, Mistress Stanhope," Hal recommended warmly. "I will lend you my strength, now and always, if you will only let me." His voice dipped low and intimate over the last few words and the young lady's expression instantly transformed to one of blushing coyness, while Penelope Culmington lifted her drooping head to glare at her rival.

Deciding he had seen quite enough of Hal's wooing, James forged grimly on to reclaim his wife.

41

The first day of the Revels' finals dawned crisp and cold. Gunnilde slipped from the bed and padded over to the window to gaze out at the December morn. It looked like a hard ground frost, though mercifully no snow had fallen to spoil the events.

Picking up her mantle, she threw it over her shoulders and returned to the bed where James was still sleeping. Bennett had not yet lit the fires and the room was chilly. She turned to look down at James's sleeping face, brushing his curling auburn hair out of his eyes. She felt so terribly proud of him.

They had not actually returned to their rooms until the early hours, as their guests had shown a remarkable reluctance to disperse. There had been much excitement over the evening's entertainment, the excellence of the food, Hal's scuffle, which to Gunnilde's surprise many ladies seemed inclined to view as the height of chivalry, and lastly the debut of "I Dare Not Show the Love I Owe," whose reception had surpassed even her wildest dreams.

There could be no doubt that this would bring an influx of new patrons. Even last night, several courtiers had approached her with a view to engaging James's services. Others had enquired when next his masterpiece was being performed, as they wanted friends or family to hear it.

Gunnilde was certain that he would soon be in great demand, and it was all down to his own merit. Even Mistress Bartree had been quite won over by his music. She had been most gracious to the musicians and when asked, had professed herself both honored and humbled by his work.

James stirred, and Gunnilde held her breath. Mistress Bartree had not been the only one who had been uncharacteristically quiet the night before. At the latter end of the evening, James had appeared quiet and reticent. Mayhap the music sapped all his energy? He rolled onto his back and flung out an arm. "What time is it?"

"Early. Bennett has not come yet."

"Hmm." He opened one eye. "Of course, he could be neglecting us again, after giving his undivided service yesterday," he suggested.

"True." Gunnilde touched the tips of her cold toes to James's leg, and he frowned.

"Have you been up already?" he asked, reaching down to seize her feet in his warm grasp. "Why are your feet so cold?"

"I just went to look out of the window," she confessed. "I wanted to make sure it had not snowed. 'Tis the first official day of the Revels after all."

He snorted. "They've been rumbling on for at least two weeks now."

"Yes, but the winners will be crowned at the end of this week."

"How do you feel this morning?" he asked, still rubbing her feet. "Happy with how it went last night?"

"Of course, how could I fail to be?"

He shrugged and looked evasive. "Bevan and his witch did not show up."

"No, they didn't, did they?" she ruminated. "But I do not think we can take offence for his invitation was issued quite late." He slanted a

426

glance her way but made no comment. "Why do you look at me like that?"

"No reason. I was just considering the original intent of the occasion," he responded.

"The original intent?" Gunnilde queried.

"Well, yes. It wasn't to debut my music, or even celebrate the impending Revels, was it?"

Gunnilde was silent a moment. "No," she agreed, withdrawing her feet from his lap. "It was for me to lord it over my former acquaintance, was it not? To make them bitterly regret spurning me." She lifted her chin. "Tell me, James," she asked quietly, "do you think I fell short of my aim?"

"Certainly not," he answered promptly. "You had two royals show up, no less. Your childhood friend was chastened, and Conway looked like he would fall at your feet given only the slightest opportunity."

"You think so? Then why do you imagine I might be disappointed with how things went?" He did not speak. "Because Sir Ned did not show up?" Gunnilde persisted. "I told you, we are now quite reconciled. I harbor no ill will toward him."

James's expression hardened. "I am not so forgiving as you it seems."

Had he woken on the wrong side of the bed this morning? Gunnilde surveyed him doubtfully. "Did you speak to your cousin Lady Gilchrist last night? Only she seemed a little preoccupied. She asked me if you had shared the contents of your mother's last letter with me, and I was forced to admit you had not."

He grimaced. "Trust me, there was precious little worth imparting. My mother is one of those distant, discontented types. Always taking offence at something or other."

What sort of things? Gunnilde wondered, pleating the bedsheets. "The Queen spoke to you a good deal last night," she ventured.

"Yes," he agreed grumpily.

"Did she mention your mother's letter at all?"

"No, she was talking about something else entirely." At her querying look, he added offhandedly, "My being appointed royal musician."

Gunnilde's heart thudded. "Really? Did she…did she offer you the post?"

"She said she would speak to the King about it. She seemed fairly confident about it, however."

"But that's…that's wonderful, James. Isn't it?" Gunnilde was puzzled. Surely this was good news. Why did he look so discontented?

"Is it?" he asked irritably. "She seemed to think you were set against the idea?"

Gunnilde stared at him. "I?"

He shrugged. "That's what she said."

"But I've never…" Vague memories drifted back into Gunnilde's head. A disagreement with Mistress Bartree where she had denied she was currying favor purely to secure such an appointment for her husband. She flushed. "Oh! But that was merely a discussion of vague ideas at that time! It was never mentioned as an actual possibility!"

No wonder he was out of sorts, Gunnilde thought, her heart sinking. He must think she had been trying to sabotage his career, not promote it. "At the time I had that foolish notion that you might achieve acclaim through writing ballads," she said desperately. "Please believe me, James. I would never have willfully jeopardized—"

A bump on the door heralded Bennett's arrival, and he pushed it open with an armful of logs, making for the fireplace, eyes carefully averted. James swung his legs out of the bed and cleared his throat.

"Is Master Neville still abed?" he enquired of Bennett.

"I've not seen hide nor hair of him this morn," Bennett answered. "Likely he's still snoring his head off, after all that dancing into the small hours. Those musician friends of yours didn't pack up until long past midnight."

"He did dance a good deal, did he not?" Gunnilde said brightly. "He danced with both Harriet and Winifred unprompted, which pleased me greatly."

"It's who your brother danced with that might cause more of an issue," James said dryly. "He will soon be getting a reputation where women are concerned if he is not careful."

Gunnilde bit her lip. She supposed by stuffy Wycliffe standards Hal had caused something of a scene. Doubtless his family would be appalled to hear of brawling at a banquet held in their family name. She knew full well her own father would only laugh and call it youthful high spirits.

Belatedly, it dawned on Gunnilde that this was yet another reason for him being out of temper. How foolish she had been thinking the night had been an unqualified success! He must think her the veriest simpleton for saying so. Likely, it was only just occurring to him how much of a liability she was proving to be as his wife.

429

Two hours later they stood shivering in the wooden stands watching the lance toss final. Even Neville, who had been so enthusiastic about the Revels, seemed somewhat depressed in spirits, though Gunnilde suspected that might be due to how much wine he had imbibed the night before.

The final two had been whittled down to Cosgrave and a young man named Willard Peyton. It was a close-run thing. Neville managed a rousing cheer when Cosgrave took the honors, then relapsed into moody silence.

Gunnilde pulled her cloak tighter about her, willing her teeth not to chatter in the bitter December air. She noticed several of her fellow ladies-in-waiting packing out the stand opposite them. Not the maturer of their number like Osanna Spencer or Margaret Pryor but the younger faction were there in droves. Even Lucy Melvin, who turned her nose up at everything.

Estrilda caught her eye at that moment and waved a scarf enthusiastically in her direction. Gunnilde waved and nodded back. She felt quite relieved about the distance between them so she would not have to answer any quizzing about Hal. According to Neville he was not particularly strong in this event and was conserving himself for the wrestling which was next.

She had caught only one glimpse of her brother so far that morning, when he had helped set up the targets for the spear throwing. He had been wearing a pale blue scarf tied about his upper arm. Nervously, she wondered whose colors he was displaying now, before casting the thought out of her mind. Hal's amours were the least of her problems.

"I cannot see Lady Portstanley here or her daughter," Neville said in desultory tones, peering out of his hood. Gunnilde wondered if there was a reason he was avoiding saying Harriet's name aloud. Her eyes met with James's before she quickly looked away. She did not want him to think she was plotting and scheming love matches once again.

430

"Did they promise to attend?" James asked after a significant pause. "Only the Revels don't really seem like their sort of thing at all."

"They may have intimated as much, depending on the weather," Neville replied with a casualness that did not seem entirely genuine. "I am surprised they find it too inclement to venture out. Despite the cold, it is a clear, bright day after all."

"Harriet has something of a weak chest, I believe," Gunnilde said. "If it is too cold, it can cause her to cough."

Neville's frown relaxed. "She is quite delicate," he agreed. "Mayhap I will call on her after and let her know how the Revels went."

Privately, Gunnilde did not think Harriet would care much who could throw a lance the furthest, but then she remembered her friend's sparkling eyes as Neville had led her into the dance. She might appreciate his visit after all.

A buzzing and jostling started through the stands, and Gunnilde turned her head to see what was causing the commotion. To her surprise it was the arrival of the King, escorted by four of his King's guard. Sir Symond was conspicuous in his absence. The King crossed to where Prince Raedan was seated under a royal canopy with Dustin sat in his lap. The King joined him there and more chairs were carried across to seat his retinue.

"Well, I never did see such a thing!" Neville exclaimed. "Have you ever known Wymer to attend the Squires' Revels before?"

James shook his head. "This will be down to your brother," he said, addressing Gunnilde.

"Do you really think so?"

431

He nodded. "Wymer arrives just as Hal's best event is about to commence. It cannot be a coincidence."

Neville coughed. "Actually, Hal is the heavy favorite for both the wrestling and the staff fighting," he pointed out with pride. "Though he has some stiff competition today. Gordon Fairfax is a strong competitor." Gunnilde hid her smile. The friendship of James's brother with her own still pleased her and gave her hope that perhaps their families were not so very incompatible after all.

"Here they come now," James announced, and Gunnilde leaned forward, laying one gloved hand on the wooden barrier before them. She would concentrate on the Revels and put all else from her mind for now.

42

"Of course, Constance always was a perfect fool." Penelope Culmington's words rang out, her voice carrying over the Great Hall.

It seemed to Gunnilde that everyone turned to look at their party as they stood on the threshold, flushed and triumphant from Hal's win. Then the whispering started, rising up toward the rafters in a great swell.

She would have come to a complete standstill if not for James, who had swept her resolutely along with him to a nearby table.

"What's to do now?" Kit whispered, clambering onto the bench opposite. "Why's everyone agape?"

"It can't just be my victory, can it?" Hal asked, glancing around. "No one's even calling out their congratulations! What's wrong with them all?"

"Simply everyone is staring!" Gunnilde muttered, reaching for bread roll to crumble between her nerveless fingers. Penelope's words had sent a thrill of warning down her spine. Constance, she had said. Why had they been discussing Constance? Her glance at this point happened to fall on Cuthbert.

His unwavering gaze seemed to hold some message, unnerving her. "Cuthbert?" She faltered. "What is it?"

"You must take heart, my lady," he said, and it sounded like a warning.

Gunnilde's heart sank down to her flimsy slippers. "Why do you say that? Whatever do you mean?"

At this moment, Neville came hurrying across the hall toward them. He had left directly after the Revels to go and visit the Portstanleys instead of coming back to their rooms. He was out of breath and red-faced by the time he sank down on the bench next to Hal.

"You will never believe what has happened!" he uttered hoarsely. "Farleigh hath returned to court with the Lady Constance and they are seeking an annulment of their marriage!"

Gunnilde gasped. "But why?" she burst out in shock.

Neville leaned forward, lowering his voice. "No one knows for sure, but the rumor is they reached the lady's estate with their union still unconsummated. Then, on arrival, her uncles persuaded her the marriage was naught but a mistake and dragged them back to court to make a formal appeal to the King."

Gunnilde felt a pang for Sir Douglas. Really, it was too bad of Constance not to stand firm in the face of such opposition! But then, perhaps her uncles had bullied or browbeaten her into it. She hoped she was not in too much distress.

"What's all this to do with us?" Hal asked, looking puzzled.

James cleared his throat. "Very little," he said. "I was betrothed to Lady Constance at one point. She eloped with Sir Douglas, and I married your sister. Kindly pass the ale jug."

Hal's expression cleared. "Oh, like that, is it?" He seized the ale jug and shoved it in James's direction. "I know Farleigh, of course. Saw him take the Newcomer's Cup at Areley Kings last year. They say he's shown a lot of improvement since Kentigern took him under his wing. He's always been good on a horse," he added judiciously.

"Bet he feels a fool being dragged back to court like that by his in-laws," Kit remarked. "I would."

"Poor Sir Douglas," Gunnilde murmured, thinking of his unwavering devotion to Constance. This must be quite a blow for him. Neville looked across at her and gave a quick shake of his head, as though in warning.

At her surprised look, he tipped his head in James's direction but when she looked toward her husband he was draining his ale cup. Neville coughed apologetically. "They say her uncles are insisting that her former betrothal is legally binding."

James slammed his cup down. "I am sure by now they must have heard of my own subsequent marriage, nullifying that."

"Aye, that's true enough," Hal reflected. "They cannot possibly remain in ignorance of it. Not now they're here at the palace. Somone's sure to have told them."

"Mayhap they think two annulments could be procured as easily as one," Cuthbert suggested.

Gunnilde's heart thudded. Two annulments? Her head reeled. She cast a quick look toward the high table but neither the King nor the Queen was in attendance tonight. Could Constance's uncles have approached them already?

For some reason she could not bring herself to look at James. What if his expression betrayed some emotion she could not face? Like hopefulness. At this point a platter of quails and larks with jelly was slammed down on their table. Gunnilde's stomach turned over and she realized she would have no appetite tonight.

It was two courses later that an attendant appeared at Gunnilde's elbow, presenting her with a letter. She took it with thanks and turned it over to peer at the seal.

"What's on that crest, an eagle?" Kit asked, proving to have very sharp eyes.

"It's a martlet," Cuthbert answered without removing his eyes from his plate.

"A martlet?" Hal repeated. "Does not Farleigh's shield feature—?"

Neville elbowed him, and her brother cut off his words as an embarrassed hush fell over the table.

"Sir Douglas and I were formerly on the most cordial terms," Gunnilde said with dignity. "No doubt he feels himself in need of a friend."

"Why not open your letter and find out?" James asked. "If he requested it to be delivered to you in person, he must consider it a matter of urgency." He did not look at her but kept his attention on his plate of roast boar.

Gunnilde hesitated, then reached for the note, breaking it open and scanning the page. The note was short and to the point.

Mistress Payne, it began. I find myself in a situation most dire and could do with your wise counsel. Could you meet me in our usual appointed place? I will be there waiting when the clock strikes midnight in the chance you can slip away. I remain your obedient servant, D. Farleigh.

Gunnilde flushed. What could Douglas be thinking? She had never before met with him at such a late hour, and though they had met several times in the knot garden, there had always been other courtiers strolling about the nearby pathways. At midnight there would be no one in the vicinity. Such a meeting would be highly improper.

Taking a deep breath, she passed the missive sideways to James, trying not to look as guilty as she felt. He took it from her and perused it with

436

a flinty expression. Seeing his eyebrows shoot up, Gunnilde took an anxious gulp of wine.

"He refers to the knot garden," she said her words almost falling over each other. "We used to meet there sometimes, to talk about, well, you know, his feelings." She threw him a look of appeal. "He—he must be heartbroken and quite desperate about his current predicament."

"He expects you to sneak out of our rooms under the cover of darkness," James said in a biting tone. "No doubt while your husband lies in blissful ignorance, sleeping."

"No! I—I don't think he can realize I am married!" Gunnilde broke in. "Only see how he addresses me as Mistress Payne!"

"Or mayhap he simply does not choose to acknowledge it," James replied in freezing tones.

"Well, I never dreamed Farleigh was such a saucy knave," Kit marveled, lowering the letter.

Gunnilde realized with horror they must have been passing it about the table. She made a grab for it. "Indeed, he is not!" she huffed.

"Hie! I never got to read that!" Neville complained as she snatched it back.

"You misunderstand the situation entirely!" Gunnilde insisted, ignoring her brother-in-law's chagrin.

"I don't know about that," Hal said sternly. "But no sister of mine is going to be sneaking off to clandestine meetings in the middle of the night, and so I shall tell him! Who's with me? He'll get the shock of his life to find us waiting for him at midnight instead!" he concluded grimly.

437

"Sorry to spoil your plans, Hal," James interrupted firmly, "but I think you'll find Gunnilde's husband is the correct person to deal with this, not her brother."

Hal deflated slightly. "Oh, er, yes," he acknowledged grudgingly. "I suppose that is so. You're sure you don't want our aid in the matter though? Only we're quite ready and willing."

"Quite sure, thank you."

"Well, how are you going to go about it?" Neville demanded. "You can't just ignore it!"

"No," Hal agreed when James did not answer immediately. "Though Farleigh would feel pretty silly sat waiting in vain in the dark, freezing his ballocks off. It's damned disheartening when a girl does that."

"Speak from experience, do you?" Neville asked slyly. Hal ignored him.

"What are you going to do, Wycliffe? Challenge him to a duel?" Kit asked hopefully.

"Of course he is not!" Gunnilde answered hotly. "James is far too sensible to act so rashly. There is not the smallest need for—"

"Quite the contrary," James answered, cutting her off. "Instead, Gunnilde is going to write back, inviting Sir Douglas to meet instead in our rooms at a more civilized hour."

Gunnilde gasped. "James," she said, grasping his arm, "that is really most handsome of you."

"Of course," he answered coolly. "Is that not what everyone says of me? James Wycliffe, the handsomest man in the realm."

438

Gunnilde regarded him with sudden misgiving. Was it just a trick of her ears, or did his words sound faintly bitter?

43

James handed a cup of ale to Sir Douglas and watched the young knight accept it with some awkwardness before settling back in his seat. He had clearly thought to meet with Gunnilde alone and, confronted with the presence of a husband, seemed pretty much at a loss how to continue.

Gunnilde leaned forward in her seat. "Now, do not let us have any constraint between us, Sir Douglas. You may speak before James as freely as you always could before me. Believe me, he is most sympathetic to your plight." James kept his features impassive as Douglas darted an uneasy glance his way. "Now, pray tell us. What has happened since you left the palace?"

Sir Douglas sighed and scrubbed his eyes with his hand. "Where to start? In truth, things went awry almost from the start. No road was straight enough for Constance, no inn respectable enough, no landlord amenable enough, no supper appetizing enough, no maidservant polite enough... I could go on." He shot a hunted look at James. "Her complaints were ceaseless."

Gunnilde's face took on a look of sympathetic understanding. "I suppose in a way it is only natural. Constance is, of course, an heiress," she said tactfully, "and moreover an only child. She is no doubt accustomed to having things her own way."

"That is one way of putting it," Douglas agreed fervently. "I think myself that we had not left court above a couple of hours before doubts started seeping into her mind." He shook his head. "We never—" He turned scarlet. "Well, she never permitted that I should share her bedchamber, that much is certain," he admitted, shame-faced.

Gunnilde sent a look of appeal in James's direction, but what the hells was he supposed to say? Bad luck, your wife is clearly not as generous and giving as mine? Realizing he was not going to come to her rescue, Gunnilde coughed. "And then, on reaching her estate?" she prompted, breaking the awkward silence.

"Oh, things really took a turn when we reached Northcott Manor," Sir Douglas said bitterly. "Her uncles came out in force, her cousins, her godfather, her steward, all of them were up in arms."

"They are all her dependents, I take it," Gunnilde commented thoughtfully. She looked across at James. "Did you ever meet any of them during your own, well, betrothal to Constance?"

James bristled. Why in heaven's name would she want to bring that up? He gave a short nod. "I met her uncle Elias," he admitted reluctantly. "I believe he is the senior guardian, and her godfather, Sir Aldo Marchmont, on one occasion."

Douglas snorted. "Aye, so you've met the worst of them, then! They've treated me like a criminal from the start and practically dragged me here in irons! At least, they would have liked to clap me in them if I'd permitted it."

James made no comment. Constance's relations had seemed amenable enough when he met them, but then again, finances and settlements had been agreed and protections put in place. None of that had been arranged for Douglas and Constance's precipitate marriage. No doubt her family had been thrown into a state of panic.

"And now they mean to put the matter before the King himself?" Gunnilde asked uncomfortably. No doubt she felt partly to blame for encouraging the pair of them in their folly. "What does Constance say about it all?" she asked.

"She barely looks at me these days, let alone talks to me," Douglas answered dispiritedly.

"I expect they keep her closely guarded at all times," Gunnilde mused. "But you must speak with her, Douglas! You must ascertain her wants and desires in the matter, not just those of her relatives."

"Trust me, I know precious little about Constance's desires," Sir Douglas retorted. "And I suspect I don't factor in them one whit."

"But Douglas—" James noticed with disfavor that she tended to drop the "sir" in moments of high emotion.

"No, Gunnilde," he said, shifting in his seat to face in her direction. "You must understand, I—I feel quite differently about things now. I was fogged before, my mind confused. Now the clouds have dispersed, I wonder if I ever really loved her or if I just got swept up in a sort of madness!"

He leaned forward, almost as though he were trying to shut James out of the conversation. "When I come to look at things, really look at them, I mean, I realize that the part I liked most about courting her was, well, the time I spent with you." He turned slowly scarlet; his eyes beseechingly trained on James's wife.

A deafening silence fell over the room as James forced himself not to spring out of his seat and fling the offending knave out of the room. Gunnilde blinked and gave a nervous laugh. "We all enjoy spending time with like-minded people, Douglas," she said soothingly. "I think I have a particular sympathy for lovers due to the fact I was disappointed at a young age. What you feel for Constance is something quite different—"

"I never even knew Constance!" Douglas burst out wildly. "Not really. I just liked the idea of her! Now I think we were likely ill-suited from the start."

442

"Oh, but—"

"What it comes down to is that she is practically a stranger to me!"

James stood up. "We seem to have reached a sticking point," he said dryly. "And I don't believe things are moving in any helpful direction. There is nothing here that my wife can help you with, Farleigh. I must now ask you to leave."

A mutinous cast came over Sir Douglas's face. "Well, but I have not finished saying what I meant to say!" he protested hotly.

"I can well believe it," James replied with quiet menace. Hostility crackled in the air. Farleigh came to his feet, sizing him up. James narrowed his eyes and took a step forward. By gods, he'd wring this scoundrel's neck given half the chance!

"It's this way, Sir Douglas," Gunnilde said quickly. "Pray do not let us detain you. You have doubtless ridden many hours this day and surely have an audience with the King to prepare for."

Farleigh allowed himself to be shepherded out of the room, with one more backward look of resentment at James, who followed close on their heels. He had no intention of giving the man a chance to importune his wife further!

"Well, good night and good luck to you, Sir Douglas," Gunnilde gabbled as he hesitated in the doorway.

"Listen, Gunnilde," he said desperately, "I've been blind but now I see that, well, that we have far more common ground! You like knights, I'm a knight, and it seems to me—"

James came right behind her, placing one hand on Gunnilde's shoulder and another on the door. "Good night," he said firmly, closing the door in the blackguard's face.

443

Gunnilde slumped against the door. "Oh gods," she moaned. "What have I done?" She turned her face toward him. "Have I ruined Sir Douglas's life?" she asked wretchedly. "I ought never to have—"

"You ought never to have been whispering in corners with him in the first place!" James said sharply. "This was bound to happen sooner or later."

She looked crushed. "But I really believed I was acting for the best! I had no notion—"

"You had no notion of anything but meddling in matters that did not concern you!" James snapped. "Moreover, if you do not mend your ways, my fine lady, you and your brother will be gaining reputations as the most hardened flirts to ever appear at court!"

The color drained from Gunnilde's face. "James, please," she whispered, reaching for his hand. He snatched it back.

"Do you even realize what that bastard was hoping for?" he demanded angrily. "To resolve this situation with some kind of exchange of wives! A proposal that would make us all look quite ridiculous before everyone!"

Gunnilde stared at him. Her lips trembled. "James—"

A roaring started in his ears. If she told him now that she loved Sir Douglas, he did not know what he would do. "Is that what you want?" he hurled at her. "To be a figure of infamy and conjecture for the rest of your life? Or perhaps you do not care. After all, you like attention riveted to your person, do you not?"

Something about the look in her eyes suddenly halted him. He swallowed the harsh words pouring from his tongue. "Let's to bed," he said abruptly. "I believe I've had quite enough to contend with for one day."

Gunnilde nodded, blinking back tears. The worst of it was, seeing her this upset just made James feel even worse, he realized as he washed and undressed. Farleigh was probably right, damn his eyes. Probably right for Gunnilde.

She would have been thrilled to marry a tournament knight, even one who was not a champion. She would have cheered him on at every tournament and consoled him sweetly after every loss.

Her father, Sir Aubron, would doubtless have rejoiced at such a son-in-law, while he barred his doors against James. Her family would have understood the match. He would have fitted right in with their company, where James would have to struggle for years before they would accept his presence and likely always remain an outsider.

James lay in bed beside his silent wife seething until the early hours. Neither one of them spoke another word. James could not speak by this point, for jealousy twisted his gut and poisoned his tongue.

He ran back and forth over the words that had been exchanged, torturing himself that Gunnilde might not have been averse to hearing the other man's avowals of love. It was downright obvious Farleigh had finally noticed Gunnilde was the more enticing prospect, and small wonder. Even he, oblivious as he was, had come to that realization on his wedding night.

Gunnilde was warm and lovely where Constance was, well, he did not know precisely what Constance was, other than a little spoiled. He had not taken the trouble to get to know her on anything but the shallowest of terms. He had not cared to then, and he did not care to now.

It should not matter in any case, for Gunnilde was his. Unlike Douglas and Constance their marriage had been most satisfactorily consummated, and he would not stand for anyone trying to posit otherwise. He had been hard-pressed not to tell Farleigh as much but

445

that would have been indelicate, he supposed. Gunnilde might not have liked it thrown in the fellow's face like that.

It was plain she harbored kindly, even tender feelings toward Farleigh, he thought, scowling into the darkness, but she would just have to get over that. She was his wife and so she would remain. She might chafe about that in the years to come but he would just have to find some way to make the fact more palatable to her. She could dress him how she pleased, throw all manner of elaborate banquets, spend all his money on velvets and silks. He would deny her nothing.

The wretched matchmaking would have to come to an end though, he fumed. He had been wrong to soften about that. It stood to reason any bachelor's eyes would start to turn her way if they spent too much time in her intoxicating company. She was too damnably enticing.

Mayhap he would have to brush up on his knightly skills again. Forty days in the King's service was likely not enough in Gunnilde's eyes. No, he needed to let her see him in his suit of armor more oftentimes than that, brandishing both sword and shield. He might not be a tourney-goer but he was a knight, damn it all! And clearly his wife needed reminding of that fact.

44

Gunnilde woke as Bennett lit the fire the next morning and lay there feeling miserable and alone, despite the fact James lay beside her still. She had made such a wretched mess of things, she saw that now. Her foolish meddling in the love affairs of others had led to disaster. She had wrecked three people's lives—Constance, Douglas, and, worst of all, James.

If she had been a sensible woman, it might have occurred to her that Douglas's admiration for Constance was a thing of no substance that would have faded in time, but no! She had been enchanted with the idea of his perfect, chivalrous love, encouraging him to believe it some grand and lasting passion.

And Constance…poor Constance, who had been betrothed to a truly estimable man. Gunnilde had wrought havoc on her life. Instead of congratulating her in the match, Gunnilde had viewed his suit as an inferior thing because he had not spouted pretty words or gazed longingly in her direction.

The fact was that regardless of this, James would have made Constance an excellent husband, as he had made her one. Only she was not deserving of her good fortune, she thought guiltily. James had been forced to marry her and his family, apart from Neville, considered it an affliction on their family name.

Feeling much chastened, she crept from the bed, washed in cold water, and pulled on her most sober-hued gown, a plain dress of dark blue which she had not worn since she came to court. Instead of wrapping and pinning her hair into her distinctive horns, she simply drew her hair back from her face, braided it, and donned her plainest veil, pinning it in place.

James stirred at this point, and Gunnilde made her escape, practically fleeing the bedchamber in her haste. She could not face him this morn. Not until she had fortified herself with sustenance.

She was surprised on entering the sitting room, for despite the early hour she found it full of people and the buzz of conversation in full swing. Neville, Harriet, Hal, Cuthbert, and Kit all had their heads bent together in an apparent counsel of war. They looked up as she entered the room, murmuring cautious greetings.

"Oh, Gunnilde!" Harriet said, jumping to her feet. "Right sorry I am that you are having all this worry!" She approached and they embraced warmly before Harriet drew her aside from the others to sit in the window seat.

Hal stood up to pour her a cup of foaming ale. "Thank you," she murmured, taking it from him, and he squeezed her shoulder before returning to the others.

"Why are you all here so early?" Gunnilde asked before taking a sip. "Surely the boys should be preparing for today's Revels, not sitting cloistered here."

Harriet hesitated. "They would not dream of being left out of proceedings, and things are progressing apace with Sir Elias Northcott's appeal. My mother heard that the King has granted an audience to his party first thing this morning. It is most unfortunate for Lord Vawdrey is not here to, well, guide the King as it were. He has journeyed to his brother's seat for the Solstice."

"Yes, I know but the King has other advisers, surely?"

"Yes, but my mother says none of them are so wise as Lord Vawdrey," Harriet answered, looking worried.

"Do you really think that James and I will be dragged into proceedings?" Gunnilde asked in hushed tones. "I mean, even if the annulment is granted…" She could not find the words to continue her line of thought. Unless it was decided she was culpable in the matter, she thought with a fresh rush of panic. Oh gods, was it really all her fault?

"It is too bad of Constance!" Harriet burst out, surprising her greatly. "I always held her in such high esteem, but I declare I am quite vexed with her!"

"Vexed? With Constance? But why are you so upset with her?" Gunnilde asked in dazed accents.

"Because she has no right to say such things about you!" Harriet said indignantly. "It is being whispered all over court that she holds you to blame! Margaret and I were discussing the matter last night and how ridiculous it is to try and apportion blame elsewhere. Indeed, I have always thought Margaret, the most sensible of the Queen's ladies, apart from yourself."

Harriet thought she was sensible? "Margaret Pryor, you mean? Yes, she was kind to me on my wedding night."

"I daresay she was, and why should she not be?" Harriet continued hotly. "It was not due to your machinations that you ended up at the altar that day, whatever they may say. The Queen demanded it by way of reparation, and you may be sure I informed Mistress Margaret of that fact."

"But Harriet, you must not be so cross," Gunnilde said, reaching for her hand, for her friend looked quite flushed.

"How can I be anything but cross when I hear the rumors circulating and Constance saying such undeserved things about you?"

Gunnilde's heart quailed. "What exactly has she been saying?" she forced herself to ask.

"Why the most ridiculous things, apparently! That it was all a plot from the start and that you schemed to steal James from her!" Harriet began, then halted, seeing Gunnilde's expression. "Forgive me, I did not mean to distress you."

"No, it is better that I should know, rather than remain in ignorance," she replied quietly.

Bennett entered at this point with a large tray of bread, fish, and butter. When the boys failed to fall on the provisions at once, Gunnilde realized they must really be concerned for her fate. Neville detached from their group and came across to ask if she and Harriet would join them in breaking their fast.

"No, I thank you," Harriet responded swiftly. "For I am meeting with Winifred and her cousin. We have much to do this morn." It occurred to Gunnilde that her little friend group would be countering any gossip as best they could. She felt a wave of gratitude wash over her.

"You must not despair, Gunnilde," Neville said kindly. "Indeed, the tide of feeling has not yet turned against you here at court. Many people point out that Constance, and Constance alone, has brought this upon herself. That you, a country-bred girl can have had no undue influence over a powerful heiress raised in the first circles."

"Yes, that is true," Harriet agreed. "My own mother said that Constance made her bed and must now lie in it. And after all, you did not counsel her to elope. I refuse to believe you did that. Constance must face up to her own headstrong folly."

"I did encourage their romance," Gunnilde admitted, "but I swear it was in good faith. I promise you, I knew nothing of their plot to elope until after the fact."

450

"Well, there you have it, then!" Harriet cried. She stood up and straightened her circlet and veil in a determined fashion. "I must go and make sure it is known far and wide," she said grimly as one riding into battle.

"Harriet, you must not become embroiled in any scandal on my behalf," Gunnilde started nervously. "Indeed, I should not wish for you—"

"Of course I must do my part to defend one of my dearest friends!" Harriet responded fiercely. "Winifred and I are quite determined that we shall give short shrift to any falsehoods spoken against you in our hearing! I go to meet her now and formulate our plan."

"Well, yes, but addressing something spoken in your hearing is one thing. You should not be actively seeking out my detractors to tackle them about it!"

"It is the least we can do, in the spirit of true friendship," Harriet said with a note of finality in her voice. "Winifred and I are quite agreed on this."

"Most noble Harriet," Neville said, catching hold of her hand. "Your friendship is indeed a prize worth having." They gazed at one another, and in another lifetime Gunnilde would have been enthralled. Today, however, she turned away to let them have a moment of privacy.

Harriet bade her farewells, and the squires finally took their seats at table to break their fast.

"Something looks different about you today, Gunnilde," Kit spoke up, lowering his ale cup. "I can't quite put my finger on what."

James emerged at this point from the bedchamber, his gaze seeking her out at once. He looked rumpled and distracted as though he had not enjoyed a good night's sleep. Ignoring the others, he came to a halt in front of her.

451

"Where are your horns?" he asked frowningly. "And your tippets?"

Gunnilde blinked up at him. "Oh, I did not—that is, I—"

"Horns?" Hal repeated. "Oh, you mean those hair puffs at her brow. Tired of them, have you, Gunnilde? Ah well, I daresay you will think of something new soon enough."

"As a leader of fashion, she will have to," Cuthbert said around a mouthful of bread.

"I noticed a few ladies in the stands yesterday had started affecting them," Kit said breezily as he helped himself to more fish.

"Really? Who?" Neville asked with curiosity.

"Can everyone be quiet for just one moment?" James asked with exasperation. "Come!" He held a hand out to Gunnilde in his most autocratic manner.

"But where are we going?" she asked in bewilderment.

"To dress," he said, sweeping her out of the room.

"But we are already dressed!" she pointed out.

This did not seem to signify to James, who immediately flung open the lid to her trunk. "Something bright, I think. You must wear your pearls too, and that ruby brooch the Queen gave you."

Gunnilde regarded him with exasperation. "I thought you did not like me drawing attention to myself?"

He shook his head. "I never said that. Why don't you wear the gown we were wed in?"

She scoffed. "Do not pretend to know which—"

"It was a deep rose in color and had many slashes revealing glimpses your underrobe." She was still reeling from this when he added, "This time I want you to wear it with your unicorn tippets."

"Anything else you require, my lord?" she asked tartly.

"Yes, since you ask. Scarlet stockings and those ridiculous flimsy shoes of yours with the ties."

"I see." In spite of herself, Gunnilde was impressed he possessed such an inventory of her wardrobe. He had been paying more attention to her attire than she had ever realized. "After that we can address your hair," he added coolly.

An hour later they were in the stands watching Kit compete in the long jumping final. Gunnilde's hair was once more dressed in her signature style. She even wore ribbons twined about them to add a finishing touch.

In return for his high-handedness, Gunnilde had requested James don once more his new doublet and another pair of paneled stockings. He had complied without complaint, and they now looked as fine a pair as any present as they sat side by side in the audience.

So fine, in fact, that Viscount Bardulf had appeared at her side during one of the frequent breaks to complain. According to him, it was too bad of her to make Wycliffe so polished and presentable. Gunnilde had managed a genuine laugh at this and was grateful for his display of friendship, for she fancied she was being eyed with a good deal of speculation by the crowds.

The King was not in attendance today, so after Prince Raedan, the most celebrated spectators were probably the Marquess and Marchioness of Martindale. They had come to watch their squire, Robin Geddings, compete and were very vocal in shouting their encouragement to him.

"Yes, Rob!" shouted Lady Martindale. "Do not spare him!"

"Northerners," Bardulf tutted. "So barbarous in their ways! I do like Lady Martindale's headdress though, what say you?"

"It gives her a pleasing effect of height," Gunnilde agreed. "But I think the black velvet is too conservative. She should wear brighter colors. Perhaps the same in a blue silk would be pleasing to the eye."

"Hmmm," Bardulf considered. "You could be right. She will end up losing it, if she does not refrain from hanging over the side of the stand like that."

It seemed her husband agreed, for Lord Martindale drew her back, wrapping a protective arm about her shoulders. Gunnilde sighed. "They are a handsome couple, are they not? Lady Bardulf did not accompany you this day?"

"Alas, my poor Jane is recovering from a head cold at present." His cynical expression softened. "I will permit her to do nothing but sit around wrapped in blankets, drinking syrup. I want her well for the Solstice."

He stayed a good ten minutes before drifting away, and Neville got up to go and fetch them some refreshment leaving her and James alone in their box.

"Were you in love with Sir Douglas?" he asked her suddenly, his conversational tone so at variance with the question that it took a moment for its meaning to sink in. "I will not take offense if you were," he continued in a measured voice, "for it happened before my time with

454

you. Last night, I overreacted. I was…rude. I hope you will accept my apology."

"I am not, and have never been in love with Sir Douglas!" Gunnilde burst out.

His shoulders relaxed. "I am glad to hear it."

"What about you? Were you in love with Constance?" She really ought to have asked him this before, but gods, she had never actually considered that possibility at the beginning. She had been so sure that he was cold and unfeeling. Then later on, she had been too scared to ask.

"No, I was not," he answered firmly.

They both stole sideways looks at one another. "Well, that's alright, then. We have neither one of us ruined the other's life," she said, swallowing.

"Ruined?" He seemed surprised by her words. "No, I should say not."

At this inopportune moment, they heard footsteps tramping down their stand. James looked over her shoulder and Gunnilde saw his look turn wary. She turned and found Sir Palmerston du Vrey, a senior member of the King's guard, approaching, accompanied by two soldiers.

"Is it my imagination or are they heading toward us?" she asked nervously.

"It would appear so," James answered grimly.

Sure enough, the footsteps came to a halt at the end of their line, and Sir Palmerston cleared his throat. "Sir James," he greeted him. "The King has sent me to request your presence, and that of your good lady wife, imminently."

455

"He did, did he? Where?" James enquired coolly.

"His Majesty awaits you in his throne room."

Gunnilde's heart sank. If the King was in his throne room then he was still presiding over Sir Elias Northcott's appeal. They were being dragged into proceedings. And there would be an audience too, she thought numbly. An audience to this catastrophe.

"Very well," James answered in a level voice. "We will accompany you there."

"Wait!" cried Neville, who was clattering down the steps, wine jug in hand. "You must not proceed without your friends and family!" Setting down the wine on the steps, he started gesturing madly to the squires down on the field.

Immediately Hal, Cuthbert, and Kit detached themselves from the other squires and vaulted over the barrier to enter the crowd.

"But they will miss the last event," Gunnilde pointed out. "Was Cuthbert not competing in it?"

"It is of no matter," Neville answered dismissively. "We had decided all this beforehand. In any case, Kit has won his event."

Accepting James's proffered hand, Gunnilde stood up and allowed herself to be shepherded out of the stands to the accompaniment of much whispered speculation.

45

Gunnilde glanced over her shoulder a few times during the procession to the throne room. She was sure they must look a ragtag bunch. Kit had mud splattered up his legs, Neville carried a brimming wine jug, and as for Hal, he wore his mystery lady's favor upon one arm and had his little dog tucked under the other.

Cuthbert must have changed his outfit in preparation for the next event, for he wore a padded gambeson instead of a tunic. Still, none of them looked remotely abashed about their appearance, so Gunnilde decided she, too, would have to shrug off her unease.

On reaching the throne room, the guards saluted Sir Palmerston and stood aside to grant them entrance. Things were set out very formally within. The King was sat upon his dais, a forbidding frown upon his face. Next to him stood Lord Schaeffer, one of his senior advisers.

Lord Schaeffer had an expression of distaste upon his face and looked as though he had swallowed something nasty. Gunnilde thought it was plain he was not enjoying proceedings so far. A large crowd of courtiers were packed into the back of the room with guards placed at intervals to keep them at a sufficient distance.

Stood in the middle of the floor facing the King was a group of disgruntled-looking men who Gunnilde guessed must be Constance's kinsmen. They were bearded, wore old-fashioned cotehardies and matching expressions of belligerence.

Beside them stood Constance, dressed modestly in a blue gown and holding a devotional book clutched in one hand. Despite the studied demureness of her appearance, her head was flung back, her eyes flashed with scorn, and her color was high. She looked, Gunnilde thought enviously, the very image of a haughty beauty.

Stood at some distance again was Sir Douglas, holding himself aloof from the Northcotts. He looked uncharacteristically bad-tempered. These clearly consisted of the principal players in the matter. Now their party was escorted to the fore, and made another grouping, at least as large as the Northcott faction.

"Your Majesty," Sir Palmerston announced, "the Wycliffes have answered your summons."

"Approach, approach," King Wymer said, rotating his hand.

James took a step forward and bowed. "What is your will, Your Majesty?"

"Well, well," the King said, his eye traveling over them. "Brought the family along, have you? Only fair, I suppose." He brightened a little on spotting Hal. "Hah, young Payne, is it? Won any ribbons this morn?" he asked with a flicker of interest.

"Not today, Your Highness, but Montmayne here just took the win for the long jump."

"Did he indeed? Well, good for you." Kit bowed. "Hear you caught the Queen's eye last night, Montmayne. She tells me she wants to see more of you and Ames at court." Cuthbert bowed too, but the King's attention had already returned to his own favorite. "Hear you struck my fine Sir Symond a blow last night." He chuckled. "He's a fiery temper and took it very ill, or so I hear."

"I believe I had cause," Hal replied mildly.

"Insulted your dog, did he?" the King replied, striking his thigh and then bursting into loud guffaws at his little joke.

Lord Schaeffer coughed, and the King cleared his throat. "Ah, well, best return to this matter at hand, I suppose." He sighed. "Heard about

458

this wretched business, have you, Wycliffe?" he asked, turning back to James.

James hesitated. "I have heard a rumor, Your Highness, that an annulment is being sought of the union of Sir Douglas and his bride."

The King nodded. "True enough. True enough. And what say you to that, sir?"

"Me, sire?" James's eyebrows rose. "Why very little, Your Majesty. What business is it of mine?"

The Northcotts started rumbling at this, but the King swung around and bent a ferocious glare on them. "You have already had the floor, sir!" he roared in Sir Elias's direction. "If I wish to hear from you further, I will let you know!" They relapsed into chastened silence.

"It has been suggested," the King began cautiously, "that you might be an interested party. That in fact, you might feel similarly about your own wedded state."

"I dare assure you, sire—" James started, but the King had already turned to Gunnilde.

"And you, Hilde?" he boomed. "What have you to say in the matter?"

Gunnilde curtseyed and stepped forward to stand beside her husband. "I am heartily sorry to hear that Sir Douglas and Lady Constance's match has not worked out," she began contritely, "but—"

"There will be no annulment of our marriage bond," James's words rang out clear as a bell.

Gasps and whispers had started toward the back of the room. Lord Schaeffer made a hushing motion with his hands that was largely ignored.

459

Gunnilde made another attempt. "You see—" she began desperately.

"In any case, there are no grounds," James cut in smoothly. "Our marriage has been consummated. Many times, sire," he added just in case there was any doubt on the matter.

Gunnilde's face flamed at the titillated gasps of the ladies and the barely suppressed chortles of the men.

The King gave an approving grunt. "Well, I'm glad to hear it! At least someone here behaves as they ought!"

Gunnilde could not believe how shamelessly James was acting. His usual reserve seemed to have gone quite out of the window! She cast an open-mouthed look his way, but he met her incredulous gaze quite calmly.

"I must also add that if anyone were to attempt to wrest my wife from me, I would be forced to take measures to counteract them," he continued calmly.

"Oh, yes?" The King stirred in his seat with interest. "What sort of measures might those be?" he asked with grudging curiosity.

"I would be forced to fly with her," he replied at once. "And put up somewhere fortified until the issue was resolved in my favor. I have kinsmen and friends whose sword arms I could rely upon." He turned back to indicate Hal, Cuthbert, Kit, and Neville. Their hands clapped at once to their daggers; all save Neville, who carried none. Still, he straightened up with his wine jug, looking grimly resolved.

"Is that so?" The King sounded entertained. "Well, well. Good for you. Good for you, Wycliffe. You're not chicken-hearted, I'll give you that." He looked across at the other party. "What about you, Farleigh?" Sir Douglas, looking pale, pressed his lips together and shook his head.

460

"Speak up, I say!" roared the King. "This man says he'll guard his wife with his sword and his honor. What say you to that?"

Sir Douglas lifted his chin, looking resolute. "Naught, save this, Your Highness. You can have mine, and welcome."

Again, the crowd erupted with gasps and laughter. Constance, who had been trembling with suppressed fury and mortification at his side, finally snapped.

"You hateful beast!" she screamed and flew at Douglas, raining blows upon his chest. Sir Douglas stood there still as a statue, until she finally collapsed against him, sobbing and spent. Awkwardly, he closed his arms about her, supporting her, though he would not look at her face.

The crowd pressed closer, all agog. "Well, whoever would have thought that prim Lady Constance was such a shrew?" Gunnilde heard Lady Schaeffer say with relish.

"If I'd known she wasn't a crushing bore I'd have cultivated her company sooner," her friend replied dryly.

"Silence!" the King bellowed. "I can't hear above all this noise." He glared beadily at the courtiers until they fell silent, then turned back to Douglas. "You don't want the troublesome wench anymore, is that it?" he asked, pursing his lips. "I can't say as I blame you."

Douglas's face hardened. "In truth, she has given me little right to protect her or call her mine. She no longer wants me and she's made that much plain." Constance's breathing hitched and she lifted her head to look at him, her eyes still swimming with tears.

Gunnilde's nose quivered. She did not think it looked so plain at this moment in time. She went to take a step forward, but James's hand closed firmly about hers, holding her fast. He gave her a warning look, as though to say Do not interfere.

461

"Mmm, and now you're tired of her," the King pronounced with a gusty sigh. "Well, this is a pretty state of affairs. If you're going to elope with a man you need to have made up your mind from the outset, madam! You can't be shilly-shallying about with one foot in and one foot out!"

"Take this pair for your example," he said, gesturing toward James and Gunnilde. "They made up their minds to have each other and nothing stands in their way. That's what you need to stand the test of marriage. Grim determination. It's a bloody business and not for the faint of heart, I can tell you that much!"

Constance gave a muffled sob, and the double doors at the other end of the chamber burst open. It was Queen Armenal with her attendants.

"Make way for the Queen!" Piers Winstanley called out, leading the way. The crowd gasped and reluctantly fell back, leaving the newcomers a clear path through to the front. Even from a distance Gunnilde could see Queen Armenal was in a high temper.

"What is all this, occurring without my presence?" the Queen demanded, her eyes raking over them all. "This affair is one of my own making!" she asserted. "How dare you all try to cut me out of proceedings at this late point in the day!"

"Well, my dear, you were indisposed," the King said significantly, waggling his eyebrows. "I didn't wish to have you bothered at such a time."

Armenal turned very pink at this mention, even indirectly of her morning sickness. "Nonsense!" she spluttered. "I needed only an hour or two for it to pass! You have been high-handed, abominably high-handed in this matter, Wymer!"

"No, no," he placated her hastily, standing up from his throne. "I have made no final ruling, that is your province." He descended the three steps and offered the Queen his arm, leading her up onto the dais, murmuring soothing words into her ear. "Bring my Queen's throne forward," he shouted.

Soldiers hastily mounted the dais to fulfil his bidding, and in a short time the Queen was enthroned beside him. Gunnilde watched as Piers, Mistress Bartree, Unwin, and the Queen's guards stood unobtrusively to one side. Looking somewhat mollified, the Queen inclined her head. "Lord Schaeffer, you may provide me with a summary of all that has passed," she said grandly.

Still looking deeply unhappy, that gentleman stepped forward and gave a summing up of the key points. Once he reached James's repudiation of the claim he might be an interested party, she sat forward in her chair.

"But this part interests me greatly," she said, holding up a finger. "For recently, I have wondered if I might have erred in my original solution to the problem of Lady Constance's elopement." She turned to James as all the air expelled from Gunnilde's lungs. The Queen could not be saying what she thought she was saying, could she? That she had been mistaken to arrange their match in the first place? "Sir James, you maintain that you have no interest in pursuing an annulment of your own marriage."

"Certainly not, Your Majesty," he pronounced loudly.

"Such an idea is distasteful to your honor, perhaps?" she suggested delicately.

He hesitated. "Distasteful is not the word that I would use. It is not strong enough. I would say myself that the notion is revolting to me on every level."

For a moment the Queen looked taken aback, then she seemed to recover. "Your finer feelings do you credit, Sir James." She smiled. "You are a high-minded individual, and your scruples show your

463

superiority of conscience. Yet I cannot help but think that in many ways, the issue could be redressed to bring about an outcome which would suit everyone a good deal more satisfactorily."

"That is what we assert, Your Majesty," cried Sir Elias, bowing low.

"Quiet, you!" the King growled.

"For instance," the Queen continued serenely, "quite mistakenly it seems, your current wife felt you did not care to perform in front of an audience." Current wife, thought Gunnilde incensed. Current wife? "This shows a basic lack of understanding of your character which—"

"She was not remotely mistaken," James interrupted the Queen forthrightly, quite taking Gunnilde's breath away. "I don't care for it."

"Well, but you performed the other evening, most beautifully, to the acclaim of all!" the Queen protested.

"I was merely filling in that part due to a last-minute absence. I will do that when the occasion demands but I will never choose to perform."

The Queen smiled thinly. "Be that as it may, Sir James, I cannot help but be aware of several points of incompatibility between my good Gunnilde and yourself. She is a simple, straightforward soul and you are an artist. I did not appreciate this sufficiently when first I championed your match. Had I but realized, I would never have proposed such a thing."

But James had already turned toward the King. "If the position of royal musician is considered a bar to my marriage, then I hereby refuse the honor, Your Majesty."

"Is that so?" the King asked looking diverted.

464

"Sir James!" the Queen burst out, sitting up very straight in her chair. "Am I to understand that you refuse our generous offer?"

"There can be no question, Your Highness. If I have the option of keeping my wife by my side or accepting the position of royal musician, then I will never hesitate as to my choice. I will choose her every time."

Queen Armenal appeared quite dumbfounded by this. As for the spectators, they were positively agog. The buzz of their whispers seemed to rouse her from her stupor. "Forgive me, Sir James," she said rallying, "but you are clearly ill-suited for the writing of popular ballads. Are you aware," she asked with a tight smile, "that was the path your wife envisaged for you? What say you to that, sirrah?"

Well! Gunnilde fumed to see the way the Queen thought to use her previous confidences against her. I will never confide in her again! she thought, bosom heaving. If it had not been a punishable offense, she would have dragged off her shoe and flung it at her royal head! Only James's calmness, his composure of manner held her back from the brink of disaster.

"I am well aware that my wife thinks I could turn my hand to any musical endeavor," he answered. "And while flattered by her faith in me, I must respectfully leave the ballad writing to my brother-in-law."

"Payne writes ballads too, does he?" the King asked with a flicker of interest.

A spasm of annoyance crossed Queen Armenal's face. "We are not speaking of your Master Payne right now, but of Sir James!"

"Well, well," the King said indulgently. "I must admit Payne is a lad after my own heart. Must get him to sing me his ballad sometime."

"Right gladly, Your Majesty," piped up Hal cheerfully.

"I believe you would like it, sire," James asserted. "It is more comedic than dramatic in theme."

"Oh, yes?" Clearly the King thought this a point in its favor.

"If you have quite finished," the Queen said tartly, "then I must insist we return to the matter at hand."

"Your Majesty," James said, lifting his voice. "You must appreciate, I would be entirely useless in the role of royal musician if you were to take Gunnilde from me." He paused to let this point sink in as the audience jostled for a better position to observe him. Gunnilde watched him, wondering what he would say next.

"The music you wish me to write will never be written without her," he continued. "The tales you wish me to commemorate mean naught to me without her interpretation. I have examined the tapestries you mentioned, and they conveyed precisely nothing to me."

There was another stirring in the room. "I was not moved to write the piece of music you so admire until my wife relayed the story to me. It was through her words alone that I was inspired."

The Queen's expression of disbelief momentarily lifted. "You mean," she said hesitantly, "that Gunnilde is your muse?"

"I suppose you could put it that way," he answered after a heavy pause. "Another way would be this." He turned to draw Gunnilde close, wrapping a possessive arm about her waist. "This woman is mine and I'll take no other to wife while I live and breathe. This I vow."

Gunnilde's heart flew right out of her chest. That James should say such a thing, should act thus, in front of a packed room of spectators! She could scarce believe it. Then he gave a brief bow and started to pull Gunnilde away as if they had been dismissed already. As if the matter was closed.

466

"Wait!" the Queen called out desperately. "There is still much to be settled!"

"Seems to me he's made his position abundantly plain," said King Wymer. "Best content yourself with dismantling this other marriage." He gestured toward Constance and Douglas. "This one's standing. Wycliffe's not giving her up and I can't say as I blame him. Sensible fellow that, in spite of the, er, artist thing." He gave a motion of his hand to indicate the guards should let them pass, and James and Gunnilde made their escape.

46

"Let us get out of here before we get besieged and halt proceedings," James murmured in her ear, urging her forward. She spared one more glance over her shoulder for Constance and Douglas and then pushed on.

On their way out, both Harriet and Winifred detached from the crowd, darting out to joyfully embrace her. Much to her surprise she had also received a tight-lipped smile and an approving nod from Mistress Bartree. Everyone else had been a blur.

"I think they will remain married, you know," speculated Kit as they hurried down the corridor. "Despite everything. What say you?"

"Of course they will!" Hal huffed. "Did not my brother-in-law make that plain? If anyone disputes it, we're to take up arms!"

"Not your sister and Wycliffe, you dolt! No question about that. I mean the Farleighs."

"Doubtful, very doubtful I should say," Neville chimed in. "Sir Douglas looked as if he was heartily sick of the pack of them. He's more likely to take an oath of chastity than to e'er say wedding vows again!"

Cuthbert, Gunnilde noticed, said nothing. She debated asking his opinion on the matter, but one glance at James's face changed her mind. Clearly, Douglas and Constance's fate was very far from uppermost in his mind. He practically dragged her up the stairs to their quarters and on reaching their rooms, made straight for their bedchamber, towing her in his wake.

"I think the others—"

"Neville can play host," James cut her off. "I need to speak with you, Gunnilde. Alone."

"Yes," she agreed, and he shut the door behind them, crossing to light the fire, which was laid ready. Gunnilde donned her woollen mantle, removed her shoes, and took a seat on the bed as James lit two candles. Though the hour could be no more advanced than four o'clock, darkness was already falling fast.

The room soon took on a cosy hue, and James drew a chair up before the fire, turning it to face her before sitting himself down. "I will tend the fire until it gets properly going," he said, taking up the poker and giving it a prod.

Gunnilde was not entirely sure this was the reason for him putting distance between them, but she nodded anyway. "Shall I speak first?"

"I would rather unburden myself, if you are willing to hear it." She assented at once and he took a deep breath. "Thank you," he said in a low voice. "For letting me say my piece before the King and for standing by me, whatever it cost you. I know I am far from your ideal, but I want you to know how much it means to me that you can overlook this and put our vows first and foremost.

Gunnilde stared at him. "James—" She faltered but he held up his hand.

"Allow me to say this, Gunnilde. Permit me to promise you a good life, despite the fact I am far from the type of husband you always dreamed of growing up."

"Far from…?" Gunnilde repeated, sitting up straight on the bed. "Why do you say so?"

"Because," he answered, "I know that I am not." She gazed at him in bewilderment. "I'm not some…strapping knight riding off into battle," he flung at her. "I'll never make you tournament queen."

469

"Oh, that, but I do not mind that at all! Eden made me tournament queen once, so I have already realized that ambition."

"Eden?" he echoed, plainly startled. "Eden Vawdrey? How could she have—?"

"I dreamed of marrying a knight, it's true, but you are a knight, James. We have already had this discussion, have we not? There are different kinds. I certainly never dreamed of marrying one so handsome as you. None of the knights who competed at my father's tournament ever were," she admitted frankly.

"The kind of knight I am married to resides at court and serves his king and country forty days out of the year. I am more than happy with my lot. In fact…" She hesitated. Would a confession of love be acceptable to him at this point? It was not like her to be so reticent, but she could not seem to help it. Her love felt like a thing that should be protected and nurtured at all costs, not exposed to the elements. "In fact," she repeated breathlessly, "my concern is that you do not share my contentment in our match. I mean, not really. After all, how can you?"

He frowned. "Explain," he said shortly.

She heaved a great sigh. "You see, I meant to work so hard on your behalf," she said sincerely. "I knew from the start that I had a good deal of work to do to make up for all you lost. Constance's fortune, I mean," she added when he continued to look blank. "And the connections she would have brought you, which would have been so valuable to your advancement."

"What are you—?"

"Please let me say it, James. I am aware that you never intended to wed one such as I, you wanted someone quite different for your bride, and our marriage was a huge shock to you." She swallowed. "And yes, a disappointment too."

"Gunnilde, don't!" he burst out. "Do not say such things. Even at the time I never thought of it like that."

"James, you do not need to spare my feelings," she insisted. "I want us both to speak freely and to—to—" Sadly at this point her courage failed along with her speech.

"Very well, if I am to speak freely, then I will confess I am not as content as you," James said confrontationally. "Shall I tell you why?"

Gunnilde forced herself to return his steady gaze. "Please do," she said, even though it cost her dearly. This was going to hurt, she thought, far more than Sir Ned's words ever could, but she owed it to James to bear the pain stoically.

"I am not content because you do not harbor the same depth of feeling for me that I feel for you. There, now I have said it!" he said with a challenging lift of his chin. "One day, I hope I will inspire such feeling in your bosom, but until that day—"

"Wait!" Gunnilde started up off the bed. She took a step toward him, then hesitated. "You mean respect and admiration and things like that?" she asked cautiously.

Slowly, he shook his head. "I'm not even speaking of love that grows sensibly over time," he admitted. "I'm talking about the fact that I have fallen headlong, recklessly, inexorably in love with you, Gunnilde Payne."

Gunnilde's hands were covering her mouth though she did not remember placing them there. She whispered his name against her fingers.

"I never intended to," he carried on. "It just happened. It happened and it changed me, and I cannot regret it. Even if you never really return it in the same spirit."

471

"Oh, but I do!" Gunnilde burst out, closing the gap between them. "I do love you!" Her eyes filled with tears. "And ever since I realized it, everything has been ruined!" she wailed. "It has all been so difficult and I have not known how to behave around you anymore!"

One minute she was standing beside him and the next she found herself seized and pulled into his lap. "Say it again," he said appealingly, staring into her eyes. His hands cradled her face. "Please."

She took a deep breath. "I love you, James Wycliffe. So very much. What I feel for you so far surpasses any liking I ever felt for Arthur, or any other passing fancy, that it feels an entirely different emotion altogether. In fact, I don't think I ever truly knew what love was before you, even though I considered myself an expert."

"Yes," he said raspily, and she could see how her words had affected him, for he looked quite choked with emotion, his throat working and his eyes welling up. She dropped a gentle kiss on his lips and his arms tightened around her.

"Again," he murmured.

"Again the words, or again the kiss," she laughed shakily.

"Both."

"I love you, James, as I have never loved another man before or ever will again. I am quite sure of that."

He nodded. "That's good," he breathed. "I feel the same way about you." They kissed again, sweet and slow. He shook his head. "I can't believe you couldn't tell what a fool I am for you."

"Sometimes you are a little hard to read," she admitted fondly. "Though, looking back, perhaps I should have realized sooner."

472

"I'm so sorry about last night," he said, his gaze falling. "I was sick with jealousy over Farleigh, but that's no excuse for how I behaved." He hesitated. "What I said about you being a hardened flirt…"

"Do not regard it," she laughed. "I am adding it to your 'flaunting siren' comment. You intended it for an insult but I do not choose to take it that way." She kissed him again. "You have no need to be jealous over Douglas. I always thought he was sweet, and I loved to see him blush and stammer over Constance, but I never wanted him for my own. I promise you that."

His arms tightened around her again. "I am glad," he said tersely. "And I will work harder to be gracious around Bevan and Conway next time we cross paths."

"You were not precisely discourteous to them," she said perhaps a shade generously.

"I did not feel remotely courteous toward any of them."

Gunnilde gave a gurgle of laughter. "Well, now you know my feelings I am sure their company will become easier to bear." She twined her arms about his neck and sighed. "I know exactly when I realized I had fallen for you. It was after that night we frequented those taverns together. I woke up the next morning and I just knew. I had been quite at ease in our marriage until that point, but then suddenly I just felt so unsure of myself and…and well inadequate."

"Inadequate?" He frowned. "Why?"

"I suppose I feared you did not feel the same way about me."

"Shall I tell you how it was for me?" She nodded and he took a deep breath. "Even when I thought you would make me the most unsuitable wife in the kingdom, I still thought you were the most provocative, the most enticing, and the comeliest woman I'd ever seen."

473

"James! Really?" she asked in high delight. "Sometimes you make me quite giddy."

"And then you started with your talk of marriage pacts and helpmeets. I found I really wanted you." His throat closed over the words. "You saved me from that jester, then you saved me from the wretched existence I had eked out for myself. I was—" He broke off frustratedly. "I did not even know what I was missing out on until you came into my life. I was…miserable. I felt totally alone. Every connection felt like a burden to me, even my brother, if I am honest." His eyes avoided hers and he looked heartily ashamed.

Gunnilde considered. "Neville told me once that he guilted and plagued you for money as the rest of your family do. He said you were overburdened with cares."

"Did he say that?" She nodded, and he was quiet for a moment. "He has improved greatly since your brother and his friends came into our lives, you know. He has not even complained of any maladies plaguing him of late. He was constantly imagining himself ill at one time, mostly from boredom and lack of purpose, I suspect."

"I think he should take on some responsibilities. It is high time."

"You mean marriage?" James asked, slanting a look at her. There was the ghost of a smile playing about his mouth.

Gunnilde started guiltily. "James, I promise you," she said fervently, "I meant what I said. Never, never again will I interfere or meddle with the love lives of others. I have learned my lesson. I wrought so much disaster upon everyone." She shuddered. "Today was proof enough of that."

"What are you talking about?" he interrupted. "I do not care one whit if you take up your matchmaking again. Not now I feel assured of your

474

heart. I think you should find husbands for Harriet and Winifred and even Mistress Bartree, should it please you!" She stared.

"It only irritates me that fool Farleigh now gazes after you like a lovesick swain but that is hardly your fault. If he was too stupid to realize his feelings before it was too late, then that is his own tragedy. Besides, I am glad he was oblivious, that worked out all the better for me."

"Sir Douglas is not in love with me," Gunnilde said sensibly. "He is merely tired of strife and contention and looks back to a time in his life when he found sympathy and comfort from another. Me. There was nothing remotely lover-like about his behavior when we used to meet. He used to spend the whole time sighing over Constance."

James pulled a face. "Constance!" he uttered with disgust. "If you ask me, I was damnably lucky that you convinced her to run off with another!"

"James!" she gasped. "Surely you do not think—?"

"Oh, I know you did not actually recommend she should elope," he assured her with a wave of his hand. "I just mean that if your espousing Sir Douglas's cause enabled me to escape that fate, then I am both relieved and grateful."

"I myself feel quite sorry for Constance," Gunnilde said truthfully. "Her family are clearly more concerned with preserving the status quo than they are securing her future happiness. Do you think their marriage will end up being annulled?"

"I have no idea and I would rather not speculate," James responded smartly. "Instead, I would rather we continued talking of ourselves. Did you really mean what you said just now? About your being content married to a mere musician instead of a tourney-goer?"

She snorted. "I don't see that there is any 'mere' about it! You are likely soon to become the foremost musician in the land! And I want to make it plain once again that the Queen quite misrepresented me earlier. I never intended to give the impression that you would not accept a royal appointment. If I did that, then I am heartily sorry for it."

"I know," he said dismissively. "You already explained."

"Yes, but I was not sure you entirely understood," she said earnestly. "James, you must believe that I support your career fully and am very proud of your talent and achievements." When he hesitated, she was filled with dismay. "What have I ever done to make you doubt that fact? Please tell me."

"It was only that you have felt so distant these past few days. I thought perhaps you were bored that day we spent at Barnabus Hall. I would not blame you if that was the case," he said hurriedly.

"Oh no! Not at all!" she answered with spirit. "You must never think that, James. I thought it was wonderful. I liked Master Gregory and the others a good deal, I assure you."

"Then why did you retreat from me directly after?" he asked simply.

Gunnilde dropped her gaze as she tried to vocalize her thoughts. "I suppose I was somewhat awed by the experience," she admitted softly. "I had no idea about the sheer enormity of your talent." He gave a short laugh as though she jested. "I am in deadly earnest, James!" she exclaimed, feeling stung.

He stared at her. "You are, aren't you?" he said slowly. She nodded, tears gathering in her eyes before she wiped them away impatiently.

"But why should it make you sad?" he asked in confusion.

476

"I do not know," she replied in a choked voice. "Because of the disparity I felt opening up between us. Because at the time, I felt that you were too wonderful to belong with someone so ordinary and forgettable as I." She swiped her eyes again, and James pulled her hands away from her face.

"Forgettable?" he repeated incredulously. "My horned temptress who flaunts herself in the halls of palaces? I hardly think so! Don't you know how infatuated I am with you, Gunnilde? How I have been from the start? How truly loved you are by your family and your friends? How influential you are here at court?" He shook his head. "Being buffeted with lances and repeatedly knocked off his horse has doubtless scrambled what little brains Bevan ever possessed. He needed a lesson in humility, and I for one am glad Mistress Fern has delivered him one."

"It was not Mistress Fern who cursed him but some old crone in the marketplace."

"Whoever it was, he is deserving of his punishment."

"Well, hopefully it will not be of too long a duration. I honestly wish him well."

When James narrowed his eyes but did not speak, she gave a watery laugh. "I was not thinking of Sir Ned's words when I described myself just now. Just...my own mediocrity."

"Do not speak of yourself like that," he said sternly. "I would not suffer anyone else to speak of you thus, and neither should you."

She considered this a moment. "No, you're right," she concluded. "And truth to tell, I did not really suffer it that time either. Did I never tell you how I responded to Sir Ned that day?"

"No. Tell me now." So, she did. "Tell me again," he said at once. She repeated the story, and he nodded slowly. "I can almost picture their faces when you whipped back that curtain."

"You're not going to write a piece of music about it, are you?" she asked with misgiving at the end of her tale.

"I almost think I could, you know," he said, looking suddenly thoughtful.

"Really?"

He nodded. "Now tell me, was it immediately after that incident you came to court?"

"I did."

"You're magnificent, Gunnilde, you must know that. Come here," he murmured, drawing her against him, holding her close. "I want always to be as close to you as this," he said, "all the time."

Gunnilde closed her eyes and let herself enjoy the moment and the sentiment. James did not think she was forgettable. He thought she was magnificent. "When you say it started early for you, I was wondering…how early?"

"Our wedding night," he answered at once, so promptly that Gunnilde caught her breath. "I thought it would take years for me to accustom myself to having a wife," he carried on. "It was always my plan to send any bride to Wycliffe Hall as soon as I could do so, without causing comment. But it was nothing like that with you. And I was so shocked. Shocked at my own reaction to your lying in my bed." He huffed out a breath of air. "I had no idea it would affect me so."

"But you…you did not wish to consummate our marriage at the time," she reminded him in confused accents.

478

He snorted. "Oh yes I did. I was in an agony that first night."

"On our wedding night?" She was incredulous. "I had no notion!"

"I know. You were chattering away, all friendly and sweet, and I was lying there with a cock-stand, feeling guilty and damnably confused."

"Oh, James!" she chuckled. "You poor thing!"

"I was such a fool," he said, smoothing her hair back from her face. I knew I found you damnably attractive, but I was still trying to pretend to myself I did not."

"And so you lay there in the dark suffering," she tutted.

"Yes."

"I would have taken pity on you, if you had only told me."

"Would you?" He caught his breath.

"Oh yes."

"What would you have done?" he asked.

"Hmm…" She appeared to consider this. "Perhaps found some way to alleviate your suffering. Let you touch me. Perhaps…touched you."

"Touched me?" he asked, his voice raspy.

"Yes."

"Where?"

"Wherever you wanted."

"You did not like me then though," he reminded her with a frown. "I would not have wanted you to feel…obligated."

"I started to like you a little at our wedding banquet," she admitted. "You were so…skittish and awkward that my heart quite went out to you."

He groaned. "You felt sorry for me, you mean, that is not the same as liking."

"You also trembled when I flung my arms about you," she reminded him shyly. "And you were so handsome, and your body was throwing out so much heat it kept me toasty warm beside you. You…well, I did not dislike it. Maybe I did realize a little that your reaction to me was not, well, not of repulsion even from that point."

"Repulsion? I should say not! You drove me wild."

"Then, you were always saying things," she said vaguely.

"What kind of things?"

"Like those times you told me the way I dressed or wore my hair would look ridiculous if I was not so pretty."

"I thought you would grow angry every time I let something tactless like that slip," he confessed. "But whenever you laughed or told me you meant to take it for a compliment, I realized how bloody nice you were, and my attraction to you increased tenfold."

"Really?"

He nodded. "I told Neville the way you dressed was indecent, but it was only because of the nature of my own thoughts toward you."

"Do you still have them?" she asked curiously.

He turned his head. "Indecent thoughts? About you?" She nodded. "All the damned time," he groaned. "When I started to realize how much I liked you, I became so clumsy, blundering about like a fool. I was supposed to be a polished courtier but all that went out of the window where you were concerned. I don't know how you put up with me or ever formed a good opinion of me, in truth. You were so patient."

"You poor, poor thing," she breathed. "Shall I take pity on you now?"

He caught his breath. "It would be a mercy."

They moved over to the bed, and after hurriedly undressing one another, spent a very delightful twenty minutes finding out exactly what Gunnilde could have done to alleviate James's suffering on their wedding night. "Ah gods," he panted, "I do not want to spend in your hand. It's…it's a good deal messier than when I touch you. You might not like it."

"Oh, but I would not mind the messiness," she assured him with perfect composure. James looked horribly conflicted for an instant. "In fact, I should like to see it," she said, tipping the balance.

He made a noise deep in his throat and then he came apart in her hands completely. Gunnilde, fascinated by his masculine beauty in the aftermath, watched him closely as he recovered.

"My gods," James groaned. "Did that—was that—?"

"I loved touching you," she said with perfect truth.

"Let me get cleaned up." He rolled off the bed and crossed to the basin. When he was done, he refilled the it and motioned for her to come over and join him. "Come and wash your hands." He stood behind her, his hands entwined with hers as they shared the soap flakes between them.

481

"It's probably as well I did not touch you like this on our wedding night," Gunnilde reflected. "For you would not have been so free and comfortable with me afterward as you are now."

He laughed. "No, I think it is safe to say that I would not." He kissed the back of her neck.

"It is good that I gave you time to get warmed up to me," she continued, wiping her hands on the drying cloth.

"Warmed up? I was burned to crisp from the outset! Let's get back into bed."

Hand in hand, they sauntered over to the bed and clambered under the covers, immediately coming back together again underneath them.

"I used to wonder, you know, what it would be like to have someone look at me through the eyes of love," she admitted quietly. "To wonder what it must it feel like to be able to wield such an effect on someone. And now I know," she concluded wonderingly.

He ran a finger down her cheek. "And how does it feel?"

She smiled at him. "Don't you know?"

Hesitantly, he answered her smile. "Yes, I know." They kissed again, and Gunnilde felt her heart skip in her chest. Maybe she would be the one fainting this time. She could not hold back her smile at the thought.

"What are you smiling about?"

"Nothing, just...remembering things. They appear in an altogether different light now that I know you love me."

"What things?"

She ducked her head. "Things like you swooning that time."

"I did not swoon!"

"You did, you know, James," she said earnestly.

"I know," he admitted at once. "I won't do it again though."

"And you rubbing my feet in that inn."

He appeared to consider this. "Yes, I would not do that for anyone else," he said, flopping onto his back. He extended his arm so she could lie on it and Gunnilde shuffled in close.

"Did you hear what the King said as we left the throne room?"

"He told the Queen to mind her own damned business." James scowled. "Someone had to."

She gave a watery chuckle. "Well, I am not likely to argue with you on that score. She was rather awful, wasn't she? I will own I was put quite out of humor with her. Indeed, I've decided I no longer want to be the Queen's favorite after all," she declared, her eyes kindling. "She presented what I said to her in the worst possible light and made me sound quite ridiculous, as if I did not know you at all, and I find I cannot forgive her for it. Besides, it is not at all what I thought it would be like."

"You mean, being a lady-in-waiting?" he enquired.

She nodded. "Strange to say, Mistress Bartree is probably the only one I shall bother to maintain a friendship with in future. Some of them are pleasant enough, but they already have their own particular friends, and no room for me. I find I do not care enough to try anymore. I have my own friends after all."

"Well, I do not mind if you are not the Queen's favorite, but I would rather you did not become the King's," James admitted, angling a wry look her way. "He called you Hilde again, I noticed."

"He did," she acknowledged, "but I think in truth it is Hal who is his new favorite. Though King Wymer is definitely warming up to you now." She shot a speculative look his way. "I believe in spite of everything, you will end up with the post of Royal musician."

"Yes, though if I do, it will be at least partly due to his partiality for you Paynes. Wymer has not heard one note of my compositions to my knowledge."

"No, but he said he thought you were sensible and a man of honor even if you were an artist."

A smile tugged at James's lips. "High praise indeed. But the only reason he thinks that is because I had the good sense to hold on to you. I heard what he said at our wedding feast. He thinks me fortunate indeed to have got my hands on you."

Gunnilde's eyes opened wide. "I do not think I am at all the sort of woman to catch his eye!" she spluttered. "Besides, he is quite devoted to the Queen."

"These days he is," James corrected her. "But it has not always been so."

"That was before my time." Gunnilde shrugged.

"Well, if he starts to get too fond, we may have to retreat into the country."

"To Wycliffe Hall?"

"Yes, I suppose." He spoke without enthusiasm.

484

"If you get terribly successful, we might be able to buy a second residence and live there instead."

He propped up on one elbow. "That might not be such a bad idea," he said slowly.

"Did you mean what you said about needing me to inspire you?"

"I don't think you realize how wearied I felt of everything before you," he said frankly. "How irritable and tired. And now I feel quite different. I feel…invigorated. Inspired. Like I could write anything, so long as you were at my side. Somehow when you describe even palace events, they sound more vivid, more real to me."

She liked that. Really liked it. "Just think…" He waited patiently for her to finish her thought. "Think of all the pieces you could write, of all the royal events you could commemorate with me there to inspire you. Maybe I will propel you to success after all."

"There is no 'maybe' about it," he answered sanguinely. "You are my salvation. Even if they do not appoint me royal musician, I suspect we will be inundated with patrons and requests."

"Sure to be," she agreed, "after the huge success of 'I Cannot Show the Love I Owe.' And the scandal of today, of course." She bit her lip. "Everyone is sure to be talking of it for months and months to come. James?" He turned his head to look at her. "You are not worried about becoming a figure of ignominy and scandal anymore, are you?"

He shook his head. "No, I've decided I rather like it." Gunnilde gasped as he rolled her onto her back and shifted over her. "After all, what did I expect? Marrying one of those horned temptresses the bishop warned us all about."

Gunnilde started to laugh, but as his lips descended on hers, he soon put a stop to that.

Epilogue

Five Months Later

Tranton Vale Tournament, Payne Manor

Carefully, Gunnilde adjusted the draping of her veil over her new double-horned headdress. Lately, she had been experimenting more with headdresses than hairstyles. Her new friend Lady Schaeffer had introduced her to some wonderful artisans. Horns were still very much her signature style though.

Settling back into her seat, she glanced down in satisfaction at the new jeweled girdle encircling her waist. It was James's latest gift to her and flashed with an array of beautifully colored stones. Since he took up his position as royal musician, the Wycliffes' monetary woes were a thing of the past.

His handsome allowance alone would have been enough to sustain them in comfort, but on top of that he had been inundated with requests and new commissions from his fellow courtiers. Even the Bishop of Badsbury had communicated his desire for a new piece of music. James had added him to a long list.

She squeezed James's hand as the combatants entered the field, and he turned to look and smile at her. "Here they come." The crowd cheered as the two knights saluted the so-called "royal box." The Paynes had never had a "royal box" before. Until the previous year they had not even had a stand designated for the family to watch proceedings. Everyone had just sat on benches.

This year, however, was different. This year, thanks to the connections of Gunnilde, James, and Hal, they had a royal prince in attendance. It had meant a good deal of scrambling and last-minute preparations to accommodate such an honor. It had also meant Payne Manor was overflowing with Prince Raedan's personal guard, and they had had to designate three more fields for pavilions to fit all the attendants in.

More knights had shown up to compete this year than in the last five years combined. Her father, Sir Aubron, was half proud and half panicked by the swell in numbers. He kept consulting with her or James to check if he had the protocol right when it came to seating or if some matter of etiquette was lacking.

Her stepmother was not much better. Poor Bess felt quite overwhelmed by so many courtiers milling about the place and had taken to deferring completely to Gunnilde in almost every household matter. "Let me just consult with the daughter of the house" had become her favorite refrain in moments of doubt, which were frequent.

Gazing out now at the sea of tents and banners fluttering in the breeze, Gunnilde felt her heart swell with pride at all they had achieved. Never had she dreamed that her father's rural tournament could become such a grand affair.

James's hand landed on her knee, and she shuffled closer to him, peering at the long list of shields he held in his hand. James had entered into the spirit of the tournament beautifully and had even written a piece of music to commemorate the event called "The Pride of Tranton Vale." It had been debuted at court and the King had pronounced it "Not bad, not bad at all. Better than anything old Palmore ever wrote at any rate."

Only she knew that the piece was really about her. Oh, and perhaps Cuthbert, who always seemed to know these things. James and four of his musician friends from Aphrany were performing the music at tonight's feast, much to the excitement of her father's guests. They were highly honored that the King's own "Music Master," as they insisted on referring to him, was playing for their entertainment.

Sir Aubron was still somewhat awed by his new son-in-law, even more than his royal guest truth be told, for the prince was still a boy. A strange sort of boy, he felt privately, but a boy nonetheless. Around James, Sir Aubron watched his manners and refrained from his usual ribald jokes. He boasted a good deal to his friends and neighbors of James's position at court, and of his daughter, who was now "one of the Queen's ladies."

"Sir Maurice de Courcey and Sir Phillip Linley," James read aloud after checking their coats of arms. "What do we know of these two? Can we expect a good showing?"

Hal looked up from where he sat next to the prince. "Linley is a solid prospect, steady and seasoned but de Courcey is a vicious little brute. You cannot trust him an inch. He paid out more in fines than he gained in winnings last year. Set a new record in fact."

"Some might call that an unprofitable strategy." Prince Raedan yawned, reclining back in his seat. He seemed more relaxed when away from court, especially when he was permitted to travel with his menagerie, which today consisted of his huge hound, Balto, and his sparrowhawk, Igraine, who rested on her perch by his side.

Balto sat at his feet, his tongue lolling out of his massive mouth and drool dripping down liberally from his jaws. The prince affected not to notice when the beast splattered his spit liberally over the nearby benches and cushions, and indeed why should he when everyone made haste to mop it up for him?

Behind his chair stood the hulking Sir Col, who was almost as muscular and ugly as Balto and who had been the prince's guard since he was a babe in arms, and who no one could get more than three words out of altogether.

"Why is Sir Maurice so vicious, I wonder?" mused the prince, his eyes half-closed against the bright summer sun. "Does anyone know?"

489

Cuthbert stirred where he stood, leaning against one of the pillars, decked out in the Vawdrey colors of red and black. He held Dustin in his arms, for the little dog was always nervous in the vicinity of Balto.

"Sir Maurice is the only legitimate son of a dissolute house, Your Highness," he volunteered. Growing up the youngest and weakest of his father's vast progeny, he had much to prove."

Prince Raedan's eyebrows rose. "And so, he chooses to prove he is the least honorable of any man present?" he asked.

Cuthbert shrugged. "None of his half brothers care to tangle with him anymore, Highness, put it that way."

"I see," the prince murmured, and they all turned back to watch Sir Maurice taunt the older man as they circled one another, swords drawn.

"Gunnilde," her father muttered out of the corner of his mouth. "Your stepmother is worried the canopy is not the correct shade of blue for the House of Argent. What say you?"

In truth, it did not match the blue of the royal standard, but there was precious little they could do about it now. "'Tis somewhat late in the day for that, Father," Gunnilde answered. "The prince is seated beneath it and did not raise any issue, so tell Bess not to worry."

Sir Aubron nodded and turned to relay the message to his wife. Kit entered the box puffing and panting, decked out in the Twyford colors of black and white, for later he would be acting as squire to his master, Lord Twyford.

Behind him scrambled in Neville, dressed in his court finery and limping slightly. "Sorry," Kit said, looking straight at Gunnilde, for he clearly counted her their hostess. "Promised Wycliffe here I'd give him a tour of the stables and introduce him to Bria'ag," he said, referring to Garman's horse.

490

"Magnificent beast!" Neville said eagerly. "Trod on my foot though." He winced. "These court shoes might have been a mistake!"

They walked over to take their seats next to Cuthbert, and Neville accepted Dustin onto his lap.

"Can we expect any of the more famous knights to compete today?" the prince asked. "Or are they saved for later in the competition?" His own knowledge of knights was limited and only ran to the more famous of their number.

"You need only wait till this afternoon, Highness, to see two of the most famous knights in the realm compete in the melee," Gunnilde's father put in eagerly. "Vawdrey and Orde," he pronounced with satisfaction, quite disregarding their newer titles. "And we expect de Bussell and de Crecy to arrive before the end of the day, gods willing, for they mean to compete in the jousting tomorrow."

"I do hope you have left a good spot in the field for the de Bussells, my dear," his wife fretted. "For Sir Armand is sure to bring his wife who you know is really—"

Hal coughed loudly, preventing his stepmother from saying anything treasonous within the young prince's hearing. "We all look forward to receiving the Lady Una," he said, stressing her lack of royal status, "and a prime spot has been marked out for their pavilion."

"Eden and Lenora promised to join us here in the box this afternoon," Gunnilde said cheerfully, for she was already looking forward to their presence very much. Both were currently waking up in their husbands' pavilions but had promised to break their fasts in Payne Manor at midday.

"Oh dear, I felt so very sorry that we could not offer them rooms inside," Bess said in a plaintive voice. "But there are so many guards—"

491

"I see a good prospect this morning for Your Highness," James said loudly, covering her tactlessness. "Sir Renlow d'Avenant is scheduled to compete shortly. He is certainly worth watching and has no small fame attached to his name. You have heard perhaps of his reputation?"

Prince Raedan considered this. "Ah, Sir Renlow, my father says he leads a charmed life," he answered at last. "Is there not some tale of his walking away unscathed from a night spent in the company of murderers and thieves?"

"Sir Renlow is plucky as a gamecock, but he'll surely struggle against this company," said Neville, frowning. "Why, he's only half the size of Twyford or Kentigern!"

"Only physically," James responded. He had recently become much interested in his old acquaintance Renlow's progress through the lists, and Gunnilde had been happy to tell him all she knew.

"What other way, pray tell, is there in which to measure a man?" the prince asked, looking intrigued.

James hesitated, but Cuthbert came to his rescue. "You can measure a man in spirit, sire, and in his heart," he said with quiet conviction. "If Renlow is competing, then you may be sure he will give his all to any tournament, big or small. Moreover, he knows no fear, no doubts, and no hesitation. That is an opponent you should never take lightly. On the right day, he has beaten every knight in the kingdom."

Prince Raedan frowned. "Even Vawdrey?"

"Even the King's champion."

"Even Kentigern?"

"Name any knight of the realm, my prince," Cuthbert offered with a smile. "My answer remains the same."

492

Hal frowned. "On the right day, 'tis true," he conceded. "But overall…" His words trailed off as he noticed the prince sitting up straight.

"They call my father the lion of all Karadok," Prince Raedan said, and there was an uncomfortable stirring in the stand, for Wymer was certainly not a large man. Cuthbert looked pointedly at James, as if prompting him to speak again.

"They do, Your Highness," James agreed. "And with good reason. Your father is fierce in battle and a formidable foe. Moreover, he is a good judge of men. He puts his faith in the best and does not flinch from hard decisions."

Raedan nodded, clearly not displeased by this description. He looked out over the field in silent contemplation. After a moment he said quietly, "I should like to meet Sir Renlow d'Avenant."

"That can certainly be arranged, Highness," Gunnilde said, giving her father a significant look. "Sir Renlow will be attending tonight's feast. We can have him seated at the high table with us."

"You have my gratitude, Lady Wycliffe," Prince Raedan said, and relaxed again.

Gunnilde's father passed a hand over his sweaty brow. "I can look to you to arrange this thing, daughter?" he asked hoarsely. She could see he was already panicking about whereabouts on the table this new addition should be placed.

"Of course, Father, do not worry yourself. It can be most easily arranged."

"So…Sir Renlow dines with princes as well as thieves and murderers," James murmured under his breath. He had a faraway look in his eye that Gunnilde had come to know well.

"You're going to write a piece of music about him, aren't you?" she whispered excitedly, squeezing his arm.

"Perhaps," James muttered, but Gunnilde could already tell it would be so.

"And you can name it after his family motto," she said with satisfaction. "If I breathe, then I strive. I expect the King will like it very much."

Funnily enough, she and James had lately become great favorites of the King, more so than the Queen. They were often sat with Earl and Countess Vawdrey at functions to denote this fact and seated on the King's half of the table.

Since Gunnilde had accepted her place among the rank and file of the Queen's ladies, she had found herself becoming fast friends with Emma Thackeray, a country-bred girl like herself, and Patience Stanhope, whose position as Hal's beloved had been as short-lived as all the others.

Now Gunnilde was no longer vying for top spot with Mistress Bartree, that lady, too, had softened toward her and showed her a consideration she did not afford the other ladies-in-waiting. Gunnilde was now permitted to fold the Queen's underclothes on occasion and even tidy them away.

Hal had fallen in love with practically every lady-in-waiting in the palace by the time the Solstice celebrations were over, and he had left court to resume his duties as a squire. Fortunately, he seemed to remain on friendly terms with all of them, and at the award ceremony for the Squires' Revels, he had been afforded the loudest cheer. At the subsequent feast, he had been proudly accompanied by the elderly Ashdown sisters, one on each arm.

494

Neville and Harriet had become betrothed in the spring with very little interference from Gunnilde. It was true, she had needed to pave the way with Lady Portstanley a little, and she had achieved this by inviting her to supper parties with the likes of Earl and Countess Vawdrey and Lord and Lady Schaeffer to show off their superior connections.

In truth, she and Lady Schaeffer had bonded over their mutual love of fashion, and they now vied with one another to obtain the tallest steeple hennins and the most elaborate veils at court. Whenever Gunnilde triumphed, Hester Schaeffer pouted and declared it was because she was "thick as thieves with that wicked creature Bardulf and privy to the latest news from overseas."

James had so far written two of the pieces the Queen had requested. One about the de Crecys called "Undone by Love's Cruel Arrow" and one inspired by an incident concerning the Kentigerns called "The Spurning of Love and Beauty." The Queen had been highly delighted with both, though the subjects of the music had seemed rather less thrilled.

Strange to say, Lady de Crecy had been more offended than Sir Jeffree, declaring it "a great impertinence." When it had proved a huge success at court, the de Crecys had finally consented to attend a performance and Sir Jeffree had wound up liking it so much he had paid for Masters Billingsley and Chamberlain to travel all the way to Ganfordshire and perform it at his uncle's prestigious seat, Ganford Chase.

As for Lord Kentigern, he had turned quite purple with rage and looked set to cause an ugly scene until his wife had graciously declared herself charmed with the music. Baroness Kentigern claimed she had been quite jealous that her sister-in-law Mistress Bartree should have such a beautiful piece of music dedicated to her, and now she, too, had one, she was vastly content.

Gunnilde had been most impressed with the way she had handled her infuriated spouse. Shortly after, a grumpy Lord Kentigern had requested a private meeting with James. At this, he had demanded James write a companion piece called "The Acceptance of Love and Beauty," which James had promised to do, finally mollifying the warlike Kentigern.

After this, James had lost his enthusiasm for completing the Queen's collection, declaring they gave him nothing but headaches and strife in the aftermath. Instead, he had turned his attention to private commissions taking advantage of their popularity at court, for "who knew how long it would last." Gunnilde did not find herself too worried about this, personally.

James's private commissions had proved so lucrative that he had suggested they buy Master Gregory's townhouse from him, so that the impoverished musician and his daughter might have access to some ready monies without having to worry about a roof over their heads for the foreseeable future.

This suggestion had gone down very well indeed, and Justina had insisted they had the largest of the bedrooms allocated for their use "whenever they might get sick of that palace" or have friends come to Aphrany and need a place for them to stay.

In addition to this, she and James intended to look for a summer place in Caer Lyoness so they could also escape from the summer court when the need arose. They made many plans for traveling around the countryside over wherever their fancy might take them.

They were finally visiting Wycliffe Hall in June after several months of frosty communications, where James had told his mother unequivocally that she held no sway over his marriage. After hearing various favorable reports from her acquaintances at court, including her niece Lady Gilchrist, his mother had started to thaw and write much friendlier missives.

Finally, she had enclosed a note to her daughter-in-law graciously welcoming her into the family and stating they looked forward to receiving her at Wycliffe Hall when court returned to Caer Lyoness. Gunnilde was not deceived but assured James she was more than equal to dealing with his mother on the occasions where they would meet.

"Fie! For shame!" bellowed an enthusiastic spectator from the crowd below.

"I do not think the crowd approves of Sir Maurice taking the win," James observed wryly.

"Whoever beats him in the next round will receive a hero's welcome," Gunnilde predicted.

"Are any of your old friends the Conways here today?" James asked, placing a hand at her middle back. "I never thought to ask. Old neighbors of your father's, aren't they?"

"Only old Lady Conway now. She is coming to tonight's feast, for Father said she hinted quite shamefully until he extended her an invite. She is quite desperate to see if you are as handsome as her daughter described you, or at least that is what Bess says."

"Thought me handsome, did she?" James asked mildly.

"Of course! Muriel has eyes in her head, whatever else her shortcomings."

"Well, so long as I do not need to guard you against Sir Arthur, I will make no complaint to his mother ogling me."

Gunnilde laughed. "She probably will stare but you must be used to such things by now. And when we get back to court, we must look into getting your portrait done, James."

"Why, so it can be hung in the long gallery and everyone else can ogle me?" He did not sound amused.

"It is only fitting that you should have one," she responded sternly. "Now you are officially appointed as royal musician, I mean. Besides, you once promised me a miniature, and it is practically the same thing."

"I'm not having one done unless you do too," he responded immediately. "One for my own personal enjoyment."

"Oh, yes?"

"You must be horned for it and wearing a flaunting gown," he said with relish. "Perhaps a new one with lots of slashes and open sides. I see it quite clearly in my mind's eye." His hand slid up and down her back.

The crowd cheered and Gunnilde realized two new combatants had entered the field, but she could not bring herself to look away from her husband's warm gaze. She cleared her throat. "Now you are just trying to bribe me, husband, for you know I never can resist a new gown."

"I do like buying you gowns," he admitted.

"And new shoes. And new stockings. In fact, everything you led me to expect from a frugal husband turned out to be entirely false," she pointed out lightly.

He smiled. "Oh, I am not remotely sensible where you are concerned, wife. Now bestow on me a kiss. It would be a kindness."

Gunnilde leaned forward and planted an obliging kiss to his lips before drawing swiftly back. James still looked so startled whenever she did such things, it never failed to make her laugh.

"I expected to have to convince you," he protested when she succumbed to mirth.

"You should know by now that I am never reluctant to kiss you. Did I not boldly kiss you at our wedding feast, immediately securing your love?"

"You did," he agreed in a low voice. "But do not try to evade me now, come close again."

Gunnilde shook her head. "We must concentrate our attention on the field," she said primly. "Everyone else is paying close attention but we two."

"Did you see who is listed for the next bout but one?"

"No, who?"

"Sir Douglas."

"Ah yes." Gunnilde sobered. "I did see his name on one of Father's lists. He has not brought Constance along with him though. A shame."

"You think so?"

"Her heart might soften if she were to see him compete."

"From what I hear, it is not *her* heart that needs softening."

"You mean, Sir Douglas now holds her at arm's length?"

James shrugged. "So the rumor says."

"Poor Constance," Gunnilde sighed.

"She was extremely lucky the annulment did not go through. He wanted it to, you know."

"I know. But I think that was a matter of hurt pride." He shrugged but said nothing, his eyes still on the competitors. Gunnilde found she was the one who could not concentrate on the tourney now. "Maybe you should write them a piece of music?" she suggested. "'The Failed Annulment,' something like that?"

He winced. "Gods no, do not forget how close we came to finding ourselves dragged into that whole mess!"

She took his hand between her own and patted it reassuringly. "I know, but all that is now passed. We are one of the most celebrated couples at court, you and I."

He relaxed at her words and closed his fingers around her own. "True, and rightly so. Did I tell you I have a surprise for you? It's packed away in my trunk. I shall retrieve it for you later."

"Another present? James, you shouldn't have!"

"It's nothing that you wear," he told her. "You will never guess. Shall I give you a clue?" She nodded and he traced a fingertip over her wedding ring.

"But you wear jewelry," she pointed out.

"Think of the inscription," he hinted.

"To my beautiful rose from your undeserving worm?"

He laughed, "Precisely."

"What is it?" She hesitated, glancing around and lowering her voice. "Not…lewd poetry?"

He nodded. "From Master Shadbolt's own pen."

"James, you did not pay him to write me a poem!"

"I did. I had to. I mean to court you in all the ways I never got to during our nonexistent courtship."

"Really?" He nodded. She gnawed her lip. "I hope it is still about the rose and the worm, or I will not be able to make out its meaning at all."

His smile broadened. "You can hardly mistake it, my love. This time, I told him to make it more appreciative and less punitive in tone, but the metaphor remains the same."

"So, it is about a happy worm and a beauteous rose living together in perfect harmony?" she ventured.

"It is about an ecstatic worm and his most remarkable rose, living together blissfully forever and ever," he assured her.

"Well, that does not sound so bad," she admitted, snuggling into his side.

"Bad?" His arm closed around her, drawing her close. "It is the most wonderful thing in the world."

THE END

I do hope you enjoyed this story. If so, perhaps you would be kind enough to leave me a rating on Amazon, Goodreads, or Bookbub or wherever you leave reviews.

Join my mailing list for a monthly newsletter and updates by visiting my website: www.alicecoldbreath.com

Other series by Alice Coldbreath you may enjoy:

THE VAWDREY BROTHERS SERIES

Book 1 – Her Baseborn Bridegroom

Lady Linnet Cadwallader has been raised a helpless invalid in her own castle. Brought up to believe she will "never make old bones" she lives a quiet and lonely existence, hiding away her excessive freckles and red hair from a world that believes her to be hideously misshapen and ugly.

Until one day her uncle arranges a marriage of convenience for her, a marriage in name only with a young puppet groom…but Sir Roland does not show up. In his place turns up his baseborn brother Mason Vawdrey. And dark, forceful Mason is no one's puppet.

Things are about to get interesting at Cadwallader Castle. And Linnet is about to discover that maybe a golden leopardess does not need to change her glorious spots.

THE VICTORIAN PRIZEFIGHTER SERIES

Book 1 – A Bride for the Prizefighter

Mina's well-ordered life is thrown into disarray when her father drops a bombshell on his deathbed: she has a brother she never knew of. Not only that, he is on his way to rescue her from the collapse of their school under a mountain of debts.

A wild journey across the country later, Mina finds herself thrown at the feet of the brutish William Nye, prizefighter and owner of a disreputable inn, The Merry Harlot. Respectable Mina is appalled to find herself obliged to wed this surly stranger!

Forced to draw on reserves of inner strength she never knew she possessed, Mina uncovers perilous secrets and bravely carves herself a new life at the side of this man as she proves herself a more-than-worthy partner for the prizefighter.

THE VICTORIAN REVERSAL OF FORTUNE SERIES

Book 1 – A Foolish Flirtation

At eighteen, Emmeline Ballentine's father splashed out on one London season to introduce his daughter to polite society. Sadly, for Emmeline, polite society was not terribly receptive to a city trader's daughter.

She only ever caught one gentleman's fancy, the dishonorable Jeremy Vance who made her head spin as he singled her out for attention at the balls and assemblies. Her worldly chaperone warned her he was making a May game of her, but Emmeline had not heeded her warning. Consequently, her dreams were dashed, when at the close of the season, Jeremy announced his engagement to another.

Ten years later, their paths cross again in Bath. Emmeline is older and wiser, and a good deal poorer, and Jeremy is divorced. There is absolutely no chance of him making a fool of her again with his shocking offer of marriage. Is there?

www.ingramcontent.com/pod-product-compliance
Lightning Source LLC
Chambersburg PA
CBHW020458020726
47493CB00001B/82